BUT WHO WILL HAVE MERCY ON BAHZELL?

"Your skill at arms has vanquished me, yet your mercy has spared my life," the young knight Vaijon forced himself to go on, "proving your right to the honor to which the War God has called you." His pain-tightened mouth quirked a wry smile within his helm, and Bahzell withdrew his sword entirely.

"Ay, well as to that, lad," he said with a ghost of a laugh, "you'd not *believe* what it took for my father to hammer a lesson into my own head. I'd not want to say I was *stubborn*, you understand, but—"

"But *I* would," another voice interrupted, and Vaijon's eyes went huge and round as another armed and armored figure flicked suddenly into existence behind Bahzell. The newcomer stood ten feet tall, with a sword on his back and a mace at his belt, and the deep, bass thunder of his words made even Bahzell's powerful voice sound light as a child's.

Every person went instantly to one knee, all but one. As the others knelt before the power and majesty of Tomanak Orfro, Sword of Light and Judge of Princes, Bahzell turned to face him with a quizzical expression and cocked ears. "Would you, now?" he said.

"I would," Tomanak told him. "It seems to me that Vaijon will need a proper example to keep him from losing any of the ground he's gained, so perhaps I should entrust Vaijon to your keeping—as your trainee, as it were."

"Now just one minute, there!" Bahzell began, "I'm thinking—"

"*Trust* me, Bahzell," Tomanak soothed. "It's an excellent idea, even if I do say so myself. And now that *that's* settled, I'll be going."

"But—" Bahzell began, and then closed his mouth with a snap as Tomanak vanished as suddenly as he'd appeared. *Just like himself to be popping in and out like a cheap candle flame*, he thought moodily.

"Not a *cheap* candle, Bahzell," a voice chided out of thin air. "And don't you think it would be a good idea to heal Vaijon's arms? You *did* break them, after all."

The War God's Own

DAVID WEBER

BAEN

Copyright © 1998 by David M. Weber

A Baen Books Original

Baen Publishing Enterprises
P.O. Box 1403
Riverdale, NY 10471

ISBN: 0-671-57792-1

Cover art by Larry Elmore

First paperback printing, February 1999

Distributed by Simon & Schuster
1230 Avenue of the Americas
New York, NY 10020

Library of Congress Catalog Number: 98-13871

Typeset by Windhaven Press, Auburn, NH
Printed in the United States of America

For Clarence A. Weber,
my father.
A man who loved books and taught me to, as well.

*I wish you were here to read this one
like you promised.*

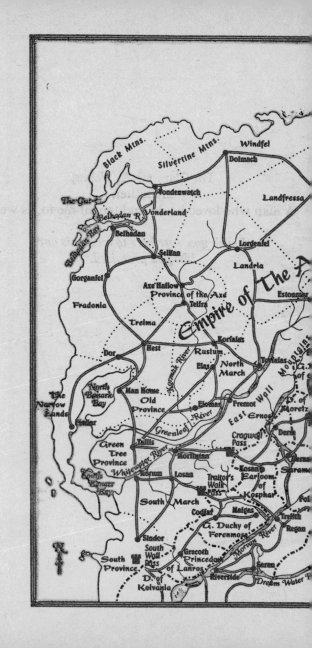

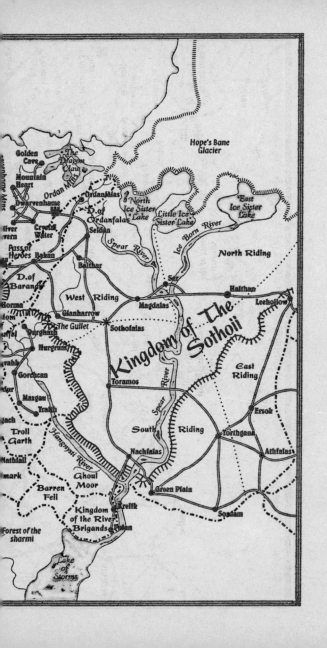

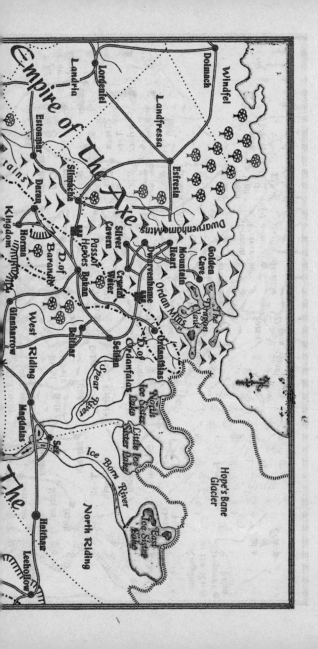

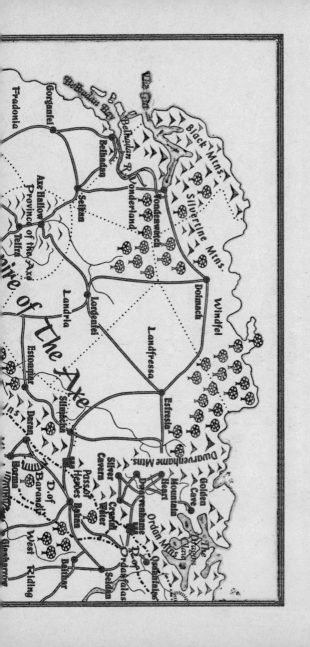

The War God's Own

PROLOGUE

Slate-gray seawater blew back in explosions of white as the twin-masted schooner sliced through the swell. The eastern sky ahead of her was brushed with rose and gold, a dawn that offered beauty to the eye if no warmth to cold-pinched fingers and noses, and ice glittered on her stays. The low, sleek vessel's flag—green, badged with a golden seagull—and black hull proclaimed her Marfang Island registry. Not that any flags were needed. A prudent seaman would have taken at least one reef, but she leaned well over to the wind, driven hard by a captain who was, to say the least, confident. Others would have used a less complimentary adjective as they watched white water cascade over her leeward rails like a tide race.

Some argued that Marfang Islanders took risks sane people went far out of their ways to avoid specifically because of their small size, as a sort of compensation for standing little more than three feet tall. Others held that they deliberately courted danger in an effort to prove that the reputation for cowardice which clung to other halflings did not apply to them, while still others claimed that it was all because of something in Marfang Island's water. Any or all of the theories could well be true, yet in the end the "why" mattered less than the "what," and any deep-water sailor who saw that schooner's driving approach to Belhadan Bay would instantly proclaim that her skipper and crew must be Marfangers.

And he would have been right . . . mostly. But not entirely, for two of the figures working about her deck were hradani who towered above their companions. One was perhaps an inch or two over six feet, which was quite enough to make him loom over the ivory-horned halflings about him, but the other was at least seven and a half feet tall. That made him a giant even for his native Horse Stealer tribe, and someone like him had no business on the deck of a vessel scaled to halflings, yet he moved among them with a nimbleness at odds with his stature, lending his massive weight and strength wherever it was most needed.

"Don't just stand there like a whore at a wedding, Master Holderman! Trim that foresheet! It's slacker than those idlers you call seamen!"

The words roared from the quarterdeck through Evark Pitchallow's leather speaking trumpet, and his first mate grimaced. Then he waved acknowledgment aft and began snapping orders of his own. The schooner's crew had just finished shaking out the reefs that even Evark carried overnight in these waters in winter, and the mate was pleased with how efficiently they'd done so. In fact, there were at most a few inches of slack in the offending foresheet, but the word panache might have been coined specifically for Captain Pitchallow, and Holderman knew better than to argue with him. Nor did the seamen who hurried to obey his orders show any inclination to dawdle, for Belhadan Bay was the largest (and busiest) port of the Empire of the Axe. Every professional seaman in the world passed through it sooner or later, and Pitchallow's crew knew he wasn't about to stand for their embarrassing him in front of his peers, even if they did have two out-sized, half-trained landlubbers getting in their way.

Something between a word and a grunt came through the speaking trumpet in an expression of what was probably satisfaction, and Holderman drew a deep breath and nodded to the men about him. Several grinned at him, as accustomed as he to their captain's ways, and he was hard put not to grin back. But he'd earned his own master's ticket last year, and he had high hopes of winning command of his own ship when *Wind Dancer* returned home. The city of Refuge boasted Marfang Island's only true deep-water harbor, and for all its inhabitants' small size, that made it the home port of the finest seamen in all Orfressa. Evark Pitchallow stood high among that select company, and his recommendation would almost guarantee Holderman a captain's berth. Which meant it was time to begin practicing his own captain's demeanor, and so he simply repeated his nod and made his way to the rail.

He crossed the deck carefully. Marfangers were daring and intrepid, but reputation notwithstanding, they weren't foolish. Or not totally so, at least. Holderman used the safety lines rigged across the treacherously wet planks with as much care as he insisted any of his seamen take, then clung to a stay and peered ahead along *Wind Dancer*'s course.

The wind of the open sea cut like icy swords, striking tears from his eyes and offering to freeze his very skin off. Showers of lashing spray made it no more pleasant, but these northern waters were as familiar to Holderman as the warmer, milder ones around his southern homeland, and compared to what conditions *could* have been at this time of year, this was an almost balmy day.

He sucked in a huge lungful of the sea's brutal freshness and watched the mountains looming steadily higher above the eastern horizon. There was snow on the taller of those peaks year round, but now their heads glittered a rose-tinged white as they loomed against the dawn, and the masthead lookouts kept a close watch. Belhadan's location as the northernmost ice-free port of the Empire helped explain its importance, but it wasn't so far south that drift ice or icebergs were unheard of. Indeed, given his own preferences, Holderman thought he might actually have reduced sail, or at least left the night's reefs in rather than shaking them out, if only to give himself a little more time to avoid any ice his lookouts spotted. But the decision wasn't his, and at least visibility was excellent.

He felt rather than saw a huge presence looming up behind him and turned to glance over his shoulder at the taller of the two nonhalflings in *Wind Dancer*'s crew.

"And how long would it be to reach yonder mountains?" a cavern-deep bass rumbled in a wind-whipped cloud of steamy breath.

"Oh, we should fetch the harbor in another two or three hours," Holderman replied. He turned, still maintaining his grip on the stay, and looked up at the other with frank curiosity. "Have you and Brandark given any more thought to your plans?"

"No, but not for want of trying. We've nothing at all to be basing plans on, you see, and I'm thinking the Axemen may be after being just a *wee* bit unhappy to see us."

"How unreasonable of them," Holderman said dryly. "Why, I can't think of anything that would make me happier than having a couple of hradani come ashore in *my* port."

A deep, booming laugh answered him, and a shovel-sized hand thumped him on the shoulder. It was a gentle thump, given the size and strength of the hand's owner, but Holderman staggered anyway. He glared up at the huge hradani, yet his heart wasn't in it, which kept him from generating the intended power.

"I'll thank you not to knock me over the rail, lummox! I've spent ten years at sea without drowning yet, and I'd just as soon not start now."

"Drown, is it? And here was I, thinking as how Marfang Islanders learned to breathe water when they were no more than wee, tiny fellows!" The hradani paused just a moment, then added, "But then, you're *always* wee, tiny fellows, so it might just be I'd the wrong of exactly when you're after learning, mightn't it?"

He tilted his head and cocked his foxlike ears at an angle that mirrored the devilish sparkle in his brown eyes, and Holderman snorted.

"I'd spend some time watching 'wee, tiny' sharks finish off a whale before I got too complacent about *my* size, Bahzell Bahanakson!" he said, and the hradani raised a hand in the gesture of a fencer acknowledging a touch. He gave the first officer another white-toothed smile, then turned and crossed to his fellow hradani's side, and Holderman watched him go.

It wasn't easy for someone that huge to maneuver about *Wind Dancer*'s decks, but Bahzell moved with an easy balance which seemed profoundly unnatural, especially to a halfling, in anyone his size. Either of his legs alone would easily have outweighed Holderman, and the blade of the sword he carried ashore was at least a foot longer than the tallest halfling aboard, but he could fit into amazingly tight quarters when he had to. His companion Brandark was over a foot shorter than he, yet Bahzell had made himself much more quickly at ease aboard the schooner. Perhaps, Holderman mused, that was because Bahzell, at least, could swim. Brandark couldn't, and the first officer suspected that had made him more than a little tentative when it came to finding his sea legs.

Yet he'd found them in the end, and he'd learned much more about *Wind Dancer* than Bahzell had. Not that Bahzell had been disinterested or tried to avoid doing his share and a little to spare aboard ship. But the Horse Stealer saw the schooner mainly as a means of getting from one port to another, while Brandark saw deeper than that. Bahzell had learned to obey the orders of the skilled professionals about him; Brandark had learned why those orders were *given*.

Holderman watched the two hradani talk with their heads close together while water creamed up over the lee rails and raced at their feet. He couldn't hear them through the sound of wind and wave, the creak and groan of timbers, and the high-pitched song of the rigging, but he'd heard them chaffering often enough to have a shrewd notion of what they were saying, and he shook his own head.

Marfangers knew more than most people about hradani, for their homeland lay directly across the Wild Wash Channel from the hradani clans of the same name. Yet for all their fierceness in battle and predilection for carrying off anything not nailed to the earth, the Wild Wash clans' reputations were but shadows of those of the Horse Stealers or Brandark's native Bloody Swords. *Wind Dancer's* crew had heard all about their savagery and mutual hatred, despite their northern homelands' isolation, long before Bahzell and Brandark had come aboard. In fact, *every* Norfressan (with the possible exception of a few hermits among the desert-riding Wakūo nomads) had heard about the Horse Stealers and Bloody Swords, and no one wanted a thing to do with either of them.

And that was what puzzled Holderman whenever he looked at *Wind Dancer's* passengers. They should have gone for one another's throats on sight, which made their deep and obvious friendship confusing enough, but neither was remotely like their people's reputations in most other ways, either. That, Holderman reflected, might indicate that hradani reputation was as misleading as some of the wilder tales told about his own folk, but it didn't explain why these two differed so . . . profoundly from the stereotypes.

Brandark was bad enough. The kindest description of the Bloody Swords emphasized their contempt for the weakening influence of anything smacking of civilization, yet Brandark favored lace-fronted shirts and embroidered jerkins which would have done a Purple Lord proud. Worse, he was the best educated person aboard *Wind Dancer*, although he was entirely self-taught. And to top things off, he was a skilled musician, despite the loss of two fingers, who could play the bawdiest tune a seaman could name or spend hours staring into a lamp flame while he stroked soft, haunting beauty from his balalaika. His voice, unfortunately, was something else again. Not even his closest friend would call *it* beautiful, and Holderman was almost relieved that it was so. The notion of a hradani scholar and dandy was hard enough to cope with; he rather doubted he could have gotten his mind around the concept of a Bloody Sword *bard*.

On the other hand, even that idea might have been easier to adjust to than that of a Horse Stealer champion of Tomanāk. Like the rest of *Wind Dancer's* company, Holderman had felt nothing but scorn when seven and a half feet of stark naked hradani had swum half way across Bortalik Bay, climbed over the rail, and calmly claimed to be one of the war god's chosen champions. The assertion had been preposterous and probably blasphemous, given the fact that there hadn't been a single hradani champion of *any* God of Light in the twelve centuries since the Fall of Kontovar. Besides, every Norfressan child knew the hradani had served as the Carnadosan traitors' shock troops in the war which had destroyed the empire which once ruled Orfressa's southern continent. That was why they were universally distrusted and shunned, if not actively hated. Well, that and the berserk, uncontrollable bloodlust Bahzell's people called "the Rage." No one, after all, wanted to get too friendly with a gigantic barbarian who might suddenly take it into his head to chop one into teeny, tiny pieces for no particular reason.

Holderman was prepared to admit that stereotypes tended to be exaggerated, yet he'd found it impossible to believe that Tomanāk Orfro, Keeper of the Scales of Orr, the Sword of Light, God of Justice, and Captain-General of the Gods of Light as well as God of War, would pick a champion from such unpromising material. But Tomanāk had done just that. The powers of the champion's blade Bahzell bore had proved it, and Bahzell's champion status, even more than the fury he'd waked among the Purple Lords whom Captain Pitchallow hated with every fiber of his being, explained the speed with which *Wind Dancer*'s master had granted him and Brandark passage to Belhadan. Not that Pitchallow wouldn't have cheerfully rescued *anyone* who could infuriate the Purple Lords. Under most circumstances, however, he would at least have required them to pay their passages—he *was* a Marfang halfling, after all—and he'd flatly refused to take a copper kormak from Bahzell.

That hadn't kept him from insisting that they pull their weight aboard ship, but it was a sign of his high regard for the hradani, and he and Bahzell had spent many a late night with their heads together. No one else—aside, perhaps, from Brandark—had any idea precisely what the captain and Bahzell had found to discuss so earnestly, but Pitchallow's devotion to Korthrala, the sea god, was as well known as it was strong. And although even his own followers admitted that Korthrala wasn't overblessed with wisdom by divine standards, he *was* Tomanāk's younger brother and firm ally, so perhaps it wasn't so very surprising that one of his churchmen should have a lot to say to a brand new champion of the war god. Especially one who needed advice as badly as Bahzell Bahnakson was likely to need it.

Now, as he watched the two hradani shade their eyes with their hands, gazing at the approaching mountains while they talked, Holderman said a small, sincere prayer of his own for them. He might be less devout than his captain, but given what *Wind Dancer*'s two guests were likely to face when they set foot ashore in Belhadan, he reflected, even *his* prayers couldn't do any harm.

CHAPTER ONE

"So, Vaijon. Are you ready?"

The question came in a gently sardonic voice, and the golden-haired young man standing before the mirror in the chapter house's entry vestibule turned quickly. A faint flush touched his cheeks as he recognized the voice's teasing edge, but he bent his head in a small bow.

"I am, Sir Charrow."

His reply was proper enough, but irritation lingered in his expression. Not overtly; it was more subtle than any scowl, little more than an extra bit of tension in his jaw, more sensed than seen, perhaps, with just the tiniest edge of challenge under his courteous words. Sir Charrow Malakhai, Knight-Captain of the Order of Tomanāk and master of its Belhadan chapter, hid a sigh as he wondered if the youngster even realized that edge was there. Sir Charrow had seen other arrogant young sprouts—more of them, in fact, than he had any desire to contemplate—during his years with the Order. Fortunately, Tomanāk's Order, as a rule, had a way of knocking that sort of attitude out of its brethren; unfortunately, the process seemed to have gone awry this time.

"Good, my son." The knight-captain made his words a gentle reprimand and was rewarded by seeing the younger man's flush darken. Whatever else he might be, Vaijon wasn't stupid. He recognized a rebuke even when he truly failed to grasp the reason for it. "This is a very important day for our chapter, Vaijon." Charrow went on in a more normal voice. "It is up to you to represent us—and Tomanāk—properly."

7

"Of course, Sir Charrow. I understand. And I'm honored by the trust which led you to select me for this duty."

Vaijon went down on one knee and bent his head once more, and Charrow gazed down at him for a moment. Then he laid one scarred hand, blunt fingers still strong and calloused from regular practice with sword, bow, and lance, upon the gleaming gold hair.

"Go then with my blessing," he said, "and with that of the God. May his Shield go before you."

"Thank you, Sir Charrow," Vaijon murmured. Charrow's mouth quirked in a small smile, for there was a trace of impatience in the younger man's voice now to mingle with his lingering irritation. Clearly, if he had to do this, he wanted to get it over with as soon as possible.

The master of the chapter considered pointing out that this was not precisely the correct attitude for one being sent forth on the War God's business, but then he thought better of it. Vaijon's attitude, after all, was one reason he'd selected the young knight-probationer for this particular task, and so he settled for patting him on the shoulder and left.

When he looked back from the doorway, Vaijon was back on his feet and gazing once more into the mirror. The knight-captain shook his head with another smile. It was a wry smile, and if the young man before the mirror had been even a little less involved with his reflection, he might have felt a twinge of alarm at the sparkle of amusement in his superior's eyes.

At twenty-five, Sir Vaijon of Almerhas, Baron Halla, fourth son of Earl Truehelm of Almerhas and cousin to Duke Saicha, Royal and Imperial Governor of Fradonia, was a handsome young man. He was also a very *large* one (he stood six inches over six feet, with broad shoulders), and as the son of a great noble and heir to a barony in his own right on his mother's side, he had begun his weapons training early. He moved with the trained grace of a warrior, his muscles had much the same solidity as well-seasoned oak, long hours on the training field had gilded his complexion with a bronze which lingered even in midwinter, and the deep green surcoat of the Order of Tomanāk set off his hair and flashing blue eyes admirably.

Sir Vaijon was well aware of all those facts. Indeed, although it would have been unbecoming to admit it, he knew he took a certain pride in them. As his father was fond of pointing out, after all, one had a duty to one's blood—and, of course, to the Order—and presenting the proper appearance was part of discharging that duty. When one looked the part of a knight of the Order and spoke with the confidence of a gentleman, one's words carried additional weight even with one's peers and impressed lesser folk into obeying one without bothersome argument.

In moments of honesty, Sir Vaijon was prepared to admit that his pride in his birth and appearance stemmed from more than a simple awareness of how they served him in the performance of his duties. To be sure, the administration of justice was the primary purpose of the Order, and it was clear to Vaijon that an imposing presence and the judicious use of his aristocratic titles would . . . encourage others to defer to him when he stepped in to settle disputes. He couldn't change who he was, anyway, so why shouldn't he embrace his identity and use it to the Order's benefit?

Yet as he listened to the door close behind him and used the mirror to check his grooming one last time, Vaijon knew Sir Charrow disagreed with him. The knight-captain considered his firm sense of who he had been born to be a flaw, though Vaijon had never been able to see why. Or, at least, to see that it detracted in any way from the performance of his duties. Not even Sir Charrow could fault his passion for truth and justice; indeed, the master was more likely to suggest in his gentle way that Vaijon might want to temper his quest for justice with a bit more compassion. Nor could he fault Vaijon as a warrior, for it was a simple fact that no one had ever bested him—in training or actual battle—since his seventeenth birthday. Which was only to be expected in an Almerhas of Almerhas, of course. And in one who had known almost from the day he learned to walk that he was destined to be a knight of the war god.

Yet the master seemed to have reservations even there, as if he thought Vaijon's confidence in his abilities constituted some sort of overweening pride, even arrogance. But how could simply admitting the truth of one's own capability be *arrogance*? And it wasn't as if Vaijon thought that he alone deserved all the credit for his prowess. He knew how much he owed his instructors for his superlative training, and he was well aware of how fortunate he was in terms of the size and native strength with which Tomanāk had blessed him. Indeed, that awareness of the favor the Sword of Light had shown him was one of the reasons he longed to administer justice among the little people of Orfressa, which was why he was often baffled by the master's concern when all he sought was to be worthy of the trust Tomanāk had chosen to repose in him.

When Sir Charrow spoke, Vaijon always listened, of course. It was his duty as a knight-probationer, and no Almerhas of Almerhas ever failed in his duty. Yet closely as he listened and hard as he pondered the master's words, he could not convince himself Sir Charrow was right. Justice was justice, truth was truth, and skill at arms was skill at arms. To deny or compromise any of them was to undercut all the Order stood for.

And as far as his birth was concerned, Vaijon had never claimed precedence over any other member of the Order, however low born those others might be. Indeed, he took a certain pride in the fact that he never had. Unlike many other chivalric orders, the Order of Tomanāk stood open to all, and fitness for membership was judged solely on the applicant's merits. It was, perhaps, regrettable that such a policy allowed the occasional lowborn embarrassment entry, but it also meant that only the most qualified warriors from the ranks of the gently born were admitted, as well. And however common some of his brother knights might be, Vaijon knew their hearts were in the right place, else they had never been admitted in the first place, which made up for a great deal. Besides, the better born and more sophisticated members of the Order—like, for example, Sir Vaijon of Almerhas—could normally cover their occasional public gaffes, and Vaijon defied anyone to name one time when he had treated any of them with less than true courtesy.

And so far as those who were not one's brothers were concerned, neither Tomanāk's Code nor any law or rule of the Order specifically required one to actually *socialize* with inferiors so long as one saw to it that they received justice. Still, he couldn't escape the notion that Sir Charrow felt he should be more . . . more—

Vaijon couldn't lay his mental grip on the exact word to describe what Sir Charrow wanted of him, but he knew it was there. The knight-captain didn't lecture him—that wasn't the way of the Order—but there had been enough elliptical references to the character traits of a true knight to leave Vaijon with no doubt that Sir Charrow was unconvinced he possessed them all in proper proportion. More, Vaijon remained only a knight-probationer after almost three full years. He knew his failure to advance beyond that status had nothing to do with his prowess, which could only mean Sir Charrow had delayed his promotion for other reasons, and Vaijon had noted (though no proper knight could admit he had) that the master had a tendency to single him out for particularly onerous duties from time to time. Not dangerous ones, and certainly not ones to which a knight of the Order could object, yet subtly . . . demeaning? No, that wasn't the word either. It was as if . . . as if Sir Charrow hoped that by burdening him with tasks better fitted to the more humbly born he could force Vaijon into some sort of insight.

If that was, indeed, the master's purpose, Vaijon had no intention of objecting, for Sir Charrow was his superior in the Order. He was also one of the noblest, and certainly one of the holiest, men Vaijon had ever met, and the younger knight did not even blame the knight-captain for his own lack of promotion. He might not *agree* with it, but decisions on advancement were properly made by the master of a chapter, and it was the mark of a true gentleman to accept the decisions of those placed in authority over him whether he agreed with those decisions or not. And if Sir Charrow wished Vaijon to learn some lesson or attain some insight which had so far eluded him, then the younger knight was earnestly willing to be instructed by him. That, too, was one of the traits of a man of noble birth, and hence, by definition, of an Almerhas of Almerhas.

Unfortunately, he had yet to obtain so much as a glimpse of whatever Sir Charrow intended him to learn, and there *were* times when he found the knight-captain's notion of his proper duties more objectionable than others. Like now. Not that there was anything ignoble about *this* task, but the morning was little more than an hour old, and six inches of fresh snow had fallen overnight. A knight must be hardy and inured to discomfort, yet there were very few places Sir Vaijon of Almerhas would rather be on a morning like this than buried in a nice, warm nest of blankets. Certainly the *last* place he wanted to be was down at dockside, and in the full regalia of the Order to boot.

He gave the set of his surcoat one last, finicky twitch of adjustment and grimaced as he listened to winter wind moan just beyond the stout front door. His silvered chain hauberk (a gift from his father when he earned his probationary knighthood) glittered brightly, and the gems studding his white sword belt (a gift from his mother on the same occasion) sparkled, yet he suspected he was fiddling with his appearance at least in part to delay the moment he had to step outdoors. The deep green surcoat, woven of the finest silk, emphasized the splendor of his accouterments . . . but it wasn't very thick. Just this once, Vaijon thought longingly of the plainer, cheaper surcoats the Order provided for those knights who lacked his own family's private resources. They were far more plebeian—rather drab, in fact, with minimal embroidery in barely adequate colors—but there was no denying that they were warmer.

Perhaps so, he told himself, but a nobleman must hold to a higher standard, especially on important occasions. And if his surcoat was thinner than he might have wished, at least he had the arming doublet under his hauberk and the otter-trimmed cloak his mother's ladies had sewn for him. Of course, once the wind moaning outside the chapter house had a chance to sink its teeth into the steel links of his mail they would nip right through his arming doublet, but—

He shook his head and scolded himself for thinking about such things at a time like this. However much the weaknesses of the flesh might make him long to avoid exposing himself to the chill— and this early, to boot!—the task he had been assigned was a great honor for a knight-probationer, and Vaijon drew another deep breath, swept his cloak over his shoulders, picked up his gloves, and headed for the door.

Evark Pitchallow laid his schooner alongside the pier with a master's touch. *Wind Dancer* ghosted in under a single jib, then kissed the fenders guarding her hull from the pilings like a lover, and a dozen longshoremen caught the lines her crew threw ashore. Thicker hawsers followed, and it took no more than a handful of minutes to wrap them around the mooring bollards and lower a plank from the pier. It angled steeply downward, for the schooner's deck was much lower than the edge of the wharf, but heavy cross battens promised plenty of traction for those who had to use it.

Evark spent a few more minutes making certain *Wind Dancer* was properly snugged down, then tucked his thumbs in his belt and marched over to where his passengers stood in the waist of the ship with their meager belongings at their feet. He paused in front of them, rocking back on his heels to regard them properly, and Bahzell smiled down at him.

"Well, I've seldom seen a scruffier pair," the halfling allowed after a moment, and Bahzell's smile grew broader. "Aye, all very well to stand there with a witless grin, fishbait! But this is the big city, not some ratty little town in the back of beyond, and the Belhadan Guard's not exactly known for viewing vagrants with affection. If you want *my* advice, you'll lie up somewhere out of sight and see about at least getting yourselves some clothes that pass muster."

"'Vagrants' is it, now?" Bahzell laid a hand on his massive chest, and his foxlike ears flattened in dejection. "You're not after being one to smother a man with flattery, are you now?"

"Ha! Calling *you* two that probably insults *real* vagrants!" Evark snorted, and there was more than a little truth to his words.

Bahzell's gear had been passable enough when he fled the Bloody Sword city of Navahk, but since then he'd covered the full length of Norfressa, north to south, on foot, through a particularly rainy autumn and the onset of winter. Having the Assassins Guild and the adherents of at least two Dark Gods competing to kill him had added a bit more wear and tear to his equipment. The rents various swords, daggers, and demon claws had left in his cloak had been mended competently enough, but the repairs would never win any prizes for neatness, and his boots had been beyond salvation weeks ago. His armor had seen better days, as well. There were gaps in his scale shirt's overlapping steel plates, and despite his best efforts, the survivors wore a faint patina of rust.

Yet grubby as Bahzell was, Brandark was almost worse. For one thing, he lacked the towering inches which lent his companion a certain imposing presence regardless of what he wore. Indeed, having Bahzell for a friend actually made Brandark look even scruffier. The Bloody Sword was taller than most humans, with far broader shoulders, yet no one really realized that when he stood next to Bahzell, for his head didn't even top the Horse Stealer's shoulder.

But shorter stature was only a part of what made him look so tattered. He'd lost a bigger share of his personal gear during the last wild, scrambling stage of their journey than Bahzell had, and what he had left had once been more splendid than anything his friend would ever have worn. Which meant, of course, that the damage it had suffered was even more apparent. And the right ear tip and the two fingers of his left hand which he'd lost along the way only made him look even more battered and bedamned.

In short, Evark Pitchallow could scarcely imagine a pair who looked less like prosperous, gainfully employed souls, and that didn't even consider the fact that they were hradani—a detail which was hardly likely to escape the observation of the first guardsman they encountered.

"I mean it, lads," he said in a quieter, far more serious tone, and jerked his head at the longshoremen already peering curiously at them from the safety of the dock. "There's those in Belhadan of the opinion that the only good hradani's one who's had a foot or so of steel shoved through his throat, and there's no reason in looking any more like their notion of brigands than you have to. You'd be wiser to bide aboard while I have a word with a tailor I know." He paused, regarding them shrewdly, then went on slowly. "If it's that you're short of money, I could—"

"Listen to the man," Bahzell said, shaking his head with yet another smile, and looked at Brandark. "Were you ever hearing a kinder offer? And here he's been to such lengths to make folk think he's a ball of old pitch where others keep a heart! It's enough to make a man come all over teary-eyed."

Evark glowered up at him, and the Horse Stealer laughed softly in a cloud of vapor and reached down to rest a hand on his shoulder.

"Jesting aside, it's grateful I am for the offer, Evark," he said, "and I'm thinking you've probably a point or three, as well. But we've no lack of funds—" he gave the fat belt purse which had once belonged to a Purple Lord landlord a jingling shake "—and we'll not be wandering about Belhadan all unescorted."

"You won't?" Evark sounded surprised.

"We won't?" Brandark echoed, and raised an eyebrow at his towering friend. "That's nice to know. Ah, just when were you planning to tell *me* we wouldn't be? And while I'm thinking about it, how in Fiendark's name d'*you* know we won't?"

"I wasn't after telling you sooner because himself only got around to telling *me* on the way into the harbor," Bahzell said reasonably, and Brandark and Evark closed their mouths with perfectly synchronized snaps. He gave a deep, rumbling chuckle at their reaction, and Brandark shook himself.

"I don't recall seeing any deities standing around the deck," he remarked mildly, and Bahzell shrugged.

"If he'd been minded to show himself he'd have been bringing along a chorus of trumpets and appearing in a flash of light, I'm sure," he explained kindly. "Given as he didn't do either, why, the only thing I can think of is that he wasn't all that wishful to be seen."

"Oh, *thank* you for explaining!" Brandark replied, and this time Evark joined Bahzell's laughter. Brandark let them chuckle for several seconds, then poked his friend in the chest.

"All right, Longshanks," he said firmly. "Now stop laughing and explain just what you mean about not wandering around on our own."

"There's no mystery in it, little man," Bahzell replied. "We're after being met, and unless I'm much mistaken—" he raised his hand to point "—that's the lad looking for us now."

Brandark followed the direction of Bahzell's index finger, and both eyebrows rose as he took in the apparition striding down the dock.

Others were turning to look, as well. Actually, *gawk* was a better word, for seldom did such splendor grace the warehouse district of the Belhadan waterfront with its presence. The handsome, golden-haired newcomer was taller than Brandark, which made him very tall indeed for a human, but despite broad, well-muscled shoulders (once again, for a human) he was almost slender compared to the powerfully built Bloody Sword. His silver-washed mail glistened, the white sword belt that marked a knight of one of the chivalric orders was studded with faceted gems that flashed with eye-watering brilliance, as did those adorning the scabbard of his sword, and his high, soft boots had been dyed the same forest green as his fur-trimmed cloak and surcoat.

A surcoat which bore the crossed sword and mace of Tomanāk in gold and silver thread.

"Korthrala!" Evark muttered, pulling at his magnificent handlebar mustache while he stared at the glittering vision. "I could buy a whole new suit of sails out of what he's wearing on his back!"

"Aye, he *is* after being a mite . . . spectacular, isn't he just?" Bahzell agreed with a wicked smile.

"Did you know what was coming?" the halfling asked, unable to tear his eyes away.

"No, I'm thinking himself was after deciding I'd enjoy the surprise," Bahzell replied, and Brandark sighed.

"Wonderful. I wish someone had thought to warn me about gods and their senses of humor."

"How's that?" Evark asked.

"I know all the legends and lays," the Bloody Sword said plaintively. "I've learned just about all the songs, read most of the chronicles, and studied everything I could get my hands on about the Fall."

"And?" Evark prompted when he paused.

"And not one of them *warned* me," Brandark complained. The halfling looked at him, and he shrugged. "Oh, there's plenty of warning that Hirahim Lightfoot enjoys bad jokes, but that's his *job*. According to the lore masters, Tomanāk is supposed to be a serious, high-minded sort of god . . . not the kind of person who'd send *that*—" he waved at the oncoming martial fashion plate "—to meet *us*."

"Aye? Well according to the tales, he's not one to be having hradani champions, either, now is he?" Bahzell demanded. Brandark shook his head wryly, and Bahzell smacked him on the shoulder. "Then I'm thinking that either your precious lore masters weren't quite the 'masters' they thought, or else there's changes being made. Either road, I've more than a feeling there's a reason himself was after sending 'that' to be meeting us."

"Oh, I'm sure of that," Brandark muttered. "What I'm *not* sure of is that it's a reason I'll *like*."

❖   ❖   ❖

It was even colder on the docks than Vaijon had feared. He had the distinct impression his nose was about to freeze off, followed by other portions of his anatomy in order of exposure, but he looked about with interest despite his discomfort.

He'd never been a good sailor. The mere thought of a winter voyage could tie his stomach in knots, and he'd managed to avoid visiting the docks more than twice in the entire time he'd been assigned to the Order's Belhadan chapter. Those two trips had been made in the middle of summer, unfortunately, and in addition to its importance as a shipping hub, Belhadan was home port to the largest fishing fleet in Norfressa, and his business had taken him right to Fisherman's Wharf. The stench from the midsummer fishery sheds had turned Vaijon a darker green than his surcoat, which was why he'd gone to such lengths to avoid repeating the experience. Luckily, today's business took him to a different part of the waterfront. Even better, the winter cold seemed to have frozen the stench out of the air, for which he was devoutly grateful.

He consulted the scrap of paper Sir Charrow had handed him and nodded as he matched the numbers on it to those painted on the dockside pilings. He'd been told to look for a schooner (whatever a "schooner" was) at Berth Nine at the Produce Pier, and he shoved the note into his belt pouch as Berth Nine came into sight. He couldn't see much of the ship moored there—it appeared to be lower than the side of the pier—but it had only two masts and seemed quite small. He felt a spurt of indignation that a champion of Tomanāk should be forced to travel aboard such a lowly vessel, but he stepped on it quickly. A true knight went where honor and his duty to the God took him, and a champion's presence touched even the least prepossessing ship with the shadow of Tomanāk Himself.

He quickened his pace, reassured by that thought, and squared his shoulders as the crowd of roughly dressed longshoremen turned to stare admiringly at him. He was accustomed to that reaction, and he inclined his head at precisely the right angle—enough to acknowledge their admiration but not enough to appear overly proud—as he headed for the gangplank.

"Gods!" Brandark muttered as the magnificent young man drew closer. "D'you think Tomanāk would be *too* upset if we dropped him in the harbor for a few minutes? I'd pull him back out— promise!"

"Will you just listen at that, now!" Bahzell replied. "Why, I'm thinking he could be teaching you a thing or two about dressing sharp, Brandark my lad."

"*Him?*" Brandark snorted. "All this time together, and you still haven't learned to appreciate the elegance, the restrained style and cut, the carefully selected fabrics of my wardrobe?" His hand swept a graceful gesture at his tattered finery, and he shook his head sadly. "*Anyone* can sew fistfuls of jewels onto himself, you uncouth barbarian, but that doesn't mean he has a sense of fashion! Besides, I won't *have* to drop him in the harbor if he's not careful. If he pokes his nose an inch or two higher, he's going to trip over his own two feet, go over the edge, and drown out of pure self-admiration."

"Ah, so that's it! I was thinking I'd heard a note of jealousy there," Bahzell observed, and grinned at his friend's expression. Brandark started to reply, then stopped as the newcomer walked to the edge of the pier and looked down at *Wind Dancer* with a puzzled air.

Vaijon looked out over the boat—no, he corrected himself, the *schooner*—in confusion. He knew he'd come to the right berth, but there was no champion in sight, nor even any sign of his proper entourage. Seen close up, the schooner was less pedestrian-looking than he'd feared. In fact, it had a certain undeniable grace, a long, lean set of lines which looked indefinably *right* somehow, but its crew appeared to consist entirely of halflings. Well, halflings and two—

Sir Vaijon of Almerhas froze. He'd never encountered a hradani in his life, for such savages were never seen among *civilized* folk, but he couldn't mistake the mobile, foxlike ears. Or, for that matter, the sheer size of the bigger one. The mountainous hradani would have made at least two of any man Vaijon had ever seen— he must weigh four or five hundred pounds, all of it bone and muscle—and a more evil-looking villain would have been impossible to imagine. His cloak looked to have been looted from a dead brigand, his crudely made scale mail had obviously been scrounged from the same source, and his boots and breeches were little better than rags. The hilt of a sword thrust up behind his raggedy cloak's left shoulder, and the sort of warrior's braid favored by backward human frontiersmen blew in the icy wind. The smaller hradani was just as tattered looking, but beside his companion's hulking menace he looked almost civilized.

Ancient tales of the hradani rape of Kontovar and more recent stories of border warfare and bloodshed here in Norfressa flashed through Vaijon's mind, and he stared at the hradani as if he'd opened his closet and found it full of vipers. There was no sane reason for two members of the most feared and reviled of all the Races of Man to suddenly appear in the middle of Belhadan, but there they stood, gazing up at him, and his hand dropped instinctively to the hilt of his sword.

He started to draw, then made himself stop while he battled his confusion. He was only a knight-probationer, but it was the duty of any knight of Tomanāk to defend the helpless against hradani and their like. He got that far without difficulty. The problem was that no one else on the pier seemed to realize they were in danger. In fact, they were gawking at *him*, not the hradani, and as he stood there with six inches of his sword out of its sheath, most of them began to grin and one or two actually laughed aloud.

His ears might be half frozen, but they weren't too cold for him to feel them burn as the loutish bystanders chuckled at his expense, and he shoved his blade back home with a click, kicking himself mentally for reacting without thought. The hradani were simply standing there on the schooner's deck, with two equally travel-stained packs at their feet. They were obviously passengers, not raiders sailing into Belhadan on the quarterdeck of a Shith-Kiri corsair, and however fearsome their kind might be as fighters, a single pair was hardly enough to threaten one of the King Emperor's largest cities! No wonder no one else seemed concerned. No doubt the Guard would keep a close eye on them—Vaijon would pass the word to the authorities himself after he guided the champion to the chapter house— but the very thought of the champion reminded him that he had more important duties this morning, and he shook himself impatiently. His lungs ached, protesting the cold as he drew a deep, calming breath, and then he settled his cloak more neatly about his shoulders and stalked down the gangplank with icy dignity.

Or as close to icy dignity as he could come. The plank was much springier than he had imagined, and he found himself doing an awkward hop-skip-and-stumble over its battens as it flexed under his boots. More guffaws rose from the idlers on the dock, and Vaijon muttered a few words Sir Charrow would not have approved of as he felt his ears burn afresh. What he *wanted* to do was take the flat of his blade to the buffoons who dared laugh at him, but his oath to the Order, not to mention the Code of Tomanāk, forbade any such thing. In an intellectual way, Vaijon could agree with the restriction—it wasn't as though anyone had offered him physical violence, after all—but his blood boiled and his teeth grated as he forced himself to swallow the insult of their low-born hilarity.

He made it to the schooner's deck in one piece and managed

to hide his relief as he felt relatively stable footing underfoot once more. He took another moment to settle himself and be sure he had control of his temper, then turned to the halfling he assumed was the ship's master. It was unfortunate that the halfling in question was standing right beside the two hradani, for their proximity made it difficult for Vaijon to ignore them, but he managed.

"Excuse me for intruding," he told the presumed captain, "but I was told to meet a passenger on your vessel."

"You were, were you?" The halfling's gruff, accented Axeman sounded harsh and uncouth beside Vaijon's polished, aristocratic enunciation, and his short ivory horns gleamed against his chestnut hair as he folded his arms and tilted his head back to gaze up at the young knight. "And who might you be?"

Vaijon blinked, unaccustomed to so direct and challenging a query. He started to reply with the hauteur such impertinence deserved, but he stopped himself in time. The Order of Tomanāk taught respect for even the most humble, and those of gentle blood bore a special responsibility to avoid treading upon those who didn't realize they were being insolent.

"I am Sir Vaijon of Almerhas, son of Truehelm of Almerhas, Knight-Probationer of the Order of Tomanāk and Baron of Halla," he said, infusing all the dignity of his ancestry into his tenor voice. "And you are, sir?"

"Nothing so special as all that," the halfling replied, then snorted. "Evark of Marfang, master of this ship," he said brusquely.

"I am honored to make your acquaintance, Captain," Vaijon said with a gracious bow.

"Charmed myself, I'm sure," Evark said dryly as Vaijon straightened. "Now, what were you saying brings you aboard *Wind Dancer*?"

The knight drew himself to his full height once more and rested one hand regally on the hilt of his sword.

"I've come on the business of the Order of Tomanāk," he said. "I was sent to meet one of your passengers."

"And which one would that be?"

"I wasn't given his name, Captain. I was simply told that you would have a champion of the Order on board and instructed to guide him to our chapter house."

"Oh! It's a champion of *Tomanāk* you're looking for, is it?" Vaijon nodded, raising his eyebrows encouragingly as the halfling finally grasped the reason for his presence. "Well, why didn't you say so?" Evark went on. "That's him there," he explained, and waved at the bigger of the two barbarians standing beside him. "The tall one," he added helpfully.

Vaijon felt his jaw drop, and then bright spots of anger blazed on his frozen cheeks. Blue eyes flashed dangerously as the halfling mocked him, and the bystanders' howls of laughter only made it worse. His gloved hand clenched on the hilt of his sword, and he took a half step forward, opening his mouth to lash out angrily. But before he got the first word said, another voice spoke.

"Gently, my lad," it rumbled, and Vaijon paused. It was deeper and more powerful than any voice he'd ever before heard, and amusement flickered in its depths. Amusement at *him*, he realized with a raw burst of fury, and spun towards its owner.

Vaijon of Almerhas was accustomed to looking even the tallest human in the eye, but he felt the strain in the back of his neck as he glared up at the hradani. He expected to see a mocking expression, but the brown eyes that met his were almost gentle— twinkling with amusement, yes, but oddly sympathetic. Which only made it worse, of course. Bad enough to be mocked by a halfling without having some unwashed barbarian *sympathize* with him for being made the butt of someone else's bad joke!

"I beg your pardon?" he got out through gritted teeth. "Were you addressing me?"

"Aye, I do believe I was," the hradani agreed in that rustically-accented subterranean bass.

"When I require your advice, *sir*, I will inform you!" Vaijon said with freezing hauteur.

"No doubt," the hradani replied easily. "But the problem with that, I'm thinking, is that most often by the time a man's *realized* he's after needing advice, he's past the time when it might have been doing him some good." Vaijon's teeth ground audibly, but the hradani went on calmly.

"Take this very moment, for example," he suggested. "There you stand, thinking as how Evark here is after making light of you, when he's done naught at all, at all, but answer your questions. It's best you be thinking over the answers before you've the doing of something you'll not be so happy about after."

Vaijon's nostrils flared and white-hot fury pulsed in his veins. Yet much as he hated admitting it, the hradani had a point. No doubt he thought it was amusing to mock a knight of the Order, but his very mockery had reminded Vaijon of who and what he was. He had a responsibility to protect the Order's honor from public insult and ridicule, but much as he longed to punish Evark's insolent excuse for a sense of humor, thrashing someone as much smaller than he as a halfling, however badly he deserved it, was hardly the act of a true knight.

"I shall take your advice under consideration," he told the hradani after two or three incandescent seconds, but his eyes were back on the halfling. "In the meantime, however, I would advise *you* to direct me to the person I'm here to meet!" he said coldly.

The halfling only shook his head with a curious mixture of amusement, derision, and sympathy, then looked up at the hradani.

"I've my ship to look after," he said, "and this un's one of Scale-Balancer's lot, gods help us all. *You* deal with it." Then he turned and stalked off, leaving a stupefied Vaijon staring at his back.

"I— How dare— Come *back* here!" he spluttered, and started to charge off in pursuit. But a huge hand closed on his mailed shoulder, stopping him, and he felt himself being turned as easily as if he were a child.

He found himself staring up at the hradani once more and reached for the hand which gripped him. That hand's wrist was as broad as his own biceps, and a strange little shiver of disbelief went through him as he realized how powerful it truly was, but his eyes flamed.

"Gently, now!" the hradani said, and his voice was sharper than before, edged with command. "I told you to be thinking over Evark's answers, Sir Vaijon of Almerhas, and you should have done it."

"What d'you—?" Vaijon began, and the hradani shook his head.

"I'm thinking I've begun to see why himself wasn't after warning *you*, my lad," he said. "You've a way of going at things without thinking at all, at all, don't you just?" Vaijon opened his mouth again, but the hradani gave him a gentle shake.

"Stop now, and take it slow," he advised. "I've no doubt the notion comes as a shock, but old Evark told you true, you see."

"Told me—?" Vaijon froze, and the hradani nodded.

"Aye," he said almost compassionately. "It's sorry I am to be telling you this, Vaijon of Almerhas, but my name is Bahzell, son of Bahnak, Lord of Clan Iron Axe of the Horse Stealer hradani and Prince of Hurgrum, and it's me you're after meeting."

"Y-*you're* a-a cham—?" Vaijon couldn't force the words out of his mouth as he stared in horrified disbelief, all color draining out of his face, and the enormous hradani nodded gently.

CHAPTER TWO

It couldn't be true. Vaijon *knew* it couldn't, yet something in the hradani's eyes, something in the timbre of his voice, whispered otherwise. But that had to be Vaijon's imagination. Tomanāk *had* no hradani champions. The very idea was . . . was . . . It was *blasphemous*, that was what it was!

He started to stay so, then stopped and fought to think his way through the impossibility. As a knight of the Order, he was honor bound to challenge any who falsely claimed membership in it, and the thought of matching himself against the hradani didn't worry him particularly, despite the other's size. He worked out daily with the Belhadan chapter's best trainers, even in midwinter; none had ever bested him, and big as the hradani was, he had to be slow, especially with any weapon as ponderous as the two-handed sword he wore across his back. But Vaijon couldn't issue challenge without proof the other had lied, and until he had that proof, his own honor required him to treat the hradani with the same courtesy he would show an honest man.

"Forgive me, sir," he said finally, "but since the master of my chapter house was unable to give me either the name or the description of the one I was sent to meet, I must seek some proof of identity."

He was rather pleased by how close to normally that had come out, but the hradani's unflustered nod puzzled him. There was no defensiveness in it, and he held his empty right hand out in front of him. Vaijon felt his eyebrows rise in confusion as the other flexed his fingers, and then that earthquake voice uttered a single word.

22

"*Come*," it said quietly, almost coaxingly, and Vaijon of Almerhas jumped straight backward in astonishment as five feet of burnished steel leapt into existence. One instant the hradani's hand was empty; the next the sword which had been on his back was in his grip, flashing with razor-edged wickedness in the morning light.

Vaijon's backwards stumble ended with him half-crouched, eyes huge while a panic no opponent had ever waked pulsed within him. But the hradani only looked at him with those same compassionate eyes and lowered his blade until its tip touched the deck before him, then turned it so Vaijon could see it clearly. The knight quivered, still lingering on the edge of that totally unexpected panic, but then he sucked in air and forced himself back under control. He was a knight of the Order of Tomanāk, and whatever else he might be, he was no coward. And so he reexerted his self-mastery and looked at the sword, then leaned abruptly forward, blue eyes wide once more as he stared at the crossed mace and sword etched deep into the blade below the quillons.

A profound silence stretched out. Vaijon had never actually seen a Sword of Tomanāk. Such a blade was the ultimate emblem of the Order, a weapon only the mightiest of champions might bear and the symbol of the obedience every member of the Order owed to its bearer. Even among champions such blades were vanishingly rare, for they came only from the hands of Tomanāk Himself, and He bestowed them only upon those who had proven themselves worthy to stand at His own side in battle. But rare though they might be, every servant of the Order, down to the rawest squire, knew each was imbued with its own special powers, and what the hradani had just done combined with the burnished, unmarred and unmarrable perfection of the sword's blade and those perfectly formed emblems of Tomanāk to tell Vaijon *exactly* what he looked upon.

For an instant, he looked whiter than the snow behind him, despite his weathered complexion, but then the color came back in a scalding flood of scarlet. It was still impossible. His emotions insisted that this hradani couldn't possibly be a champion of Tomanāk. Yet his intellect knew better . . . and that he'd made a colossal fool of himself into the bargain.

He forced himself to straighten and cleared his throat, gloved hand still locked on the hilt of his own sword. It was remotely possible that the blade he'd been shown was a wizard-wrought forgery, but Sir Charrow would be the best judge of that. For now, his own duty was clear, and he made himself look the hradani squarely in the eye.

"Pray pardon me for questioning your identity . . . Sir Bahzell," he got out.

"As to that, I've no doubt I'd be a mite surprised in your boots my own self," Bahzell replied. "Which, come to think, is the reason himself was after giving me this sword. He *said* I'd have need of proof." His sudden grin showed square, white teeth that looked strong enough to bite *Wind Dancer's* hawsers in half. "And I've no need for 'sirs,' my lad. Just plain Bahzell will be serving well enough for the likes of me."

"But—" Vaijon began, then chopped himself off and managed a nod. "As you will, S— Bahzell. As I've said, Sir Charrow Malahkai, Knight-Captain and Master of the Belhadan Chapter of the Order of Tomanāk and Constable of Fradonia in the King-Emperor's name, sends greeting through me and begs you to accompany me to the chapter house that he and your brothers of the Sword may greet you properly and welcome you to their fellowship."

He knew there was a sour edge to his voice, hard though he tried to keep it out, and Bahzell cocked his head, twitching his ears thoughtfully back and forth as he gazed down at him. A handful of seconds trickled past, and then the Horse Stealer reached back over his shoulder to sheath his sword and nodded agreeably.

"That's after being the friendliest welcome I've had this whole trip," he observed, with just enough irony to make Vaijon flush anew, "and it's happy I'll be to accept it. Assuming, of course, that it's meant to include my friend here," he added, indicating Brandark with a flick of his ears.

Vaijon hesitated in fresh consternation. Bad enough to invite a hradani who *might* be a champion into the chapter house without inviting one who most certainly was not. But assuming that this Bahzell was who and what he claimed, he had the right to extend guest right to anyone he chose . . . and there *was* that sword. . . .

"Of course," Vaijon said with a sigh he couldn't quite hide. "Will you have your baggage sent after you to the chapter house?"

"I'm not after being so feeble as all that just yet," Bahzell said genially. He hung a leather rucksack over one shoulder, picked up the steel-bowed arbalest which had lain beside it on the deck, and beamed at his guide while Brandark gathered up his own pack. "We'll just be taking it with us as we go," he told Vaijon. The knight-probationer started to make another comment, then hesitated and visibly changed his mind.

"If you and your . . . companion will follow me, then," he said instead, and led the way back up the springy gangplank. Bahzell and Brandark paused only to exchange farewells with *Wind Dancer's* grinning crew, then followed docilely in his wake.

Neither hradani spoke as Vaijon led them through Belhadan's streets, and he was just as glad. It freed him to think, which was in many ways a mixed blessing, but at least it also gave him a chance to consider the conclusions which his brain persisted in drawing however much he would have preferred not to.

It was certainly possible Sir Charrow had known no more about this "champion's" identity than Vaijon had, but Vaijon didn't believe it for a moment. Especially in light of the master's frequent, gentle admonitions on the perils of pride in self, his selection of a guide back to the chapter house was too pointed to be coincidental, and Vaijon clamped his jaw tight on resentment as he reflected upon that unpalatable fact.

He longed to cling to the belief that "just plain Bahzell" was, in fact, an impostor, but he knew better, and it was no part of a gentleman's conduct to lie to himself. Yet admitting that knowledge to himself didn't make things any better. Champions were chosen directly by the God Himself. They were His true Swords, the exalted few who bore the full brunt of battle against the Dark Gods in the Light's name, and there were probably fewer than twenty of them in all Norfressa at any given moment. How could Tomanāk have wasted such honor as that upon an ignorant, blood-thirsty, barbarian *hradani*?

His soul cried out in protest at the very thought, yet even as it did, another part of him writhed in self-contempt. He had no right to dispute the choices of the god he served. Worse, the part of him Sir Charrow had worked so hard to reach—the tiny, buried part which had heard the summons of the God of Justice even through the pride of House Almerhas—knew protest was stupid. That the Order itself taught that neither birth nor blood nor family made a true knight. That the only cause which truly counted was the cause of justice, the only true treasure was the treasure of truth, and the heart of a true knight's strength must come from within. And if all those things were true of the knights of the Order, how much more must they be true for the God's own champions?

That small, inner voice would give Vaijon no peace as it whispered in the back of his brain, castigating him for his own blindness. Yet it was *only* a whisper, and youth and pride muffled it. He truly tried to work through his confusion and lay hands on understanding, but his own strength and stubborn will were turned against him in the struggle, and resentment and confusion boiled just beneath the false surface of courtesy his childhood training still presented to the world.

Brandark glanced at their guide's pike-straight back, then looked at Bahzell and rolled his eyes, flattening his ears for emphasis. His wicked expression warned the Horse Stealer that he'd just thought of a way to twit Vaijon, and a part of Bahzell wanted to sit back and watch it happen. But only a part, and Brandark shrugged when he shook his head quellingly. The Bloody Sword flipped his left hand in a small gesture, resigning responsibility for whatever happened, and turned his bright-eyed attention to the city about them, instead.

It was worth looking at, for if the Purple Lords' Bortalik was queen of the southern coast, Belhadan ruled the far north . . . and she was a more impressive monarch. Worse still, from the Purple Lords' perspective, she was only the *second* city of the Empire, as outclassed by the royal and imperial capital at Axe Hallow as she outclassed Bortalik.

The Purple Lords' festering resentment for the Empire and all its works was probably inevitable. Both the Empire's wealth and the ingenuity of its artisans and craftsmen mocked their efforts to imitate its achievements, and they hated it for that. It was bad enough to be overshadowed by anyone, but what truly stuck in the Purple Lords' craws was to find themselves so outclassed, and with such apparent lack of effort, by the "mongrelized" Axemen. It was a fundamental article of faith for any Purple Lord that his half-elvish blood made him superior to all of the other Races of Man. After all, his people's elvish heritage meant they lived as much as four hundred years, while the pragmatism of their human blood kept them focused in the real, everyday world as no dreamy elf lord could ever be. To be sure, they were less fertile than humans or dwarves, but quantity was no match for quality. Even dwarves were fortunate to live more than two and a half centuries, and if Purple Lords bore few children, their city-states boasted more than sufficient human peasants and serfs to serve their needs. From their viewpoint, their cultural and racial superiority were obvious, and they went to enormous lengths to maintain the purity of both. All of which made their persistent failure to match the Empire's achievements far worse than merely infuriating, for Axemen embraced precisely the opposite attitude. Worse, they regarded the Purple Lords' unceasing efforts to wrest away the Empire's undeserved preeminence as a source of *amusement*, not a threat.

Not that anything better could have been expected from them, for the Empire of the Axe had grown out of the even more ancient Kingdom of the Axe, and the Kingdom of the Axe had been the land to which three quarters of the refugees from the Fall of Kontovar had come. The traditional insularity which most of the Races of Man had practiced in Kontovar—and which had reemerged in many of Norfressa's younger kingdoms—had crumbled in the Kingdom of the Axe. It was difficult to see how anything else could have happened, given the desperate straits to which the Fall's survivors had been reduced, but the House of Kormak had taken pains to *nurture* what necessity had created over the centuries which followed.

As a race, dwarves were probably the finest engineers ever born—certainly their people took the deepest pleasure in working with earth and stone and iron, for it was in their blood. Historically, however, they had always been the most insular of the Races of Man, tending to keep themselves (and their secrets) to themselves. Few among them had truly valued—or even understood—the elves' soul-deep love for the beauty of poetry, art, and music or humans' restless energy and hunger for experimentation and change. But the fusion of peoples which had created the Empire of the Axe had made dwarf, elf, and human partners as never before, bringing all those qualities together in the "mongrelization" the Purple Lords so despised . . . and had never been able to equal.

And however contemptible the Purple Lords found the Empire's half-breed pedigree, the fruit of the Axemen's labors were obvious to Bahzell and Brandark as they gazed out over Belhadan on a cold winter's day. The deep bay which served the city was smaller than Bortalik Bay, but it was vast enough. There was room and to spare for twice a hundred ships on its sun-streaked, wave-wrinkled cobalt, and the city spread up the sheer mountains above it like some enormous flower petaled with steep-pitched roofs of slate and tile. It showed the unmistakable impress of dwarvish engineers, and not just in the massive breakwaters which joined the islands off the bay's mouth to protect its moorings even in the wildest weather, yet human and elvish influence was equally obvious.

No other race understood stone as dwarves did, and Belhadan was unquestionably the work of their hands. But dwarves had always favored straight lines and soaring heights fused with functionality, and their love of stone had never blunted their urge to master it and make it conform to their desires. In many ways, they were at least as intractable as their beloved rock and iron, and their solution to a problem was generally to tackle it head-on. If a hillside or mountain blocked the path of a roadway, a dwarvish engineer went straight through the obstacle. He was quite *capable* of going around it, instead; it was simply that the idea of detouring would never enter his head unless someone else put it there.

Clearly, someone had done just that for Belhadan's architects, for the city was intimately entwined with the mountains in which it had been planted. Rather than subdue those mountains, it embraced them and followed their contours with streets and small, intimate plazas, brick-paved squares and terraced courts. But it also *shaped* those contours, utilizing them with a subtle efficiency which allowed them to be themselves yet bent them to the service of Belhadan's citizens, as if a "normal" city had been divided into portions and inserted with loving care into mountains untouched by mortal hands. Natural cliffs and steep slopes furred with ever-greens loomed above broad squares and avenues designed for commerce, trade, and places of government. Satellites of homes and shops swept up those slopes, like surf spouting up through fissures and flues, while residential avenues trickled down to meet the wide roadways required by freight wagons and merchant caravans. Regularly placed street lamps—not the torches most cities Bahzell had seen used for street lighting (if they used any at all) but big, square lanterns on green-painted pillars—stood like sentries, joined by waist-high chains which separated the streets from wide, flagged sidewalks, and the thought of how they must look from a distance at night as they traced the arteries of the city through the darkness like Silendros' own stars touched Bahzell with a wondering awe. And under the surface, tunnels and galleries sliced through those same cliffs, burrowing deep into their foundations to provide streets, taverns, warehouses, ropeworks, ship chandlers, and a hundred different kinds of businesses—all carved deep into living rock without disturbing the mountains' rough-spined beauty.

Nor had Belhadan's builders neglected its defense. Walls as mighty as those the Purple Lords had raised to protect Bortalik reared behind the busy wharves and docks; the huge Royal and Imperial naval base, enclosed within its own walls; and the winter-idled shipyards. A raiding fleet might ravage the docks, if it could strike with numbers enough, but no seaborne force could breach those walls so long as the defenders had strength to man them, and the landward fortifications were even more imposing. The impress of dwarvish engineers was most obvious there, for military considerations had been foremost in their design. Yet in an odd way, the harsh, uncompromising lines of wall and tower only emphasized the love with which Belhadan had been fitted into its surroundings.

Entire slopes had been quarried away into man-made cliffs, many pierced with the slits of tunneled archers' galleries. Their bare stone rose to the walls and towers which crowned them, impregnable, and yet less like fortification against outside foes than like dikes, holding in the greenery and life of the city.

Bahzell and Brandark had seen wonders few of their kindred could have imagined in the months since they'd fled Navahk. They'd passed through Esgfalas, Derm, even fabled Saramfel, where elven lords who remembered the Fall itself ruled, yet Belhadan touched them as none of those other cities had. It was larger than any of them, older than Derm yet far younger than Saramfel, and it had a strength—a sense of itself and a bright, confident vitality—wholly and uniquely its own. They felt it singing in the ice-cold air as they followed Vaijon through the rousing bustle of morning streets, the early cries of vendors, the laughter of apprentices sweeping and shoveling the night's snow from streets and walks. It took all their self-discipline not to gawk like the yokels Sir Vaijon obviously considered them, yet a part of them pitied the people about them, for Belhadan's citizens were too close to the wonder the hradani perceived so clearly to recognize how remarkable their city truly was. This was their home. They took it—and themselves—for granted as they got on with their lives, and perhaps only barbarians who knew from grim experience how thin a line stood between peaceful prosperity and ruin could truly appreciate the wondrous thing which had been created here.

Bahzell shook his head as the wish that his father could see this slid through his thoughts. Prince Bahnak would have grasped the wonder of a people so secure in the safety of their city that it never even occurred to them to think about it. He might not have fully understood something so foreign to his own experience, yet it was the end towards which he worked, the reason he had imposed his will on the other clans of the Horse Stealers. Oh, Bahzell knew his father too well to see him as a saint, and he knew how much Prince Bahnak enjoyed the game, how he relished the conflict and competition of building an empire where there had been only anarchy. Yet he also knew there were depths within Bahnak, hopes his father might never have fully defined even for himself, and he recognized the millennium-old heart-hunger of his people for the chance to be like the people bustling through Belhadan's streets, clapping their hands together against the chill, huddling into coats and cloaks for warmth, hurrying about their business and eddying aside as they suddenly recognized the hradani in their midst and gave them a wide berth.

For the chance, Bahzell realized, simply to *be*, and to let others be, without warlords and the constant need to watch and ward. That was what his father wanted to bring to the northern hradani, whether or not he'd ever put it into so many words, and Bahzell felt suddenly humbled and ashamed for all the years in which he hadn't understood. But he understood now, and in understanding that, he also understood why the Dark Gods opposed Bahnak. The Dark fed on suffering and despair, for it was those who saw no other hope of saving themselves or those they loved who turned their backs upon the Light. It was those conscious only of their helplessness who would make *any* bargain with anyone who promised them strength, and who could blame them if they did?

That was why the Dark Gods hated Bahnak: because he would take that sense of helplessness, that despair, from his people if he succeeded in his efforts.

It was odd, Bahzell reflected, to see it all so clearly three hundred leagues from home among the people of a city who regarded all hradani as blood-drinking barbarians, but perhaps he'd *had* to come here to see it. Perhaps it was only the combination of all he'd seen and experienced since leaving Navahk which made the vision so clear. But none of that truly mattered. What mattered was that he *had* seen it and, in the seeing, understood yet another reason Tomanāk Orfro had chosen a hradani champion at last.

"Ah! *There* you are, Prince Bahzell!"

The ill-assorted trio had just turned up the steep slope still called Tannery Hill (although the city fathers had banished all tanneries and their stench from Belhadan proper to share quarters with the fishery sheds decades ago) when someone called to them. It took Vaijon a moment to realize the voice was addressed to them, for they were halfway to the chapter house and his mind had been busy with how he was going to explain two hradani to the door wardens, but then he stopped and turned to see the speaker . . . only to blink in fresh astonishment.

The man striding briskly towards them wore a knee-length coat. That wasn't uncommon in Belhadan, where most people preferred such garments for winter wear. They were less fashionable than cloaks, and they almost always made Vaijon think of bankers and merchants and moneylenders, but they were also warmer and more practical. And he felt no temptation to curl a mental lip in disdain this time, for *this* coat was darkest midnight blue, trimmed in white. Those were the colors of the magi, and the golden scepter of Semkirk glittering on its right breast said the man who wore them held high rank in the mage academies. He was of no more than middle years, though snow-white streaks shone like burnished silver in his thick brown hair and neatly trimmed beard. He wore a huge smile and carried the traditional polished white staff of a mage, and Vaijon inhaled sharply as he recognized him.

Bahzell had also stopped, and his ears cocked in question as the newcomer walked up to them.

"And a good morning to you, too," the Horse Stealer said politely, then tilted his head to one side. "I'm hoping you'll forgive the asking, but should I be knowing you?"

"Not yet," the mage said, still smiling. "My name is Kresko. I'm the senior master of the Belhadan Mage Academy."

"Are you now?" Bahzell murmured, and his eyes narrowed. There had been a time when "mage" and "wizard" meant the same thing, but that had been long ago. These days, a mere suspicion of wizardry was enough to get a man lynched places—understandably, given what the dark wizards had done in Kontovar—but magi were as trusted as wizards were feared. Unlike a wizard, a mage's skills and talents were those of the mind, and he could draw only upon his own strength, or that of other magi linked in mutual support, not upon the enormous power wizards routinely sought to manipulate. But the true reason they were trusted was the Oath of the Magi, the code which bound them to use their talents only to help and never to harm . . . and made them mortal foes of any black wizard.

"Yes," Kresko said, answering the Horse Stealer's question. "Mistress Zarantha told us you and Lord Brandark would be arriving today and asked us to greet you, but I'm afraid her precognition wasn't equal to telling us the precise time of your arrival, and I missed you at the docks."

Vaijon stood mutely to one side, listening, and fresh confusion flickered through him. Master Kresko was one of the most important people in Belhadan—or, for that matter, in the entire province of Fradonia—but he seemed totally unaware of it as he smiled at both hradani and extended his right hand to clasp forearms with Bahzell.

"We of the academies owe both of you an enormous debt," he said more seriously. "Zarantha is still new to her talents. When they reach full maturity, she'll be one of the most powerful magi we've seen in generations, and she and Duke Jashân have already begun construction of their own academy. But if the two of you hadn't saved her life—"

Bahzell made a small, uncomfortable gesture, and Kresko stopped what he'd been saying. He gazed quizzically at the two hradani for a moment, then shrugged.

"She warned us about you, you know," he said, and let his smile grow a little broader as Bahzell and Brandark exchanged glances. "She *said* you wouldn't let us thank you properly, and I see she was right," he went on. "But that was only part of why I hunted you down this morning. The main reason was to deliver three messages."

"And what messages might those be?" Bahzell asked with a touch of wariness, and Kresko chuckled.

"Nothing too sinister," he assured the Horse Stealer. "First, Duke Jashân asked me to remind you and Brandark that you're now sept to Jashân, and he knows from Zarantha that you lost most of your gear to the Purple Lords. Accordingly, he's used the mage relays to establish a line of credit in his name with House Harkanath's local factors, and he expects you to draw upon it. And Zarantha said to tell both of you that she doesn't want to hear any nonsense about refusing the offer. She says she *told* you her father would reward you for helping her get home, and all your new relatives will be mightily insulted if you make a liar out of her."

He paused with an expectant air, and the two hradani looked at one another once more. Then Brandark grinned.

"She did tell us that, Bahzell," he said. "Neither of us believed her, but she *did* say it."

"Aye, and I'd not like to see what she might be doing if she took to feeling 'mightily insulted,'" Bahzell agreed wryly, and flicked his ears at Kresko. "All right, Master Kresko. It's pleased I'd be if you'd tell Lady Zarantha we're glad to accept the Duke's kindness."

"Good. Now, for the second message. Wencit also asked us to thank the two of you for your assistance. He, ah, said you might not be the smartest pair he ever met, but that your other virtues make up for it." Both hradani snorted, and Kresko smiled. But then his smile faded, and his voice turned more serious. "He also said to tell you he'd be seeing you again, and that he would count it an honor if you called upon him for assistance when the time comes."

"'The time comes'?" Bahzell rumbled. He reached up to scratch the tip of one ear and frowned. "And did he happen to be saying just what 'time' he's after talking about?"

"I'm afraid not." Kresko shrugged wryly. "You know how Wencit is. It's like pulling teeth to get him to tell you *anything*. I think it's part of his 'mysterious, all-knowing wizard' act."

"Aye, isn't it just?" Bahzell muttered. He frowned down at the cobblestones, clearly thinking hard, and Vaijon swallowed. It had been bad enough to hear Master Kresko throwing around the name of a duke, even a foreign one, who claimed *hradani* as members of his own family, but this was worse. There was only one person to whom Kresko could be referring: Wencit of Rūm. But that was ridiculous! What in Tomanāk's name did a pair of hradani barbarians have to do with the last and greatest white wizard of them all?

"Well," Bahzell said finally, "he's a right pain in the arse with his acts and games, but he's a knack for turning up when things look worst, too. If he's after contacting you again, I'd be pleased if you'd tell him I'm still thinking he's one as knows too much for my peace of mind, but I'll not turn him down if he wants to help."

"He'll be delighted, I'm sure," Kresko said dryly. "But that brings me to my third message. When Duke Jashân had us contact House Harkanath to establish credit for you and Bahzell, their factor sent word to Dwarvenhame, and Kilthandahknarthas sent back a message of his own."

"Ah?" Brandark smiled. "And what did the old thief have to say?" he asked.

Repeated shocks, Vaijon observed, seemed to be stunting his ability to feel surprise. Kilthandahknarthas dîhna'Harkanath was the head of Clan Harkanath of the Silver Cavern dwarves and of the vast trading house of the same name. There *might* be three wealthier individuals in the entire Empire of the Axe; there couldn't possibly be four, and hearing a rag-clad hradani call him an "old thief" should have stunned him speechless. Now it seemed almost minor, and he waited for Master Kresko's response.

"He said to tell the two of you you were still idiots to leave him in Riverside, but that his offer still stands. And if either of you need a reference with merchants here in Belhadan—or, knowing you, with the Guard—you should mention his name and his factor will post bail for you. At a slight interest rate, of course."

"Aye, he would be saying that." Bahzell chuckled.

"Yes, he would," Brandark agreed, "and while you're doing whatever a champion of Tomanāk does in the middle of the winter, I think I'll just take him up on his offer."

"You will, hey?" Bahzell cocked his ears quizzically, and Brandark shrugged.

"I actually learned a little something on *Wind Dancer*. I'd like to learn more, and I imagine old Kilthan has pretty good contacts here in Belhadan. Maybe they can vouch for me and give me an introduction to one of the shipyards."

"I wasn't after noticing a lot of activity in those yards," Bahzell pointed out, and Brandark shrugged again.

"No, but there's bound to be something going on, and even if they're not actually building or rigging anything, there have to be brains I can pick."

"And you the lad who's never learned to swim," Bahzell marveled with a grin.

"No, I haven't," Brandark replied with dignity. "And if it's all the same to you, I think I'll wait to learn until I don't have to melt the water to practice in, thank you. But there's no reason I shouldn't get started on the rest of my education, now is there?"

"Not a reason in the world," Bahzell agreed cheerfully, and smiled at Kresko. "Our thanks for your messages, Master Kresko. It's a pleasing thing to be finding so warm a welcome here."

"No warmer than you deserve," Kresko said.

"That's as may be, but it makes it no less pleasing. And truth to tell, I'm minded to learn a mite more about magi while we're here. Would it be overimposing to be inviting myself to visit your academy?"

"Of course not! You'd both be welcome any time. Just give us a little warning. There's always a class of new magi, and their shielding and control aren't all they might be during training, so we need to warn their mentors if nonmagi are coming on campus, but we'll be delighted to see you."

"Thank you," Bahzell murmured, and Brandark nodded in agreement.

"In that case, I'll be on my way," Kresko said cheerfully. "I've got several more errands to run this morning. I'm delighted to have finally met you both, and I look forward to seeing you again Friday when I drop by for my regular chess game with Sir Charrow." He clasped forearms with both hradani once more, nodded briskly to Vaijon and set off about his business.

Vaijon stared after him for several long seconds, then looked back at the hradani. Brandark grinned impudently at him, ears weaving gently back and forth, but Bahzell met his eyes with that same wry, oddly compassionate expression, and Vaijon closed his eyes while he tried to digest the violence Master Kresko had done to his worldview in such a tiny handful of minutes. Master magi, dukes, dwarvish merchant princes, and white wizards couldn't possibly have anything to do with hradani. But they did. And quite a lot, to judge by the tone of the messages Master Kresko had delivered. And that meant—

He shook himself. Just for the moment, he decided, he wouldn't think about all that it might mean. There would be time enough for that later . . . assuming he could get these two to the chapter house without the Lord Mayor and the entire City Council stopping by to announce that *they* were old friends, as well.

CHAPTER THREE

"Ah! *There* you are, Vaijon!"

Vaijon paused halfway through his formal bow of greeting as Sir Charrow's tone registered. It confirmed his suspicion that the knight-captain had deliberately sent him out to be humiliated, and fresh anger flared within him. But he snuffed it sternly and rose, and the touch of color in his cheeks could easily have been put down to the cold wind outside the chapter house. He doubted Sir Charrow would be fooled into thinking any such thing, but the two of them could pretend.

"Yes, Knight-Captain," he made himself say formally. "Permit me to introduce Sir Bahzell, son of Bahnak—" his voice stumbled over the unfamiliar names, though not as much as on the next three words "—Champion of Tomanāk."

"I see." Sir Charrow rose from behind his desk and examined the two hradani. They stood just inside the door to his study, the taller of the two with his head bent to clear the ceiling of what was normally a comfortably large chamber, and the lips half-concealed by Charrow's snowy beard quirked in a smile. "Ah, Vaijon," he said delicately, "just exactly *which* of them is Sir Bahzell?"

Vaijon inhaled a jagged breath, yet once again the knight-captain had asked no more than a courteous question he should have answered without asking. Despite his undertow of fury at being rebuked, he knew he had drawn it upon himself . . . and the fact that he was actually failing even in the courtesy his parents had taught him long before he joined the Order, far less that expected of a knight-probationer, only proved he had, however hard it bit. Whatever Vaijon might think of the idea of a hradani champion, a gentleman owed it to *himself* to treat even the most basely born with courtesy.

"Forgive me," he said with a very creditable effort at a calm tone. "This," he gestured at the huge Horse Stealer, "is Sir Bahzell, Sir Charrow. And this—" He started to gesture at the second hradani, and his face went crimson as he realized he hadn't even asked the other's name. But Master Kresko had called him by name, hadn't he? Vaijon thought frantically for a seemingly interminable moment, hand frozen in midair, then—finally—completed the gesture.

"This is his companion, Lord . . . Brandark," he said, and made himself face the smaller hradani. "Your pardon, Milord, but I failed to ask your full name so that I might make you properly known. The fault was mine. Would you, of your courtesy, make yourself known to Sir Charrow?"

Brandark's eyebrows rose as Vaijon's exquisite, aristocratic accent rolled out the words. He hadn't really believed there were people who actually spoke the way bad bards wrote dialogue, and the devil in him longed to twit the youngster. But he also heard the gritted teeth in the young man's voice, and compassion won out. He didn't know if someone could die of mortification, but "Sir Vaijon" seemed to be headed in that direction, and Brandark didn't want his death on his conscience.

"Certainly, Sir Vaijon," he said instead, projecting all of his considerable suavity, and bowed to Sir Charrow. "My name is Brandark, Sir Charrow, Son of Brandark, of the Raven Talon Clan of the Bloody Sword hradani, until recently of Navahk."

"Oh, yes." Sir Charrow nodded. "The poet."

Brandark blinked, then smiled crookedly. "Say, rather, the *would-be* poet, Milord," he suggested. "I'll claim the title of 'scholar,' but more than that—" He shrugged, and Charrow nodded once more, in understanding.

"As you say, Lord Brandark, but know that you are welcome in this house as the companion and sword brother of Sir Bahzell. Accept hearth right and come under the protection of our shield."

Brandark bowed once again, much more deeply, at the ancient words of welcome he had never actually encountered outside a book, but Bahzell shook his head beside him.

"It's grateful I am for your welcome, Sir Charrow. Aye, and for your welcome of this worthless Bloody Sword, as well. But as I was after telling the young fellow here," he nodded sideways at Vaijon, "it's just plain Bahzell."

"I beg your pardon?"

"There's no 'sir' on the front," Bahzell explained with a hint of exasperation.

"But I—" Charrow broke off, looking for just an instant as confused (although far more poised about it) as Vaijon. Then he cleared his throat. "Excuse me," he said, "but the God *did* say you were properly *Prince* Bahzell, didn't he?" he asked carefully.

"Aye, I've no doubt himself would be doing just that," Bahzell replied, and this time resignation had replaced exasperation. "He's the sense of humor for it, now hasn't he just?"

"But . . . Are you saying you're *not* a prince?"

"Oh, well, as to that, I suppose I am," Bahzell said a bit uncomfortably. "That's to say, my father's after being Prince of Hurgrum, and I'm after being his son, so—" He shrugged. "Still and all, my folk are minded to see clan lordship as more important than 'princes,' and there's three brothers betwixt me and any crown, so there's small enough point in putting on airs."

"Perhaps not from your perspective, Milord," Charrow said with a hint of dryness. "Still, for those of us whose sires aren't princes of anything, it seems worth noting. But my point was that even if you've never been formally pledged to the Order, there *are* secular orders of chivalry. Surely, as a prince, you were knighted by your father, so—"

The master of the Belhadan Order broke off in astonishment as Bahzell began to chuckle. Sir Vaijon was inclined to bristle, but the Horse Stealer's expression made it obvious he was fighting hard not to laugh. Unfortunately, he was failing. Brandark at least managed to turn *his* laughter into a fit of coughing that looked almost natural, but Bahzell couldn't stop himself, and he pressed one hand to his ribs as his huge, chamber-shaking guffaws broke loose.

It took him only a few seconds to strangle his mirth once more, and he wiped tears from his eyes while he shook his head as penitently as the low ceiling allowed.

"I beg your pardon, Sir Charrow, and I'm hopeful you'll forgive me, for my father would be after fetching my skull a fearful rap for laughing so free. But it wasn't you as I was laughing at so much as the notion of him knighting *anyone*. It's not the sort of thing hradani are like to spend much time in doing, d'you see."

"You mean—?" Vaijon was stunned into the indiscretion. He tried to cut it off, but something else seemed to command his tongue as all eyes swung to him, and he heard his own voice blurt out the question. "You're not even a *knight?*"

It came out in a half-wail, like a child's protest that something

an adult had just said couldn't possibly be true, and a blaze of
scarlet swept over his face and burned down his throat. Yet he
couldn't tear his eyes from the Horse Stealer, just as he simply could
not wrap his mind around the thought of a champion of Tomanāk
who had never been knighted. Who wasn't even a knight-*probationer*
like Vaijon himself!

"Unless my tongue's taken to saying other than I tell it to, that's
the very thing I was just telling you," Bahzell said after a moment
and, for the first time, Vaijon heard an ominous rumble in the deeps
of his voice.

"But . . . but—"

"Peace, Vaijon!" Sir Charrow spoke with a sharpness Vaijon had
seldom heard from him, and the flicker of true anger in the older
knight's brown eyes did more than anything else to shock Vaijon
into silence.

"Forgive me, S— *Prince* Bahzell," he said, and bent his golden
head in contrition.

"Let it be," Bahzell said after half a dozen aching heartbeats, and
Charrow inhaled deeply.

"I thank you for your patience with us, Milord," he said gravely.
"As I'm sure you must realize, we of the Order have no experience in how properly to address a hradani champion. And I fear
that the God was . . . less than fully forthcoming when He advised
me of your arrival, shall we say?"

"Oh, aye! Himself's a rare one for having his little joke," Bahzell
agreed with a snort, ill humor banished. "And as for that, I'm
thinking there must be a deal he wasn't after telling *me* either. Not
least that there ever was an 'Order of Tomanāk' in the first place!
I've no more notion what you do, or how, than a Purple Lord has
of charity."

"He didn't tell you about the Order?" Even Charrow seemed taken
aback by that, and Bahzell shrugged. The old knight gazed at him
for several seconds, obviously considering what he'd just been told,
then shook himself. "Well! I see we have a *great* deal to discuss,
Milord. First, however, I think it would be well for Vaijon to escort
you and Lord Brandark to your quarters and see you settled. After
that, if you would be kind enough to join me in the library, I'll
try to fill in the blanks He neglected to deal with."

An hour later, Vaijon, divested of his mail and dressed in the
simple tunic and hose the brethren normally wore within the
chapter house (although *his* were of the finest silk), guided Bahzell
and Brandark into the library. After showing them to the quarters

set aside for them, he'd used the intervening time to get his thoughts into some sort of order, and his expression was composed as he ushered them through the stone-walled passages. Internally, however, he remained imperfectly reconciled to the entire concept of a hradani champion. Especially—it pained him to admit it, yet it was true—of a backwoods, uneducated hradani champion whose Axeman came out sounding remarkably like that of the unlettered foresters who served on the Almerhas estates in backward Vonderland. He knew it shouldn't matter to him if it didn't matter to *Tomanāk,* but it did. It truly did, and try as he might, he couldn't quite swallow his resentment that so high an honor should be wasted on such a person . . . or his disdain for the one on whom it had been squandered.

And then there was Bahzell's companion. Clearly, Brandark was better educated than Bahzell. Indeed, *his* Axeman could have been that of any well-educated citizen of the Empire of the Axe. It lacked the aristocratic finish with which Vaijon himself spoke, yet it was better than, say, Sir Charrow's. But for all that, Vaijon wasn't at all certain he ought to be leading Brandark along with Bahzell. Sir Charrow had said he had much to explain to *Bahzell;* it didn't automatically follow that he intended to explain the Order's business to an outsider.

Unfortunately, Bahzell clearly wanted Brandark along, and the smaller hradani equally obviously saw no reason why he shouldn't come. And so, yet again, Vaijon found himself doing something he was positive he ought not to do at the unspoken behest of the totally unsuitable creature Tomanāk had seen fit to choose as His champion.

That thought carried him into the library, where Sir Charrow sat beside a crackling coal fire. Despite the large chamber's lofty dimensions, the hot air flowing from furnaces in the cellar through the vents of the hypocaust hidden under the stone floor and buried in the walls went far to drive off the chill. But the fire on the hearth was still welcome, particularly to Sir Charrow. The Belhadan master remained fit enough to hold his own in the field at need, yet there was no denying that he'd slowed with age, and he felt the cold more keenly than once he had.

Now he looked up from the tongs he held in one scarred, sinewy hand, and the fresh coal he'd positioned in the flames crackled wildly as he smiled at his guests.

"Thank you for coming, my lords," he said. "Please—be seated."

The library's walls were lined with high bookshelves, and a second-floor-level balcony ran around them to give access to still more shelf space. As a result, the ceiling was far higher than that of Sir Charrow's study, and it was obvious he'd used the intervening hour to make some preparations of his own. The chair to which he waved Brandark was no different from the one in which he himself sat, although the Bloody Sword filled a seat which made most humans look undersized just about to capacity. But no one in Belhadan had ever built a chair to Bahzell Bahnakson's stature, and so Charrow had ordered a cushioned, high-backed bench brought in to replace the chairs on the other side of the polished table by the library's diamond-paned windows. It was a little low for the Horse Stealer's long legs, but it had been built for several pages to sit abreast while awaiting the summons to duty, so at least it didn't squeeze in on him from the sides.

"We're pleased to be asked," Bahzell replied as he took his seat, "but if it's all the same to you, I'm thinking Brandark is as wishful as I that you'd be after leaving aside the 'sirs' and 'my lords.'"

"But I—" Charrow began, then stopped. "Very well, my friends. If that's truly how you prefer to be addressed, it's certainly not my place to argue with you. Besides—" he chuckled dryly "—traditionally, champions of Tomanāk are noted for their . . . um, determination."

"You mean rock-headed, stiff-necked, bloody-minded obstinacy, don't you, Sir Charrow?" Brandark asked politely, and the white-haired knight-captain laughed.

"Of course not, Mi— Brandark. It would be *most* improper for me to say such things about a champion!"

"I see." Brandark's eyes laughed at Bahzell, and he tilted his ears impudently. "Fortunately, it's not at all 'improper' for *me* to describe him accurately."

"That's as may be, little man," Bahzell rumbled, "but just you be thinking about all the nasty accidents as might befall a man too busy working his mouth to watch where he's walking."

"Oh, I will. I will," Brandark promised with a laugh, then looked back to Charrow. "But I believe you'd invited us to join you so that you could explain the Order of Tomanāk to this anointed lout of yours?"

Beside Charrow, Vaijon felt his hands close into fists behind him. He didn't care at all for the mocking levity with which these two addressed Sir Charrow, even if Sir Charrow did seem perfectly comfortable with it. And despite his own doubts about hradani champions—or perhaps *because* of them—hearing Brandark describe Bahzell as "this anointed lout" was infuriating. Yet no one but him seemed to care, and he forced himself to stand calmly erect beside the chapter master's chair.

"So I did." Charrow leaned forward to pour wine into wrought silver goblets and passed one to each hradani, then poured a third for himself and leaned back in his chair.

"If you will, Bahzell," he went on, sounding almost comfortable using the bare name without honorifics this time, "I thought it would be wise to give you a quick, brief description of the Order. I'm sure you'll have questions about the details, but I'd like to lay a broad foundation for them first. Does that sound acceptable to you?"

"Aye," Bahzell said. The single word came out just a bit shortly, as if he found the older man's continual deference an uncomfortable fit.

"Very well, then. Essentially, the Order was established shortly after the Fall—initially in the old Kingdom of the Axe, at Manhome, though we now have chapters in many lands—as the secular arm of the Church. There are, in fact, suggestions in our earliest records that the Order had existed in Kontovar for thousands of years *before* the Fall, but as with so many other institutions, the Church lost by far the greater part of its written history during the flight to Norfressa. We cannot be sure if the 'Brothers of the Sword' which historians tell us held the Anvil of Tomanāk in Kontovar to the very end were, in fact, members of the Order which we still serve. We would like to believe that they were, but we have no proof."

He paused for a moment to sip wine and gaze into the flames seething on the hearth, then shrugged.

"Be that as it may, the organization—or reorganization—of the Order in Norfressa took many years. There was enormous confusion in those early days, of course, with refugees flooding in from Kontovar and Duke Kormak trying frantically to find places just to put them all."

"Aye, so I've been told," Bahzell rumbled, and his deep voice was dark, almost cold. Charrow looked up quickly, and the hradani shrugged his shoulders impatiently. "Ah, don't be fretting yourself," he said. "It's just that hradani have little enough use for your Duke Kormak. I've no doubt at all, at all, that he was a good man, after doing the best he could, but never a single thing did he do for *our* folk. Saving, of course, to order our throats slit if we were after washing up on his coast."

"Bahzell, I—" Charrow began in a troubled tone, but the hradani waved a hand.

"Don't fret yourself, I said, and meant it," he said in a more normal voice. "What happened twelve hundred years and more ago bears small enough weight today. Aye, and truth to tell, I was no more there then than you or Kormak's heirs. Let the past be burying the past."

"I— All right." Charrow paused a moment longer, then resumed. "At any rate, it took us quite some time to get organized, and, as I say, the Manhome chapter, as the first founded, is the Mother Chapter even today, although our administrative headquarters were transferred to Axe Hallow when the royal and imperial capital moved there. We're not the largest chivalric order in the Empire, but we *are* the oldest, and, unlike most of the others, our membership is open to anyone who hears the God's voice and proves worthy to serve Him. Which, as a rule—" he darted a sudden, eagle-eyed glance at the Horse Stealer "—includes His champions."

"Ah?" Bahzell asked mildly.

"Ah, indeed," Charrow replied in dust-dry tones. "There have been a handful of exceptions, over the centuries, but for the most part, the God chooses His champions from within the Order. Nothing *requires* Him to restrict His choices to our membership, of course. He's a god, and *we* serve *Him*. We certainly don't sit around telling Him what to do! Nonetheless, we're always taken a little aback on those rare occasions when He selects someone from outside the Order. Like you."

"Why is it I'm thinking himself was after going just a mite further 'outside the Order' than usual when he decided to go pestering *me* into signing on?" Bahzell murmured.

Pestered? Vaijon thought indignantly. *Did he just say the God pestered him into accepting the greatest honor a man could possibly receive?!*

"Ah, yes, I suppose you could put it that way," Charrow agreed through pursed lips. "Which creates something of a problem, I'm afraid. Some of our members—" the chapter master's eyes might have flitted sideways at Vaijon, but Bahzell couldn't have sworn to it "—are going to find the idea of a hradani champion just a trifle difficult to deal with."

"I'm not wishful to be upsetting anyone," Bahzell said seriously. "Mind, I'm not after apologizing for who or what I am, either, but I've no mind to be putting myself forward or sticking my spoon into someone else's stew. If there's those as wish me elsewhere, well, I've been wished elsewhere before, and will be again, no doubt."

"No," Charrow said so flatly the hradani blinked. "It doesn't work that way," the human went on in firm tones. "Champions are rare, Bahzell. You may not realize just *how* rare, but according to the Order's rolls, there are currently, not counting you, only seventeen

living champions in all of Norfressa. Only *seventeen*—eighteen with
you—and the entire purpose of the Order is to support *your* work
in the world."

"*My* work?" Bahzell stared at him, ears flat in astonishment, and
the old knight nodded.

"Precisely. Oh, I have no idea at all what your particular task
is. That's between you and Tomanāk, and the qualities which *make*
it something between you and Him are the same ones which made
you a champion in the first place. You and those like you truly
are Tomanāk's Swords. It is your task to lead, and ours to follow
you. Not blindly, but as we would follow any captain set in command of us by our liege lord." The human's voice rang with iron
pride—not arrogance, but the fierce determination of the warrior
he was. "We are not forged of the same steel as His champions,
but it is we of the Order who hold the frontiers *they* conquer,
Bahzell Bahnakson. As He commands you, so you may command
us—any of us—for we were created as your shield arm, and however high you may fly in His service, wherever you may go under
His command, there we will be also."

"Here now!" Bahzell tried to bring the protest out quickly, lightly,
but the old man's sincerity hushed his voice. "Himself was never
after saying all that! I've no mind to command any man to follow me—no, nor to fight my battles for me, either!"

"Of course you don't. If you did, you wouldn't *be* a champion.
But that doesn't mean you can escape it, either. Oh, you can try
to run from us. Others have, on occasion, but the Order has a way
of finding His champions sooner or later. Yet I don't think you're
the type who *would* run," Charrow added thoughtfully. "Not once
you've thought it over. You're not so proud or arrogant—or cowardly—as to turn your back on the aid you may need to do whatever it is He's called you to do."

Bahzell winced, but he shook his head, as well. "That's as may
be, Sir Charrow, but I'll not go seeking it, either! I told himself
I'll do what I do because I *choose* to do it—because it's the right
as *I* see the right. I'll not 'command' anyone to follow where it may
be naught but my own stiff-necked pride leads!"

"Which is probably the reason He picked you in the first place,"
Charrow said serenely. He met Bahzell's fierce gaze for several
unflinching seconds, then smiled and poured more wine into the
goblets.

"Well, that's the bare essentials of the Order—and how it relates
to you," he said more lightly. "As for the details, our commander
is Sir Terrian, Knight-General of the Order, and we currently count

a total of ninety-six chapter houses. Each chapter house consists of at least five knights-companion and their squires and from three to five knights-probationer, which is the minimum strength allowed under our charter. Most are larger, of course, like our chapter here in Belhadan. We have myself, as knight-captain, four knights-commander, and thirty-one knights-companion, all with their squires, plus twelve knights-probationer and two hundred lay-brothers as our men-at-arms. In addition, another ten knights-companion and fifty lay-brothers are headquartered here but assigned to roving duty across the border in Vonderland, where things tend to be somewhat less, um, orderly than here in Fradonia. Our chapter is somewhat larger than others because of Belhadan's importance to the King Emperor, and—"

Bahzell Bahnakson sat back on the bench, holding his wine and listening to Sir Charrow describe the size and organization of the Order, and a sense of rebellion bubbled within him, leavened by a feeling of futility. Charrow's attitude made it plain that the choice to have nothing to do with the Order had been taken out of his hands the moment he agreed to serve Tomanāk as his champion. It was too late for him to evade the authority Charrow was determined to cede him, but even as he listened to the chapter master's voice, he felt Vaijon of Almerhas' eyes and knew not all of the Order's brethren would accept his presence as calmly as the Belhadan chapter's master seemed to have done.

CHAPTER FOUR

Well, you seem to have settled in comfortably enough," Brandark observed as he tipped his chair far back on its rear legs. The heels of his brand new boots rested easily on the table Bahzell had moved in front of the fire in his assigned quarters, and his hands lovingly oiled the wood of the balalaika in his lap. Sir Charrow—or, to be more accurate, Mistress Quarelle, the chapter house's chatelaine—had wanted to put the visiting champion in a considerably larger set of chambers, but Bahzell had put his foot down at that. After the past several months spent mainly in the field, this much smaller suite offered him all the space and comfort he wanted, and he continued to feel awkward about his status with the Order.

"Well as to a roof to keep the snow off, aye, I'm after being comfortable enough," he rumbled now, looking up from the whetstone he had been carefully applying to his dagger. The sword lying on the table no longer required honing. He still found that unnatural, and though he continued to check it religiously—he winced at his own choice of words—it was almost comforting to turn his attention to more normal steel.

"But not with your new brothers, eh?" The question could have come out with Brandark's normal astringency, but instead it was asked almost gently, and Bahzell's expression turned grim as his ears flattened in agreement.

"Aye. Though truth to tell, it's less that I'm feeling awkward with *them*—though there's something to that, for a fact—as that they're still after trying to decide what himself was after thinking. That pompous nit Vaijon's not one to make it any easier, but he's scarcely

46

the only one who's wondering. It's in my mind that Yorhus and Adiskael are at least as ill-pleased as he is, and with less cause. Worse, they're older than him, and senior to boot. If they're minded to send whispers marching back and forth to set folk against me—and I'm thinking they are—then like as not they'll do more damage in the end. And just for now, Vaijon's after making himself so spectacular a fool that not even Sir Charrow's noticed what the pair of 'em are about."

"Um." Brandark flexed his legs, rocking his chair back and forth precariously, and frowned into the flames on the hearth, hands resting motionless on the balalaika while he considered. Bahzell was certainly right about how obvious Vaijon had made his own angry resentment, but the Bloody Sword hadn't paid Sir Yorhus or Sir Adiskael much heed. Now he berated himself for his lack of attention. Yorhus and Adiskael were both knights-commander, ranked fourth and fifth in the Belhadan chapter, respectively, and soft words from them could do more damage than the most impassioned tirade from an arrogant young hot-head. And while Brandark might not have noticed anything of the sort from them, he knew Bahzell too well to believe the Horse Stealer was inventing enemies. That had never been his way, even in Navahk.

The Bloody Sword's ears cocked thoughtfully. Perhaps it wasn't all that surprising he hadn't noticed Yorhus or Adiskael. He was even more an outsider than Bahzell, and though he'd begun to find a place of sorts for himself among the bards and minstrels who entertained in Belhadan's taverns—and with the Royal and Imperial University scholars to whom Master Kresco had introduced him—the Order's members were unlikely to confide in him when they hadn't even made up their minds about Bahzell!

And in fairness to the Order, Brandark had to admit that Bahzell might have been more than a bit hard for them to accept even if his race weren't hated and reviled. There were innumerable things Brandark had yet to figure out about Bahzell's relationship with Tomanāk—which, he reflected wryly, also seemed to be true for Bahzell—but he could certainly see why the Horse Stealer might disturb the Order's more orthodox members.

Most importantly, he supposed, was the way Bahzell spoke about Tomanāk. There was never anything disrespectful in his tone or manner—not by hradani standards, at any rate—but Brandark doubted the rest of the Order saw it that way. Sir Charrow clearly did, but it was hard for any of the other Races of Man to understand the hradani's ways, and especially those of the Horse

Stealers. Like his own Bloody Swords, Horse Stealers were capable of exquisite courtesy, but (even more than among his Bloody Swords) having one of them be polite to one was usually a sign of serious trouble. As a rule, formality on their part was a sign of distrust, and they were most polite of all to people they detested. Personally, Brandark suspected that politeness was yet another defense against the Rage, a way of using courtesy to defuse tension and keep swords sheathed.

On the other hand, the Horse Stealers were inclined to be a bit more . . . informal under normal circumstances than even other hradani. Brandark had never been to Hurgrum, but he'd heard reports of Prince Bahnak's "court," and he shuddered at the very thought of how someone like Vaijon would have reacted to it. Not because of any "barbarian squalor" or crudity, but because any of Bahnak's people had the right, by custom and law, to appear personally before him to present petitions directly. And, as Bahzell had told Sir Charrow, Bahnak's position as lord of Clan Iron Axe was more important to his own people than any princely title. By a tradition stretching back to the days when only the clan's swords stood between its people and extinction, a clan chief was the true source of its cohesion, the embodiment of its joint survival. Nothing and no one could be *more* important to Bahnak's folk, and he had proven himself one of the greatest chieftains in the Iron Axes' history. Which meant, of course, that his people *addressed* him as they would their clan chief, with an earthy succinctness utterly at odds with Vaijon's notions of proper courtesy.

And that was precisely how Bahzell spoke of *Tomanāk*—with the devotion, loyalty, and familiarity of a Horse Stealer for his clan lord. In its own way, that was a supreme compliment, the highest honor Bahzell could bestow, yet too many of these citified, over-civilized knights seemed unable to grasp that fact.

"Well enough for *you* to be sitting there saying 'um' while you're after toasting your arse in front of *my* fire," Bahzell said moodily, breaking into the Bloody Sword's thoughts. "It's not you as has to deal with them directly!"

"Not directly, no," Brandark agreed, "but your relationship with them rubs off on me, you know, Longshanks. I get the bad with the good—second-hand, as it were." He waved a hand as Bahzell darted a dangerous look at him. "Oh, don't worry! They're too civilized for their own good, and they'd never dream of offering me even the tiniest insult. But they *do* tend to look at us a bit askance, don't they?"

"A bit and then some," Bahzell growled, looking back down at his dagger and testing its edge on his calloused thumb. "But that's not to say as how they've done aught but see to our needs with rare speed," he admitted.

"That's true enough," Brandark agreed, for it was.

The hradani had been in Belhadan for a mere twelve days, but anyone looking at them now would have found it difficult to envision the ragged state in which they had arrived. In Brandark's case, that was due in no small part to the line of credit Duke Jashân had set up for them. The Bloody Sword had confined his buying spree primarily to the funds he and Bahzell had brought with them, but the Duke's credit had allowed him to indulge himself without worrying about what happened when his cash ran out. He'd not only replaced his lost and ruined equipment but commissioned new garments from one of Belhadan's foremost tailors, and his elegant shirt was made of the finest silk while the embroidered doublet which covered it would have done credit even to Sir Vaijon's relatives. In fact, the only place he'd spent more money was in Belhadan's bookstores. He had no idea how he was going to get his mountain of books home, but that was the least of his worries. Printing presses and movable type were two more things the Axemen had and hradani did not. Of course, there were very few *hradani* books—printed or hand-copied—of any kind. Most of the foreign volumes he'd managed to acquire had been printed, but he'd been able to assemble his library back home in Navahk only in bits and pieces, and almost all of his books had been damaged, many badly, before they ever fell into his hands. Here in Belhadan, though, he felt like a miser loosed in someone else's gold mine, and he intended to pry up every nugget he could lay hands on.

Bahzell, on the other hand, had never been much of a reader, and he continued his utter indifference to fashion. He had allowed the Order to replace his ruined clothing, but he'd refused anything remotely like Brandark's finery. His breeches were warm and serviceable, but they were cut for comfort, not style. His full-sleeved shirt was made of first-quality linen, but without a trace of embroidery, and the warm tunic he wore over it was of the same plain green wool as the Order's field-issue surcoats, as was the quilted Sothōii-style poncho he'd insisted upon instead of a cloak. Most of the lay-brothers who served the Order as men-at-arms were better dressed than he, and he must certainly be the drabbest "knight" ever to grace these halls.

Except, of course, that he *wasn't* a knight.

"You know," Brandark said slowly, adjusting a tuning peg with exquisite care rather than looking at his friend, "it *might* put these people a bit more at ease with you if you'd let them knight you. Sir Charrow, at least, is just aching for the opportunity, and I don't see how Tomanāk could object. They *are* his Order, after all."

"Ha!" Bahzell snorted, and sheathed the dagger with a sharp *click!* as if for emphasis. "Wouldn't *that* just look wonderful, now. Me, decked out like some cursed knight from one of your fool tales! Oh, no, my lad!"

"But if it would make *them* happy—"

"No, I said, and no, I meant," Bahzell said flatly. "Himself was after telling me he needed a champion. He said naught at all about knights and lords and titles, and I've no mind to be taking such on, either. And—" his brown eyes hardened ominously "—if these folk can't be accepting what's good enough for himself, then I've no mind to be catering to their prejudices, either!"

"I hadn't thought about it in that light," Brandark admitted. He pursed his lips and half-flattened his ears, then plucked a string, listening critically to his instrument's voice. "So if you're not going to let them knight you, what *are* you going to do?"

"Now there you've got me." Bahzell sighed. He rose and clipped the dagger sheath to his belt, stretching in a huge yawn despite the limitations of the chamber's ceiling, then crossed to the rack on which he'd hung the armor Sir Charrow had insisted the Order was duty bound to provide him. A kite-shaped shield, dark green and bearing the emblems of Tomanāk in gold, hung on the wall behind it, beside his arbalest, and Bahzell smiled faintly as he reached out to brush his fingertips almost reverently across the mail. It was by far the finest he'd ever owned, dwarvish chain with a steel breast-and-back, though he felt certain Sir Vaijon would turn up his nose at it. The mail was of honest steel rings, with no silver wash or fancywork, and the burnished breastplate was equally plain, without even the green enamel most members of the Order preferred. But Bahzell knew the quality of that armor's workmanship, and Bahzell Bahnakson had little use for flash and glitter.

Yet happy as he was to see it and to once again have boots which not only fitted but kept out snow and wet, the price seemed high. It was obvious Vaijon could scarcely force himself to be civil even now. In fact, the young man's unhappiness seemed to be growing still worse, as if some poison festered deep inside him. Yet Bahzell almost preferred Vaijon to the reservations and resentments behind the exquisitely courteous facades of all too many of his new "brothers." He'd identified Yorhus and Adiskael, but he suspected there were others, as well. Others who were far harder to identify because they were older and more restrained. More . . . cautious than Vaijon's desperate youthful ardor permitted the golden-haired knight-probationer to be. Yet they were there. He often wondered whether or not Vaijon realized that, but he doubted it, somehow. Young Vaijon was too wrapped up in his own unhappiness and disappointment to realize that he was serving—perhaps even being *made* to serve—as the focus of the unstated resentment of so many of his seniors, as well.

"I've thought on it, this last week and more," he went on to Brandark after several thoughtful seconds, while his fingers unconsciously caressed the high-combed helmet with the special openings for a hradani's ears. "To speak truth, I've been more than half minded to take myself off. Old Kilthan's factor could find work enough for the two of us, or Master Kresco's one as would be after putting us up at need, and I've had a bellyful of sideways looks. Mind you, I've naught at all against Sir Charrow, and most of the rest've *tried* at least, but there's no skirting 'round it, Brandark. But for Sir Charrow and two or three others, most of 'em are ready enough to be seeing my backside."

He paused, staring moodily into the fire once more, then sighed heavily.

"Just betwixt the pair of us, I'd as soon show it to 'em, too," he admitted, "and maybe the sooner the better." Brandark glanced up quickly at his words' bitter undertone, and Bahzell looked back at him with an expression not even the most charitable could have called a smile. His hand caressed the hilt of his dagger, and a dangerous glitter, like chips of cruel ice, flickered in his usually mild eyes. Perhaps only another hradani would have understood that glitter, but Brandark *was* a hradani, and he drew a deep breath before he spoke very carefully.

"Was there a specific person who brought you to that conclusion?" he asked.

"Aye," Bahzell said grimly, and knuckles whitened as his hand clenched on the dagger.

The ice in his eyes burned suddenly hot with remembered passion, and his nostrils flared as a razor-edged echo of his people's curse shivered at his core. He and Brandark had learned more about the Rage than any other hradani had ever suspected there was to learn. They had mastered the trick of summoning it at need—of using it in their times of darkest peril—but that hadn't lulled them into forgetting its dangers, for having accepted that it *could* be used, the temptation *to* use it might well become even greater. It wasn't something they discussed, but there were times when both of them feared that their new knowledge might actually weaken the chains with which they held their demon pent. And as Brandark gazed at his friend, he suddenly wondered how much of Bahzell's apparent calm was no more than a mask for something else. There were dark and dangerous places in any hradani's soul, even that of a champion of Tomanāk, and it was chillingly obvious that someone, at least, had come perilously close to pushing his way into one of them.

But then Bahzell closed his eyes, shook himself, and exhaled noisily. When he looked back at Brandark once more the sick, hungry fury of the Rage had been banished from his eyes, and he took his hand from his dagger. Brandark said nothing, but the Horse Stealer needed no words to read the thoughts behind his eyes, and he chuckled harshly.

"Aye, it was after being 'specific,' right enough," he agreed, "and the fool not even guessing how close he'd come to seeing his guts spilled on the floor before him, either!" He bared his strong, white teeth. "It was near as near, Brandark—that close—" he raised his hand, holding index finger and thumb a bare quarter-inch apart "and but for himself, I'm thinking I'd've—"

He stopped himself and shook his head.

"No, let's be honest amongst ourselves. But for himself I'd *not*'ve stopped myself. I'd've killed the sanctimonious, smiling bastard and laughed . . . and wouldn't *that* have been proving as how they'd all been right to think us savages?"

"Don't blame yourself too much," Brandark said quietly, his voice for once devoid of humor. "The Rage can take even the best of us, Bahzell. You know that as well as I."

"Aye, aye." Bahzell turned his eyes back to the hearth and shrugged, but his voice was low. "Yet I'd hoped when himself told us how it was changing I'd not have to be facing it again—not in the old way. Yet there it was, like red murder in my soul, and the hunger of it. The *need* just to be reaching out and taking him by the neck and—"

He shuddered again, then stood completely motionless for almost a minute. Then he tossed his head and turned to his friend once more, and this time his smile was almost natural.

"Still and all, himself was never after promising us it would be easy, was he now? And I'm thinking he was also after warning us the old Rage lingers yet, so like as not it was naught but foolish pride made me think as how it might not be waiting for *me* these days, hey? And while I'd sooner not come any closer to it than I've done already, it's in my mind that himself is after thinking up something for me to be doing here, which means I can't be off before I've done it . . . whatever it is. On the other hand, cursed if I know what it is. And himself's not after making so very free with his little 'visits,' either," he added wryly, then chuckled. "Now *there's* a thing I'd not thought myself likely to be missing!"

"I feel sure he'll get back around to confiding in you," Brandark said dryly, as relieved as his friend by the change of topic.

"Oh, like enough," Bahzell agreed, turning back to the table and seating himself once more. "The problem is I'm not so very comfortable in my mind about waiting for the boot to fall, you see. I've the notion that when it does, there's *someone* as won't like it overmuch, and experience has a nasty way of suggesting the someone's me, like enough."

"Good!" Brandark said, and grinned as his friend looked up quickly. "I'm working on another verse for *The Lay of Bahzell Bloody-Hand*," the Bloody Sword explained, "and the *interesting* things that happen to you always provide plenty of inspiration."

"Now just you be holding up there! I thought you'd given over on that curst song!"

"Oh, I meant to, Bahzell. I truly *meant* to. But then we got here and I saw how your own brethren in the Order have failed to appreciate your towering nobility. *Surely* you see that it's my duty to repair that dreadful injustice." Brandark struck a rousing chord on his balalaika, grinning devilishly, and Bahzell glowered at him.

"What I'm seeing," the Horse Stealer said grimly, "is that I've waited overlong in wringing your scrawny neck! Not," he added, "but what that can't be seen to easy enough still some dark night."

"Why, *Bahzell!* What would Sir Charrow think if he could hear you now?" Brandark demanded with a gurgle of laughter.

"He'll cheer me on, like as not, if you've been after spreading that song of yours about," Bahzell shot back, then stabbed the Bloody Sword with suddenly suspicious eyes. "You *have* been spreading it about, haven't you?" he demanded.

"Well, it *has* proved quite popular down at the Seaman's Rest," Brandark admitted. "And at the Anchor and Trident. And, now that I think of it, I do believe they asked for an encore at the Flying Lady night before last, and Estervald—he's the resident harpist at the Jeweled Horse—wants to know when the new verse will be finished."

"I *have* waited overlong." Bahzell groaned, and Brandark laughed again. However dreadful his singing voice or the doggerel his efforts at verse normally produced, even his worst enemies—perhaps *especially* his enemies—would admit he had a gift for satire, and

The Lay of Bahzell Bloody-Hand was his personal gift to his towering friend. Unfortunately, from Bahzell's viewpoint, he'd chosen to set it to the melody of a much beloved and depressingly easy to remember drinking song.

"I don't really see your problem, Bahzell," he said now, his tone insufferably prim. "It's not as if the song *insults* you in any way!"

"No, and if one tenth of what it claims was after being true, I'd be the biggest ninny on the face of Norfressa!"

"Why, Bahzell! How can you say that? I'll have you know that no one could possibly doubt that you're a very perfect paladin after hearing my song! Your nobility of character, your selfless determination to rescue maidens, your fearless resolve when facing demons or devils, your—"

"One more word—*one* more!—and I'll crack your skull this minute!" Bahzell told him, and Brandark shut his mouth with a grin.

Sir Vaijon of Almerhas stalked into the chapter house in a black, bleak fury so deep that the door warden physically flinched away from him. In his defense, Vaijon had no idea his rage showed, which was, of course, yet another sign of its seething power. But he knew it was there, and the reasonable part of his mind told him he should take it to Sir Charrow, or perhaps to Sir Ferrik, the chapter's senior priest.

Only he couldn't. He'd done that too often in the last two weeks, and each time, they'd looked at him with that same reproach. Neither had berated him, yet it was obvious both felt the problem was his. That some failing within *him* created the terrible pressure boiling in his heart and mind whenever he faced the intolerable thought of a hradani *champion*.

Vaijon had tried. He'd truly tried, spending endless hours watching beside his armor and sword when he should have been asleep, begging the God to help him deal with this insult to the Order. To help him accept the inclusion of a *hradani* among His brightest blades. He knew other members of the Order were humbly born. Sir Charrow's father had been a brick mason, for Tomanāk's sake! But a *hradani*? An uncouth barbarian who *spoke* like a barbarian? Who refused even to allow the Order to knight him in order to regain at least some of the respect it was bound to lose when it became known *he* was one of its champions? A barbarian who didn't even appear to realize the tremendous honor Sir Charrow had offered to bestow upon him and spoke of the God Himself with such casual disrespect?

And now this! Vaijon's face flushed afresh, and his teeth grated audibly as the song replayed itself in his mind. He hadn't meant to visit the tavern. Such places were for the low born—for seamen and tradesmen and the like—but he and Sir Yorhus had been returning from an errand to Captain Hardian, who commanded the cruisers the Order maintained here in Belhadan, when he'd heard the name "Bahzell Bloody-Hand" in the snatch of song floating out the briefly opened doors and known he had no choice. He and Sir Yorhus had stepped into the establishment, wrapping themselves in their cloaks and hoping no one would note the Order's arms on their surcoats, and stood in the back to listen—first with astonishment, then with incredulity, and finally with horror and outrage.

It *mocked* the Order! It mocked everything the Order *stood* for, and all in the name of that uncivilized *dolt*. Saving serving girls from the "foul attentions" of "ill-favored overlords," indeed! And that business about rescuing noblewomen disguised as peasants— as if things like that truly happened! And fighting *demons* and evil princes with cursed swords, for Tomanāk's sake! Why, the Empire hadn't seen a proved demon sighting in over forty years! It would have been bad enough, Phrobus take it, if the song had treated it all with proper dignity, but this—! One of the bards at his father's high table might have sung such mythic deeds properly, to teach and inspire, even though all who heard his song would *know* it was myth. But this . . . this . . . this *ditty* had the sheer effrontery to suggest such things had really happened, to give Bahzell credit for them by *name*, and to do it all as if it were some sort of *game!* As if someone who claimed to be a champion of Tomanāk were no more than a topic for sport!

The insult had been too much for him, and Sir Yorhus' efforts to calm him had been worse than useless. Vaijon knew the knight-commander was displeased by Bahzell's presence, but the older knight had tried valiantly to point out that it scarcely mattered what ignorant, lowborn laborers and seamen thought about the Order or its members. Certainly their brethren had cause to be disappointed, even angry, over the insult, but it was their duty to rise above it and ignore it lest in reacting to it they bring still more ridicule upon the Order.

It had been an unfortunate choice of argument. Had Sir Yorhus tried, he could not possibly have said anything better calculated to fan Vaijon's rage, and the younger knight had stormed out of the tavern. Nor had the long, frigid hike back to the chapter house cooled his blazing anger. Indeed, it had grown only worse during his walk.

Had he been even a bit less furious, Vaijon might have recognized why the song had crystallized all the resentment and discontent—the disappointment—he'd labored under since Bahzell's arrival. But he wasn't that one bit less furious, and he *was* disappointed. It wasn't something he'd put into so many words for himself. Indeed, it was something he would not—*could* not—*allow* himself to put into words, even in the privacy of his own mind. But deep inside he knew, whatever he could or could not admit to himself, that he'd been betrayed. By choosing someone like Bahzell as His champion, the War God had broken faith with Vaijon of Almerhas. By forcing him to acknowledge the paramount authority of someone not fit to keep the Earl of Truehelm's swine, Tomanāk mocked thirty generations of the House of Almerhas.

But since Vaijon could not permit himself to blame the God, there was only one person he *could* blame, and he ground his teeth still harder as he stalked down the passage towards his small, spartan chamber. He fought his rage as he might have fought a servant of the Dark, for even in his fury he knew a knight of the Order should never feel such things. But he was only human, and he was very young, and his fight against it only made it stronger as humiliation at his inability to vanquish it coiled within him.

And then he turned a corner without looking and staggered back with an "*Oof!*" of shock as he ran full-tilt into someone coming the other way and almost fell.

"Your pardon," he began stiffly, catching his balance somehow and managing to keep his feet, "I—"

But then he saw the one he was addressing, and the words died on his tongue.

"No matter, lad," Bahzell said comfortably. "The passage isn't overwide, and I'm one as takes up a goodly bit of any road. So—"

"Don't patronize me!" Vaijon snapped.

Even as the words burst from him, he knew he was in the wrong. Such discourtesy was worse than wrong, for it violated his oath to the Order. He was a knight-*probationer*, not even a full knight-companion, and this man was a *champion*. But it didn't matter. Or, rather, it *did* matter . . . and there was nothing he could do about it. Betrayal and fury blazed in his blue eyes, and he saw the hradani's normally mild gaze harden, saw the ears fold back and the right hand steal to the hilt of the dagger at his belt, and he didn't care.

"I wasn't after 'patronizing' anyone, Sir Vaijon." The deep, bass rumble was hard, anger grumbling in its depths like boulders coming down a cliff, and the bright, hungry flicker in Bahzell's eyes would have warned another hradani of just how deep was the danger in which he stood. But Vaijon was human, not hradani, and he had never seen a hradani in the grip of the Rage. He had no concept of what he faced in that moment, yet despite his own fury he recognized, however imperfectly, the control Bahzell exerted over himself.

Yet that only made it worse, for Bahzell spoke as a grown man *should* speak, and all Vaijon heard was an adult rebuking an enraged, spoiled child by example.

"Oh, yes you were!" he spat, unable to contain the hurricane of emotions whirling within him. "Well, I don't *need* your 'understanding,' *hradani!* I don't need *anything* from you, or your stinking clan, or—"

"*Vaijon!*"

The whipcrack authority of that single word cut through Vaijon's white-hot tirade like a knife, and he froze. For one dreadful instant the entire universe seemed to hold its breath, unmoving, waiting, paralyzed between one moment and the next. But then that illusory eternity ended ... and the reality was worse than the illusion. Far worse.

"I find you discourteous, Sir Vaijon," the voice behind him continued, colder than a Vonderland winter and sharper than a Dwarvenhame blade. "You forget yourself and the honor due a champion of our God, and in the doing, you insult Him Whom we serve with blade and blood and soul."

"I'm thinking it was naught but—" Bahzell began.

"Peace, Milord Champion." Charrow's voice was respectful but harder than iron. For once, there was no hint of deference in it as the master of the Belhadan chapter asserted his authority, and Bahzell shut his own mouth, then drew a deep breath and jerked his head in an unhappy nod.

"Well, Sir Vaijon?" Sir Charrow turned back to the knight-probationer. "Have you anything to say for yourself?"

"I—" Vaijon swallowed and made himself face the older man. The mentor, he realized in that moment, whom he respected most in all the world ... and whom he had just failed. But not even that realization could quench the outrage blazing at his core, and he stared at Sir Charrow, trapped between obedience, shame, and the fury which would not release him.

"I asked a question, Sir Knight," Charrow said very, very quietly, and Vaijon's anger burst up afresh.

"Why?" he demanded bitterly. "Whatever I say will be *wrong,* won't it? He's a *champion* of the Order, isn't he? Anything *he* does is right, and whatever *I* do is wrong!"

Charrow blinked at the raw anguish Vaijon's rage could no longer disguise, and a part of him went out to the younger man. Yet only a part, for what he heard from Vaijon was the hurt and anger of a child, and no knight-probationer of Tomanāk was a child. He looked at Vaijon pityingly for a moment, but then his face hardened.

"You—" he began, but Vaijon had whirled away from him to Bahzell.

"*You!*" he snapped. "*You're* the one who insults the God! Your very *presence* is an insult to him!" He glared up at the hradani, taloned hands half outstretched, panting like a man at the limit of his endurance. "What can *you* know of what the God demands of His warriors, *hradani?* None of your accursed kind have ever served the Light—it was *you* who brought the Dark to power in Kontovar! Did Phrobus send you to ape the part of a champion? Are you here to give *Norfressa* to the Dark, as well?"

Sir Charrow froze, a deathly hush seemed to spread to fill the chapter house, and Vaijon went parchment white as he realized what he'd said. He stood there, feeling his entire life crashing down about him, and he couldn't move even when Charrow reached out and, without a word, unbuckled the belt which supported his sword and dagger.

"You have disgraced yourself and the Order," the older man grated in a voice like crumbling granite, "and we take back the weapons you bore in the God's name."

Vaijon's hands moved in small, hopeless arcs, as if they longed—needed—to snatch back the blades Sir Charrow had taken. But they couldn't, and horror filled his eyes.

"The commandery shall be summoned to determine your fate," Charrow went on. "You will be judged before the brethren you have dishonored, and—"

"Just one moment, Sir Charrow." The knight-captain looked up quickly as a voice colder than a dagger's kiss interrupted him. Sir Vaijon turned more slowly, like a poorly managed puppet, and Bahzell bared his teeth in an icy smile that belonged on something from the depths of a Ghoul Moor winter.

"Yes, Milord Champion?" Charrow spoke with the same formality, but there was a worried crease between his brows as he tried to interpret Bahzell's expression, for no more than Vaijon had he ever seen the Rage in a hradani's eyes. There was anger in those eyes, that much the chapter master knew, but there was something else, as well. A deep, terrible something—a fusion of cruelty colder than

Vonderland's ice and a dark passion crackling like heat from an opened furnace door—that reached out for all about Bahzell with talons of freezing flame.

"I'm thinking as how the insult was after being to me, not to your brethren," he rumbled.

"To you, and through you to the God Himself," Sir Charrow agreed, "but it was offered by a member of the Order, and so the *dishonor* is to us."

"As to that, himself can be taking care of his own insults, and I'm not so very interested in the dishonor," the hradani said in a voice of chill iron, and hardened warrior though he was, Sir Charrow felt himself shudder as the hungry smile that reached out almost lovingly to Vaijon drove a sliver of terror deep into him. "You've the right of it in that much, my lad," the Horse Stealer told the paralyzed young knight, "for I'm naught but what you see before you. Old Tomanāk'd split his guts with laughter, like enough, if I was to go about calling myself 'Sir This' or 'Champion That,' and my family tree's not nearly so pretty as some, I'll wager. But it's me you've made your tongue so free of—not Sir Charrow, not the Order, just me, Bahzell Bahnakson. And so I'm thinking it's *me* you should be after answering to, not your brethren."

"Milord, you can't—" Charrow began in a quick, urgent voice, but a raised hand cut him off, and Bahzell's deadly eyes froze him into silence.

"You've been after calling me a champion of Tomanāk for days now," he said flatly. "Am I such?" Charrow nodded helplessly, and Bahzell bared his teeth again. "And would it happen a champion has the right to administer his own understanding of Scale-Balancer's justice?" Charrow nodded once more. "And would that justice be like to supersede your commandery's?" Charrow had no choice but to nod yet again, and Bahzell nodded back, then jerked his chin at Vaijon.

"In that case, you'd best be giving yonder lordling back his weapons, Sir Charrow, for he'll need them come morning."

He turned that blood-freezing smile directly upon Vaijon, and his hungry voice was soft as serpent scales on stone.

"You've plenty to say about barbarians and hradani and servants of the Dark, Vaijon of Almerhas. Well, come morning, here's *one* barbarian will show you what hradani truly are."

CHAPTER FIVE

Sir Vaijon did not spend a restful night.

In fairness, his insomnia owed little to fear. Never having lost in the last eight strenuous, often brutal, years of training, he simply could not conceive of losing now, to anyone, yet there was more to it than simple self-confidence could explain. Despite the unforgivable actions he knew his fury had betrayed him into committing, he *was* a knight of Tomanāk who had sworn obedience to the Order and to those set to command him. Now he was foresworn, disbarred in his own eyes, as well as his fellows', from their ranks, and he knew that, as well. Yet whatever failings Bahzell Bahnakson might have as a champion of Tomanāk, and whether he realized it or not, he had given Sir Vaijon an opportunity to reverse that judgment by making their confrontation what was, for all intents and purposes, a trial at arms to be judged by Tomanāk Himself.

It was a trial Sir Vaijon did not intend to lose, yet he found he could not approach it as he had any other contest under arms. Not because he doubted his own prowess, but because deep inside, some little piece of him whispered that he ought to lose. Hard as he might try, he could find no excuse for his conduct. Sir Charrow was right; he *had* disgraced himself and the Order. A defiant part of his heart might still cry out in bitter disillusionment that Tomanāk had no right to waste such honor on a barbarian, but even granting that, a true knight had no excuse for such behavior. And so, even as the thought of besting the hradani and proving Bahzell had no right to the position he claimed filled him with a fiery determination, he could not escape the unhappy suspicion—small and faint, but damnably persistent—that perhaps this time he did not *deserve* to win.

At first, as he watched that night beside his weapons, he pushed away any thought of defeat whenever it surfaced. Instead, he filled his mind with memories of how Bahzell had transgressed, of how the hradani's mere presence filled him with fury, and promised himself that the morrow would see all his anger and betrayal assuaged. But as the night crept slowly, slowly past, he made himself look the possibility that he might lose in the eye, and he was almost surprised by what he saw there, for Bahzell *had* made it a trial at arms. If Vaijon lost, he would probably die. He was too young to truly believe that, though he recognized the possibility in an intellectual sort of way, but the thought that if he *did* lose he would at least have been punished for his actions was obscurely comforting. He fully intended to emerge victorious and thus expunge the stain of those acts, yet defeat would erase them in another fashion, and the deep and abiding devotion to Tomanāk which had first brought him to the Order was glad that it would be so.

"Ah, you're not actually planning to, well—?" Brandark paused delicately and cocked his truncated ear at Bahzell as his friend buckled the straps joining his breast and back plates and adjusted them carefully.

"To what?" the huge Horse Stealer demanded, not looking up from his task.

"I realize Vaijon is a pain in the arse," Brandark replied somewhat indirectly, "and there've been times enough when *I* wanted to put him out of my misery. But I was only wondering exactly what you intended to do to him this morning."

"'Do to him,' is it now?" Bahzell finished fiddling with the last strap and looked up at last, and his deep voice rumbled derisively. "Surely you've been after hearing the same as me, Brandark, my lad. Yon Vaijon is Tomanāk's own gift to mortals with sword or lance! Why, he's after being downright invincible, and my heart's all aflutter with terror of him." The Horse Stealer's smile was cold enough to confirm the suspicions Sir Charrow's oblique questions had awakened in Brandark, and he began to feel true alarm.

"Now let's not do anything hasty, Bahzell. No one could deny you've got every right to be angry, but he's only a youngster, and one who's been spoiled rotten, to boot. It's plain as the nose on your face—or *my* face, for that matter—no one ever told him—"

"It's too late to tell me such as that, Brandark," Bahzell said, lifting his sword down from the wall rack and slinging the baldric over his shoulder, and his voice was so grim Brandark frowned. "And Vaijon's no 'youngster,'" the Horse Stealer added even more grimly. "He's as old for his folk as either of us is after being for ours, and a belted knight, to boot. Well, he's always after yammering about knightly this and knightly that and chivalric the other, and the whole time he's sulking like a spoiled brat, and I'm thinking it's past time he was after finding out just what all that means. Aye, him and all the other nose-lifters minded to think like him."

"But—" Brandark began once more, then closed his mouth with a click at Bahzell's glower.

Sir Charrow Malakhai wrapped his cloak about himself and tried to hide his gnawing worry as he stood waiting in the center of the huge, echoing salle. The training room's floor had been covered with fresh sawdust, and the scent of it filled his nose with a resinous richness, spiced with the tang of coal smoke from the fires seething in the huge hearths at either end of the room.

Most northern chapters of the chivalric orders had salles like this one, and the weather raging outside the thick walls reminded Charrow of why that was. Blasts of wind rattled the skylights which admitted the gray, cold light of a snow-laced morning, and despite the fires, his breath was a thin mist before him. Outdoor weapons training in such weather was out of the question, although he supposed one could always teach courses in how to survive under blizzard conditions. But this morning the training salle would serve another, grimmer purpose, and he sighed as he checked the lighting once more.

Huge lanterns burned before brightly polished reflectors, filling the cavernous room with light that would be fair to both parties, and with the sole exception of those assigned to duty as door wardens, every member of the chapter currently in Belhadan had gathered as witnesses. Knights, squires, and lay-brothers alike, they packed the trestle benches set up down the long sides of the salle with a sea of green tunics and surcoats, and that sea stirred restlessly as whispered conversations rustled across its surface. Sir Charrow glanced at them, and his brown eyes hardened as they rested on the knot filling the center of the front two benches along the west wall. Sir Yorhus and Sir Adiskael were the focus of that knot and, if truth be told, Charrow was far more furious with them than he was with Vaijon.

Vaijon was an arrogant, willful child whose father should have spent more time tanning his posterior than spoiling him with gifts . . . or filling his head with nonsense about his family's incomparable lineage. He shouldn't be—not at this stage of his life—but he was, and today he would pay for it. Yorhus and Adiskael were senior members of the Order, both in their late thirties, who had served Tomanāk well in the field. That gave them a responsibility to lead by example, yet they were as disgusted as Vaijon himself by the notion of a hradani champion . . . and neither was as straightforward as he about it.

In every way that counted, the pair of them were far more dangerous to Bahzell than Vaijon could ever be, but Sir Charrow had been slow to recognize that, and he wondered if the hradani realized it even now.

The Order of Tomanāk had fewer factional struggles than most chivalric orders, yet the sort of people who'd chosen to sit with Yorhus and Adiskael had alerted Charrow to a problem he hadn't realized he had. One which might cut deep into the bone and muscle of the Belhadan chapter. The knights-commander weren't arrogant. They didn't see Bahzell's elevation to the status of champion as an insult to their personal honor. But they felt just as betrayed as Vaijon, for they *were* zealots who hated and despised hradani, and Sir Charrow hadn't even guessed they felt that way.

Yet now that his eyes had been opened, the knight-captain wondered how he could possibly have missed it before. Perhaps it had grown so gradually that no one would have noticed it, or perhaps he'd been *unwilling* to see it. That didn't really matter now. What mattered was that it had happened . . . and that the Order of Tomanāk simply could not tolerate the bigotry some ecclesiastic orders put up with. The Order's impartial devotion to truth and its even-handed administration of justice must be forever above question. That was what made Yorhus and Adiskael so dangerous. They hadn't shouted their disgust openly, as Vaijon had. Instead, they had used soft words—words Charrow could not believe they had chosen accidentally—to hammer home suspicion of Bahzell with a smooth rationality that was almost seductive.

Vaijon's firebrand fury only made those softer words sound even more reasonable. Indeed, Charrow felt grimly confident that the older knights had deliberately encouraged his rage, and that willingness to twist and manipulate in the name of their own prejudices made them and the half-dozen others who sat with them a cancer at the Order's heart. It attacked the very essence of their calling to open-minded, honest examination of the facts in any dispute, even among themselves, and Charrow felt a fresh stab of worry as he wondered how he was going to deal with the problem they represented. That he *would* deal with it was a given—the Order of Tomanāk did not choose chapter masters who shrank from their duties—but he was honest enough to admit he dreaded it.

Of course I do, he told himself impatiently. *What sane person wouldn't, especially with the support they seem to enjoy? But at least my eyes have been opened to the fact that I must deal with it, and for that I thank Tomanāk . . . and Bahzell.*

His mouth quirked. The Order's histories said champions had a way of bringing things to a head and that they tended to arrive for that very purpose at the times one least expected them, but he rather doubted Bahzell Bahnakson regarded himself in that light. But then his half-smile faded, and he shivered as he remembered the hunger which had echoed in the Horse Stealer's ice-cold promise to show Vaijon "what hradani truly are."

For all the young knight-probationer's flaws, and Tomanāk knew they were legion, Charrow loved him. He sometimes wondered if that was why Vaijon had failed to overcome those flaws. Had Charrow, as his mentor, taken the wrong approach? Should he have accepted that it was time someone *beat* some sense into that handsome, golden-haired head rather than persist in his efforts to *show* Vaijon the way? Yet there had been something else about the youngster, from the moment Charrow first laid eyes upon him. There truly was a strength and power inside him, hidden by the spoiled demeanor and choked in a thorny thicket of arrogance. Charrow had wanted to save that power, to awaken Vaijon to the potential he represented and train him in its use, and so, perhaps, he had let things go too far, spent too long trying to repair the weak spots in an imperfect vessel rather than hammering that vessel with the flail of discipline to see if it was strong enough to withstand the blows required to mend its flaws. Had—

His thoughts broke off as Bahzell and Brandark strode through the door in the center of the north wall. The Bloody Sword looked anxious, as if he were less concerned by how the trial might end than by the consequences of that end, but Bahzell's face might have been forged of iron. He wore no expression at all as he halted, helmet in the crook of his right arm, kite-shaped shield on his left. The hilt of his sword thrust up over his shoulder, and even Yorhus and Adiskael and their cronies hushed their murmured conversations as the lantern light fell upon him.

Seven and a half feet tall he stood, as broad and hard looking as the mountains in which Belhadan had her roots, and his brown eyes were cold. Danger clung to him like winter fog and, despite himself, Charrow swallowed. He had never faced hradani in battle;

now, looking upon Bahzell Bahnakson, he realized how fortunate he had been.

Another door opened, this one in the salle's southern wall, and Vaijon stepped through it. Like Bahzell, he was bareheaded, carrying his helmet, but there the similarities ended. Bahzell was grim and still, a towering cliff of plain, burnished steel and the muted tones of leather harness, but Vaijon glittered like the War God Himself. Silver-washed chain flickered in the lantern light, silk and gems and blinding white leather added their magnificence to his presence, and his golden hair shone like a prince's crown. He was a foot shorter than his foe, but he moved with catlike grace, and if Bahzell's eyes were cold, his blazed with determination.

A fresh mutter went up, and Charrow's stomach tightened as he heard it. It came from Yorhus and Adiskael's followers, and it carried the unmistakable echo of approval for Vaijon's cause.

But he had little time to think about that as Vaijon strode towards Bahzell, and he straightened his own spine as they approached him. Normally, there would have been at least two referees to serve as score keepers; today there were none, for this was no training exercise. The combatants were not armed with the blunted weapons of practice, and their scores would be kept only in the wounds they wreaked upon one another.

Bahzell and Vaijon stopped with a perfectly matched timing which could not have been intentional, each precisely one pace short of Charrow, and he looked back and forth between them. Under any other circumstances, it would have been his duty to attempt to dissuade them from combat even now, but Bahzell had made that impossible. The huge hradani who had been so reluctant to exert his prerogatives had never even hesitated this time, and he was right. A champion's authority *did* supersede even that of the Order's commandery. He, and he alone, could avert this confrontation, and his cold expression said all too clearly that he had no intention of averting it. And so Charrow made no effort to remind them of their brotherhood within the Order or to beg them to reconcile. He only cleared his throat sadly, then made his voice come out as clear and calm as he could.

"Brothers of the Order, you are here to meet under arms," he told them simply. "May Tomanāk judge rightly in the quarrel between you."

He took one step backwards, turned, and walked to the high-backed chair which awaited him. He seated himself in it and watched as Bahzell and Vaijon nodded coldly to one another and donned their helmets. Then steel whispered as they drew their blades, and he waited one more moment, as if engraving the tableau before him on his memory.

Vaijon's longsword gleamed in his hand, and not even the gems which crusted its hilt could hide its lethality. It was a beautiful bauble, yes, yet it was the work of a master swordsmith, as well, a yard-long tongue of steel, as deadly as it was gorgeous, and sharp enough to slice the wind itself.

Bahzell's sword boasted no such decorations. Its blade was two feet longer, but it was a plain, utilitarian weapon whose only beauty lay in the perfection of its function. The hradani held it one-handed, without so much as a wrist tremor to indicate its massive weight, yet Vaijon's body language was assured. His weapon might be shorter, but it was also far lighter. It would be quicker and handier, and he was clearly confident in his own prowess and the speed of his own reflexes.

For an instant longer Sir Charrow watched them, and then he said one last word.

"Begin."

Bahzell stood motionless, eyes glittering on either side of his open-faced helm's nasal bar, and the right side of his mouth drew up in a dangerous smile. He felt the Rage flicker in the corners of his soul, trying to rouse and take control, and he ground an inner heel down upon it. He had felt it, known he hovered on the brink of an instant and lethal explosion when Vaijon insulted him, and even now he felt the hot blood hunger calling to him. It would taste so sweet to yield himself to it. To call upon it to smash and rend the personification of all the insults and hatred he had felt from those who should have been his brothers. *He* had never asked them to become such. It was their own code, their own precious Order, which insisted that they should have, and somehow that had made their abhorrence cut even deeper. Now he had not simply the opportunity but the excuse to repay them all, and the Rage cried out to him, demanding that he set it free to do just that. But deeply as he longed to do just that, Bahzell Bahnakson refused to give himself to it this day. It was hard to fight the terrible need, the hunger—harder than any human could ever have suspected—and it took every ounce of discipline he possessed, yet he had no choice *but* to fight it. The outcome of this fight was too important for anything else.

Then Vaijon uncoiled in a lightning-fast attack. The blow came without warning, in a light-silvered blur of steel with absolutely no clue of changing expression or tensing muscles to alert its victim, and Bahzell felt a distant flicker of admiration for Vaijon's trainers.

It took years of harsh, unremitting practice to teach one's self to launch an attack in deadly earnest without betraying one's intention.

But Bahzell had been trained in an equally unforgiving school, and his brown eyes didn't even flicker as his right hand moved. His five-foot blade would have been a two-handed weapon for any human, but Bahzell wielded it as lightly as a Sothōii sabre. Steel belled furiously as he met the attack blade to blade, without even bothering to interpose his shield, and he sensed Vaijon's shock at the speed of his parry.

The human fell back a step, eyes narrowed behind the slit of his helm, but Bahzell only stood there, still smiling that small, cold smile. His ears twitched derisively, and his refusal to follow Vaijon up mocked the young knight, jeering at him as Bahzell displayed his own confidence. And then the Horse Stealer's shield made a small beckoning motion. It was a tiny thing, as much sensed as seen, yet it struck Vaijon like a lash. It dismissed him, dared him to do his worst, and he snarled as he accepted the challenge.

Yet for all its fury, his rage was not enough to betray his training. Instead, he drew upon the power of his anger, forcing it to serve rather then rule him. He came at Bahzell perfectly balanced, with a speed and brilliance which made more than one of the veteran warriors watching him hiss in appreciation. Three strides he took, with a dancer's grace, longsword licking out with viperish speed, and his shield was another weapon, not merely a passive defense. It slammed into Bahzell's shield like a battering ram, backed by all the power of Vaijon's hard-trained, powerful weight, and the sound of collision was a sharp, ear-shocking *Crack!*

Many of those watching had seen Vaijon launch the same attack in training. It had never failed when executed properly . . . and Vaijon had never executed it any other way. It came in at precisely the correct angle, and it should have smashed Bahzell's shield to the side, battered him sideways, opened the way to his body for Vaijon's blade even as it staggered him and drove his weight back on his heels.

But Bahzell wasn't staggered. He didn't even seem to shift balance. He simply took Vaijon's full weight, and all the momentum of his charge, and absorbed it. It was Vaijon who bounced, eyes wide in disbelief, as Bahzell twisted his arm and tossed their locked shields—and Vaijon—aside so that his stroke went wide . . . and left him wide open for the hradani's riposte.

Someone in the watching audience bit off a shocked shout as Bahzell's blade flicked out almost negligently. The blow seemed effortless, almost gentle, but it sounded like an axe in seasoned oak as it landed, and Vaijon staggered back another stride as Bahzell lopped a huge chunk from the side of his shield.

The younger man tried to gather himself, regain his balance, but Bahzell wouldn't let him. The hradani stood motionless no longer, and Vaijon felt a totally unfamiliar surge of panic. It wasn't *fear*, really, for there wasn't time for it to become that. It was surprise—disbelief and even shock—that anyone the Horse Stealer's size could move so quickly, coupled with the feeling that he himself had somehow been mired in quicksand. Huge as he was, Bahzell moved like a dire cat, with a deadly precision whose like Vaijon had never before encountered. His huge sword sang, impossibly quick, lashing out as if it weighed no more than a walking stick as he *flicked* the blade in strokes that looked effortless even as every one of them carved yet another chunk out of Vaijon's shield.

Other knights came to their feet as Vaijon reeled back, mercilessly driven by his unrelenting foe, and Sir Charrow watched in a disbelief as great as that any of his brother knights felt. Bahzell wasn't attacking Vaijon directly. He was attacking Vaijon's *shield*, ignoring openings to the other's body, using that huge sword like a hammer to batter the smaller, slighter human back and back and yet further back. He all but ignored Vaijon's sword, as well, using his own shield with almost contemptuous ease to brush aside the few, desperate attacks the younger man managed to launch.

If it was hard for the rest of the chapter to believe, it was even harder for Vaijon. He'd never experienced anything like it, never imagined an attack like this was possible. *No one* could maintain that furious, driving rhythm—not with something as massive and clumsy as a two-handed sword! Bahzell *had* to tire, had to slow, had to lose his cadence and give him at least an instant to regain his balance!

But that tree trunk arm *didn't* tire . . . and it didn't slow. Vaijon tried to twist his body, tried to set himself and thrust Bahzell back, and it didn't work. Then he tried to fall back faster than Bahzell could follow, tried to get outside the other's reach, open the range at least enough to rob the hradani's blows of their power, and *that* didn't work, either. Bahzell had too much reach advantage, and he seemed to sense Vaijon's moves even before the human attempted them. He followed up, hacking, hacking, *hacking* at Vaijon's shield, and splinters flew as that merciless blade reduced it to wreckage.

Vaijon panted for breath, too astonished by the boundless power of Bahzell's attack to feel fear even now, but it was obvious to every watcher that he was totally at the hradani's mercy. Bahzell was *toying* with him as he drove him back in a staggering, lurching parody of his normal, tigerish grace. The hradani battered the younger man back until Vaijon's heel caught on the hearth at the southern end of salle. The golden-haired knight staggered for balance, half-falling, and a deep, rustling sigh went up from the audience as he faltered, exposing himself for Bahzell's coup-de-grace.

But Bahzell didn't deliver it. Instead the hradani stepped back with a deep, booming laugh. The mockery in it cut like a lash, and Vaijon's half-strangled gasp for breath was also a sob of rage and shame as he hurled himself forward once more behind his shattered shield. The tip of his blade came up, thrusting murderously for Bahzell's exposed face, but the hradani's shield slammed the sword—and swordsman—aside. Vaijon bounced back from the blow and went half-way to one knee, and this time Bahzell was on him in an instant.

The hradani wasted no more time driving his enemy about the salle. He had only one purpose now, and Sir Charrow felt himself frozen motionless in his chair as Bahzell Bahnakson of the Horse Stealer hradani gave the Belhadan chapter of the Order of Tomanāk a merciless lesson in who and what he was. A single savage blow smashed what remained of Vaijon's shield into dangling wreckage, hanging from his shield arm to entangle and hinder without affording the least protection. Vaijon fought to interpose his longsword, but Bahzell's blade crashed down upon it, and steel rang like an anvil. The younger man went all the way down on his right knee, and Bahzell struck again, twisting in with brutal, side-armed power. Steel belled and clangored again, like harsh, explosive music ugly with hate, and Vaijon's sword flew through the air, spinning end-over-end. It landed in the sawdust fifteen feet away, and Sir Charrow lunged to his feet at last as Bahzell's sword came down yet again.

Yet the knight-captain's shout of protest died unspoken. Vaijon was defenseless, and the hradani would have been completely within his rights to finish him once and for all. But instead, the massive sword came in from the side, the flat of the blade striking Vaijon's shield arm like a blacksmith's sledge, and the knight-probationer cried out. His mail sleeve could blunt that blow; it couldn't *stop* it, and his forearm snapped like a dry branch. And then Bahzell struck yet again, and Vaijon cried out once more as his *sword* arm broke as well. He slumped fully to his knees, both arms broken, crouching at Bahzell's feet, and the hradani stretched out his sword once more—gently this time, with the precision of a surgeon— until its lancet tip rested precisely against his plate gorget.

"Well now, Sir Vaijon of Almerhas," a voice rumbled. It was deep

and steady, unwinded and coldly mocking. "I'm thinking I promised to show you what hradani truly are, but it's in my mind as
how you're not overpleased with the lesson. Still, there's little need
for me to be after showing you, for you already know, don't you
now? Aye, it's a rare, bloodthirsty lot my people are, so I'm thinking
there no reason at all, at all, why I shouldn't be pushing *this*—"
metal grated with a small, tooth-clenching squeal as he twisted his
wrist, grinding the tip of his blade against Vaijon's gorget "—right
through your arrogant throat, now is there?"

Vaijon stifled a whimper—of pain, not for mercy—and gazed
up along the glittering edge of the five-foot blade resting against
his throat. Absolute silence hovered in the salle, and fear flickered
in his blue eyes at last. That fear was made only sharper and deeper
by the fact that he'd never truly expected to feel it, yet he refused
to beg, and Bahzell smiled. It was a grim smile, but there was a
hint of approval in it, and he eased the pressure on his sword.

"Still and all," he said quietly, "it might just be you've a thing
or two to learn yet, Vaijon of Almerhas, and not about hradani
alone. I'm thinking himself can't be feeling any too pleased with
you just now, for I've yet to meet a more conceited, miserable excuse
for one of his knights."

Vaijon felt his face go scarlet within the concealment of his helm,
despite the shock and pain of his broken arms, as that deep, rumbling voice hammered spikes of shame into him. They hurt even
more than shattered bone, those spikes, for they were completely
deserved, and he knew it.

"If I were wanting your life, my lad, I'd already have had it," Bahzell
told him almost compassionately, "but for all you've worked yourself into a right sorry position just now with me and with himself,
as well, you've some steel in your spine and some gravel in your gullet.
Aye, and I doubt you've ever had a conniving thought in your life—
unlike some." The hradani let his eyes rest briefly on Sir Yorhus of
Belhadan's strained face, then looked back down at Vaijon. "It's a pity,
perhaps, that you've so much bone in your skull to go with the steel,
but I've been known to be a mite stubborn myself, from time to time.
I've a notion himself would think it a bit harsh to be taking someone's
head just because he's acted the fool, however well he was after doing
it. So tell me, Vaijon of Almerhas, would it be that you're minded to
be just a *mite* more open-minded about who himself can be choosing
as his champions?"

"I—" Vaijon bit his lip until he tasted blood, then sucked in a
huge lungful of air and made himself nod. "Yes, Milord Champion,"
he said, his voice loud and clear enough to carry to every corner

of the salle despite his shame and the waves of pain flooding through his arms.

"Your skill at arms has vanquished me, yet your mercy has spared my life," the young knight forced himself to go on, "proving both your prowess and your right to the honor to which the God has called you." He paused, and then continued levelly. "More, you have reminded me of what I chose in my arrogance to forget or ignore, Milord. Tomanāk alone judges who among His servants are fit to be His champions, not we who serve Him. Sir Charrow sought to teach me that. To my shame, I refused to learn it of his gentleness, but even the most vain and foolish knight can learn when the lesson is tailored properly to his needs, Milord Champion."

His pain-tightened mouth quirked a wry smile within his helm, and Bahzell withdrew his sword entirely.

"Aye, well as to that, lad," he said with a ghost of a laugh, "you'd not *believe* what it took for my father to hammer a lesson into my own head when I'd the bit between my teeth. I'd not want to say I was *stubborn*, you understand, but—"

"But *I* would," another voice interrupted, and Vaijon of Almerhas' eyes went huge and round as another armed and armored figure flicked suddenly into existence behind Bahzell. The newcomer stood at least ten feet tall, brown haired and brown eyed, with a sword on his back and a mace at his belt, and the deep, bass thunder of his words made even Bahzell's powerful voice sound light as a child's.

Sir Charrow went instantly to one knee, followed just as quickly by every other person in the salle. All but one, for as the others knelt before the power and majesty of Tomanāk Orfro, Sword of Light and Judge of Princes, Bahzell turned to face him with a quizzical expression and cocked ears.

"Would you, now?" he said, and more than one witness quailed in terror as he stood square-shouldered to face his god.

"I would," Tomanāk told him with a smile, "and I feel quite confident your father would agree with me. Shall we ask him?"

"I'm thinking I'd just as soon not be bothering him, if it's all the same to you," Bahzell replied with dignity, and Tomanāk laughed. The sound shook the salle with its power and pressed against those who heard it like a storm, and he shook his head.

"I see you've learned *some* discretion," he said, and looked down at Vaijon. "The question, my knight," he said more softly, "is whether or not *you* have."

"I . . . I hope so, Lord." Vaijon had no idea where he'd found the strength to whisper those words, for as his god's brown eyes burned into him, they completed the destruction of the arrogance Bahzell had humbled at last. He was naked before those eyes, his soul exposed to the terrible power of their knowledge, for they belonged to the God of Justice and of Truth, and their power unmasked all the petty conceits and pompous self-importance which had once seemed so important for what they truly were.

Yet there was a strange mercy in that searing moment of self-revelation. He didn't even feel shame, for there was too vast a gulf between himself and the power of the being behind those eyes, and if no secret cranny of his soul was beyond their reach, then neither did they conceal their essence from him. He was aware of his abasement, of the countless ways in which he had fallen short of the standards Tomanāk demanded of his sworn followers, yet he also felt Tomanāk's willingness to grant him a fresh start. Not to forgive him, but to allow him to forgive *himself* and prove he *could* learn, that he *could* become worthy of the god he had always longed to serve.

And as that awareness flowed through him, Vaijon of Almerhas saw at last the link between Tomanāk and Bahzell Bahnakson. They were akin, the champion and his god, joined on some deep, profound level which Vaijon glimpsed only faintly even now. It was as if a flicker of Tomanāk was inextricably bound up with Bahzell's soul, an indivisible part of him, muted and filtered through the hradani into something mere mortals could trust and follow. Someone in whom they could see a standard to which they might actually aspire, a mirror and an inspiration which shared their own mortality. And that, Vaijon realized suddenly, was what truly made a champion. The dauntless will and stubborn determination which stopped short of his own shallow arrogance—which was almost humble in admitting its limitations yet had the tempered-steel courage of its convictions *within* those limitations—and the strength to endure an intimacy with the power of godhood few mortals could even imagine. It wasn't anything Bahzell *did*; it was who and what he *was*. In that moment Vaijon knew he saw the myriad connections and cross-connections between champion and deity far more clearly than Bahzell himself ever would, and in seeing them, understood why Bahzell greeted Tomanāk upon his feet, not his knees, and the profound respect which underlay his apparent insouciance.

"Yes, I think you have learned, Vaijon," Tomanāk told him after a moment. "It was a hard lesson, but the ones which cut deepest are always hardest, and there is no resentment in your heart." Vaijon blinked, amazed to realize that was true, and Tomanāk smiled at him. "So you've learned the *entire* lesson, not just the easy part, my knight. Good!" Another laugh, this one softer and gentler but no less powerful, rumbled through the salle. "I'm pleased, Vaijon. Perhaps now you'll finally start living up to the potential Charrow always saw within you."

"I'll try, Lord," Vaijon said with unwonted humility.

"I'm sure you will . . . and that you'll backslide from time to time," Tomanāk said. "But, then, even my champions backslide at times, *don't* they, Bahzell?"

"A mite, perhaps. Now and then," Bahzell conceded.

"Hmm." Tomanāk gazed down at his champion for a moment, then nodded. "It seems to me that Vaijon will need a proper example to keep him from losing any of the ground he's gained," he observed, "and having someone to be an example *to* might just keep *you* from getting carried away with your own enthusiasm, Bahzell. So perhaps I should entrust Vaijon to your keeping—as your trainee, as it were."

The hradani stiffened, but Tomanāk went on before he could interrupt.

"Yes, I think that would be an *excellent* idea. He needs some field experience, and you'll be able to use all the help you can get in the next few months. Besides—" the war god grinned at his champion's pained expression "—think how well he and your father will get along!"

"Now just one minute, there!" Bahzell began finally. "I'm thinking it's the outside of—"

"Oh, hush, Bahzell! Or are you saying the lad doesn't have the potential for it?"

"Well, as to that," Bahzell said with a glance at Vaijon which the younger man didn't fully understand, "I'll not say yes and I'll not say no. It's likely enough, when all's said, but—"

"*Trust* me, Bahzell," Tomanāk soothed. "It's an excellent idea, even if I do say so myself. And now that *that's* settled, I'll be going."

"But—" Bahzell began, and then closed his mouth with a snap as Tomanāk vanished as suddenly as he'd appeared. The Horse Stealer glowered at the space the god had occupied for several seconds, then growled something under his breath, unslung his shield, and sheathed his sword. He stood in the center of the salle, arms folded, and then glanced up as the profound and utter silence registered upon him.

Scores of eyes looked back at him, huge with awe. The knights and lay-brothers were still on their knees, even Yorhus and Adiskael, gazing raptly at him, and he twitched his shoulders uncomfortably.

Just like himself to be popping in and out like a cheap candle flame, he thought moodily.

"Not a *cheap* candle, Bahzell," a voice chided out of thin air. "And while you're standing around feeling put upon, don't you think it would be a good idea to heal Vaijon's arms? You *did* break them, after all."

CHAPTER SIX

"Don't you get just a little tired of all that?" Brandark asked in a voice just too soft for anyone else to hear, and grinned at the deadly look Bahzell gave him. The two lay-brothers who had stepped aside with bows of profound respect to let the two hradani pass fell behind, and the Horse Stealer leaned close to his friend.

"Aye, I *do* get a mite worn out with it," he said equally quietly, "and I'm thinking as how I'd just as soon be working out my frustrations on someone."

"Oh? Did you have a specific someone in mind?"

"No, that I didn't . . . until just now."

Brandark chuckled but let the opening pass. He was reasonably certain Bahzell was only joking, but the Horse Stealer's exasperation was real, and there were times it was more prudent not to prove or disprove a theory.

The deference the lay-brothers had just shown had become the norm over the last two days, and Bahzell found it even more difficult to deal with, in a very different way, than the hostility which had preceded it. Hostility was something any hradani had no choice but to learn how to cope with if he meant to travel among the other Races of Man. Admiration, awe, and near deification were something else entirely, and very few hradani had ever been offered the opportunity to deal with *them*.

Yet there was no avoiding them now. The knights of Tomanāk knew all champions were directly and personally chosen by their god. In Bahzell's case, however, that was no mere intellectual awareness. Tomanāk Himself had manifested—*personally*—to make His

75

choice clear. Worse, from Bahzell's perspective, He had *left* once more . . . leaving Bahzell to take the brunt of His worshipers' religious awe. Even Yorhus and Adiskael—or, perhaps, *especially* Yorhus and Adiskael—had taken pains to make plain their allegiance to Tomanāk and Bahzell, in that order.

"Actually," Brandark went on as the two of them reached the larger quarters to which Charrow and Mistress Quarelle had insisted upon transferring Bahzell following "The Visitation," as Brandark had christened Tomanāk's appearance, "the situation *is* an improvement. Mind you, I can see where having everyone falling over themselves bowing to you could get, um, *bothersome*, but it's certainly better than worrying over who might want to leave a dagger in your back some fine night."

"Humph!" Bahzell snorted. He shoved the door open and nodded Brandark through it, and the Bloody Sword stopped short as Sir Vaijon looked up from the breastplate he was polishing.

"Greetings, Lord Brandark," the golden-haired knight said cheerfully, then looked at Bahzell. "Good morning, Milord Champion," he said, and inclined his head in a small bow.

"I'm thinking as how I could shine that up myself, if it were after needing it. Which it isn't," Bahzell rumbled back with a hint of disapproval, and Vaijon shrugged.

"So you could, Milord. But I had no other pressing duties, and I was taught that caring for his master's gear is a proper duty for any squire."

"Squire?" Bahzell's ears cocked and his eyebrows rose. "I've no memory of saying as how I'd take on any *squires*."

"There was no need for you to," Vaijon replied with a serenity Bahzell found very difficult, even in the wake of divine intervention, to reconcile with the arrogantly superior pain in the backside he remembered. "Tomanāk assigned me Himself." The young man allowed himself a small smile. "Even Sir Charrow agreed with me about that, Milord, when he authorized me to move my possessions to your chambers."

"When he *what?*" Bahzell blurted, but Vaijon only gave another of those serene nods and returned to polishing the breastplate. The Horse Stealer stared at him in disbelief, then shook his head.

"Now look here, lad," he began in his most reasonable tone. "I'm willing enough to admit himself had it in mind for me to be, well—" He glanced at Brandark, and his discomfort kicked up another notch as his friend adopted a painfully neutral expression, crossed to the hearth, and busied himself poking up the fire. Bahzell glowered at his back for a moment, then looked back at Vaijon and made himself continue. "Well, to be taking you under my wing, as you might say, until you've worked all that pompous fuss and feathers out of your head. But he never said a word at all, at all, about 'squires,' and I've not the least tiniest notion how to go about having one, even if he had!"

"It's not difficult, Milord," Vaijon assured him, running his cloth one last time over the breastplate. Then he lifted the burnished steel, turning it under the light to inspect it, carried it to the armor tree, and hung it carefully with the rest of Bahzell's mail. "A squire looks after his lord's personal gear and horses. If they're in the field, he looks after his lord's tent and meals, as well. In winter quarters, he keeps his lord's chamber neat and sees to his appointments and any other minor tasks that need doing."

He turned to smile at Bahzell, and the hradani crossed his arms.

"And just what is it he's after getting in return for all this slavelike devotion?" he demanded.

"Why, his lord trains him, Milord."

"How?" Vaijon's smile turned into a faint frown of incomprehension, and Bahzell shrugged. "It's new I am to championing, Vaijon, and I've still less experience at anything to do with knights and knighthoods. You'd best be remembering that when it comes time to explain about such."

"Of course, Milord." The young man—who, Bahzell suddenly realized, wore a plain, utilitarian surcoat utterly devoid of gems or bullion embroidery—rubbed his chin for a moment, as if seeking exactly the right words. "The most important things a squire learns from his lord, Milord, are skill at arms and the proper deportment of a knight. As you bested me with considerable ease, it seems painfully evident you have a great deal to teach me about the former, and—" he blushed faintly "—Tomanāk Himself made it quite plain you have even more to teach me about deportment. That's why I feel He intended me as your squire, not just a 'trainee.' I would be honored far beyond my deserts to learn from you, and the performance of such duties as normally fall to a squire would seem far too little repayment for my lessons."

Vaijon's quiet sincerity took Bahzell aback. Despite everything, including Tomanāk's intervention, a major portion of his brain had continued to think of Vaijon as the conceited, egotistical peacock who'd met *Wind Dancer* at the docks, and he felt a stab of shame as he realized that. Gods knew the original Sir Vaijon had deserved all he'd gotten, but Prince Bahnak had taught his sons better than to think that no one could learn from experience. Hradani notions of justice were severe, as they must be among a people afflicted

by the Rage, but they were also fair. Punishment was meted out
to suit the offense; once it had been administered, the account was
squared, and no wise clan lord or war leader continued to hold
the past against his followers. That, after all, was one of the functions of punishment: to teach anyone capable of learning, whether
from personal experience or from the example of others.

And as Bahzell gazed at the younger man, he realized not only
that Vaijon *had* learned but that the knight-probationer was genu-
inely grateful for his lesson. That was a sobering thought, for Bahzell
was only too aware of how seldom *he* had been grateful for the
lessons of his own past. Especially the ones which involved bruises.
Which, now that he thought about it, seemed to account for a
majority of the ones which had stuck with him.

"I'd not put it quite that way myself, lad," he said after a moment,
and waved for Vaijon to sit back down at the table while he seated
himself in the out-sized chair beside the fire. Brandark took the
opportunity to disappear into his own rooms in an unwonted
display of tact, and Bahzell rested one heel on the raised hearth
while he gazed down into the burning coal.

"It's glad enough I'll be to teach you what I know of arms," he
went on after another pause. "Mind you, I'm thinking you've been
taught well enough already. It was overconfidence and anger got
you into trouble—that, and the way you'd underestimated what I
might be doing because you were so all fired busy with what *you*
meant to be doing . . . and so sure no hradani could really measure up to himself's standards."

He glanced up and smiled as the younger man flushed in embarrassment. The flush grew darker for an instant, but there was too
much sympathy in his smile for Vaijon to resent it, and the human
smiled back hesitantly.

"I wish I could dispute your analysis, Milord," he said, and
Bahzell chuckled.

"Don't be taking it too hard, lad. It's the way of young bucks
to make mistakes. Tomanāk knows *I* did—aye, and it's lucky I was
they didn't cost me far more than yours cost you! There's no shame
in admitting past mistakes; only in making 'em over again."

"I understand, Milord," Vaijon said, and, for the first time, he
truly did.

"Well, if you're after understanding that much, understand this,
as well," Bahzell went on seriously. "I'm no knight, Vaijon, and I've
no least desire to be one. In fact, the very notion makes me come
all over queasy. I know that's not something as you find easy to
understand, but it's true enough. And I'll not take you nor anyone

else as a 'squire,' either." He held the younger man's eyes levelly. "But this I will do. I'll keep an eye on you as himself was asking, and I'll teach you whatever there is for me to teach, as *you* asked. And if I'll not have you as a servant, I *will* have you as a friend and companion."

A light began to glow in those blue eyes, and he raised a warning hand.

"Best be thinking before you leap after it like a fish after a fly, my lad, for I've been casting my mind over what himself was saying. I'm thinking it's past time Brandark and I were on our way to Hurgrum, and Gods only know what sort of trouble we'll be finding there! Not to mention that it's high winter and the snow's horse-belly deep betwixt here and there. Or that we'll have to be crossing Bloody Sword territory to get there, if we go by road, and cutting cross country in winter's as good a way as any to die. Then there's the little matter of a price on my head in Navahk. Aye, and on Brandark's, too, now I think on it. And once we get past all that—assuming we do—you'll be one lonely human amongst a crop of Horse Stealer hradani, some of whom'd just as soon cut your throat as look at you. I'll put in a word for you, you understand, but some of my folk . . . Well, let's just say they're after thinking about humans like *you* were thinking about hradani. There's some would look at all that and think two or three times before deciding as how they'd want to be *my* friend, I'm thinking!"

"I'm sure there are, Milord," Vaijon agreed, and smiled. "When do we leave?"

"You mean to *what?*" Charrow looked at Bahzell with the expression of a man who devoutly hoped he'd misheard.

"I've dallied long enough," Bahzell told the knight-captain with unwonted seriousness. He stood in the library, his back to the fire, and Vaijon stood quietly in one corner. The master of the Belhadan Chapter had been careful to take no note of the way the young knight-probationer's finery had mutated into an echo of Bahzell's utilitarian style. Nor had he drawn attention to Vaijon's new modesty of manner by praising it, although the smile he'd given his long-recalcitrant protégé had carried its own measure of approval. But Bahzell's abrupt announcement of his impending departure had snapped Charrow's attention away from Vaijon in a heartbeat.

"But . . . but it's high winter!" he protested. "And you've been here less than three weeks! There's so much we still have to tell you—and that *you* still have to tell us! And—"

"Hisht, now!" Bahzell rumbled with a crooked grin. "It's in my mind that himself already has what he was wanting out of my time here. This fine young lordling—" he jerked his head at Vaijon and winked at the younger man "—was after getting a mite out of hand, so himself had me spank him for you."

Something suspiciously like a chuckle emerged from Vaijon's corner. Under other circumstances, Charrow would have been astonished to hear it; now he scarcely noticed.

"As for the rest of your chapter," Bahzell went on more thoughtfully, "I'm thinking it was Yorhus and Adiskael and their crew himself wanted seen to." His crooked smile became something very like a grin as Charrow frowned at him. "Well, no one's ever called hradani smart, Sir Charrow, but I'd've been a right idiot not to see how the wind set with *those* two. But if they're after having the makings of good religious fanatics, I've a shrewd notion himself's little visit has, um, *redirected* their attention, hasn't it now?"

"Well, yes," Charrow admitted. In fact, he found the two knights-commander's newfound, humble piety almost more worrisome than their earlier zealotry. Charrow had seen too many people in whom humility and extremism seesawed back and forth. But at least now he realized the potential problem was there so that he could keep an eye on it, and Bahzell was right. It was the hradani's presence—and, of course, Tomanāk's manifestation—which had not only shaken them out of their previous attitude but pushed Charrow himself into seeing a problem to which familiarity had blinded him.

"Well, then," Bahzell said, holding out his right hand, palm up. "I'm thinking that was what needed doing here, and now I've other matters to see to."

"But what in Tomanāk's name is so important it can't wait until spring?" Strictly speaking, Charrow had no right to demand that information, for champions were the sole judges of where the God most needed them. He knew that, but he was also no stranger to the rigors of winter campaigning and travel.

"As to that," Bahzell said slowly, turning to stare down into the fire, "I'm not so very certain. Not as to the whole of it. But I've something to teach my folk—something himself was after going out of his way to be certain I knew, and . . ." He paused and looked up at Charrow, then glanced at Vaijon, as if measuring their probable reactions, before he continued. "The Dark Gods are meddling amongst my folk, Sir Charrow," he said quietly, "and I've no idea how deep the rot has spread."

"You're certain of that, Milord?" Charrow's question came out like the crack of a whip, and Vaijon stiffened in matching concern.

"Aye, that I am," Bahzell said. He grinned again, sourly this time.

"I've no doubt the two of you have been ill-fortuned enough to've heard that curst song of Brandark's? The one about 'Bahzell Bloody-Hand'?" Charrow nodded slowly, and Bahzell shrugged. "Well, that bit in it about the prince with the cursed sword is after being true enough. Mind, the japester who wrote it saw fit to dress things up a bit—aye, and left out the tiny little fact that *he* was after facing four of the prince's guardsmen by himself at the time, and them all in the grip of the Rage—but it happened."

"Cursed how, Milord Champion?" Charrow's voice was crisp, now, with the authority of his rank, and Bahzell shrugged again.

"As to that, I'd no experience with such before himself took it into his head to be recruiting me, but he was there, as well, and when I asked him what it was, he said as how it was forged as a 'gate' to Sharnā's realm." Both Charrow and Vaijon hissed at that name. "He said old Demonspawn meant it as a way to strike at me through Harnak, and there's no way in all the world Harnak could have been laying hands on such if the Dark Gods *weren't* meddling."

"This Harnak was heir to the Navahkan throne?" Charrow's tone made the question a statement, and Bahzell nodded. "Then 'meddling' is too weak a word, Milord," the knight-captain said grimly. "It's a classic pattern. One of the Dark Gods gets his—or her—hooks into a ruler's heir, then . . . disposes of the ruler so that the throne falls into his hand like a ripe plum. And of them all, Sharnā is best at that maneuver. Too many people in love with power are likely to employ the Assassins Guild, never realizing the dog brothers are always as much Sharnā's tool as that of whoever pays them." Charrow snorted bitterly. "For that matter, I suspect many of the *dog brothers* fail to realize they are. They're not among the most devout adherents of any god, and no doubt they see their relationship to Sharnā's church primarily as a business opportunity. But his priesthood has always coordinated the guild's activities, and the guild has always found it convenient to have the support structure the church offers. Which means that anyone who deals with the one must also deal with the other, whether he knows it or not. And once that door is opened—"

Charrow broke off with a twitch of his shoulders, and Bahzell nodded heavily.

"Aye, I was thinking the same," he admitted. "I'm hoping they were after banking on Harnak and not working on one of his brothers at the same time. If that *was* their plan, then I'm thinking killing him must've set their efforts back. And from what I know of his father, they'd not have wanted to spread their net too wide, lest he realize they were about. Mind you, Churnazh of Navahk's soul is blacker than Krashnark's riding boots, and he's no giant when it comes to thinking things through. But he's not after being a complete idiot, and he'd not have lasted as long as he has without a certain cunning. I'm thinking he'd've ripped Harnak's heart out with his own hands, son or no, had he ever guessed what Harnak was about, for he knows how his allies would react to word of it."

"How *would* they react?" Charrow asked softly, and Bahzell turned to face him fully, brown eyes hardening as he straightened his spine.

"As to that, how would *your* folk be reacting?" he challenged harshly. For just a moment, his gaze and the knight-captain's locked across the office, and then Charrow raised a hand in a small gesture of apology. Bahzell glared at him for another second or two, and then his nostrils flared as he inhaled deeply.

"That's the reason I wasn't so very eager to be babbling all about it to everyone I meet," he admitted, turning to stare moodily back down into the fire. "Even now, there's too many folk too ready to believe hradani *chose* to serve the Dark in Kontovar, and the truth is that we *did* serve. Not because we'd chosen to, but because their curst wizards gave us no choice. Few enough hradani have any use for *any* god, Light or Dark, Sir Charrow, but there's no one in all the world has more cause to hate the Dark than my folk. Yet let a whisper of even a single hradani's having dealings with the Dark slip out, and all the old hate comes back to life against *all* of us, and I'll not add to that."

"No," Charrow said softly. "No, I can see that, and I ask you to forgive me. It seems that I, too, have more of the old prejudices than I'd guessed."

"Bah!" Bahzell made a sweeping, dismissive gesture and shrugged. "How many hradani had you met before Brandark and I were after washing up at your door?"

"Well . . . none," Charrow admitted.

"Then you'd naught to measure the stories against, now had you?"

"That's a reason for my blindness, Milord—not an excuse. But you're right, I suppose. And you're right about how most people would react to your news. Yet it's the Order's business to deal with such threats when they arise."

"And so the Order will," Bahzell reassured him. "You were the one as was telling me all champions are part of the Order, whether we like it or no, weren't you?" Charrow nodded. "Well, that being so, I'd say it's after being up to me and young Vaijon here to be dealing with it."

"Just the two of you?" Charrow couldn't quite keep his skepticism from showing, and Bahzell laughed.

"Well, the two of us, and Brandark . . . and forty or fifty thousand Horse Stealers."

"I thought a truce existed between your people and the Bloody Swords."

"So it does—or did before Harnak and I were after having our little disagreement. I've had no letters from my father since Brandark and I left, and it's possible the truce holds still, but I've a shrewd notion Father wasn't any too pleased when Harnak raped a girl under *his* father's protection and laid the blame for it on me. And even if he was minded to let that pass, there's those among his captains would never let it stand. Oh, I'll not say it's *all* because of me, but no one but a fool ever thought that truce would last forever, and one thing Father isn't is a fool. I'm thinking he must have had most of his preparations in place before ever Harnak and I crossed swords. And even if I'm wrong, he'll move quick enough when he hears who Harnak had dealings with."

"So he doesn't know yet," Charrow mused.

"No. I'd meant to write him, for we've no magi for the mage relays to pass word to him through, but it's likely enough I can get there as fast as any letter. And while it's happy I'll be to have his backing, you've the right of it. This *is* the sort of job himself had in mind for the likes of you and me, and I'll not leave my clan to fight my battles for me."

"No. No, I can see that," Charrow agreed. He lowered himself into a chair and leaned back, stretching his legs out before him while he plucked at his lower lip in thought. The slow, steady ticking of the clock on the mantel and the soft crackle of flames from the hearth were the only sounds as he pondered Bahzell's words, and then he gave a sharp nod and inhaled deeply.

"Very well, Milord Champion. You scarcely need my permission, but for what it matters, you *will* have my blessings. And my aid."

"Aid?" Bahzell frowned. "If you're minded to send more folk than Vaijon and Brandark along with me, it's grateful I am, but not so certain it would be wise. We've two choices once we get closer to home: we can cross the Bloody Sword lands to reach Father, or we can strike out cross-country from Daranfel to Durghazh. I'd favor the second, except that only a madman would be crossing that stretch of ground in winter if he's a choice. Still and all, it may happen we've no choice but to try it, and either road, three men will find it easier going—and easier to avoid the notice a dozen would draw."

"No doubt you're right, but that wasn't what I had in mind. Or not exactly. I *would* like to send an escort along with you—perhaps led by Sir Yorhus or Sir Adiskael." The master of the Belhadan Chapter smiled with cheerful nastiness. "I believe a good, brisk ride through freezing cold and blizzards might help inspire them to consider the full implications of their recent, ill-judged actions, don't you think?"

"You're a cruel and wicked man, Sir Charrow," Bahzell said with a slow, lurking smile of his own, and Charrow laughed. But then he sobered and leaned forward, raising one hand to stab a forefinger at the hradani.

"That's as may be, Milord, but an escort could be very helpful to you. For one thing, it would help avoid any . . . misunderstandings you and Brandark might encounter crossing the Empire. And while I realize your homeland is at least as cold as Belhadan, and I'm sure you and Lord Brandark are well acquainted with winter travel, we can provide experienced guides to see you safely on your way. How, exactly, had you planned to make your way home?"

"The hard way," Bahzell said wryly. He smiled at Charrow for a moment, then crossed to the enormous map that hung on one wall. "I'm thinking the best route is from Belhadan down through Axe Hallow," he said, tracing the roads with a finger as he spoke, "then across to Lordenfel, south to the Estoraman high road, up to Silmacha and across the Pass of Heroes to Barandir. From there, we can skirt the Wind Plain down into Daranfel, then either sneak through the Bloody Swords' back pasture or cut straight across to Durghazh and take the main road south from there to Hurgrum."

"Um." Charrow stood and walked over to join the Horse Stealer's perusal of the map. "That's a logical enough route . . . for someone who's picking it off a map. But I've spent some time traveling through Landria and Landfressa myself, and you'll never get through the Pass of Heroes before spring. That's almost as bad as South Wall Pass down in South Province. No, Milord. If you truly intend to make the trip at this time of year, you'll either have to go clear south to Crag Wall Pass or else bear straight north from Lordenfel to Esfresia, then cross into Dwarvenhame through Mountain Heart."

"Ah?" Bahzell rubbed his chin, and his ears shifted gently in thought.

"Exactly," Charrow said, tapping the map with his forefinger. "The bit from Esfresia to the mountains will be the worst of the entire journey, but once you reach the Dwarvenhame Tunnel, it will take you under the mountains, and from there you can pass through

Golden Lode Gap into Ordanfressa and turn south to Barandir. That will take you considerably further north than you'd planned, but Golden Lode is far lower than the Pass of Heroes, and the going—especially across the mountains—will be much easier. And—" he turned from the map to regard Bahzell levelly "—I just happen to know a guide familiar with the route all the way to Mountain Heart. Ah, not to mention the fact that Sir Yorhus was raised in Landfressa and is quite an accomplished snow country traveler."

"I see." Bahzell looked back at the knight-captain for several contemplative moments, then chuckled. "I'll not take 'em any further than Daranfel, Sir Charrow, but you're one as drives a hard bargain. As long as they're all ready to be taking orders from a hradani champion of Tomanāk, they'll be welcome to come along that far."

"I thought you'd see it my way, Milord," Sir Charrow murmured, and he smiled.

CHAPTER SEVEN

The first portion of their journey was less arduous than Sir Charrow had predicted or Bahzell had expected. The skies had cleared, and their worst problem was the eye-gnawing sunlight reflected from the snowfields. Fortunately, all of them knew the danger of snow blindness, and the Axemen had better ways of dealing with it than Brandark's and Bahzell's people did. Instead of the layers of cloth in which the northern hradani swathed their eyes, the reindeer herders of Vonderland, Windfel, and Landfressa used lenses of tinted glass to reduce the glare to manageable proportions.

Bahzell approved wholeheartedly of the innovation. Snow lenses weren't cheap—even dwarves found the manufacture of unflawed, uniformly tinted glass an expensive proposition—and adjusting the goggles in which they were mounted for an exact fit could be difficult. But their only real drawback was that they tended to fog up under certain circumstances, and he could live with that. Especially since the problem was worst when the temperature was lowest, and the temperature (during the day) had actually risen above freezing and stayed there for most of the first week. That was a blessing Bahzell had not anticipated, and the quality of the Empire's roads was another.

Even a barbarian Horse Stealer had heard of Axeman engineers and their mighty projects, but those tales had sounded so unlikely that Bahzell's people tended to put them down as the sorts of wild exaggerations city slickers spread among their credulous country cousins. Bahzell might have been less scornful than some, but neither he nor Brandark were the least prepared for the reality of the royal and imperial high roads. Bahzell supposed they should have been, given the pithy comments Kilthandahknarthas' wagoneers had made about the highways beyond the East Wall Mountains. Some of those roads had seemed like marvels of engineering to him and Brandark, but now he knew why the wagoneers had been so critical, and even with the reality underfoot, he found it hard to believe in. Not even Belhadan had prepared him, for Belhadan, after all, was a city. It sat in one place, a focal point of effort. Roads were something else, for they fanned out in all directions, and the sheer length of them made even a fairly modest highway a greater project than the mightiest city wall ever raised.

But "modest" was a word no one would ever apply to any royal and imperial high road. The one from Belhadan to Axe Hallow, for example, was sixty feet wide and paved with smoothly leveled stone slabs. The hugest freight wagons could easily pass one another, and the roadbed's arrogant straightness bent around only the most intractable obstacles. Clearly, its builders had known precisely where they wanted to go, and they had cut sunken rights of way through the very hearts of hills rather than curl around them or accept slopes whose steepness would have exhausted draft animals.

Yet even as he admired the way in which the Empire's roads served the needs of freight haulers, Bahzell knew any civilian advantages were secondary to the real reason they had been built. The Empire's freight traffic was important, but those roads were built for men on foot, not wagons or the horsemen who used the Empire of the Spear's highways. They were bordered on either side by broad, firm stretches of turf which were clearly intended to spare the hooves of rapidly moving horses the pounding a stone surface would have given them, but their hard-paved centers were meant for the boots of marching men, for the Royal and Imperial Army's true strength was its superb infantry. No one else in Norfressa could match that infantry's quality, and roads such as this provided it with unequaled mobility. The men of the royal and imperial infantry called themselves "the King-Emperor's mules" with a pride as genuine as it was wry. Their peacetime training included regular marches of forty miles a day, in full kit, and they had repeatedly proven their ability to march almost any cavalry in the world into the ground.

Especially along roads like these. The Belhadan-Axe Hallow high road was almost a thousand years old. The bridges over the many streams and minor rivers it crossed wore thick moss over their ancient stones, and the bordering firs which had been planted as windbreaks had grown into giants four and five feet thick. Yet for all its age, it had none of the potholes and mired stretches, even now, in the middle of winter, that Bahzell and Brandark had encountered elsewhere. The Empire was a prosperous land, and villages and towns—the latter large enough to count as small cities in most realms—were threaded along the highway like beads on a string. The farmland which supported communities of such size obviously must be rich, yet as Bahzell counted the houses and observed the smoke curling up from chimneys and the healthy, well-fed citizens who watched their party move by, he realized Axeman farmers must know a thing or two his people didn't. Even allowing for the ability of the Empire's transportation system to ship in food, no hradani farmers could have fed so many mouths off so little land.

But these people managed it, and he made a mental note to suggest that his father see about importing a few Axeman farming experts. It was a point worth bearing in mind, and so was the way in which the local communities kept the high road cleared of snow in their vicinities. Yet Bahzell also had to admit that clear skies, sun, and the quality of the roads were only a partial explanation for the ease of the journey's early stages. Sir Charrow had provided rather more support than he had wanted, but he wasn't about to complain after he saw it all in action.

Sir Yorhus commanded the escort, and he clearly intended to wash away any stigma of his previous resentment of hradani champions. He was almost oppressively attentive, and his constant, pestering search for things he might do for Bahzell and Brandark's comfort had threatened to drive the rest of the escort mad for the first day or so. After that, however, he had calmed down—less, Bahzell was sure, because he felt he had sufficiently expiated his original attitude than because, for all his potential zealotry, he was a wise enough commander to leave others to attend to the business they knew at least as well as he did.

And they did know their business. Sir Charrow had provided two capacious wagons, drawn by teams of Vonderland reindeer completely at home in ice and snow, and the wagons—like those of Kilthan's merchant caravan—had wheels rimmed not with iron but with some thick, flexible substance. One of Kilthan's wagoneers had told Bahzell the material came from the distant jungles of southeastern Norfressa, although he'd been a bit vague about just whom the dwarves dealt with to obtain it. Wherever it came from, however, it certainly made for a far smoother ride than the grating of iron-shod wheels would have, and so did the fat metal cylinders—the "shock absorbers," as one of Kilthan's wheelwrights had called them—and steel leaf springs which had replaced the leather or rope slings a hradani wagon would have been fortunate to boast.

Yet these wagons, unlike Kilthan's, were intended for winter use, and each was provided with a set of sled runners, as well, carried in long racks along its sides. Practiced drovers like those Sir Charrow had provided could mount the runners and strike the wheels in no more than an hour, and while there had been no need to do any such thing so far, Bahzell could appreciate the advantage the runners would offer under less salubrious conditions. The winter daylight was brief enough to limit them to no more than thirty miles or so a day even with such wagons, but that was far better than Bahzell would have dared to predict before setting out.

Nor had the Order skimped on their other supplies. Aside from their inability to find a horse up to Bahzell's weight—which, he admitted cheerfully, *no one* could have done—the Order's quartermasters had provided anything he could have thought to ask for and more. In addition to grain and fodder for the reindeer and horses, there were down-lined Vonderland sleep sacks (a marvelous innovation whose worth, Brandark had loudly announced, exceeded that of any "shock absorber" ever invented), snowshoes, heavy winter tents, coal oil heaters and the fuel to feed them, rations, and even the cross-country skis Bahzell and Brandark had requested. Better yet, from Brandark's perspective, at least, the wagons provided space for the entire collection of books he had assembled in Belhadan. Tents were nice, but the ability to haul his loot home was even nicer. Still, it seemed unnatural to spend nights in such comfort, and the five knights and twenty lay-brothers Sir Charrow had added (no doubt, Bahzell thought wryly, to sufficiently impress his own importance upon any anti-hradani bigot they happened to meet), provided a degree of security the two hradani had not experienced since leaving Kilthan's employ the previous autumn.

All in all, Bahzell decided, he could become accustomed to such coddling. It wasn't something he intended to mention to Brandark, who luxuriated shamelessly in it already, yet he knew it was true, and that was one reason he insisted on working out regularly. The daylight was too short to waste, but even the best wagon was slower than a mounted man—or a Horse Stealer on foot—which meant he could train for an hour or so each morning and still easily overtake the rest of the party by midday.

The first day, he and Brandark had worked out together while Sir Yorhus, Vaijon, and two other knights kept watch, but that hadn't

lasted long. The next morning, Vaijon had respectfully reminded
Bahzell of his promise to complete his training, and Sir Harkon,
the senior knight-companion and Yorhus' second in command, had
asked if he might spar with Brandark, as well. By the third day,
all the knights and two of the senior lay-brothers had arranged
to take the duty of "guarding" Lord Bahzell in rotation while he
worked out so that all of them could get in their own drill time.
He wasn't really surprised, given that they were members of a
martial order. That sort of training had been an everyday part of
their lives for years, and they knew how serious the need to *stay*
in training was. It was also a way to break up the monotony of
the journey—and no matter how well equipped they might be, any
winter journey was always a dreary proposition.

Yet there was another aspect, as well, one Bahzell was slow to
recognize, for he remained unaccustomed to thinking of himself
as special. But he *was* special to these men. He was a gods-touched
champion of the Light, one their own God had personally appeared
to claim as His own in front of them. Whatever he might want,
however he might try to change it, he could never be anything else
to them, and so they hungered to test themselves against him and
so touch the edge of godhood, however indirectly.

And when he finally did realize what was happening, he certainly did try to change it. He didn't *want* to be a gods-touched
champion, and his stubborn refusal to fall down and worship
anyone else made him acutely uncomfortable when someone else
tried to do that to *him*. Nor did it help that Yorhus was the worst
of the lot. As Bahzell had unkindly observed to Charrow, the
knight-commander had the makings of a good fanatic. Not because
he was inherently evil or arrogant, but because he believed so
strongly . . . and tended to substitute faith for reason in a way that
made Bahzell's skin crawl. The Horse Stealer remembered the night
Tomanāk had told him it was his very stubbornness—his refusal
to do anything *he* had not decided was right—which had made
him a champion. He hadn't understood that at the time; now,
looking at Yorhus, he did.

At first, he'd thought it was part of his job to change Yorhus,
to somehow make a little of his own obstinate individualism rub
off on the knight-commander. With that in mind, he'd invited
Yorhus to spar with him in the hopes that a drubbing like the one
he'd given Vaijon (although somewhat less drastic) might batter
through the older knight's mental armor. But he quickly discovered that it was an effort doomed to fail, for Yorhus lacked something Vaijon had. Bahzell couldn't put his finger on exactly what

that something was. He had a suspicion, but it remained too vague for positive conclusions, and whatever it was, Yorhus obviously didn't have it. He also lacked the old Vaijon's egotism, for there was not an arrogant bone in his body. His problem wasn't that he valued his judgment above that of others or looked down on those who fell short of his own accomplishments, or birth, or skill at arms. It grew, in fact, out of his sense of humility. He was utterly prepared to submit to Tomanāk's will in every way. In fact, he *needed* to submit to Tomanāk's will, and that was the heart of his problem.

When Tomanāk failed to give him direct orders, he had to decide for himself what those orders ought to have been, and once he'd decided what his orders were, they had the imprimatur of Tomanāk's Own Writ as far as he was concerned. He adhered to them with unflinching, iron determination . . . and expected all about him to do the same. The possibility that he might be mistaken in what he thought Tomanāk wanted of him seldom so much as crossed his mind, for if he *were* mistaken, then *surely* Tomanāk would tell him so. In fact, Tomanāk *had* told him so in Bahzell's case, and the man was desperate to expiate his "sins." Yet Bahzell felt unhappily certain that once Yorhus had shown his contrition and—in his own eyes—squared his account for current errors, he would go back to all his old, ardent intolerance. Oh, he would never repeat the *same* mistakes, but doing penance for them actually seemed to strengthen the habits of thought which had produced his errors in the first place.

Unfortunately, a taste for blind faith wasn't something Bahzell could knock out of a man in a training bout. It was more a matter of figuring out how to knock a dose of self-skepticism *into* him, and that was a task for which Bahzell was ill fitted. Never a patient man, he was far better suited to dealing with problems which could be solved by taking things apart—usually with a certain degree of forcefulness—before putting the bits and pieces back together the way they were supposed to fit. Yorhus was a different kind of task, and Bahzell had no idea how to go about building qualities he lacked—and obviously saw no pressing need to acquire—into him.

If Bahzell found Yorhus difficult to deal with, Brandark found him almost impossible. The Bloody Sword could no more survive without needling those about him than he could without air, but the serious, literal-minded knight-commander was utterly incapable of seeing what struck Brandark as humorous in a witticism or a song or a joke. He tried—in fact, his efforts to understand were enough to drive the Bloody Sword to drink—but he simply couldn't do it, and Bahzell considered himself lucky Brandark had decided to be tactful and avoid conversations with Yorhus as much as he possibly could.

But that got Bahzell no closer to solving his own problem. Sir Adiskael was back in Belhadan, where Sir Charrow no doubt had his own ideas about how best to deal with zealotry, but Yorhus was clearly Bahzell's job, and he had no idea how to do it.

"Excuse me, Milord, but I couldn't help noticing that you have something on your mind. Is it anything I can help with?"

Bahzell looked up from his strong, steaming cup of midday tea. They were six days out of Belhadan, no more than another day or two from Axe Hallow, and there'd been a surprising amount of traffic, despite the season, as they neared the royal and imperial capital. Some of those they met had gawked at Bahzell and Brandark when they recognized them as hradani, and one or two had actually shrunk away. Compared to the welcome (or lack thereof) they'd received in other lands, that was the equivalent of a warm and hearty greeting, which probably owed a good deal to the fact that they were accompanied by two dozen armed members of the Order of Tomanāk and that Bahzell himself wore the Order's colors. Sir Yorhus, unfortunately, didn't see it that way, and he'd spent most of the morning glaring at those he suspected of harboring disrespectful thoughts where Bahzell was concerned.

"And what makes you think I've something on my mind?" the hradani asked with the air of a man sparring for time, and Vaijon shrugged.

"My father may have raised me to be arrogant, Milord; he didn't raise me to be stupid, however I may have acted in the past. I've come to know you well enough to realize when something is bothering you. Even if I hadn't, Lord Brandark certainly does, and he's been avoiding you most of the morning."

"He has, has he?" Bahzell grinned wryly. "Well, then, perhaps I've something to be grateful for after all."

Vaijon smiled back, but he also shook his head.

"Give you another hour or two and you'll miss him enough to go deliberately offer him an opening, Milord, and he knows it." Bahzell eyed the young knight sharply, surprised by the acuity of that remark. "And he isn't avoiding you because he thinks you'll bite his head off. He's staying away to give you time to chew on whatever you've been thinking about so hard all morning."

"Ah?" Bahzell cocked his ears inquiringly, and Vaijon shrugged again.

"In case you hadn't noticed, Milord," he said with just a hint of asperity, "*everyone's* avoiding you. That's why I decided to bring this whole thing—whatever it is we're talking about—up. I wanted to be certain sheer disuse of your tongue didn't cause you to forget how to speak."

"I'm thinking as how you've been spending entirely too much time with Brandark, my lad," Bahzell said with a slow grin, and Vaijon chuckled. His blue eyes sparkled with pleasure, and the hradani shook his head, trying to imagine anything less like the Vaijon he'd first met than this personable youngster. But then his grin faded as the changes in Vaijon underlined his inability to encourage any similar change in Yorhus, and he sighed.

"Something *is* bothering you, isn't it, Milord?" Vaijon asked in a softer, more serious voice, and Bahzell nodded.

"Aye, lad." The hradani paused for another moment, trying to decide how best to explain, then twitched his ears. "It's Yorhus," he sighed. "Mind you, I'd not say a word against his honesty or courage. Indeed, I'm thinking as that's the heart of the problem. He's one as goes forward full tilt when he's sure he's right . . . or spares no pains to admit his errors when his nose is rubbed deep enough in them. But that's the problem, d'you see? Wrong or right, he's *always* after being sure, with never a bit of give in him *until* someone rubs his nose in it, and questions never bother his head at all, at all."

Bahzell paused, cocking one eyebrow and both ears at Vaijon, and the younger man nodded slowly.

"I know," he said, and his eyes fell briefly. "It never bothered me before you were so kind as to break my arms rather than my head, but he's not very . . . flexible, is he?"

"A bit of the pot and the kettle in that, I'm thinking," Bahzell observed with a smile, and Vaijon chuckled in wry acknowledgment. Then he sobered.

"But not for the same reasons, Milord. I was too full of myself to listen, but Yorhus isn't like that. In most ways, he's one of the humblest knights I know. It's just that . . . that—"

"It's just that too much humility is after being the worst kind of arrogance," Bahzell said quietly, and saw understanding flicker in the blue eyes which rose suddenly to meet his once more. "You're right. I'm thinking he's a good enough man underneath it all, but I'm wishing he could've met Tothas." Vaijon looked a question at him, and he shrugged. "A Spearman I know, Lady Zarantha's personal armsman. He follows Tomanāk, and a better man—or a more understanding one—I've never met. He offered me some advice one night that was better than even he guessed, and it's in my mind that if anyone would be having the patience or wit to straighten Yorhus out, Tothas would."

"Then send Yorhus to him," Vaijon suggested. Bahzell looked at him sharply, for the younger man's voice was completely serious, as if he'd just made the most reasonable suggestion in the world.

"I don't think I was after hearing that correctly," the hradani said after a moment. "Would you be so very kind as to repeat it?"

"I only suggested you send Yorhus to this Tothas." Vaijon sounded perplexed, as if Bahzell's apparent confusion puzzled him. "If you think he could get through to Yorhus in a way you can't, then why *not* send Yorhus to him, Milord?"

"Why not?" Bahzell sat back, cradling the warmth of his mug between his chilled hands, and cocked his ears sardonically. "Why, aside from the tiny fact that Tothas is after being a good thousand leagues from here, all of them covered in snow, *and* a Spearman in the middle of an entire empire of Spearmen who aren't over fond of Axemen that I've noticed, *and* that Yorhus is after being assigned to a chapter house in Belhadan and under Sir Charrow's orders, not mine— Why, aside from all that, there's not a reason in the world that I can see why I shouldn't be sending him off to the ends of the earth in hopes a man as doesn't even know he's coming can sort him out if ever he gets there."

"With all due respect, Milord, none of that matters," Vaijon said, and smiled crookedly as Bahzell's ears flattened in disbelief. "If you'd stayed a little longer in Belhadan and let Sir Charrow finish explaining things, you'd know that without my telling you."

"Know *what?*"

"I was there when Sir Charrow told you there are only eighteen living champions in all of Norfressa. Only *eighteen*, Milord. Aside from Sir Terrian, no member of the Order can so much as dispute any order one of you chooses to give, and not even Sir Terrian could *disobey* you except on Tomanāk's direct authority. If you feel Sir Yorhus could benefit from being sent to your friend Tothas—or anywhere else in the world—you have the authority to send him there without consulting Sir Charrow or anyone else."

Bahzell blinked, and a shiver which owed nothing to winter weather ran through him. The thought of such authority was terrifying, for with it came responsibility . . . and the temptation to tyranny. The idea that his will, however capricious, could send a man across a thousand leagues of bitter winter snow and ice made his stomach knot, and he wondered what insanity had possessed the Order of Tomanāk to put that kind of power into *anyone's* hands.

"Well," a familiar, earthquake-deep voice said soundlessly in the back of his brain, "I suppose they did it because I told them to."

Vaijon sucked in a sudden, deep breath and went white as the snow around them, and Bahzell blinked again as he realized the knight-probationer had also heard Tomanāk's silent voice. There was undoubtedly a reason for that, but at the moment, the sudden revelation of his own authority was the first weight on Bahzell's mind, and he set his mug aside and leaned aggressively forward, bracing his hands on his knees as he glowered at the empty air.

"You did, did you?" he said tartly. "And just what maggotybrained reason were you having for *that*?"

Bahzell wouldn't have believed Vaijon could turn any whiter, but the knight-probationer managed. Tomanāk, on the other hand, only chuckled.

"Mine is a military order, Bahzell, and any army needs officers to command it. For the most part, the Order chooses its own officers—like Sir Terrian and Sir Charrow—and those choices serve it well. But it is *my* order, and I reserve to myself the right to select my *own* officers and place them in authority over it. As I have chosen you."

"And never a word did you say to me about it while you were *after* choosing me, either!" Bahzell pointed out.

"Of course not. If you'd asked, I would have told you the truth, of course. But you didn't, and I was just as glad of it. If I *had* told you, you would have raised even more objections, and recruiting a boulder-brained hradani was hard enough without that!"

Vaijon uttered a strangled sound and made as if to rise, but Bahzell waved him back down. The younger man settled back on the saddle bags he was using for a seat, and the hradani returned his attention to his deity.

"It may be I would have, and it may be I wouldn't," he said, "but that's neither here nor there just this moment. What's in my mind is that I'm none too happy to think such as me could be sending a man I hardly know to what might be his death on a whim!"

"Bahzell, Bahzell! You can be the most stubborn, infuriating, obstinate—" The god chopped himself off, then sighed. "Bahzell, would *you* give authority to an officer you expected to use it capriciously and carelessly?"

The hradani shook his head.

"*Then what in the names of all the Powers of Light makes you think* I *would?*"

The question was a sudden peal of thunder, reverberating with such soundless violence between Bahzell's ears that his eyes glazed. It was obvious from Vaijon's expression that he'd heard the same question, although Bahzell felt certain he'd heard it at a lower volume. *His* eyes weren't crossed, after all.

That was when Bahzell realized Tomanāk had withdrawn with as little warning as he had arrived, and the hradani's lips quirked. He hadn't considered the question from Tomanāk's viewpoint, but he supposed it *did* make sense, after a fashion. Bahzell wasn't about to award himself any accolades for infallibility, and he was only too well aware of his own myriad shortcomings. But he also had to admit that the casual abuse of power had never appealed to him, and if he knew that, how could Tomanāk *not* know it? Still, the god hadn't said a word about whether or not Bahzell would use his newly discovered authority wisely, only that he wouldn't use it *carelessly* . . . which left the responsibility squarely in Bahzell's hands. And that, too, he realized now, was a part of the measure of a champion's duties. It was *his* job to decide whether he was right or wrong. Tomanāk might offer guidance, but as he'd told Bahzell on another snowy afternoon, it was the exercise of his champions' wills and courage which *made* them champions. It was simply that Bahzell hadn't thought about the particular sort of courage it took to assume the authority Tomanāk had just confirmed was his.

"Well!" he said finally, explosively, and slapped his palms on his thighs. The loud smacking sound made Vaijon jump, and Bahzell grinned. "Heard him yourself, did you?"

"Ah, well— I mean, that is—" Vaijon stopped and swallowed. "Yes, Milord. I-I suppose I did."

"Ah, well himself *can* be a mite testy from time to time," Bahzell said blandly, then laughed out loud and leaned over to clap Vaijon on the shoulder as the younger man stared at him. "I'm not so very certain just why he was wanting you to be hearing—not yet— but you can lay to it that he had a reason. In the meantime, though, I'm thinking perhaps I should be giving your suggestion some thought."

"My suggestion, Milord?"

"Aye, the one about Yorhus and Tothas. It just might be there's some merit in that, after all."

CHAPTER EIGHT

The good weather deserted them on the morning of the day Axe Hallow should have come into sight.

Even the high road had begun to twist and turn as it threaded through the Axe Blade Hills which surrounded the Empire's capital like a huge, natural breastwork. In any other land, the hills might have been called "mountains," but the towering East Walls which formed the Empire's eastern rampart denied Axeman geographers the use of that word to describe any lesser peaks. Bahzell, on the other hand, had found himself using it in his own thoughts without reservation as he marched into an icy, cutting breeze and the scattered snowflakes which had begun to turn into something else shortly after dawn. Now it was late morning, and he gritted his teeth as what looked suspiciously like the early stages of a blizzard blew down a rocky cut, straight into his eyes. Bitter as that wind was, he had experienced worse coming down off the Sothōii Wind Plain. It was only the unnaturally easy going of the last week which made it seem like the very breath of ice demons. Not that understanding the why of it made it any more pleasant . . . and not that it wouldn't prove quite sufficient to kill any unwary traveler if it got much worse.

The sudden abatement that morning of the traffic they had been encountering as they neared the capital should have warned him something like this was coming, he thought grimly. No doubt the locals, accustomed to the weather in these parts, had exercised the good judgment to stay home. They'd probably advised any travelers who'd had the sense to ask to do the same, but Bahzell's

97

eagerness to reach Axe Hallow had pushed the pace harder than usual yesterday. He hadn't wanted to stop when they reached the last town with a good two hours of daylight left, and the result had been to leave them camped beside the road rather than sheltered in a hospitable inn whose landlord undoubtedly would have warned them against venturing out today. And knowing *that* didn't make things any more enjoyable, either.

He looked around and grimaced. Once upon a time, he'd wasted very little thought on gods of any persuasion. All he'd asked was for them to leave him alone, in return for which, he'd agreed to leave *them* alone, without nattering at them whenever things looked a little unpleasant. But his attitudes had changed a bit lately, and he considered praying for the weather to pass them by. Unfortunately, Tomanāk wasn't in charge of weather; his sister Chemalka was, and she paid very little heed to the importuning of mortals, assuming she even heard them. The Lady of the Storm did as she chose, when she chose, and it was obvious she was about to choose to drop several feet of snow on one Bahzell Bahnakson's head.

Even more unfortunately, there would be no more inns between here and Axe Hallow, for there was no place to put them. The western approach to the capital was worse going than any of the others, and the stark slopes of the "hills" were the next best thing to perpendicular. The high road wound back and forth as it climbed them like a stony serpent, yet not even that concession could make the repeated ascents anything but a long, exhausting haul, and there certainly weren't any flat places for people to live on.

From the maps, most of the towns and villages near the capital were located to Axe Hallow's east and southeast, where the Kormak River flowed out and down to reach the Greenleaf. Bahzell would have chosen to locate in the same place, given a choice between these barren hillsides and a sheltered river valley, but he could certainly see how Kormak III's councilors had convinced him to locate his new capital here eight hundred years ago. The Kormak Valley was the only true breach in the natural fortress of the hills. Tiny blocking forces could hold the strongest invading army along any of the capital's approaches, and Kormak's dynasty were dwarves, who probably found the terrain comfortingly homey.

Bahzell did not. He didn't mind mountains as such, but these barren, snow choked hills seemed to close in on him, making him feel simultaneously exposed and trapped even when no blizzard was howling through them. His fellow travelers seemed as miserable as he felt, but not one of them had complained about the way his decision to push on yesterday had left them no choice but to continue onward now. Which, since the party included Brandark, probably meant they simply hadn't reasoned it all out . . . yet. He spared a moment to hope things would stay that way, wrapped the thick Sothōii-style poncho more tightly about him, and stumped onward into the wind and gathering snow.

One good thing, he reflected wryly, was that none of his companions cared to complain about whatever pace a man on foot set. The knights and lay-brothers remained uncomfortable at having their commander walk while they rode. They understood horses simply didn't come in the right size for someone seven and a half feet tall, and they probably felt a bit like children cantering along on their ponies beside an adult on foot, but it still seemed profoundly unnatural to them . . . which was solely because they were so unfamiliar with hradani in general and Horse Stealers in particular. It never crossed their minds that *they* were far more likely to slow *him* than vice versa, for they didn't realize he could have run their horses into a state of foundered collapse. Brandark did, but he took it so much for granted that it never occurred to him to mention it, and given the weather, Bahzell was prepared to take shameless advantage of the others' ignorance to push them still harder. The last milestone had shown them only thirteen miles from Axe Hallow, and he wanted the lot of them under shelter before the real storm hit.

He topped out on another rise and turned his back to the wind long enough to look behind him. Fresh snow coated the pavement in a thin, slippery skim of white. The reindeer seemed unperturbed, but the wagoneers looked a little anxious, and the mounted men had moved their horses onto the better footing offered by the turf beside the road proper. At least snow wasn't ice, Bahzell told himself philosophically as he turned to peer back into the wind once more. Or not *yet*, at least.

From everything he'd ever heard of Axe Hallow, the watchtowers on the hilltops above it ought to be visible by now, but the flying snow reduced visibility badly, and he shrugged. They'd reach the city when they reached it; in the meantime, he had more pressing concerns, and he slapped his mittened hands together in a vain effort to make his fingers feel warmer as he started forward once more.

By late afternoon, there was no longer any question about how the weather might best be described. The day had degenerated into a howling gale, and their pace had slowed even more. The road's steepness would have made every mile feel like two even without the blizzard; with it, the thirteen miles Bahzell had expected to cover in two or three hours had eaten up every remaining scrap of putative daylight, and he was beginning to consider stopping right where they were.

It was not an appealing decision. The road passed through a series of narrow cuts bare of anything remotely like a windbreak. If they must, they could turn the wagons broadside to the wind and use them for cover, and their felted tents and sleeping sacks would keep them from freezing to death. But that wasn't the same as keeping them *warm*, and he didn't care for the feel of the wind. It had been icy all day; now the temperature had begun a dangerous plummet to sub-zero levels, and with no better cover than was offered here, they could easily lose half their horses on a night like the one they plainly faced.

He swore to himself, pounding his fists together and peering vainly into the snow. None of his companions knew precisely where they were, and even Sir Yorhus, who'd made this trip many times, had lost his bearings. The milestones had long since vanished as the snow and wind closed in, and Bahzell snarled. For all he knew, they could be within a hundred yards of the city . . . but they might not be, too, and he had to make a decision soon. They couldn't stumble on indefinitely, always hoping the capital was *just* ahead. Sooner or later a horse would lose its footing and go down, or frostbite would claim someone's fingers or toes—or worse. But if Axe Hallow *was* close at hand, it promised walls and roofs and fires.

He was about to give up and order his followers to make camp when he realized someone—or something—was coming. It was more sensed than seen, a darker blot in the gale-lashed dark, and he frowned and raised one hand, trying vainly to shield his eyes in an effort to see better. It was useless at first, but then he stiffened as a single horseman emerged from the wall of snow and came trotting straight towards him.

"Well, well! *Here* you are!"

The white-bearded rider's cheerful voice should have been torn to shreds in the heart of the blizzard, but it carried with absolute, unnatural clarity. The Sothōii warhorse under him was worth a prince's ransom, but nothing else about him suggested any particular wealth or rank. Like Bahzell, he wore a plain Sothōii-style poncho over equally plain—and warm—woolens and leather, and the scabbard of his longsword was of unadorned, scuffed leather. He pushed back the hood of his poncho with mittened hands, exposing the gay stripes of a red-and-white knitted woolen cap that looked absurdly out of place amid the blowing snow and ice, and grinned, and Bahzell planted his fists on his hips and glowered at him.

"I'm getting just a mite tired of the weather you carry about with you, wizard," he growled.

"I had nothing to do with it," the mounted man told him virtuously, then leaned sideways in the saddle to clasp forearms with him.

"Ha!" Bahzell replied, surveying the newcomer with obvious disbelief. The old man looked back with what was probably an expression of artful innocence, but it was hard to be sure without seeing his eyes, and no one had seen Wencit of Rūm's eyes in well over a millennium. The glowing witchfire which had replaced them when the wild magic came upon him danced and flickered under his craggy brows, and he chuckled.

"You have my word, Bahzell," he said. "Not even a wild wizard meddles with the weather. Besides, if I *were* going to adjust conditions, I can think of far more pleasant things than snow and ice!"

"I suppose," Bahzell agreed grudgingly and turned his head as Brandark urged his horse up beside him. "Look what the wind's blown in . . . again," he said sourly.

"You really have to work on the way you speak about ancient and powerful masters of arcane lore," Brandark told him severely, then held out his own hand to the wizard. "Hello, you old horse thief!" he said in genial tones. "Fancy meeting you here."

"Remind me to do something nasty to both of you," Wencit replied. "But not right now. Why don't we get the lot of you inside so you can at least be warm when it happens?"

"That," Brandark said with feeling, "sounds like an *excellent* idea. Of course," he went on in a more wary tone, eyes narrowing as he considered the wizard, "the *last* time we ran into you in a blizzard, there were forty or fifty dog brothers and a pair of dark wizards—one of them a priest of Carnadosa, as I recall—camped out in the middle of it. I trust you're not here to reprise that performance?"

"No, no!" Wencit assured him with another grin. "I happened to be in Axe Hallow on business of my own—business which, I'm sure you'll be relieved to know, had nothing at all to do with either of you—when this little squall blew in. Since you hadn't turned up before dark fell, I thought I should come looking for you, that's all."

" 'All,' is it?" Bahzell murmured. He studied the old man thoughtfully, but Wencit only grinned more broadly, and the hradani decided to let it drop. Wencit of Rūm was a law unto himself, and

Bahzell no more believed he'd just "happened" to be in Axe Hallow than he did that the sun would rise in the west tomorrow morning. On the other hand, he'd had ample opportunity even in the brief time he and Brandark had spent working with the old man to rescue Lady Zarantha to realize Wencit would tell him as much as he wanted him to know and no more. Bahzell would have expected that to infuriate him, given the traditional hradani attitude that the only good wizard was a dead one and his own lack of patience, but somehow it didn't. He supposed that could be because if anyone had ever earned the right to be mysterious, Wencit was certainly that anyone. Only four white wizards had survived the Fall of Kontovar. One of them had been driven quite mad, and two more had been permanently drained by the White Council's desperate, self-immolating counterstrike against the Lords of Carnadosa. Only Wencit had survived with his power intact to protect the exodus to Norfressa by the last, decimated wave of the Fall's survivors, and he was probably the only reason anyone had survived to flee. Under the circumstances, he was entitled to a few quirks.

"Well," the Horse Stealer said after a moment in tones of elaborate patience, "you're the one as knows just how far we *are* from the blasted city, Wencit. So if it's no bother, I'm thinking it would be a kindly thing for you to stop sitting on your arse and show the rest of us. In a manner of speaking, of course."

"Oh, of course!" Wencit chuckled, and turned his horse back the way he'd come. "If you'll just follow me," he invited. "And *do* try not to get lost."

In fact, they'd been barely half a mile from the city's western gate when Wencit found them, and Bahzell didn't know whether to be grateful that they'd had so short a distance left to go or disgusted that he'd been prepared to spend a miserable, icy night that close to the shelter he'd been unable to see. He decided to settle for gratitude, and craned his neck back to stare up at Axe Hallow's walls as the party approached them.

Since its founding, the capital had expanded mainly to the south and east, where there was room for homes and businesses and merchants could take advantage of the Kormak River and its canal system. The successive rulers who had made Axe Hallow the greatest city in Norfressa had insisted that the fortifications must be expanded to cover each outward bound of the city limits, however great the expense, and the expansion had gradually replaced all the other original gates. Only West Gate remained, but there was nothing at all wrong with it, despite its age. The outer wall stood more than tall enough for its battlements to vanish into the wind-blown snow, and massive, hexagonal towers flanked the gate itself. Under normal conditions, the dark stonework must look harsh and forbidding; tonight, the warm yellow light spilling out of West Gate's cavernous gullet and the towers' arrow slits promised a welcoming oasis, and Bahzell heard Vaijon's horse whinny in relief as they headed for it.

The gate was fully manned, blizzard or no, and the Horse Stealer studied the guard detail closely. The sentries looked half frozen, but they examined the travelers alertly, and though there was no challenge—probably because of Wencit's presence, Bahzell decided as he watched the wizard nod to an officer in passing—the guards clearly knew their business. And well they should, for these were troopers from the Royal and Imperial Army, not regular city guardsmen.

The sentries looked back at him and Brandark with equal curiosity, and he wondered what these Axemen made of them. The Empire's borders had no direct contact with any hradani land, but defensive treaties with the Border Kingdoms along its frontiers had brought its army into occasional contact with hradani brigands, raiders, and even one or two armies of invasion over the centuries. Bahzell had never personally faced Axemen in battle, but he'd talked to grizzled veterans who had, and they'd always spoken of the Royal and Imperial Army with profound respect, even fear. Given their choice, they probably would have preferred facing Axemen to a charge of Sothōii windriders, but it would have been a very close thing.

No other infantry in the world could match the army of King Emperor Kormak. Even before the annexation of Dwarvenhame in the middle of the last century, a quarter of the Empire's population had been dwarvish. The rest of its people were predominately human, but it had a healthy leavening of all the races (except, of course, hradani), and the unprecedented intermixing—and marriage—among the various Races of Man which had stemmed from the Kingdom of the Axe's status as the main port of refuge for Kontovar's escapees continued to hold true for the Empire. Compared to the Sothōii, the humans with whom Bahzell was most familiar, most humans in the Empire were relatively short. There were obviously exceptions, like Vaijon, but few of them would have been at all happy at the thought of engaging hradani-sized enemies on a one-to-one basis.

That was why the Royal and Imperial Army did its best to see to it that its personnel never had to do something like that. It was hardly surprising that the Army was infantry-oriented, given the Empire's strong dwarvish component. Yet even though the Axe Brothers—the elite bodyguard and personal retainers of the King-Emperor—took their name from the great daggered axes they wielded in battle, that traditional dwarvish (and Horse Stealer) weapon was restricted solely to their ranks. Dwarvish axemen had always been fearsome opponents, but the army which had been built by the hard-bitten professionals of the Royal and Imperial officer corps, most of them graduates of the Emperor Torren Military Academy right here in Axe Hallow, was even more frightening.

Bahzell's father had always insisted no organized force was ever outnumbered by a *dis*organized one, regardless of the numbers, and the fact that he'd managed—finally—to hammer that axiom through the skulls of his Horse Stealers accounted for their ability to crush Bloody Sword forces which had often enjoyed a numerical advantage of two to one or even more. Yet Bahzell nursed no illusions. For all of his father's reforms, an Axemen army would have smashed Prince Bahnak's alliance as easily as he had defeated Navahk and her allies.

The Empire's infantry were exhaustively drilled in the sort of formation fighting alien to "barbarians" (like traditional hradani warriors) who insisted on fighting as individuals. Even among Prince Bahnak's troops, that fundamental individualism persisted on an almost instinctive level which only harsh training and harsher discipline could counter. But no Axeman infantryman thought of himself that way; all of his training focused on the need to fight as a member of a mutually supporting team carefully organized to maximize the effectiveness of its members.

The Axemen's primary maneuver unit was the thousand-man strong battalion. Composed of ten hundred-man companies, each of ten ten-man squads, it formed the heart of the tactical formation known as a "torren," after the Kontovaran Emperor, who had formalized it. The two or three battle lines of a torren resembled nothing so much as a huge chessboard built out of blocks of infantry, each of whom left a gap between itself and the units on either side of it which was exactly the width of its own frontage. The line behind it was arranged in the same formation . . . but offset so that each of *its* units was immediately behind one of the gaps in the first line. The torren could be adopted by units from battalions down to the squad level. In fact, it was most common for a battalion to break down into company-sized blocks, but size as such hardly mattered, for that apparently simple formation was the secret of the Army's success. It was also, as Prince Bahnak had discovered when he began evolving his own tactics for his Horse Stealers, much less simple than it seemed, and only superbly trained troops could make it work.

For those who could employ it, the torren provided unparalleled battlefield mobility. Its square blocks could march in any direction equally well simply by changing facing, and the gaps in each line allowed units to fall back under pressure, knowing there would always be friendly units ready to cover its flanks. Or the front line could be used to hold an enemy while the second charged through its gaps to administer successive shocks to the opponent. For that matter, less sophisticated troops often saw the spaces in the torren as opportunities to break their enemies' formation and stormed forward into the gaps only to have the torren's second-line battalions charge into their own flanks.

But as if the torren's tactical advantages weren't enough, every Axeman infantryman was also issued a thigh-length chain hauberk, a steel breastplate, and steel greaves to protect his legs. That was far better than most armies—like those of the Empire of the Spear, which relied upon feudal levies for its military manpower—could manage. Even the wealthiest Spearman baron or count would have found it difficult to match the standard-issue armor of the Royal and Imperial Army, yet excellent as their armor might be, the most important defense of "the King-Emperor's mules" were the tall, cylindrical shields designed to protect them from throat to knees and to overlap into an impenetrable defensive wall in close formation.

Protected behind those shields, they engaged their foes with light spears and shortswords. Their spears could be thrown as they charged, showering an opponent with a deadly hail of missiles as they closed, but they were used as hand-to-hand weapons just as often, with each man thrusting out through the narrow gap between his shield and that of the man to his own right. The length of his spear gave him a reach few sword-armed foes could match, but even when it had been cast at the enemy or broken, no one could get at him past his shield as long as his unit's formation was unbroken, and his shortsword was designed for thrusting. Little more than eighteen inches long, it was deadly in the hands of a well-trained veteran.

Of equal, if less spectacular, importance, the Empire's quartermasters and military engineers were the finest in the world. Indeed, the Axemen's single weakness was their lack of cavalry. The Royal and Imperial Mounted Infantry were just that—mounted *infantry* whose horses (or mules) provided them with greater mobility, but who fought on foot. They were *not* cavalry, although they were trained to fight mounted (after a fashion) in cases of dire necessity. There *was* some light and medium Axeman cavalry, but it accounted for less than ten percent of the Empire's total standing army.

Unfortunately for the Empire's foes, the House of Kormak didn't really need a powerful cavalry force. Or, rather, it already had one that simply belonged to someone else. The Empire and the Kingdom of the Sothōii had been allies for over eight hundred years, and only a madman would willingly face Axeman infantry supported by Vonderland longbowmen and Sothōii cavalry.

Personally, Bahzell had no desire to see any Royal and Imperial army advancing towards *him* whether it had Sothōii cavalry in support or not, but at the moment he found the sight of the tough, seasoned looking sentries almost as reassuring as the sight of West Gate itself. He recognized their surprise as they took in his own livery, and he hid a smile as he wondered what they made of a hradani in the colors of the Order of Tomanāk. But they were too well trained to react openly, and the unflappable lieutenant commanding the guard detachment returned Bahzell's raised-fist salute as if he saw hradani every day.

The long gate tunnel seemed unnaturally hushed, despite the clatter of hooves and the jingle and creak of weapons harnesses, to say nothing of the wagons and *their* teams, but the blizzard was waiting when they reemerged inside the walls. The city's buildings broke some of its force, but the wind continued to howl like souls trapped in Krahana's hells. It seemed even worse after the brief respite the tunnel had provided, and Bahzell shivered as he turned to Wencit once more.

"Would it happen you'd someplace in mind to lead us to when you were after deciding to come out and fetch us?"

"As a matter of fact, I did," Wencit admitted. "Follow me."

He touched a heel lightly to his horse and trotted off through the snow blowing down the deserted street, and Bahzell and his companions followed him into the city.

CHAPTER NINE

Bahzell formed only fleeting impressions of Axe Hallow that night. He had a sense of spaciousness, of wide avenues whose ruler-straight broadness contrasted sharply with Belhadan's more intimate streets, and bits and pieces stood out with startling clarity—like the magnificent statuary group which loomed suddenly out of the whirling whiteness as they reached a major intersection, or the snow-covered fountains (turned off for the winter) which seemed to stretch endlessly across an immense, paved square. But the visibility was too low (and he was too frozen) for anything more. It wasn't that he didn't realize he was walking through the greatest city in the known world; he simply had too much on his mind and too much snow in his eyes to appreciate the scenery properly.

But that changed abruptly when they reached Wencit's destination.

The wizard drew rein, halting them in another square, even larger than any through which they had already passed. Twin rows of street lamps marched off through the snow, continuing the line of the avenue by which they had entered until they met with two more rows which crossed them at right angles. The wicks in the glass lanterns burned steadily, despite the wind, and still more street lamps stretched out to either hand, outlining the entire square in light. Despite that, its far side was invisible, but the building directly before them stood out like a cliff of marble, and glorious color spangled the snow as more light streamed through huge stained glass windows. Frail-looking flying buttresses arced through the night, gossamer as moth wings as the street lamps and windows turned the airborne snow about them into a mysterious, glowing fog, and Bahzell could just make out the graceful, indistinct blurs of the towers and domes looming high above him.

Shallow steps stretched the full width of the magnificent portico which fronted the building, and the columns supporting the portico's roof wore the shape of the war god's mace, with the weapon's flanged head for a capital. The lintel of the doorway which centered the facade, carved in the shape of two enormous crossed swords, was at least forty feet across, and the door below it was closed by panels of hammered steel. Even through the snow, he could make out the bas relief frescoes of warriors locked in mortal combat with demons, devils, and other creatures of the Dark which adorned those massive doors, and the majestic, stern-eyed face of Tomanāk himself looked out from above it, flanked on either side by the immense stained glass windows, shaped like point-down swords, which spilled their glory into the night.

The two smaller entrances to either side of the main portal were scarcely less magnificent, and fully armed warriors in the green and gold of the Order of Tomanāk stood watch before all of them. They were motionless as statues despite the night's flaying cold, and Bahzell felt something unpleasantly like panic as the colored light from the windows flowed over them and he realized Wencit had led them directly to the High Temple of Tomanāk. Combat against dog brothers, demons, or god-cursed swords was one thing; facing something like *this* was another thing entirely.

"By the Harp!" The reverent whisper sounded unnaturally clear in a fleeting lull in the storm, and Bahzell turned to look at Brandark. It was an oath he'd heard his friend use only twice in all the time they'd known one another, and for once the urbane, aggressively sophisticated Bloody Sword looked as awestruck as Bahzell felt.

"Impressive, isn't it?" Wencit's dry tone could have sounded ironic, or as if he were mocking the hradani's stunned reaction. Instead, its simple matter of factness only underscored the fact that mortal hands had no business raising a structure with the power and presence of this one.

No one else spoke. Sir Yorhus and most of his fellows had been here before, yet they seemed as awed as Bahzell and Brandark. In a way, the hradani's reaction had made them stop and look at the Temple with fresh eyes, seeing it once more for the very first time, and it had struck them to silence. Those burnished doors and glowing windows promised warmth and comfort, yet not one of the half-frozen travelers hurried forward to claim their protection. They only sat their horses or stood there, gazing up at the temple as if they were afraid to break some magical spell.

But then, suddenly, the central doors opened. More light poured out, cascading down the broad steps like a golden carpet, and a dozen armed and armored figures strode down that carpet. The chestnut-haired man at their head was a few inches shorter than Vaijon, with a curly beard and powerful shoulders. The sword and mace on his surcoat were worked in thread of gold, he carried a plumed helmet in the crook of his left arm, and rubies and sapphires glittered like fire on the scabbard of the broadsword at his side.

There could be no question of who commanded that group of warriors, but the woman following a half-pace behind him was at least as eye-catching. Bahzell was surprised to see her, for she was the first female warrior he'd laid eyes on since entering the Empire. Among his own folk, women were routinely taught at least the rudimentary use of weapons, but that was primarily as a precaution, for hradani women were far too valuable to risk in combat. Unlike their men, they were immune to the Rage, which made them the guarantors of what stability most hradani tribes clung to, and some of the other clans regarded the Horse Stealers as heretical for training them with weapons at all. He was aware that other lands and peoples had other customs, of course. The Sothōii war maids, for example, might be considered outcasts by "proper" Sothōii, but they were widely acknowledged as the finest irregular light infantry in the world, and dwarvish women routinely fought shoulder to shoulder with the men of their clans. But most of the Races of Man reserved warfare primarily for their menfolk, if for no other considerations than physical size and strength, and he'd assumed that was the case among the Axemen.

Until now. The woman descending the steps towards him reminded him suddenly and almost overpoweringly of Zarantha of Jashân. But that wasn't really true, he realized almost as quickly. Or was it? Zarantha and her maid Rekha were the only human women he'd had the chance to truly come to know, after all. Was that the reason for his strange sense of familiarity, or was there something more to it? Zarantha had always radiated a certain presence, a sense of assurance and self-knowledge, and this woman did the same, yet aside from that and her hair—the same midnight black as Zarantha's—there was no true physical similarity. This woman wore *her* hair in a warrior's braid which matched Bahzell's own, her eyes were a dark, startling blue, not brown, and

she stood just under six feet in height, almost a foot taller than
Zarantha. She also moved like a hunting dire cat, yet even though
Bahzell had never seen her before, he couldn't shake off the eerie
sensation that he knew her. It was if he had met her in some other
place and time, even though he knew with absolute certainty that
he never had.

The welcoming party reached the bottom of the steps, and the
chestnut-bearded man strode forward, still accompanied by the
woman, to where Bahzell stood frozen with more than the cold.
He smiled and nodded up at Wencit, but his gray eyes never left
Bahzell, and he held out his right hand.

"Welcome, Bahzell Bahnakson!" The resonant baritone, lighter
than Bahzell's but deeper than most humans', carried with the
clarity of a voice accustomed to the field of battle. "I am Sir Terrian,
Knight-General of the Order of Tomanāk, and I bid you welcome
indeed in the War God's name."

Bahzell clasped the proffered arm, and Terrian grinned almost
impishly.

"We were warned you were on your way, and Kaeritha and I—"
he twitched his head sideways at the woman "—were concerned when
the weather closed in. We were about to assemble a party to go looking for you when Wencit 'happened by' and offered to find you for
us. Under the circumstances, we decided to stay home by the fire and
let him amaze us afresh with his accomplishments."

"Did you now?" Bahzell returned Terrian's grin, pushed back the
hood of his poncho with his free hand, and twitched his ears in
amusement. He felt an instant, powerful liking for Terrian—even
more than he had for Sir Charrow—and he gave the knight-
general's arm another squeeze before he released his grip. "I'm
thinking I'd've chosen the same, like enough," he allowed. "Besides,
Wencit's quite a way with finding folk in the middle of blizzards."

"So I've heard," Terrian replied dryly. Then he shook himself
and indicated the armored woman beside him. "But allow me to
complete the introductions, Bahzell. This is Dame Kaeritha Seldansdaughter." The woman held out her arm in turn, and Bahzell's
eyebrows rose at the strength of her clasp. "Like yourself, Kaeritha
is a Champion of Tomanᤥk," Terrian continued, and chuckled at
the flicker of surprise Bahzell couldn't quite keep from showing.
"I imagine you and she should have quite a few notes to compare," the knight-general added. "I believe her elevation to champion status was greeted with almost as much consternation as your
own."

He looked up at the mounted members of the party, and his

gaze located Sir Yorhus with unerring accuracy. The Belhadan knight-commander flushed, twitching his shoulders uncomfortably, but made himself meet the eyes of the commander of his Order with commendable steadiness.

Bahzell hardly noticed, for he'd suddenly realized why Kaeritha felt so familiar to him, and it wasn't any imagined resemblance to Zarantha. There was something inside her, like an echo of Tomanāk, which called to a matching echo deep within *Bahzell*. He hadn't realized that tiny bit of the god's presence was there until he saw its twin in Kaeritha, but he recognized it now, and his eyes softened as he gazed into her face.

"Well met, sword brother," she said, and her soprano voice cut even more cleanly through the storm than Terrian's had. "He told me He'd found me a new brother I'd like."

"Did he now?" Bahzell smiled at her, and his grip on her arm tightened as he savored the accuracy of her greeting. He *was* her brother, and she was his sister, more surely than if they had been born of the same parents. He'd never before experienced anything like that moment of instant awareness, of complete certainty in the capacity and fidelity of another, yet there was no room at all for doubt. "Well, I wish himself had been after thinking to warn *me* about *you*, sword sister," he rumbled back, "but I've no doubt he just wasn't wishful to spoil the surprise."

"This is all very touching," Wencit interrupted, "but as Terrian says, I *did* go find you lot, and my backside is pretty nearly frozen to this saddle. Do you suppose we could move this conversation indoors and conduct it in front of a fire like civilized people?"

"Civilized, is it?" Terrian snorted. "And since when have *you* been 'civilized,' Wencit?"

"Since I started freezing in place," the wizard replied tartly, and Terrian laughed.

"I'm relieved to see *something* can turn your thoughts in the direction of civility! But if that's what you really want, I suppose we can accommodate you." He nodded to three of the Temple guardsmen who had followed him and Kaeritha down the steps, and the designated men stepped forward. "If you and Lord Brandark—and you, Sir Yorhus—will let these gentlemen have your horses, they'll see to stabling all your animals and getting your baggage unloaded while we continue our conversation under those more civilized conditions you wanted."

"So how may the Order serve you, Milord?" Sir Terrian asked the better part of an hour later, and Bahzell lowered his huge tankard of hot cider with a slight frown. The blizzard's unabated fury was faint through thick walls, and his feet were propped in front of a roaring fire in the large office-cum-sitting room which served as Terrian's study. The room was as well heated as anything in the Belhadan Chapter House, and the Horse Stealer's toes—and nose—had thawed considerably. He was actually beginning to believe he might enjoy having survived the storm, but Terrian's question pulled him back from the raw sensual pleasure of being warm again and required him to think.

"As to that, I'm thinking the Order's done just about all I might have been asking of it already, Sir Terrian," he rumbled after a moment. "Leaving aside the little matter of today's weather, which was none of their doing, Sir Charrow and Sir Yorhus between them have made this the least unpleasant winter march in my memory."

"I'm delighted to hear it," Terrian said, sipping from his own mug of cider. Then he gave Yorhus another of those sharp, stabbing looks. "I'm particularly pleased to hear it given some of the reports Sir Charrow has forwarded to me through the mage relays. I understand there was some, ah, *difference of opinion* over your status, shall we say?"

Bahzell began to reply, but Yorhus spoke before he could.

"There was, My Lord General," the knight-commander said formally. He bent his head, but that strange note, as if he found some obscure pleasure in admitting his fault, was back in his voice. "To my shame, much of the making of that difference was mine. But Lord Bahzell and Tomanāk have shown me my error, and I trust to so amend my behavior that neither they nor you shall have reason to find fault with me ever again."

Terrian's eyes narrowed, and he pursed his lips, then threw Bahzell a sharp glance and raised his eyebrows. Bahzell flicked his ears to acknowledge the silent question. He was pleased Terrian had recognized the compulsiveness of Yorhus' admission, and he fully intended to discuss sending the knight-commander to Jashân in the hope that Tothas could straighten him out. But he had no desire to begin that discussion before so many others. Common courtesy dictated that he speak with the knight-general about it in private, and so he turned his attention to Kaeritha with a grin.

"Aye, Sir Terrian. 'Differences of opinion' is one way to be putting it. And from what you were saying earlier, I've the impression Dame Kaeritha could tell us about a few 'differences of opinion' of her own."

"Indeed I could . . . if I were inclined to bring up old misunderstandings. Which, of course, no true knight would ever do," Kaeritha replied in a devilishly demure tone.

Bahzell chuckled, and she smiled back at him. In the better light of the office, Bahzell could see the pale line of a scar, thin but obviously the legacy of a deep wound, which ran down her oval face from the top of her right cheek to the side of her throat. Another ran from her forehead back and up across her hairline, and a streak of startling white traced its course further back into her hair. Despite its scars, hers was a face well suited to the smile it wore, but then her expression grew more sober.

"Unlike some of the other chivalric orders, ours has always been open to women," she said seriously. "That's caused some problems in places like the Empire of the Spear, where the very notion of a woman choosing to train at arms is anathema, but Tomanāk was rather firm about it when he ordained the Order's existence."

She paused, and Bahzell nodded, once again reminded of Zarantha. It was fortunate Duke Jashân had chosen to give his heir, daughter or no, the sort of training which would have horrified his peers. Without it, she would have possessed neither the dagger which had helped keep her alive the night she and Bahzell met nor the skill to use it, nor would she have known how to use Tothas' bow against the dog brothers in the Laughing God Inn. But Kaeritha was right: the mere notion of a woman warrior, much less a belted knight, would strike most Spearmen nobles as an abomination.

"Despite Tomanāk's decree, however, relatively few women actually join us," Kaeritha continued. "I'd be surprised if more than one or two percent of our members have been women." She glanced at Terrian, as if for confirmation, and the knight-general flicked one hand.

"I haven't checked the numbers, but I'd imagine you're right. In fact, you're probably *over*estimating the numbers," he said, and looked at Bahzell. "It's not because we discourage women from taking our vows, you understand—though I suspect some of our brethren do so unofficially. Relatively few women ever express a desire to take up the sword, and we have our own share of men who think *none* of them should. But the main reason the numbers are so low is that most of the women who *do* seek admission to one of the militant orders turn to either the Sisterhood of Lillinara or to the Axes of Isvaria."

He cocked an eyebrow at Kaeritha almost challengingly, and she shrugged.

"True enough. In fact, *my* first thought was for the Sisterhood.

I suppose it's only natural for a woman to feel drawn to the service of a god*dess*, and both the Sisterhood and the Axes are at least as good in the field as our Order is, now aren't they?"

She held Terrian's eyes with a bland challenge of her own, and he laughed.

"If they aren't, *I'm* certainly not brave enough to say so!"

"That's because the Order chooses its knights-general for wisdom as well as skill, Milord," Kaeritha said, and grinned as he chuckled. But then she turned back to Bahzell, and her smile faded.

"As I say, I was strongly drawn to the Sisterhood in the beginning. I come from Moretz peasant stock, Bahzell, and my life had been . . . unpleasant." Her blue eyes went even darker, but her voice was calm. "My father was an Esganian, actually, but he had a way with horses, and he was a drover for a Hildarth merchant for many years. I don't remember him well. I think he was a good man, but he was killed by brigands when I was three or four, and my mother—" She paused, then twitched her head. "My mother had left her own village when she married him. She had no family near the one we lived in when he died, and she . . . did whatever a 'foreign' woman with three children and no man had to do to survive. I loved her, and I never stopped loving her, but it was hard for a child to understand the decisions she had to make. There are things I thought—things I actually said to her—which I would give all I may ever own to take back. I can't, of course. All I can do is honor her memory and seek to protect others like her."

She took another long sip of cider, gazing into the fire, and Bahzell heard Yorhus stir restlessly behind him. He glanced back over his shoulder and saw the anger in the knight-commander's face. Not at Kaeritha, but at her mother's fate. He must have realized where Kaeritha's tale was headed as well as Bahzell had, and outrage flickered in his expression. But Kaeritha seemed unaware of it, and her eyes remained fixed on the dancing flames when she spoke once more.

"I was thirteen when my mother died. My younger sister had already died of some wasting disease—I'm not certain which one; I was too young to know at the time—and my brother had been drafted for military service when our local baron decided to raise troops for a fishing expedition in the Ferenmoss civil war. I was alone, but I was tall for my age and prettier than most, and some of the local men decided I was old enough to . . . take my mother's place. I disagreed, and when one of them tried to force me—" her right hand rose to trace the scar on her cheek, and Bahzell heard the sharp, sibilant hiss of Yorhus' indrawn breath "—I took away his dagger and killed him with it." She looked up from the fire to meet Bahzell's eyes. "I'm afraid I didn't let him die very easily, either."

"And a good thing," Bahzell rumbled. Among most hradani, rape was the one crime which not even the Rage could excuse. That held true—publicly, at least—even in Navahk, where Prince Churnazh ruled through terror and brutality. The fact that Churnazh and at least three of his four sons were rapists was well known, although few dared say so openly. Yet it had been the public knowledge that Bahzell had beaten Crown Prince Harnak almost to death for raping a servant girl which had truly driven Harnak into pursuing him across the width of a continent. Not even the Navahkans would have followed Harnak while those rumors persisted, and the only way to silence them had been to kill Bahzell and his victim. Unfortunately for his plans, both of them were still alive and he *wasn't*, and Bahzell doubted that even Harnak's father regretted his death very deeply, considering the embarrassment he'd become.

But Bahzell had come to realize that rape was much more common among the other Races of Man. It disturbed him deeply, for it was a crime he simply could not understand and for which he had the utmost contempt, but he knew it happened . . . and he had no sympathy at all for anyone who committed it.

Kaeritha looked a bit startled by the firmness of his approval. She gazed at him for a moment, and then the corner of her mouth quirked.

"If the local magistrates had shared your view, I'd probably still be living in Moretz," she said wryly. "As it happened, I doubted they'd see things my way, so I fled. I won't bore you with the details, but eventually I wound up in Morfintan down in South March. I was two-thirds starved and filthy, my cheek was badly infected, and the City Guard snapped me up for vagrancy. I'd had no experience of Axeman justice, and I was scared to death when they marched me into the courtroom. The only magistrates I'd ever met had been my natural enemies—I certainly wasn't prepared for one who took one look at me, then sent the bailiff out to fetch his wife so he could hand me over to her to 'wash her and feed her up so I can't count her ribs anymore, for Orr's sake!'"

The grim darkness in her eyes faded, replaced by happier memories.

"That was how I met Seldan Justinson and his wife, Marja," she said, the warmth of her eyes leaking over into her voice, as well. "They took me in as casually as if I were a stray puppy, and I'm not the only stray they saved. I may not have any idea where to find any of my blood relatives—assuming I have any—but I've got six brothers and eight sisters, most of 'em still living in Morfintan, and four of them still living with Seldan and Marja. He's Mayor now, and he and Marja are the parents who saved my life . . . and my soul." She met Bahzell's eyes fully, and her smile was gentle. "They taught me love again, you see," she said simply, and the Horse Stealer nodded.

Silence hovered for a long moment, and then Kaeritha inhaled deeply.

"Well, Seldan and Marja washed me, fed me, called in a healing mage for my face, sent me off to school each day—kicking and fighting every inch of the way—and generally set about civilizing me. They even got me to stop complaining about the silliness of a peasant girl learning to read by enlisting the aid of Mistress Sherath, the mage who served as the school's headmistress. She recognized something in me and decided I needed some specialized training. She was a mishuk herself, but I was clearly unsuited to a weaponless technique, so *she* enlisted Dame Chaerwyn from the Morfintan chapter of the Order of Tomanāk. I'd never dreamed that anyone would offer me that sort of training—it's illegal to teach a peasant the use of edged weapons in Moretz—and it was as if someone had offered me all the gold in Norfressa. I didn't think a great deal about *why* I was learning weapons craft. All I thought about then was that if I learned to fight, I'd never have to whore as my mother had . . . and that anyone, man or woman, who ever tried to force me to do something against my will would find a foot of steel in his or her belly."

She paused, her eyes momentarily dark and grim once more, then wrinkled her nose and raised one hand, palm uppermost, as if tossing something away from her.

"Whatever my motive for learning might have been, I soon realized I had a natural aptitude. My progress pleased Dame Chaerwyn, though she was always ready to cut me down to size when I got too impressed with myself, but she and Mistress Sherath were firm. If I wanted to continue my weapons lessons, then I had to spend at least an equal amount of time with my other studies, which is how I came to lose the wretched Moretz accent I'd brought to Morfintan with me.

"I don't think Mistress Sherath picked Dame Chaerwyn because she felt I was destined for the Order. It was just that she was the best weapons master in Morfintan who also happened to be a woman, and Mistress Sherath wasn't about to put me into a training salle with a *man* with a weapon in my hand. I don't blame her, either. There was still a lot of hate in me, and I think—no, I *know*—that bothered Dame Chaerwyn. But she taught me *self*-discipline along with weapons skill, and by the time I was nineteen, she was prepared to sponsor me to the Order.

"I almost refused. She was the only woman in the Morfintan chapter, and she'd already told me how few women there were in the Order as a whole. I also knew she still had problems with some of the Order's other members, despite the fact that she'd been the Morfintan chapter's senior weapons master for almost ten years. Besides, the Sisterhood of Lillinara seemed more suited to my needs."

She smiled once more, and this time the flash of white teeth was like an icy wind that sent a chill through Bahzell's bones. He saw the remembered bleakness in her dark eyes, still and blue as deep ocean water in that moment, and he understood. Lillinara was the patron of *all* women—the laughing maiden, the loving mother . . . and the avenger.

"But then I realized something," Kaeritha said softly. "Something Seldan and Marja and Mistress Sherath and Dame Chaerwyn had been trying to teach me for almost six years." She leaned back in her chair and looked not at Bahzell, but at Sir Yorhus.

"Vengeance is a poison," she said in that same soft voice, "and vengeance was what I wanted from the Sisterhood. I wanted the Silver Lady to accept my sword so that I could use that sword on the men who'd turned my mother into a whore and tried to do the same to me, and it didn't matter at all that *those* men were all back in Moretz. *Any* man who transgressed in *any* way against *any* woman would have done for me, because I didn't want justice. I wanted an *excuse*."

Yorhus twitched, and then his eyes fell, as if unable to bear her gaze. She continued to look at him for several moments, then shrugged and turned back to Bahzell.

"I realized that even if the Sisterhood had been willing to accept my oath—and I'm not at all sure they would have—I would have given it for the wrong reasons. Yet I also knew that what had happened to my father, my mother, my sister and my brother—and to *me*—would happen to others, again and again. That it would go right on happening until someone made it stop, and *that* was what should truly be important to me: making it *stop* whenever and wherever I could. Not avenging myself on men who hadn't had a thing to do with what happened to me, whatever they might have done to someone else, but keeping those same things from happening to others and in administering *justice*, not vengeance, when they did. And when I realized that—" she shrugged "—there was only one place to take my sword."

"I'm thinking Dame Chaerwyn must have been pleased by that," Bahzell said after a moment.

"Oh, indeed she was!" Sir Terrian said before Kaeritha could reply. Blue eyes glinted at him dangerously, but he only shook his head with a smile. "But I don't think she was quite prepared for what she got. You see, no sooner had Kerry completed the required vigil over her arms and been knighted than Tomanāk Himself appeared and promoted her directly from knight-probationer to champion."

"It wasn't quite *that* simple," Kaeritha said tartly.

"No? Well, it came close enough," Terrian returned, unabashed by her tone, "and I have Chaerwyn's dispatch describing the entire affair in my files if you'd care to see it, Kerry, so don't think you can intimidate me into changing my story."

"You're absolutely hopeless, Terrian. Do you know that?" Kaeritha demanded.

"It's been said," the knight-general replied comfortably, and Bahzell laughed.

"Aye, and with reason, I'm sure," he observed, setting his empty cider tankard aside, and smiled at Kaeritha.

"It's grateful I am for the tale, sword sister, and honored you'd tell it to me," he told her, "but I'm also a mite curious about something else. From what Sir Charrow was telling me, there's but eighteen champions in all Norfressa." He cocked his ears questioningly, and Kaeritha nodded in confirmation. "Well, in that case, I can't help wondering why it is that two of us are after sitting in front of the self-same fire drinking cider while Wencit of Rūm just 'happens' to be in the same room at the same time. No doubt it's naught but the suspicious barbarian in me, but I've the oddest notion there's a *reason* for it."

"Well, of course there is," Kaeritha agreed cheerfully. "You and Brandark and Vaijon are on your way home to Hurgrum, and Wencit has business of his own in the area, so he thought he might just travel along with you."

"Oh, he did, did he?" Bahzell gave the wild wizard a withering look, but Wencit only smiled benignly. "And yourself?" the hradani said, returning to Kaeritha.

"Well, I have a little job of my own to see to," she told him.

"Amongst *hradani?*" Bahzell couldn't keep the doubt out of his tone, but she only laughed and shook her head. "Well, if not with my folk, then with who? There's naught where we're bound but hradani and Soth—"

He stopped, staring at her in sudden speculation, and she gave him a sunny smile. She had to be joking, he thought. If Spearmen were hostile to the notion of woman warriors, the Sothōii were infinitely worse. Despite all the honor they *officially* showed the war maids, most Sothōii—men and women alike—privately considered them beyond the pale. They weren't truly "women" at all, for every one of them had renounced the ties of blood and family in order to *become* war maids, and that acutely unnatural act could never have been committed by any *properly* reared woman. The fact that the windriders regarded the war maids as invaluable allies and their only true peers meant little against that sort of bone-deep prejudice, and a female knight of Tomanāk would be only marginally more welcome than a Horse Stealer invasion. Not to mention the fact that Bahzell's father might be less than thrilled by the notion of having one of his son's companions wander off to hobnob with the Horse Stealers' most implacabale foes.

But as he looked into Dame Kaeritha Seldansdaughter's eyes, he knew she was completely serious. One might almost have said *dead* serious, he reflected, and shuddered at the thought.

CHAPTER TEN

Sir Yorhus wasn't with them when they left Axe Hallow two days later. Somewhat to Bahzell's surprise—he still hadn't quite come to terms with the authority a champion wielded—Terrian hadn't even questioned his decision to send Yorhus south. In fact, the knight-general had seemed downright relieved by the notion.

"If you think this Tothas has a chance to get through Yorhus' skull, then of course we should send Yorhus to find him," Terrian had said firmly.

"Even though Spearmen aren't so very fond of Axemen as all that?"

"First of all, the Spearmen's dislike for Axemen—and vice versa—is more a tradition than a burning hatred," Terrian had replied. "It's not like, oh, the way the Purple Lords feel about us. Second, the Order has quite a strong presence in the Empire of the Spear. We may be headquartered in Axe Hallow, and our charter may have been confirmed originally by Kormak I, but our loyalty is to Tomanāk—who, you may recall, is also 'Judge of Princes.' That means we don't take sides in wars unless one party or the other has clearly violated Tomanāk's Code. And—" he smiled faintly "—since everyone knows that, most reasonably sane rulers go to considerable lengths to *avoid* open violations. But the point is that Spearmen don't automatically think of us as an Axeman organization or of our knights as spies for the King-Emperor."

"Um." Bahzell had leaned back in his chair and rubbed his chin, ears half-flattened. Terrian was probably right, he reflected. The Empire of the Spear's hostility towards Axemen sprang from the fact that the Empire of the Axe was the true bar to the Spearmen's unbridled expansion. They resented the fact that the Axemen's matchless power was committed to blocking all efforts to push their borders further north. Still, they understood that the King-Emperor had treaty obligations to protect the Border Kingdoms' sovereignty, and they also knew the Axemen had no objection to their expanding into the vast, unclaimed lands east of the Spear River. Besides, as Terrian had said, the Order of Tomanāk was neutral in the empires' rivalry . . . and its role as administrator of Tomanāk's justice served the rulers of both well.

"Besides," Terrian had gone on while the Horse Stealer pondered, "whatever his other failings, Yorhus is as energetic, competent, and determined a field commander as you're ever likely to find. As a matter of fact, he's much too valuable for us to make a desk man out of or demote to subordinate duties unless we absolutely have to. The problem is keeping him away from positions in which his particular brand of piety might shape the Order's policies . . . or convince those outside the Order that it has. That means that sending him to Jashân will let us kill two birds with one stone, as it were."

"And how would that happen to be?"

"As I'm sure you know even better than I do, Zarantha of Jashân is in the process of establishing the first Spearman mage academy under her father's protection." Terrian's tone had made the statement half a question, and Bahzell had nodded back. "Well, there's been some fairly noisy resistance from a handful of Spearman reactionaries. The fact that Mistress Zarantha's a woman is enough to make some of *them* recalcitrant; the fact that she was educated in Axe Hallow only makes it worse, and some of them are rattling a few swords. I don't think they'd care to face Duke Jashân in open conflict, especially since their Emperor would certainly support the Duke, but they wouldn't be above encouraging a little 'brigandage' which just happened to run over Mistress Zarantha. Even more ominously, they have some very peculiar allies for conservative Spearman nobles."

Bahzell had pricked his ears questioningly, and Terrian had shrugged. "There would appear to be a good bit of Purple Lord pressure being brought to bear, including what looks like the beginning of an effort—unofficially, at this time—to embargo Jashân's trade through Bortalik."

"The Purple Lords, is it now?" Bahzell had murmured, and Terrian had nodded.

"Indeed, Milord, and that was enough to make us look very closely at the situation, especially in light of what you and Wencit have told us of Duke Jashân's and Mistress Zarantha's suspicions about the Purple Lords. No doubt many of the city-states would oppose the notion of Spearman magi simply because anything that contributes to the Empire's independence from the Purple Lords threatens their profits, but I believe Duke Jashân is correct in believing there's more to it than that. And given that the magi and the Order of Semkirk are our best counters to the activities of dark wizards, we have an unhappy suspicion of what that something more is.

"Which," the knight-general had gone on, "is why the Order of Semkirk has asked us for aid. They have a solid core of mishuki, but they aren't a true military order, as we are, and asking us to take a hand makes sense. Jashân needs help, and it would be best if that help came from a third party. If the Duke can step back from his role as the primary protector of Mistress Zarantha's new academy and assume a more 'neutral' role, it should help ease the purely political and economic tensions in the area."

"And you're thinking as how using the Order's troops to protect Zarantha would be after letting him do that."

"Precisely. We don't envision it as a permanent responsibility. Any established mage academy is quite capable of looking after itself, thank you, and once Mistress Zarantha has *her* academy properly organized, we should be able to withdraw our people with a clear conscience. But that will take several years, and in the meantime, we'll need a good field commander to handle the situation."

"And if that should just *happen* to be taking Yorhus into Tothas' neck of the woods . . . ?"

"Precisely," Terrian had said again, and smiled. "Best of all, if we don't tell Yorhus that Tothas is supposed to be straightening him out for us, he won't have any reason to get his defenses up the way he does whenever one of *us* tries to talk to him. And from what I've heard of Mistress Zarantha, she'll probably do as much to get through to him as your friend Tothas."

"Aye, she would that!" Bahzell had chuckled, and nodded. "All right, then, Sir Terrian. Mind you, I've a few reservations yet about this notion of sending people off on a whim, and I'll want to send Tothas a letter of my own, warning him what we're about to drop on him. Whatever your lot may think, Tothas is no member of the Order, and he's no reason at all but friendship to be doing as I ask. But I'm thinking he'll do his best for me still, and you're right about the number of birds we have to kill. And even if Yorhus *can* make himself a right pain in the arse, I've no doubt at all that you're right that he's the makings of a good field commander, as well. If

Zarantha's after needing help, then it's grateful I'll be if we can be sending her *good* help."

And so it had been decided. It hadn't actually been necessary for Bahzell to write Tothas, for the Axe Hallow Mage Academy had established a dedicated relay to Zarantha long since. The magi were able to relay the Order's offer of troops—and Bahzell's request of Tothas—to her, and she sent back her thanks and acceptance of both almost immediately.

Yorhus had seemed a bit surprised by his new orders, but his eyes had positively glowed as he promised he would personally see to the safety of Bahzell's adopted sister. The Horse Stealer could have wished for a bit less enthusiasm and a bit more rationality, but he felt confident the long, cold ride to Jashân would cool his ardor. And if it didn't, Zarantha and Tothas would sort him out in record time.

With that taken care of, Bahzell and Brandark, their remaining escort, and Wencit and Kaeritha had resumed their own journey as soon as the weather allowed. Bahzell would have liked to spend more time in Axe Hallow and actually see something of the city, but an ominous sense that time was becoming shorter and shorter oppressed him. It didn't make a great deal of sense to him, since he still had no idea exactly how he intended to deal with his various problems when he got home, but the conviction that he had to get there as soon as possible wouldn't permit him to tarry.

Brandark was inclined to twit him about it, but no one else was, and even the Bloody Sword had no true objection to setting forward once more. And so it was that Bahzell found himself at Axe Hallow's East Gate, clasping forearms one last time with Sir Terrian while a cold breeze sighed down from a cloudless, painfully blue sky.

"It's thankful I am for all your help, Sir Terrian," the towering Horse Stealer said gravely. "And that I've seen the High Temple. I'd like to've been seeing more of it—and you—but there's never enough time, and weather like this is too good to be wasting."

"That's true enough," Terrian agreed. "And I'm grateful your journey brought you through Axe Hallow . . . even if you *won't* let us knight you."

"Another time, maybe," Bahzell said with a grin, releasing the knight-general's arm, and looked around at the people waiting to travel with him. Clouds of breath rose like smoke in the crystal-clear morning, and despite the cold, he felt suddenly eager to be back on the road once more. It showed, and Terrian laughed.

"You'd best be off then, Milord Champion! But we'll expect you back again someday soon. And until then—" the knight-general sobered "—may Tomanāk's Shield go before you and His Sword strike through you."

"And the same to you," Bahzell responded gravely. He nodded once more to the commander of the Order of Tomanāk, then turned his back on the magnificent walls of Axe Hallow. He threw out an arm to gesture at the high road before them and grinned at his companions.

"Let's be going, then," he said.

The weather was almost perfect over the next several days, as if Chemalka were feeling generous now that she'd worked off her tantrum. Bahzell wasn't about to trust her to stay that way, yet for the moment, at least, the sky was all smiles. The temperature remained bitterly cold, but there wasn't even a hint of additional snow. Instead, a few white puffball clouds, too brilliant for the eye to rest on long, floated in a sky so blue it hurt, and the reflected snow-dazzle made them grateful for their snow lenses once more.

Once they worked their way free of the Axe Blades, the high road straightened out again and the long, steep slopes eased. They also left the deepest accumulations of snow behind, and the going was almost as good as it had been on the road from Belhadan to the capital. The party quickly settled back into much the same routine as in the earlier stage of its journey, except that Wencit and Kaeritha joined the morning training bouts.

The wizard claimed it was simply a way to stay warm, since a man of his advanced years had no business using a sword with serious intent, but Bahzell doubted his disclaimer fooled anyone. And the Horse Stealer *knew* it didn't fool anyone who'd ever had the dubious pleasure of crossing blades with the "old man," whether it was merely for practice or not. The expression on Brandark's face when Wencit disarmed him three times in five minutes had been priceless, and although Bahzell himself managed to hold his own against the wizard, it was a very near thing. In fact, Wencit managed to "kill" him almost as often as the Horse Stealer managed to "kill" the wizard. Bahzell would have liked to think it was because Wencit's sword was enchanted, which—as anyone who'd ever seen him confront dark wizards knew—it most certainly was. Unfortunately, the hradani couldn't quite convince himself that magic explained what Wencit could make that sword do. For all his vast age, the wild wizard remained hard-muscled and supple (no doubt the wild magic had a little something to do with that), and he'd had over twelve centuries to pick up tricks of swordplay Bahzell hadn't even heard of yet.

But much as Bahzell enjoyed sparring with Wencit and adding some of those same tricks to his own repertoire, his bouts with Kaeritha gave him even greater pleasure. His respect not only for her but for her teachers was enormous. She was more than a foot and a half shorter than he, and she might weigh a third as much as he did when she was wringing wet. Most of his weight advantage was muscle and hard bone, as well, and there was no way she should be able to stand up to him in one-on-one combat.

Yet no one had ever told *her* that, and if he was far stronger, with a much longer reach, she compensated for those disadvantages with speed, skill, and raw aggressiveness. A blow from a sword the size of Bahzell's, even if it was a blunted training weapon, could break bone, mail or no, but that didn't faze Kaeritha. She dove straight in at him with an apparent disregard for possible injury which turned his blood cold the first time he saw it—especially when he considered what would happen to her if she did the same thing against *edged* weapons. But even as he was thinking that, her toe hooked behind his right ankle, she heaved, and he went down in the snow to find the tip of her sword pressed firmly against his gorget.

Or, rather, the tip of *one* of her swords, for she used a technique he'd never before confronted, although he'd heard something like it described by Horse Stealers who'd faced Sothōii war maids. Rather than one sword, or even a sword and a dagger, she fought with a sword in each hand. They were light blades which he suspected she'd designed herself, somewhere between the eighteen inches of the Royal and Imperial Infantry's shortsword and the three feet of Vaijon's longsword, but she wielded them with a speed and dexterity which had to be seen to be believed. She couldn't use a shield with them, but Bahzell quickly discovered that her technique more than compensated for the lack of one. Even more impressive, she seemed to use either hand with absolute impartiality, and she could shift the emphasis of her attack between them with devastating speed. It was rather like fighting a whirlwind, and once she got inside an opponent's sword, her victim usually ended up wishing a whirlwind was *all* he'd been fighting.

She was equally skilled with the quarterstaff she carried upright in her stirrup as another knight might have carried a lance. She was the only person Bahzell had ever met who actually used a staff from horseback, and she spent at least twenty minutes practicing with it every day. Brandark, who had never had the misfortune to

encounter a quarterstaff in skilled hands and so tended to look
down upon the weapon, made the mistake of chuckling over her
antics with it one morning. Fortunately for the Bloody Sword, she
decided to treat his amusement as the product of ignorance, not
an insult, so instead of cracking him smartly over the head, she
made him a wager. She bet him that she could strike a dozen eggs
out of the air as quickly as he could throw them at her, and then,
for an encore, cracked—not *broke*, but simply *cracked*—a half-dozen
more with overhead strikes while they lay neatly lined up on a
wagon tongue. The wager cost Brandark two gold kormaks, but it
also cured him of any misplaced contempt for her chosen weapon.

Bahzell, on the other hand, who had never felt any particular
temptation to laugh at staff play, found that it took him several
days to adjust to her style. And despite the difference in their sizes,
he was the one who had to adopt the more defensive stance until
he began to get a feel for it, for her speed and skill offset much
of his advantage in reach and raw strength. She was like a terrier
worrying an elk hound, charging in and pressing an attack so fast
and furious he had no choice but to defend himself. But her technique also required her to parry every attack *he* could launch with
one of her primary weapons, since she used no shield, and if he
could hold off her initial, all-out assault, his longer reach, stronger muscles, and heavier blade came into their own once more.

In most ways, the time he spent sparring with Wencit—or, for
that matter, Brandark or the male knights and lay-brothers of the
Order—was more valuable to him. He was never going to adopt
Kaeritha's style, and he'd probably never run into an enemy who
used the same technique. Certainly he was unlikely to encounter
anyone who used it as furiously as she did! He was much more
likely to pick up some new move to add to his own style from
the more conventional swordplay of one of the other male members of the party, and he knew it, but the sheer pleasure of seeing her in action made all that irrelevant. Her sleek, deadly speed
was a joy to watch, and for all the apparent fury of her technique,
it was actually wrapped around a core of lethal precision.

No doubt he should have expected that from someone who'd
been chosen as one of Tomanāk's champions on the very day of
her knighting, but that made it no less impressive. Even more to
the point, perhaps, that sense of kinship he'd felt from the start
grew stronger with each day. She settled effortlessly into place in
the party, slipping into a friendship not simply with Bahzell but
with Brandark, as well, which was as deep as it was inevitable. In
fact, the one complaint Bahzell had was that, like Zarantha, Kaeritha

actually encouraged the Bloody Sword's efforts to improve upon *The Lay of Bahzell Bloody-Hand*, and she had a dismayingly good singing voice which she insisted upon using to help him along. She'd gone into whoops of hysterical laughter the first time Brandark played it for her, and he could get her to start giggling simply by humming it. Hearing an anointed champion of Tomanāk who could easily have cut almost anyone else in the party into dog meat *giggle* would have been unnerving under any circumstances, but to have her take such unmitigated glee in suggesting fresh rhymes to Brandark was the outside of enough. Even worse, she soon discovered that Vaijon had a splendid tenor singing voice, and when she got *Wencit* into the act as well . . .

They made very good time from Axe Hallow to Lordenfel, but somehow the spritely notes of a balalaika and the tuneful trio singing along with it managed to make the trip seem very, very long.

CHAPTER ELEVEN

They reached Lordenfel six days out of Axe Hallow. Unlike the capital's sentries, those at Lordenfel's gates were barely a token presence, and casual about their duties to boot. Sir Terrian had sent word ahead that Bahzell and his companions were on their way, but it wouldn't have mattered if he hadn't. The tubby, middle-aged sergeant in charge of the gate detail scarcely bothered to look up at their approach. Not even the sight of two hradani seemed to rouse his interest. All that seemed to concern him was spending as little time as possible outside the warmth of the guardhouse, and he only waved them through, then disappeared back to his waiting fire.

Kaeritha and Bahzell glanced at one another with matching scowls while the rest of their party passed through the gates. Bahzell, in particular, had mixed feelings. It was the first time since leaving home that a gate guard hadn't at least eyed him askance simply for being a hradani, which he supposed should have pleased him. Unfortunately, it hadn't happened because the sergeant was fairminded enough to reject stereotypes; he simply didn't care that someone with the reputation prejudice assigned Bahzell's people had walked into his town.

The security of a town Bahzell had never called home was hardly his responsibility, but the gate guards' obvious disinterest in their duties grated on his nerves. He glanced sideways at Kaeritha and saw a matching disgust in her eyes, as well.

"I'm wondering," he murmured, leaning closer to her as the second wagon passed them. "What d'you think would happen if you and I were after creeping up on the guards tonight?"

"Creeping up—?" Kaeritha looked at him for a moment, then chuckled. "Why, Bahzell! What a dreadful thing to suggest. You might get them into all *kinds* of trouble!"

"What's that? Did I hear someone say 'trouble'?" Brandark demanded from where he rode on Kaeritha's far side. He looked speculatively at her and Bahzell. "Are you two contemplating some despicable deed such as no decent person would even consider committing?"

"Well, as to that—and in a word, as you might say—aye," Bahzell replied with a grin.

"Sounds like a marvelous idea! Ah, just what despicable deed were you contemplating?"

"Bahzell was simply thinking aloud," Kaeritha explained. "It struck him that the gate guards here in Lordenfel aren't exactly the most alert ones in the world."

"I noticed that myself." Brandark grimaced. "I don't imagine too many eight-horse teams or invading Spearmen armies would get by them unnoticed, but anything smaller than that—" He shrugged, and Kaeritha nodded.

"Exactly. And, as any good champions of Tomanāk, Bahzell and I have a responsibility to help insure the safety of the peaceful citizens of a city like this. So it follows that we labor under something of a moral imperative to do anything we can to, um, *motivate* their guardians to attend to their duties, now doesn't it?"

"You can sound dreadfully virtuous when you want to," Brandark said admiringly.

"It's not my fault if simply reflecting on my duties makes me sound virtuous," Kaeritha replied with dignity.

"So just how do you two virtuous champions intend to ginger up the sentries?"

"As to that, I'm thinking it's not that difficult," Bahzell said comfortably, glancing back as the gate disappeared behind them. "There's no moon tonight, and a strange thing it would be if Kaeritha and I couldn't be creeping up on the lot of them unseen."

"And then?"

"Well, I'm not so very certain as to that," Bahzell admitted, scratching his chin and squinting thoughtfully up at the sky. "I suppose we *could* simply leap out and shout 'Boo!' or some such thing. I've no doubt at all that such as that would be getting the lot we jumped on back on their toes for a time, but I'm wishful to make a more . . . lasting impression on *all* the City Guard."

"Don't worry your head about it, Bahzell," Kaeritha advised him kindly. "I know *exactly* how to achieve your objective. You just follow my lead."

"And don't think the two of you are going to keep all the fun to yourselves," Brandark warned them with a grin.

"I hate to interrupt you three when you're plotting," Wencit put in, urging his horse up on Bahzell's other side, "but I believe that gentleman is looking for you." He pointed, and Bahzell followed the gesture with his eyes. A young man in the Order's colors made his way towards them, and Kaeritha's eyes lit as she saw him.

"That's Lynoth!" she said. "Seldan wrote me he'd been transferred here as one of Sir Maehryk's squires," she went on, then paused, eyes narrowing as she noticed the young man's white belt. "I stand corrected. That's *Sir* Lynoth, one of the Lordenfel chapter's newest knights-probationer."

The youngster reached them a few seconds later, and Kaeritha smiled hugely, reaching down from the saddle to offer him the clasped-arm greeting of equals.

"So, Nuisance! They finally broke down and made *you* a knight, did they?"

"Nobody 'broke down,'" Lynoth replied with enormous dignity. "It was simply time to improve the Order's quality. And I have it on the best of authority that they scoured all of Norfressa searching for the squire with the best qualifications, too."

"And a sad disappointment it must have been that they had to settle for *you* instead!" Kaeritha shot back, and dismounted to throw her arms around him. She hugged him firmly, then turned to Bahzell, one arm still draped around his shoulders. "I'd like you to meet another of Seldan's and Marja's strays," she said. "Bahzell, this is Sir Lynoth Seldanson; Lynoth, this is Bahzell Bahnakson, Champion of Tomanāk."

"I'm honored to greet you on behalf of the Lordenfel chapter, Milord Champion," Lynoth said soberly. "Sir Maehryk sent me because he knew Kerry was with you."

"Did he, now?" Bahzell ran thoughtful eyes over the youngster and nodded mentally in approval. Lynoth wasn't very tall, even for a human, no more than five-eight or five-nine, but he had a wrestler's powerful physique. He couldn't possibly be more than a year older than Vaijon, and Bahzell liked his open, infectious smile. "Well then, Sir Lynoth," he went on after a moment, "why don't you just lead the way home?"

Lordenfel was much smaller than Belhadan, and downright rustic compared to Axe Hallow. In fact, it was little larger than Esgfalas,

capital of the Grand Duchy of Esgan. Bahzell had thought Esgfalas
a large city when he first saw it, but he'd learned better since. Now,
to his more experienced eyes, Lordenfel looked like a sleepy, provincial town, despite its walls and battlements. Winter probably
contributed to its sleepiness, but the energy of its people and
economy would never approach those of Belhadan. Yet the Lordenfel
Chapter of the Order was almost twice the size of the Belhadan
Chapter. That struck Bahzell as odd, at first, but Sir Maehryk
explained it simply enough.

"Yes, we're larger than the Belhadan Chapter, Milord Champion,"
he agreed. He was about Sir Charrow's age, but his dignified—"stuffy"
was the word which actually sprang to Bahzell's mind—manner made
him seem older. He also had a pronounced tendency to lecture, and
Bahzell felt vaguely betrayed by how Kaeritha had abandoned him
to Maehryk's undivided attention. He wouldn't have minded her
eagerness to visit with her younger brother if he hadn't been pretty
sure she knew Maehryk of old and had deliberately used the nov-
elty of a brand new hradani champion to distract the chapter master from her own disappearance.

"But big as we are," Maehryk went on now, "less than half our
people are here at any given moment. As I'm sure you'll notice when
you move on into Landfressa, towns and villages are few and far
between from here to the mountains. The soil's good enough, but the
growing season is short, and most of our country folk are herdsmen
of one sort or another. I'd guess that as many as half the villages in
Landfressa shut down entirely in the winter when the cattle and sheep
move south, and that leaves us with two problems."

He paused, one eyebrow raised, like a tutor waiting to see if his
student knew the answer, and Bahzell snorted.

"Wilderness breeds brigands—or hiding places for 'em, at least,"
he said shortly, "and without city guards or local militias to root
'em out, then it's up to the army . . . or someone else."

"Exactly," Maehryk agreed. "And that's especially true here. Once
winter closes the Esfresia-Dolmach high road, anything shipped
out of Dwarvenhame has to follow the southern route through
Lordenfel and Axe Hallow to Belhadan. There may not be much
traffic compared to what passes through during the summer, but
the pickings are still rich enough to draw bandits. So we lend a
hand to keep the roads open. In fact—" he paused, frowning while
he stroked his short, gray beard "—we've been busier than usual
this year. The stretch just the other side of the border into
Landfressa's been particularly bad. You might want to watch yourselves when you get to it, Milord Champion."

"We'll do that." Bahzell managed to keep from sounding short—again—but it was hard, and he felt a twinge of guilt. Maehryk was a conscientious man, or he would never have been chosen for this post, far less left in it for going on eight years. But he was obsessively formal and had about as much liveliness as a salted cod, and Bahzell simply couldn't warm to him as he had to Charrow or Sir Terrian.

He started to say something more, but the sound of the dinner bell interrupted him, and he rose with a bit more haste than was strictly courteous. He tried not to feel grateful for the reprieve—or glad they would be spending only a single night in Lordenfel—and ordered himself to be pleasant over supper as Maehryk led him to the dining hall.

Sir Lynoth was waiting in the morning to escort them on their way once more. Bahzell and his friends had risen early, eager to make as much distance as the short winter daylight permitted, but Lynoth and most of the rest of the chapter house clearly had already been up for quite some time. Whatever had roused them had upset Sir Maehryk, too, and there seemed to be quite a few uniformed members of the City Guard about. The prim and proper chapter master could scarcely be accused of discourtesy, but he was plainly preoccupied and perilously near to abrupt with the Guard lieutenant who followed him about so closely that he seemed to have been grafted onto his left shoulder. He didn't even put in an appearance until after the travelers had broken their fast, and when he did arrive to bid them formal farewell his attention was clearly elsewhere.

But whatever had upset Maehryk seemed to have had an opposite effect on other members of the chapter. The younger knights-probationer and knights-companion, in fact, appeared to experience some difficulty in maintaining straight faces, and Lynoth looked like someone who'd swallowed a bumblebee. Kaeritha gave him a glance of sisterly repression, but even so he broke out in coughing fits suspiciously like camouflaged laughter three times while Maehryk was bidding the chapter's guests farewell.

"—and may Tomanāk's Shield go before you until He brings you back to us once again," the knight-captain finished his formal speech at last, nodded briskly, and then hurried off once more with the Guard lieutenant bobbing in his wake. Lynoth watched them go, then started to turn and look at his sister once more, only to stop, as if he didn't trust himself to meet her gaze while Maehryk might still be in earshot.

"W-we'd better go now," he said in a curiously breathless voice, and walked quickly down the chapter house steps to where the rest of their party waited, along with horses for Wencit, Kaeritha, and Brandark. The young knight swung up into his own saddle and deliberately looked anywhere but at Kaeritha while he waited for the others to mount. Bahzell watched his performance with a small, crooked smile, then waved to the others and strode off down the street while they followed in a clatter of hooves.

"And what, pray tell, has your drawers all knotted up this morning, Nuisance?" Kaeritha asked sweetly, and Lynoth instantly lost his battle not to laugh. He leaned forward in the saddle, roaring with laughter, and his horse tossed its head in disgust at the hopeless mirth of the feeble, two-legged creature on its back.

Kaeritha watched with the exasperated patience of a sister and let him laugh for several minutes. Then she drew her right foot from the stirrup and kicked him none too gently on his left hip. His startled horse crow-hopped away from her, but the kick had the desired effect, and Lynoth managed to drag himself back under control.

"S-sorry," he got out, wiping tears of laughter from his eyes. "It's just that some of us have been so pissed off for so long with—" He stopped again and drew a deep breath, then looked his sister straight in the eye. "You wouldn't happen to know anything about what happened at South Gate last night, would you?"

"South Gate?" Kaeritha's dark blue eyes were innocent as a new dawn. "Whatever makes you think I'd know anything about South Gate? For that matter, what *did* happen?"

"Well, that's part of the mystery," Lynoth told her. "Tell me, did you notice anything about the gate guard when you arrived yesterday evening?"

"Aside from the fact that they were more concerned with toasting their backsides than doing their duty, you mean?"

"That's precisely what I mean." Lynoth's humor faded, and there was very little mirth in his voice when he continued. "Sergeant Gosanth—he was the sergeant of the watch who passed you through—has been sitting on his fat arse all fall and winter. It's bad enough when a guardsman does that out of sheer lard-butt laziness, but quite a few of us have suspected there was more to it in his case."

"Ah? And what more would that have been?" Bahzell put in mildly, cocking his ears at the young knight.

"Let's just say certain individuals seem to have been departing with property whose title was in doubt on nights when Gosanth had the watch," Lynoth replied.

"I see." Bahzell shook his head. "Sure and it's a sad shame to know anyone might so much as *think* a fine, upstanding sergeant of the Guard would be having truck with such as that," he said piously.

"To be sure," Lynoth said dryly, and his mouth quirked in a fresh smile. "Sir Maehryk felt much the same as you, Milord Champion. And despite certain, um, rumors which reached his ears, he also felt very strongly that it was not the Order's business to interfere in the internal affairs of the City Guard."

"And very properly, too," Brandark put in. "Why, what would the world come to if just everyone went about poking his nose into other people's business?" he added, stroking his own prominent nose for emphasis.

"No doubt you're right, Lord Brandark. But apparently *someone* decided to poke his nose—or, rather *their noses*—into it last night."

"How so?" Kaeritha asked.

"Well, I've only heard bits and pieces of it so far, and I'm fairly sure it's grown in the telling," her brother said, and paused to give her a sharp look. She returned it blandly, and he grinned. "I can only hope that someday the individuals involved will give us the details," he went on, "but from what Gosanth is claiming, at least two dozen masked brigands appeared out of nowhere and set upon him and his valiant squad with clubs."

"No! Two dozen? With *clubs?*" Kaeritha shook her head, and Lynoth shrugged.

"That's his story, and he's sticking to it. As a matter of fact, I think I did hear someone else say something about quarter staffs," he said, glancing at the staff braced upright in Kaeritha's right stirrup. "And there was something else about giants summoned up by spells," he went on, glancing in turn at Bahzell, who looked back with an air of total innocence. "And someone else said something about hearing music coming from the guardhouse," Lynoth added with a glance for Brandark's balalaika.

"Goodness gracious," Kaeritha said comfortably. "What a dreadful experience it must have been, to be sure."

"Well." Lynoth gave a lurking smile. "From all accounts, the really *dreadful* part didn't begin until whoever was playing the music started trying to sing."

"Oh, it didn't, hey?" Brandark growled. Bahzell's innocent expression seemed to crack momentarily, but he had it under control by the time Lynoth glanced back his way.

"So what were these mysterious brigands after doing?" he asked. "I'm hoping no one was hurt too badly?"

"Oh, hardly at all, Milord. Aside from a few bruises and one or two contusions, the 'brigands' seem to have been very careful not to, ah, *damage* anyone. But whoever they were, they appear to have walked in while some of that mislaid property I mentioned was in the process of walking out, because it was all piled in a heap in the center of the guardroom when Gosanth's relief turned up. And the relief also found Gosanth's entire detail—plus six burglars and a fence the Guard's been hunting for months—wrapped up in rope like moths in so many cocoons and hanging from the rafters."

"My goodness!" his sister murmured. "But why was Sir Maehryk so perturbed?"

"Well, I'm sure most of it was no more than a perfectly understandable state of shock that members of the Guard could possibly be involved in criminal activity," Lynoth said gravely. "But I suppose part of it could be the fact that someone chalked the Sword and Mace on all the stolen property. That, of course, suggests the Order was somehow involved—which, as we all know, couldn't *possibly* be the case without Sir Maehryk's knowledge. And you saw the lieutenant who was with him this morning?" Kaeritha nodded, and Lynoth shrugged. "That was Sergeant Gosanth's platoon commander. I gather his superiors are none too happy with him, but he comes from a *very* prominent family, and he seems determined to nag Sir Maehryk into confessing that the Order was behind the whole thing and that *he* had nothing to do with Gosanth's . . . activities. But since the Order *didn't* have anything to do with it, there's nothing Sir Maehryk can confess to—or say to clear the lieutenant. Only the lieutenant doesn't want to accept that, and Sir Maehryk's too polite to have him tossed out of the chapter house by force."

"Dear, dear, dear," Kaeritha sighed, and shook her head sorrowfully. "I do hope they get to the bottom of it . . . eventually."

"Oh, I'm sure they will . . . eventually," her brother agreed. The two of them grinned impishly at one another, but then Lynoth looked up and his grin faded. North Gate lay before them, with traffic flowing smoothly in and out in the chill morning sunlight. The corner of his mouth quirked again as he observed the industry with which the Guard detail attended to its duties. No doubt the two lieutenants, one captain, and the major looking over its sergeant's shoulder had something to do with that.

"It looks like the rest of the Guard's heard about Gosanth's adventure," he observed. "Do you suppose that was what whoever it was had in mind?"

"Now how would such as us be knowing a thing about the twisted minds of those as could treat poor Gosanth in such a way?" Bahzell demanded.

"Forgive me, Milord Champion. You couldn't possibly understand how such depraved individuals must think," Lynoth apologized.

"And don't you forget it, Nuisance!" Kaeritha admonished, then urged her horse alongside his to throw an arm around him. She hugged him tight, then released him and waved a finger under his nose. "And don't forget to write Seldan and Marja, either, you ungrateful whelp!"

"I won't, I won't!" he promised, and drew rein. The rest of the party flowed past him to pass through the gate under the Guard detail's eagle eye, but Bahzell paused to clasp arms with him.

"Look after yourself, youngster," the hradani advised him. "And don't go making too much mock of Sir Maehryk," he added in a sterner tone, lowering his voice so that no one else could hear. "I've no doubt he's an old stick-in-the-mud at times, but he's also the head of your chapter. It'll do him no harm to be shaken up from time to time if he's getting too stuffy, but it's not the place of a knight to undercut his commander's authority without better cause than stuffiness."

"Of course, Milord. I didn't mean—" Lynoth began with a dark blush, then cut himself off, and Bahzell smiled at the youngster's refusal to try to wiggle out of the implicit rebuke.

"I wasn't thinking you meant aught by it, lad, and I'd not give two coppers for a youngster as didn't want to see his elders brought down a peg or two *once* in a while. But it's not something as sits well in a chain of command."

"No, Milord. I can see that." Lynoth nodded soberly, and Bahzell reached out to squeeze his shoulder.

"Good! And now, if you'll forgive it, your sister and I have a ways to go yet."

"Yes, Milord. May Tomanāk ride with you."

"And with you, Sir Lynoth." The massive Horse Stealer nodded once, turned, and walked away after his friends. Then he paused in the gateway and looked back with a grin. "And I'll see to it *she's* after writing to Seldan and Marja, too!" he promised.

CHAPTER TWELVE

Bahzell was no city boy. In fact, he preferred wilderness to towns, yet he found the sheer emptiness of northeastern Landria depressing, especially since the stretch from Lordenfel to Esfresia was the longest leg of their journey across the Empire. Both Landria and Landfressa were populated primarily by freeholders and the herdsmen Maehryk had mentioned, so there were few of the large estates found in other provinces. There *were* occasional large family farms whose owners stayed put year round, but they were rare, with fortresslike homes and outbuildings, fierce and well-trained dogs, and inhabitants who were less than happy to see strangers.

Not that the towns were any better. In fact, they were worse. The travelers were barely thirty miles outside Lordenfel when they passed the first village whose inhabitants had headed south for the winter. It was a small place which no doubt housed a relatively small total population even in summer, and its few permanent residences all clustered around the town square, thick-walled and built very solidly of stone or brick. Most were at least two stories tall, with no windows on the ground floor, and several were enclosed within sturdy outwalls, as well. They might have been home to eight or ten families, but no more than that could possibly have been crammed into them, and it was clear people who chose to stay the winter out in these parts were used to looking after themselves.

The lack of local year-round populations also explained the harder going the travelers began to encounter. With towns so much further apart and so denuded of people, there were simply too few warm bodies available for snow clearance. The high road remained just as impressive as a feat of engineering, but the terrain in this region tended to be flat, with only occasional patches of forest. There were few landmarks, and there were many places where fresh snowfalls would have left the roadway impossible to pick out without the rows of firs which marched along on either flank. The wagoneers had stopped two days out from Lordenfel to replace their wagons' wheels with the sled runners. They made much better time over the snow-covered road that way, and when they hit one of the rare patches of bare pavement, they simply moved onto the turfed sections and kept right on going.

Bahzell and Brandark were northern-bred and no strangers to snow country, although the city-raised Brandark had less experience with cross-country travel in winter. Yet not even Bahzell had ever experienced such open, lonely, emptiness in what was supposed to be an inhabited land. In an odd sort of way, the existence of the high road actually made the emptiness worse. Its straight line, nailed down by its rows of windbreak trees; the occasional stretches of bare paving, rising up through the snow like whales surfacing to breathe; the stone bridges which appeared suddenly to leap across streams winter had turned into sheets of ice; and, most of all, the villages whose inhabitants had disappeared bag, baggage, and family . . . all of those things were like relics of a vanished people. They had been abandoned to the armies of winter, and there seemed no hope spring would ever drive those armies back. The air was so cold it ached, and when they woke in the blessed warmth of their down-lined Vonderland sleeping sacks each morning, they found the outsides of those sacks coated in frost. There was something almost sentient about the implacable power of winter here, and the squeak of fresh snow under Bahzell's boots and the jingle of harness or thud of hooves or occasional snatch of conversation were lost and tiny in the vast stillness.

"I never imagined anyplace this . . . empty, Milord," Vaijon said quietly one morning. He had abandoned his showy cloak for the thick, wooly warmth of the Sothōii-style poncho most of the others wore, and he pounded his gloved hands together as he swept his eyes over the white, sterile landscape. "It's hard to imagine anyone lives here even in the summer!"

"And you from Fradonia!" Kaeritha teased. The young knight turned to her with a grin the old Vaijon would never have shown an ex-peasant whose mother had been no more than a common whore, champion or no, and she shook her head at him. "Didn't you say your family had holdings in Vonderland, as well?"

"We do, Milady. But villages tend to stay put in Vonderland. They certainly don't up and move away when the snows come!"

"No, but their people also tend to be foresters, farmers, trappers, and fishermen, not herdsmen," Kaeritha replied, "and the population density is much lower in Landria and Landfressa. Over half those who do live here are herders whose herds and flocks simply can't winter successfully in these conditions, which means they *have* to move, and they don't want to leave their families behind when they take the herds south. If you could be in two places at once, you'd be amazed by how many people seem to have suddenly migrated to northeastern Rustum and the North March about now. But that's not where the majority of them have gone."

"Excuse me?" Vaijon looked puzzled. "I thought you just said they were herders and followed the herds."

"No, I said they were herders who didn't want to leave their families behind when they can't be with them. That's why it's been customary up here for—oh, the last four or five centuries, since the Dwarvenhame Tunnel was cut—for those families to move in with the dwarves for the winter. They pay their way with beef, mutton, and venison, and they also provide an annual influx of hands for the dwarves' manufactories. Weather may make it difficult for them to get their products to market until spring, but winter's always been one of the dwarves' most productive times of year."

"I didn't realize that," Brandark put in. "That the dwarves use other sources of labor during the winter, I mean."

"Those in Dwarvenhame didn't, before the Tunnel went in." Kaeritha shrugged. "From what I've been told, all the dwarves in Kontovar refused to share their secrets with nondwarves, and the Dwarvenhame clans followed that same tradition for six hundred years. But once the Axemen expanded up to their borders and they saw what good use their cousins in the Empire made of nondwarvish additions to their work forces, they couldn't afford not to follow suit. By now, the humans in eastern Landfressa are as much part of Dwarvenhame's industry as the dwarves are. You'll see what I mean when we get closer to the Tunnel. None of the towns up *there* close down for the winter."

"Um." Bahzell nodded, then cocked an eyebrow at her. "From what Sir Maehryk was saying, I'd understood as how half or more of his chapter's troop strength was up here." She nodded, and he waved a hand at the emptiness about them. "That being the case and all, would you mind so very much telling me just where they are?"

"We should meet some of them in the next day or two," she reassured him. "There's nowhere near enough of them to make patrolling the roads practical, so they're concentrated in forces large enough to do some good and based on the larger towns—the ones that don't lose so many people each winter. Given road conditions, anything that travels out of Dwarvenhame is going to do so in a caravan, and each force is responsible for seeing each caravan in turn safely from its own base to the next one along the road. After that, it turns around and heads back to pick up the next one to come through." She shrugged once more. "It's not particularly exhausting duty. Actually, the Order's main duty up here is to provide security for the folk who choose to winter over, and our people run patrols through the smaller villages at irregular intervals to make sure somebody we wouldn't like hasn't settled into them."

"It still seems awfully empty to me . . . and *big*, too," Vaijon observed.

"Does it, then?" Bahzell asked, and something about his voice made Vaijon look at him sharply. The Horse Stealer's tone was mild, but his eyes had narrowed behind the darkened glass of his snow lenses, and he'd tugged the mitten off his right hand. As Vaijon watched, he reached behind his head, as if to scratch his neck, and unobtrusively unbuttoned the retaining strap from the quillons of his sword.

"Milord?" the young knight asked tautly.

"I'm thinking you should be riding on ahead a little, Vaijon," the hradani replied in that same mild voice. "Don't be making a show of it, but warn Sir Harkon that something nasty is waiting in those trees yonder." He made no obvious gesture, but his ears flicked at a thick mass of snow-crowned hemlock and yew, well to the north of the road at present, but curving closer ahead of them.

"Of course, Milord." Vaijon nodded casually and pressed with his knees to urge his horse to a trot.

"And you, Brandark. It's grateful I'd be if you'd be so very kind as to drop back and pass the same word to the wagons," Bahzell murmured as the youngster moved away. "And tell 'em to get their bows strung, if they can do it without anyone seeing."

"Done," Brandark agreed. He drew rein and dismounted, making a show of checking his girth while the wagons caught up with him. Bahzell and Kaeritha continued moving at the same pace, and she glanced at him as she rode along at his side.

"And what makes you so sure there's something waiting up there?"

"I could be saying instinct," he replied, moving his eyes back to sweep the suspect trees, "and it might be there'd be some truth to that. But the fact is that my folk are after having better sight than you humans, and mine is better than most hradani can claim."

"And?"

"And if you were to be looking just about in the center of those trees, and maybe forty or fifty yards back, it might be as you'd notice there's a break in the snow cover. And if you were after having a low, suspicious mind as notices things like that, you might look a mite closer and be seeing just the tiniest wisp of smoke rising from them."

"You saw a wisp of smoke from *here*?" Kaeritha's tone was that of a woman trying very hard not to imply disbelief, and he bared strong, white teeth in a fierce grin.

"Lass, my folk are after cutting their eyeteeth in raids on the Wind Plain, and there's naught at all, at all, up there for cover ... especially in winter. Which isn't to say the Sothōii don't manage to hide anyway, whenever they've a mind to. Truth to tell, a Sothōii warrior or war maid could hide on a card table, like as not, if they put their minds to it. So any Horse Stealer who's minded to live to a ripe old age had best learn to keep his eyes peeled and his wits about him . . . especially when things are after looking safest. And with tree cover as scattered and far about as it's been these last two or three days, I've been paying closer heed to the patches we see than I might otherwise."

"I'll take your word for it," Kaeritha said, unobtrusively loosening her own blades, one by one, in their sheaths. She thought longingly of the cased longbow slung beside her saddle, but there was no way she could reach for it without any watcher noticing. Besides, it was a weapon to be used on foot, not from horseback. Bahzell, on the other hand, had casually eased his arbalest off his shoulder. As she watched from the corner of her eye, he slipped the iron goatsfoot from his belt and spanned the steel-bowed weapon one-handed. It was a prodigious offhand display of strength, and he looked up at her with another grin as he slid a square-headed quarrel onto the string.

"You're certain they'll attack?" she asked, a bit bemused even now to realize she had accepted Bahzell's warning without question.

"As to that, I'll not say as how whoever's up there has wickedness in mind. In fact, *I'd* be letting us go unmolested for certain if it was me over there. We've the better part of forty swords over here, counting the drovers, and only two wagons. Come to that, we're headed north, not south, so it's like enough any wagons we do have are riding empty. They'd get little loot and plenty of hard knocks from such as us, and your average brigand's not one as likes a fight unless there's plenty of profit in it. All I'm after saying is that there *is* someone up yonder, and I'm not minded to be taking any chances on their being as smart as I about picking targets, if you take my meaning."

"I was thinking the same thing," Kaeritha murmured. "But you *do* expect them to hit us, don't you?"

"Aye," Bahzell replied quietly, and flicked his ears. "But if you're asking *why* I do, well, that I can't tell you."

He watched Vaijon reach Sir Harkon, who had succeeded Yorhus in command of their escort and now rode at the head of the party. The older knight glanced at Vaijon, then stiffened in his saddle. Bahzell doubted anyone would have noticed if he hadn't been looking very closely, and Harkon didn't so much as turn his head to look back at Bahzell, but his hand dropped to his side and inconspicuously flipped the skirt of his poncho back from the hilt of his sword.

The Horse Stealer nodded in satisfaction. The dangerous stretch of forest was already well within bowshot or he would have opted for stopping where they were to reorder their own ranks and let the enemy—assuming there *was* an enemy—come to them. Unfortunately, not even his eyes could see into those dark, impenetrable trees, and he had no idea what precisely was waiting for them. Had *he* been planning an ambush, he would have brought along all the bowmen he could find and opened the assault with a storm of arrows, and it was possible that was precisely what would happen. But there was nothing his people could do except hope their armor turned any arrows—a likely outcome, unless they faced longbows or heavy crossbows—and keep moving. Assuming that someone intended to hit them, the attack would undoubtedly come at or near that bend ahead, where the trees came closest to the road, and all they could do was ride right into their enemies' arms.

But *not*, he thought with an evil smile, the way those enemies expected them to ride. The one thing more devastating than an ambush which completely surprised a target was the counterattack of a target which the ambushers only *thought* they'd surprised. Bahzell knew, for he'd been on both ends of that particular stick, and he knew that men who were certain they'd achieved surprise *expected* that momentary advantage, that brief period when their opponents stared at them in shock and tried to get a grasp of what was happening. And when the ambushers didn't *get* that moment of consternation, the advantage shifted instantly in the other direction.

It took veteran troops to ride into a trap without any indication they realized they were doing so, but he'd come to know these men well, and he'd been impressed by their quality. Which, he supposed, he shouldn't have been, considering whose Order they belonged to. Here and there the loose column closed up a little, but so slowly and casually not even he would have suspected why it was happening. The two extra drivers on each wagon had disappeared back under their vehicles' felted covers, and he had no doubt they were stringing bows for themselves and the men left at the reins, as well. The six lay-brothers who'd been riding on the south side of the wagons had also strung their short horsebows, using the wagons for cover, and he nodded in satisfaction. If an attack did come—

Vaijon and Harkon came abreast of the forest's nearest approach, and movement flickered under the trees. Lesser eyes than Bahzell Bahnakson's might not have seen it, but his had, and his arbalest was already moving up to his shoulder even before he realized they had. It steadied, the string snapped, and the crossbowman who'd been taking aim at Vaijon screamed as the quarrel nailed his shoulder to a tree.

Someone shouted, and a dozen more crossbows fired from the trees. The knight riding directly behind Vaijon pitched out of his saddle without a sound, the lay-brother beside him cursed and clapped a hand to the short, stubby shaft suddenly standing out of his left thigh, and yet another quarrel struck Vaijon himself in the chest. Fortunately, it came in at an oblique angle and skipped off his mail, ripping a huge tear in his poncho without inflicting any other damage. Harkon was less lucky, for his horse went down, shrieking as a quarrel drove home just behind its left foreleg. But at least the knight-commander had known something was coming, and he kicked out of the stirrups. He landed rolling and came upright, his sword already in his hand, just as another horse reared in agony and collapsed, spilling yet another lay-brother from the saddle. But that was all the damage the crossbowmen managed to inflict, and someone else shouted under the trees—this time in consternation—as the entire "unprepared" column wheeled sharply to its left and charged.

The woods loomed before them, motionless and menacing for several moments, and then figures began to spill out of the trees. They came in dribs and drabs, like water spurting through leaks in a dike, their surprise obvious in their lack of formation. These were men who had expected to emerge from cover only to confront victims who'd already lost men to crossbow fire and whose survivors were half-broken by the surprise of ambush, and Bahzell shook his head in disgust as he spanned the arbalest once more.

If *he'd* been in command over there, he would have broken off and fled the instant it was apparent surprise had been lost, or at least stayed put in the trees. The ambushers' only missile weapons appeared to be crossbows, which were notoriously slow-firing in most people's hands. Prince Bahnak's Horse Stealers had adopted weapons like Bahzell's own arbalest, but they had the strength of arm to span them like *light* crossbows, which let them maintain a rate of fire no one else could match. Still, even human crossbowmen could have gotten off at least one more shot each while their attackers came at them and, at the very least, they could have forced their enemies to come into the trees after them, where mounted troops would be at a severe disadvantage. Coming out into the open, especially without even taking time to shake down into coherent formation, was stupid.

Still, he allowed as he raised the arbalest and sent another deadly bolt through the throat of an attacker, the brigands did have a marked advantage in numbers. There must be forty or fifty of them, and their decision to leave the sanctuary of the trees might not be quite so addlepated as it first seemed.

Most of the Order of Tomanāk's knights were medium or heavy horse who fought with lance, sword, battleaxe, or mace. There were exceptions—those who, like Bahzell or, for that matter, Kaeritha, preferred to fight on foot—but almost all of the Order's warriors were horsemen. At the moment, that was a disadvantage, for the greatest weapon of a mounted man was normally his horse's momentum. But the snow off the high road was more than horse belly-deep in places, and however willing their mounts, that snow slowed them as they floundered towards their enemies. It was a problem for anyone on foot, as well, of course, but less of one, relatively speaking.

Fortunately, however, Tomanāk's Order rejected the nose-lifted disdain some chivalric orders felt for missile weapons. Unlike those orders—whose members, as far as Bahzell could figure, regarded war as some sort of game in which an arrow was a rank breach of etiquette—Tomanāk's followers used whatever weapon served best, and the Order's lay-brothers were mounted archers. Few of them carried the heavy Sothōii horsebows which made the windriders so deadly, but the lighter version they did use was lethally effective in expert hands, and they were experts.

Now the wagoneers and the lay-brothers who'd strung their bows while concealed behind the wagons—a full dozen of them in all— laid down a deadly fire that did to the ambushers what the brigands' abortive crossbow volley had failed to do to the head of the column. Men screamed and fell, thrashing in the snow as needle-pointed pile arrows slammed into them. Blood spattered the snow, shocking in its redness, and Bahzell dropped his arbalest, drew his sword, and went racing after Kaeritha's mount.

The snow was an impediment to him, as well, but not nearly as much a one as it would have been to another footman, and he drew even with Kaeritha just before she reached the enemy. She might prefer to fight on foot, and a quarterstaff might not be a typical mounted weapon, but that didn't seem to faze her. She dropped her reins, guiding her horse solely with knee and heel, and the staff blurred as she sent it hissing through the air in a two-hand stroke. She took her first victim squarely in the forehead with a perfectly timed strike, and blood sprayed as the impact shattered his skull.

Bahzell had little time to notice. The snow and heavy going had deprived his own people of any sort of formation, as well, and what had been intended as a nice, neat ambush turned into an ugly, sprawling melee. Knots of combat coalesced out of the confusion as two or three men on each side came together, and the Horse Stealer's lips drew back and his ears flattened as he met his first foe head-on.

The brigand in question slithered and skidded in the snow, trying to stop himself as he realized what he faced, but it was too late for that, and Bahzell's sword came down two-handed. Razor-edged steel slammed into the angle of neck and shoulder, and the bandit didn't even have time to scream as it sheared clear down through his torso to emerge below the opposite armpit. The mangled corpse flew aside, blood steaming in the cold, and Bahzell turned as three more brigands came at him.

"*Tomanāk!*" he bellowed, and a soprano voice shouted the same name beside him. A quarterstaff licked out, striking with deadly precision, and one of his three opponents fell headlong, temple crushed. He took the second man himself, blade flashing in a long, blood-spattering arc to send his victim's head flying, and Kaeritha— who had parted company with her horse somewhere along the way—blocked the last man's desperate cut with her staff. She drove the brigand's blade to the side, then brought the lower end of the staff up in a strike to his face. He saw it coming and leapt back to avoid it, but he lost his footing in the snow and fell, and she smashed the staff's butt down in a short, savage arc that sent splinters of his shattered forehead deep into his brain.

She and Bahzell whirled, backs to one another as if they had fought together for years, as still more brigands came at them. Bahzell caught a fleeting impression of Brandark and Vaijon, converging to fight side by side, driving hard to reach him and Kaeritha, and another of Wencit of Rūm, forbidden the use of sorcery against nonwizards by the Strictures of Ottovar, carving bandits into bloody ruin with deadly efficiency. But there were even more attackers than he'd thought and, for some reason, he and Kaeritha seemed to draw them like lodestones. None of them so much as tried to get at the wagons; instead, thirty of them drove at the two champions in a wave while the others foamed forward to prevent anyone else from aiding them.

Bahzell had no time to worry about why it was happening, and he snarled as he reached out and deliberately gave himself to the Rage.

For twelve hundred years, the Rage had been the darkest, most terrible curse of the hradani. The sorcery the Lords of Carnadosa had used to compel them to fight under the Dark Gods' banner in Kontovar had sunk into their blood and bone, marking them with a berserker's fury which could strike anywhere, anytime, without warning. As it still could today. But as Tomanāk had told Bahzell one terrible evening in the Empire of the Spear, the Rage had changed over the centuries, and when a hradani deliberately *summoned* that new Rage to himself, it became his servant, not his master.

And so Bahzell called it now, as he had refused to call it for his duel with Vaijon, and felt it explode through him, crackling in his muscles as all restraint, all doubt vanished. Pure, elemental purpose filled him, and the deep-throated bellow of his war cry rose like thunder as he went to meet his enemies.

Kaeritha came with him, and the icy clear precision of his mind knew exactly where she was at every moment. There was no berserker in him. There was only that focused purpose, as pitiless as winter itself, and he went into the bandits like an avalanche, huge sword crunching through chain and leather armor with equal disdain, cleaving flesh and hurling aside bodies. He didn't worry about his flanks or rear. Kaeritha was there, as dependable as his own arms or legs and just as deadly, and the two of them went through the brigands like a dwarf-designed killing machine of steel and wire.

The ambushers' headlong drive towards the champions slowed as the men who'd led it disintegrated in broken wreckage. None of them had ever faced a hradani in the grip of the Rage, and very few men had ever seen two champions of Tomanāk fight side by side. Fewer still had survived the experience of *facing* two champions, and these men lost all stomach for the chance to confront them. Those nearest Bahzell or Kaeritha were too terrified to turn their backs yet desperate to get out of reach, and they began to slip and stagger backwards as they tried to disengage. Those further away took advantage of the distance to turn and run, but the champions' companions had their own ideas about that.

The furious combat redoubled as the knights and lay-brothers of the Order closed in on the knot of bodies which had congealed around Bahzell and Kaeritha, and the way those attackers had clumped to attack the champions proved their undoing. The Order's horsemen had managed to envelop them, and Brandark and Vaijon launched one prong of a driving attack, riding shoulder to shoulder as their horses trampled their victims. Sir Harkon and Wencit led the other prong, hooking in from the far side, and war cries cut through the ugly sounds of steel in flesh and the shrieks of dying men as the early winter afternoon fell apart in slaughter.

And then, suddenly, it was over. The handful of surviving bandits threw down their weapons—many of them screaming "Oath to Tomanāk! *Oath to Tomanāk!*" as they begged for quarter—and Bahzell drew himself up with a snarl. A flash of terrible disappointment went through him for, summoned or not, the Rage was a sweet and dreadful drug. The need to finish the job, to kill and destroy until no living foe remained, pulsed in him, hammering with the beat of his heart. But he was the Rage's master, not its slave, and he drove the hunger from him. He closed his eyes for a long, quivering moment, sending the Rage back to its sleeping place until he needed it once more, and then drew a huge, lung-stretching breath and opened his eyes once more.

He looked down at his sword, coated with blood and hair and more horrible things, then turned to look at Kaeritha. She'd lost her quarterstaff somewhere, and someone's blood had sprayed over her right shoulder and the side of her face. Her shortswords were both bloody to the hilt, the fire of her own battle lust still burned in her eyes, and she limped from a gash on her left leg, but she met his gaze and nodded to him, then bent to wipe her swords one by one on the cloak of a fallen bandit.

Vaijon and Brandark were there, too. The Bloody Sword raised his blade in salute to Bahzell, and the Horse Stealer saw the echoes of the Rage in his eyes, as well; knew that Brandark, as he, had summoned their people's "curse" to him. Vaijon was pale-faced and grim, clearly shaken by his first true taste of combat, but he'd stayed shoulder to shoulder with Brandark throughout, and Bahzell knew how few warriors could have done that.

Now the Horse Stealer turned where he stood and grimaced as he saw the trail of bodies strewn over the trampled, bloodstained snow. His own path was a ruler-straight line of corpses, headed directly for the woods from which the attack had come, and it was obvious which had fallen to him and which to the precise, lethal thrusts of Kaeritha's lighter weapons. The two of them alone had probably accounted for a third of their attackers, he realized, but, then, they'd had an advantage the others had lacked: those enemies had come to them—initially, at least.

But their companions had fought just as hard . . . and some had been less fortunate. He saw a dismounted lay-brother sitting up in the snow, shoulders propped against another brother's knee while a third tightened a tourniquet on a left arm which had lost its hand. Other bodies in the Order's colors lay still and unbreathing in the snow, and more knights and lay-brothers bent over other wounded friends.

But there were far more bandit bodies, he noted grimly. His original estimate had been low; there had been more like sixty than forty attackers, but less than fifteen had survived, and he gazed at them bleakly as he promised himself the opportunity to . . . discuss their actions with them. Yet for now there were other things to concern him, and he looked back at Kaeritha.

"Well fought, sword brother," she told him, sheathing her cleaned swords, and he nodded.

"You, too, lass," he agreed, and ripped a poncho from another corpse to wipe his own blade. He cleaned the steel, then sheathed it. "But now I'm thinking it's time I was having a look at that leg of yours, sister," he rumbled more quietly, "and after that—" he twitched his head at the other wounded "—we'd best be talking to himself about healing our friends."

CHAPTER THIRTEEN

So none of them have the least idea who hired them, eh?" Kaeritha sounded as skeptical as Bahzell felt, and the Horse Stealer snorted.

"If they do, none of 'em's minded to be telling *us*, at least," he rumbled, and turned his head to spit into the snow in disgust. "Mind you, if it wasn't for that 'Oath to Tomanāk' nonsense, Brandark and I'd soon have the truth out of them."

"It's not 'nonsense,' Bahzell," Kaeritha said, her tone mild but firm.

One knight—Sir Erek—and four lay-brothers had been killed, and six more had been wounded, two severely. Given the odds they'd faced, that was a low casualty list, but that made neither the deaths less painful nor the suffering of the wounded easier. Now the two champions sat apart from the others, wrapped in blankets while they recovered from the exhaustion of healing those wounded men. It wasn't simply physical weariness, but a champion's ability to heal depended on three things: his faith, the strength of his own will, and his ability to directly channel the power of his deity. As joyous as that was, it was also as strenuous, in its own way, as any battle. The focused will and faith, the ability to *see* the wounded man whole as he ought to be, produced the exhaustion, but the direct communion with their god produced its own sense of . . . bemusement and almost dreamy wonder. Still, they'd had time to recover from the stronger aftereffects, and Kaeritha gave the hradani a moderately stern glance.

Bahzell grimaced, but he also nodded. There was no question that he commanded their party—which, after all, had been assembled to get him home to deal with Sharnā's meddling in

Navahk—but Kaeritha had been a champion for almost eight years. It was hard to remember sometimes that she was senior to him, for despite her formidable height (for a human woman), she was of less than average height and delicate compared to hradani women, and she was almost ten years younger than he. Yet senior she was . . . and no one who had seen her in action this afternoon would ever think of her as a fragile flower of sheltered femininity.

"Aye, I know," he agreed after a moment, "but if the boot were on the other foot, these bastards wouldn't be caring less what *our* lot might have sworn. And if *they* hadn't been after swearing it, and if all our people weren't after being in the Order's colors, then Brandark and I could convince them easy enough . . . and without laying a finger on 'em, either." Kaeritha raised an eyebrow, and he grinned evilly. "We're hradani, Kerry, and all the world knows as how hradani would sooner slit a man's throat than look at him. Trust me. If these lads weren't after knowing as how calling on Tomanāk protects them from us, we'd scare 'em into loosening their tongues quick enough."

"I see." Kaeritha considered for a moment, then chuckled. "You know, I think I'd like to see that. And as far as I know, *scaring* them into talking isn't against the Code."

"As far as that goes, Milady," Vaijon said, crossing from the fire to bring the two of them steaming mugs of tea, "we can always hope they violate their oaths of surrender."

"I don't think that was precisely what Tomanāk had in mind when he ruled that a prisoner's violation of the terms of surrender frees His followers from the Code," Kaeritha told him dryly as she accepted a mug. He acknowledged her point with a nod, but the wistful longing in his eyes didn't fade, and she shook her head. "You two deserve each other," she said, waving the mug at them. "Either Bahzell is a corrupting influence on you, Vaijon, or else there was always a nasty streak of peasant practicality in you and you just didn't know it."

"Please, Milady!" Vaijon protested, drawing himself up and looking down his nose at her. "Practicality if you like, and 'nasty' is fair enough. But '*peasant* practicality'? My father would die of apoplexy! I *am* an Almerhas of Almerhas, you know."

"Don't we all?" Kaeritha returned, and he chuckled. He was about to say something more when Sir Harkon walked up behind him. Wencit and Brandark were with Harkon, and the knight-commander looked grim as he held out one hand.

"We found this on one of their dead, Milord," he told Bahzell in a flat voice, and the Horse Stealer stiffened as he saw the golden chain and pendant. He hesitated a moment, then took it gingerly, holding it up for Kaeritha to see, as well. The pendant was an icon in the shape of a scorpion, as long as a man's index finger, crouched atop an oval cut emerald a half-inch across. The creature's stinger-tipped tail was raised to strike, and its eyes were tiny rubies. It was an exquisite piece of work, and Kaeritha hissed as she saw it.

"Sharnā *here?*" She glared at the symbol of the god of demons and assassins.

"Why not?" Brandark demanded with mirthless humor. She looked at him, and he shrugged. "Old Demon Breath took quite a dislike to us—well, to Bahzell, to be honest, though it tended to spill over onto everyone in the vicinity—last fall. From all I've heard, he isn't one to give up grudges easily, and he doesn't seem to be particularly blessed with inventiveness, either. He spent a thousand leagues or so and several dozen dog brothers trying to ambush us. It never quite worked, but he *did* seem determined to keep trying until he finally got it right."

"That's not what I meant." Kaeritha reached out and took the scorpion from Bahzell. It was obvious she didn't enjoy touching it, but she turned it up and tapped the emerald on which it crouched. "This isn't something a dog brother would wear, Brandark. For all its official connection to Sharnā, the assassins' guild isn't particularly pious, and this is the emblem of one of Sharnā's priests." She glanced at Harkon. "Did you find any dog brothers among the dead?"

"None," Harkon replied, and looked at Wencit for confirmation.

"There weren't any," the wild wizard agreed. "And we looked very carefully for tattoos after we found that—" he jutted his chin at the scorpion "—too."

"I see." Bahzell leaned back on the rock upon which he sat. He took a long sip of hot tea, then rubbed the tip of his nose while his ears flattened in thought. He felt the others watching him, but he took his time considering the scanty information they had.

"I'm thinking," he said at last, "that there's naught but one possibility. Scummy as he is, Demon Breath is still a god . . . of sorts. Like as not, he's after knowing what we're about, and like Brandark says, he's not been shy about trying to scrag us both in the past. On the other hand, it's in my mind that himself said not even the Dark Gods dare meddle too directly." He cocked a questioning eyebrow at Kaeritha, who nodded. "Well, I suppose it's possible, then, that he's not told his lot just *why* he's wanting us dead. Come to that, the way these fumble wits went about it may mean as how he's not even told them who we are. I'm thinking this lot had no notion they were about to cross swords with the Order of Tomanāk until they saw our colors."

"I'd say you're right about that last bit, at least, Milord," Harkon said. "The scum who follow Sharnā have never cared to meet us in battle, and certainly not in anything like equal numbers. They only outnumbered us by three to two here, and if they'd known what we were, they would have bought a lot more swords to help them out."

"They've certainly avoided this sort of thing in the past," Kaeritha agreed.

"Aye, and Sharnā's not exactly noted for keeping faith with anyone," Bahzell pointed out. "He'll send his own worshipers to their deaths and laugh unless there's after being something of special value for him in keeping 'em alive, from all I've heard. Like as not the notion of setting them on us without warning them would actually amuse him."

"But that doesn't mean he doesn't really want to stop us—or you, or the *two* of you, or even the *three* of you, counting Wencit," Brandark said. The Bloody Sword rubbed the tip of his truncated ear for a moment, then grimaced. "Phrobus! If *I* were Sharnā, I'd want the whole lot of you as far away from *my* plots as I could keep you."

"Which only emphasizes the importance of our not letting him get away with delaying us," Wencit put in, and Bahzell nodded.

"My very own thought. But what to do with this lot in the meantime?"

He twitched his head at the miserable prisoners. The fact that Tomanāk's Code protected them from abuse by their captors didn't seem to have made them feel a great deal better, and he didn't blame them. The code wasn't binding on the Royal and Imperial courts, and brigandage was a hanging offense.

"I don't see any option, Milord," Harkon said almost apologetically. "We'll have to take them along at least until we meet one of Sir Maehryk's patrols. I don't think they'll slow us, though. We only lost three horses, and our scouts rounded up all of theirs from their camp to replace the losses. Maybe the local magistrate can get more about their employers out of them. Once they're face to face with the courts—and the hangman—they may decide to strike a deal and turn King-Emperor's evidence."

"I'm afraid Harkon's right about taking them along," Kaeritha said. "But we might be able to get just a *tad* more information out of them. While I would never encourage anyone to violate the Code,

this—" she held up the scorpion "—puts a different color on things."
Bahzell looked at her quizzically, and she shrugged. "*They* don't
necessarily know that working for Sharnā doesn't change their status.
As servants of Tomanāk it would never do for us to actually *lie*
about that, but if they just *happened* to get the notion that the Code
doesn't protect those who give their allegiance to the Dark Gods,
well—"

She shrugged again, and Bahzell gave an evil laugh. Vaijon and
Harkon looked at her as if they weren't certain they'd heard correctly, and Wencit only shook his head, but Brandark sighed. The
others looked at him, and he raised one hand to wag an index finger
under Kaeritha's nose.

"Bahzell is clearly a bad influence on you," he told her severely.
"The very idea of a champion of Tomanāk suggesting such a sub-
terfuge! I'm shocked—*shocked!*—that you could so much as think
such a thing!"

"Oh?" Kaeritha's dark blue eyes glinted challengingly. "Does that
mean you disapprove?"

"Of course I don't disapprove—I'm a *hradani*, Kerry! I just can't
help wondering how *Tomanāk* is going to react to this."

"Oh, I've a notion he'll grow accustomed," Bahzell said, reclaiming
the scorpion and dangling it in front of him while he considered
it once more from all angles, then he grinned. "Now what do you
suppose would be the best way to begin?" he mused almost dreamily. "Should we let Brandark be showing this little bauble to them
one by one while he plays with his knife, or should old Wencit
be after making sure they've seen his eyes and then give them all
a lecture at once?"

Kaeritha's plan worked to perfection. Unfortunately, the surviving hired swords truly didn't know much about the people who'd
hired them. No brigand in his right mind would have *admitted* he'd
known he was working for Sharnā, yet Bahzell was inclined to
believe their protestations of ignorance. Somewhat to his surprise,
Kaeritha agreed, for their anger—and fear—when they discovered
the truth seemed completely genuine. Any mercy they might have
anticipated from the courts would evaporate instantly if they were
proven to have knowingly served the Dark, and they appeared
desperate to offer any information they could in an effort to buy
some sort of clemency.

Only they didn't actually *have* any true information. The few who
weren't regular out-and-out brigands were mercenaries of the sort
Tomanāk did not approve of, and none had asked many questions

when they hired on with their now deceased employer. Nor had they been told they were waiting for a single, specific target. They'd thought they were going to pillage anyone who happened along, and they hadn't even realized the travelers were in Tomanāk's colors until the first crossbow bolts were fired. The only thing all of them agreed on was that the man who'd hired them had been accompanied by an inner cadre of ten others, all of whom had appeared to be seasoned fighters . . . and none of whom had survived.

It wasn't much. In fact, it was worse than nothing in many ways, for it simply confirmed that Sharnā was involved without providing a single additional hard fact. But at least they knew now that their enemies knew enough about *their* plans to attempt to stop them, and that lent a new urgency to their journey. They decided to press on as quickly as possible in hopes of reaching Dwarvenhame before Sharnā could organize something more effective than a botched ambush. And while none of the attackers they'd killed or captured had borne the dog brothers' telltale scorpion tattoo, they couldn't be positive the assassins wouldn't be called in. Given that fact, Kaeritha agreed with Bahzell that it would be wise to avoid any town or city. It was easier to watch one's back in the wilderness than among an entire town's worth of people one didn't know from Hirahim's house cat and, as Bahzell had demonstrated, sneaking up on a Horse Stealer hradani in the open was a difficult task, at best.

The champions transferred their prisoners to one of Sir Maehryk's detachments at the first good-sized, permanent village they passed, but they barely even slowed down to turn them over. The detachment's senior knight seemed a bit miffed by their haste, but none of their own companions so much as complained, despite their longing to spend at least one night under a snug roof. There were a few wistful sighs when they circled Esfresia itself without even entering the provincial capital, however, especially when the clear, cold weather which had accompanied them from Lordenfel decided to disappear. There were no fresh blizzards, but the sun vanished. The temperature actually rose a bit, but the rising humidity which came with it only made the damp cold bite even deeper, road conditions were miserable, and they were plagued by dense fog and frequent flurries of wet, soggy snow for days on end.

Their pace slowed once they'd passed Esfresia, and not simply because the roads were worse. The ambush had inspired Sir Harkon to put out scouts, and the wretched visibility restricted the distance at which those scouts could stay in visual contact with the rest of the party. A part of Bahzell longed to overrule the knight-commander, but he couldn't. Not only was Harkon right about the need to have someone sweep for enemies, he was also the senior member of the Belhadan chapter still present, and Bahzell was not about to undercut his authority simply because he wanted to move a little faster.

The trip from Esfresia to the Dwarvenhame Tunnel was the shortest leg of their journey so far, little more than thirty-seven leagues, but it seemed much, much longer. The terrain changed once more as the land began to climb towards the eastern mountains, and the high road passed through forest as dense as anything in Vonderland. Trees pressed in on either hand, further aggravating the scouts' problems, and the first few leagues east of Esfresia were particularly hard going as the horses pushed through the deep snow. It took them the better part of three full days to cover barely thirty miles, and Bahzell began to despair of reaching Hurgrum before midsummer.

Fortunately, conditions began to change on the fourth day. The deserted villages with which they had become all too familiar disappeared, and they saw little of the abandoned pasture lands which had stretched across Landria and southern Landfressa. There were more farms, with stout, winter-tight barns and brick silos, but it was clear that most of those living in the towns they passed now had other things on their minds than farming. The high road was clearer than it had been since Lordenfel, and teams of woodsmen were busy in the forest through which it passed. Ox-drawn sledges laden with trimmed tree trunks moved steadily along beside the road, all headed east, and Kaeritha smiled when Bahzell wondered aloud at seeing so much industry in such bitter weather.

"Think about it," she suggested. "What's the one thing folk who live underground have the least of?"

"Ah?" Bahzell scratched an ear, then nodded. "Trees," he said.

"Exactly. Dwarvenhame is as greedy for forest products as Purple Lords are for gold, and these people make an excellent living supplying them. And not just with lumber or pitch or turpentine, either. Dwarves have a deep craving for fine woodwork, but it's not something they're particularly skilled at producing. And this is a good time for these people to do their timbering. There's less need for farm labor, and without rivers big enough to float logs down, winter actually makes it easier to move them. Timber sleds move much better over snow."

Bahzell nodded again, though he remained bemused by the shouts echoing through the forests from the labor gangs. The occasional crashing thunder as trees came down and the cheerful profanity bellowed by drovers as ox teams leaned into their harnesses were a far cry from the icy, deserted silence he'd seen further south, yet he still felt taken aback initially when the locals called out cheery greetings as he and his companions passed. It was good to once more find themselves among people who felt secure enough to greet them, yet after their earlier experiences, and especially after the botched ambush, it seemed unnatural for these people to view any large, armed band with anything other than wariness, regardless of whose colors they wore.

But a little thought helped explain the difference between the attitudes of these industrious foresters and the inhabitants of the largely deserted towns and villages. Landfressa's foresters, like those of Vonderland, were a hardy and independent lot, and most were hunters as well as loggers. There were undoubtedly dozens of bows in their work camps, and given the probable skill of those bows' owners— not to mention the fact that woodcutters were inevitably accompanied by extremely sharp axes—only fools would offer them violence. Besides, however valuable timber might be in Dwarvenhame, it wasn't exactly something brigands could seize and ride off with.

Not that there weren't plenty of other temptations to lure potential raiders, for Kaeritha had been right about the relationship between Landfressa's humans and the dwarves of Dwarvenhame. Winter might have frozen them for now, but in warmer weather dozens of brawling mountain streams ran down to the northernmost tributaries of the Greenleaf River. They were too shallow to be used for transport, but every town the travelers passed boasted its own holding ponds, as if an army of beavers had descended upon the land, and Bahzell and Brandark marveled at the scores of waterwheels those ponds served. Many were idle now, but some still turned, and it didn't need a hradani's ears to hear the sounds of hammers, saws, chisels, and other tools coming from the large brick buildings clustered about them. Among hradani, waterwheels were used only to drive the grinding stones of grist mills, but these people obviously used water to power a whole host of other tools, as well, and Bahzell watched in fascination as they passed an open-sided structure where a water-driven saw as tall as many men slabbed enormous tree trunks neatly into planks and timbers. Neither he nor Brandark had ever imagined such an improvement on the slow, laborious saw pits their own people used, yet the fact that the locals seemed totally unaware that winter was supposed to be a time when the pace of life slowed until the spring thaw was almost more bemusing to them.

The humans in their party seemed to take that in stride, but then, with the possible exception of Wencit—who, as a wild wizard, might or might not be properly classed as a "human" to begin with—they were all citizens of the Empire. Bahzell and Brandark were not, yet the comments their companions let drop told them that busy as all this seemed to *them*, it was commonplace to the others. Indeed, compared to the more populous provinces further south, all of this bustle and industriousness, however impressive to two barbarian hradani, was downright rustic.

That was an almost frightening thought for Bahzell. His father had worked for years to build a place where merchants and artisans could survive and prosper, and the result had been to make Hurgrum crushingly superior to her foes. By hradani standards, Bahnak's realm was incredibly prosperous, able not only to feed and clothe its people but to arm them and equip them for war with weapons of their own manufacture. It had been an enormous achievement, one which had played a decisive role in Bahnak's rise to the threshold of empire, yet the prosperity and productivity of this area which Bahzell's human friends clearly regarded as a backwater dwarfed all his father had achieved. It put the wealth and power of the Empire of the Axe into stark perspective . . . and made him realize how incredibly far his own people still had to go.

Or, rather, those busy, productive towns made him *begin* to realize the length of the journey to which Prince Bahnak had committed his Horse Stealers. It took their arrival at the western end of the Dwarvenhame Tunnel to make the realization complete.

CHAPTER FOURTEEN

"Phrobus!"

Brandark's soft-voiced curse, rich with wonder, expressed Bahzell's own feelings almost perfectly. The Horse Stealer glanced at his friend, but only briefly, for the sight before them wouldn't let him look away for long.

The stonework of Belhadan and the Empire's roads had been marvel enough, but this was the first time the hradani had seen the work of dwarvish engineers untouched by the influence of any of the other Races of Man, and they knew it. No one could have looked at the western face of the Dwarvenhame Tunnel and *not* known it, for no one but a dwarf could have conceived and executed such a project.

The entire face of a mountain had been sliced away to create a sheer, vertical wall of smooth rock eight hundred feet high at the least. There was something merciless about the perfection of that sweep of stone, a purity of line and plane which nature could never have produced. It had been imposed by a hand and eye which thought in straight lines and the consummation of function, and it loomed above the puny mites at its feet with a majestic severity too intense for beauty.

The mouth of the tunnel itself was a black dot against that vast backdrop. Only as they approached its portcullis-fringed maw and the flanking bastions carved from the rock to either side of it did its size truly become apparent. Those bastions were garrisoned, as was the battlemented traverse work cut to overhang the full width of the gate. Sentries looked down on the travelers from embrasures, murder holes for heated oil and banefire, and arrow slits, but the duty officer must have been warned they were coming, for the stocky dwarf only raised his axe to Bahzell in salute and waved them past.

Truth to tell, Bahzell had paid the guards little heed, for his attention was riveted to the tunnel itself, and he felt a fresh sense of awe as hooves clattered on the hard-paved approach and he strode under its massive vault. As a rule, he disliked underground spaces. He wasn't exactly claustrophobic; it was just that most caves and tunnels made someone his size feel hemmed in. But the Dwarvenhame Tunnel was fifty yards across, with a stony roof so high above the roadway that it seemed to float suspended rather than press down upon him, and a reassuring breeze flowed through ventilation shafts on silent feet of chill, fresh air. The light within was dim compared to the daylight without, but it was much brighter than he would have expected. Wall-mounted lanterns burned every twenty yards, and even though they lacked the reflectors he'd seen in places like the Belhadan chapter's training salle, they threw powerful spills of illumination along the tunnel. It took him several minutes to realize why, and then he inhaled sharply.

They didn't require reflectors because the walls themselves served *as* reflectors. The stone wasn't simply smooth; it was polished almost to the quality of a mirror, without a single tool mark to mar its surface, and he shook his head in baffled wonder.

"What?" Wencit asked quietly from beside him, and Bahzell turned his head. The wild wizard's eldrich eyes looked eerier than ever in the subdued lighting, floating like twin pools of witchfire under his brows. Their shifting glow was so bright Bahzell thought he could almost have read by it, yet not even that unnatural sight could distract him from the odd sense that the tunnel didn't truly exist. That it *couldn't* exist.

"The walls," he said after a moment, his voice soft, almost hushed, as if he felt some compulsion to speak without the tunnel's creators overhearing him. "There's not a tool mark on 'em."

"No, there isn't," Wencit agreed, turning to cock his head and consider the walls himself. He studied them almost critically, then shrugged. "Actually, I think this may be even better than some of the work I saw in Kontovar," he mused. "Of course, it's been a while. I suppose my memory could be playing tricks on me."

Bahzell swallowed, jarred by the casualness of the wizard's tone. He could forget Wencit's age and reputation for days on end—or no, not *forget* so much as set them aside or fool himself into thinking he'd come to grips with them—and then some offhand remark would drive the old man's sheer antiquity home like an arbalest bolt. Like now. No one else in the world could possibly refer to twelve hundred tumultuous years as "a while," yet to Wencit of Rūm, that was precisely what they had been.

For an instant, Bahzell was terrifyingly aware of the age and knowledge—and power—riding peacefully along at his side. This was the man who had strafed Kontovar. Who had fought the Lord of Carnadosa himself, and all his inner council, to a standstill in the first, desperate days of the war which had doomed the Empire of Ottovar. Whose protection had prevented the Dark Lords from pursuing Kontovar's refugees to Norfressa to make an end of them. Bahzell Bahnakson was not a man who felt awe easily, but there was not—could not be—a more perilous being in all the world, and for just that instant, a fear-touched awe was precisely what echoed through Bahzell's bones.

But the moment passed. Not because the Horse Stealer felt any less respect, but because Wencit had *chosen* for it to pass. It would have been impossible for Bahzell to imagine anything less like the dark and terrible wizard lords of the ancient tales than the plainly clothed old man on the horse beside him. No one who ever met Wencit of Rūm could mistake the steel at his core, but the wizard had never sought wealth or pomp. His was a quiet authority which came from who he was and what he had done, not from the sort of mailed fist which could impose obedience. He was a wanderer, moving about on missions of his own, often inscrutable and mysterious to those about him, who turned up unexpectedly and then disappeared as unexpectedly as he'd come. He was as comfortable with barbarian hradani as at the King-Emperor's own court, and for twelve hundred years he had been a law unto himself.

Now he looked at Bahzell, raising one snowy eyebrow, and smiled. It was an oddly intimate little smile, as if he knew what the hradani had been thinking and found it amusing, yet there was a wry twist to it, as well. Perhaps, Bahzell thought, the real reason Wencit had never built himself the sort of wizard's tower the old tales described or established himself in luxurious wealth and authority in Axe Hallow or Midrancimb or Sothfalas was far simpler than most people had ever imagined.

He was lonely. Could it truly be that simple, the Horse Stealer wondered? And yet, how could it not be? This man's flame-cored eyes had witnessed the fall of the greatest empire in history. He'd seen the wreckage of that empire washed up on Norfressa's shore, watched over and guarded it as it painfully and laboriously set about putting its pieces back together. And aside from some of the elves of Saramantha in their self-imposed seclusion, he was the *only* one who had. How many people—how many friends—had he known across that vast sweep of years? How many times had death washed them away and left him alone once more to pursue his lonely task as a continent's guardian? The grief of so much loss must eat at a man's soul, yet the only way to avoid that sorrow would be to isolate one's self as Saramantha had—to erect barricades and defenses against feeling—and that, Bahzell somehow knew, was something Wencit simply could not do. And so he took people as he met them. *All* people, on their own terms, accepting them for who and what they were, for he *needed* them to remind him of who he was . . . and why he had given and sacrificed so much to protect them for so long.

"You were commenting on the walls?" The old man's voice prodded Bahzell with unusual patience, and the Horse Stealer shook himself, then grinned.

"Aye, so I was," he replied, grateful to Wencit for breaking the train of his thoughts. "I'd not've thought anyone would spend the effort to polish them this way. Tomanāk! I'd've said no one *could* do it!"

"Ah, but they didn't—polish them, I mean," Wencit said. Bahzell looked at him for a moment, then flicked his eyes back to the glass-smooth stone.

"And just how would you describe whatever they *were* after doing, then?" he asked politely.

"Oh, the stone's smooth enough," Wencit agreed, "but they didn't have to 'polish' it. This—" he flicked a hand to indicate the entire wide sweep of the tunnel which surrounded them "—is *sarthnasik* work."

"*Sarthnasik?*" Bahzell repeated carefully. The word was obviously dwarvish, though it seemed overly short for their language, but he'd never heard it before.

"It translates—roughly, you understand—as 'stoneherd,'" Wencit told him.

"Does it, now? And what might a stoneherd be?" Bahzell felt Brandark urging his horse up behind him and sensed the Bloody Sword leaning towards Wencit with his ears cocked. Vaijon wasn't far behind, and Kaeritha smiled crookedly as she moved her own mount to the side to make room for the young knight-probationer. Clearly she was already familiar with the term, but Bahzell wasn't, and he eyed the wizard intently.

"A stoneherd is a dwarf who practices *sarthnasikarmanthar*,"

Wencit explained. "That's the traditional dwarvish discipline—or art, perhaps—which allows them to command stone."

"*Command* stone?" Brandark repeated, sounding as dubious as Bahzell felt, and the wizard chuckled.

"That's the simplest way to put it," he said dryly. "I can give you a more technical explanation if you really want one, but I doubt it would mean a great deal to you." The Bloody Sword raised an eyebrow, and Wencit shrugged. "Do you remember the night I tried to explain how wizardry works?"

"Yes." Brandark rubbed his nose. "You said something about the entire universe being composed solely of energy, however solid it may look."

"Precisely. And if you'll recall, I also said that all wizardry consisted of was a set of tools or techniques with which to manipulate that energy?" It was Wencit's turn to cock an eyebrow, like a professor checking to see if his students followed him.

"Oh, aye. We *recall* it, right enough," Bahzell assured him. "Which isn't to be saying we're after *understanding* it, of course, but we do recall it."

"Good. Because *sarthnasikarmanthar* is simply a specialized version of the same thing—one which applies only to stone and which only the dwarves have developed. A *sarthnasik* doesn't 'dig' or 'cut' a tunnel. He visualizes it in his mind—much as I suppose you or Kerry visualize the mending of a wound when you call on Tomanāk for healing—and then imposes that vision on the energy other people see as 'solid stone.' "

Wencit shrugged, as if what he'd said was self-explanatory and as simple as baking a cake, and Bahzell stared at him, appalled by the implications.

"D'you mean to be telling me," he said very slowly after a moment, "that a dwarf can simply *wish* something like this—" he waved at the tunnel again "—into being?"

"Hardly!" Wencit snorted. "It takes a great deal of concentration and imposes a tremendous drain on the life energy of a stoneherd. Something like this tunnel or some of the other tunnels and cuts *sarthnasiks* have produced for the Empire aren't anything they do casually, Bahzell. But the ability is undoubtedly the real reason dwarves seem so much more comfortable underground."

"And they still do it today?" Brandark sounded uneasy, and Wencit turned to look at him. "I mean, there's no White Council—hasn't been one for twelve hundred years." Wencit cocked his head, and the Bloody Sword frowned. "I don't think I like knowing that a bunch of wizards have been running around unsupervised all that time!"

"They're not wizards," Wencit said, and sighed at Brandark's expression of disbelief. "*Sarthnasikarmanthar* is no more wizardry than the elves' long life spans are, Brandark. Rock is the *only* thing a stoneherd can impose his will on, though most *sarthnasiks* do seem to have a greater affinity for metal work than even other dwarves do. I think it has something with their sensitivity to the ores in their raw state. But a stoneherd could no more 'visualize' a hole through *you* than Vaijon here could."

"Sounds like wizardry to me," Brandark said stubbornly, and Wencit shook his head.

"I suppose that—in a *very* specialized sense—you can define it that way if you absolutely insist," he said, "but no wizard would. It's a natural talent no one can learn to duplicate without the same inborn talent. In fact, most wizards would agree with the historians that *sarthnasikarmanthar* was the very first cleft point for the Races of Man."

"'Cleft point'?" Bahzell repeated. Wencit nodded, and the Horse Stealer rubbed his jaw. "And what would a cleft point be?"

"A cleft point—" Wencit began, then paused. He rode in silence for a few seconds, scratching his own beard thoughtfully, then looked around at his audience. "How many of you are familiar with the works of Yanahir of Trōfrōlantha?" he asked.

Brandark started slightly, but the others only looked blank. The Bloody Sword waited to see if anyone else would speak, then shrugged. "I've come across the name," he said cautiously. "I've never seen any of his actual writings, but I've seen some older works cite him as a secondary source. He's supposed to have been a historian and philosopher from the time of the First Wizard Wars, isn't he? Frankly, I always thought he was a myth."

"He wasn't," Wencit assured him. "And you're right about when he lived. In fact, he was court historian for Ottovar the Great and Gwynytha the Wise."

Brandark's weren't the only eyes that went wide and round at that. Ottovar the Great had lived over ten thousand years ago, and the wizard smiled wryly as he saw the unvoiced thought behind their eyes.

"No, I *wasn't* around at the time," he told them in a dry tone. "I did, however, have the opportunity to read his works before the Fall. The Imperial Library in Trōfrōlantha had an almost complete collection." He paused again, meditatively, and his voice was thoughtful when he continued. "You know, I haven't thought about

Yanahir in centuries. I'd forgotten that no one in Norfressa ever had the chance to read him." He shook his head again. "Maybe I should find the time to sit down and jot down what I remember. It certainly couldn't hurt . . . and it might do quite a bit of good, now that I think about it."

His voice trailed off, and he gazed into space, looking at something no one else could see. The others glanced at one another, waiting for him to resume, but over a full minute dragged past without his saying another word, and Bahzell cleared his throat.

"I'm sure that's all very well, Wencit, but would you be so very kind as to be getting on with whatever it was you were telling *us* before you came all over historical?"

The wizard twitched, then grinned at the hradani's acerbic tone.

"Forgive me, Bahzell. When you have as many memories as I do, you sometimes get a bit lost sorting through them. As for what I was about to say, Yanahir was a wizard himself, as well as a historian, and he was fascinated by the Races of Man. Of course, there were only three then: humans, dwarves, and hradani."

"Three?" Brandark looked up sharply. "What about the elves?"

"Oh, they didn't even exist until after the First Wizard Wars," Wencit told him. "In fact, it was watching them come into existence that started Yanahir wondering about the original three races."

"The elves '*came into existence*' after the Wizard Wars?" Brandark sounded stunned, and Wencit nodded.

"Of course. Ottovar and Gwynytha created them."

"*What?*" Bahzell stared at the wizard in disbelief, and Wencit sighed.

"I see I *do* have to get as much of Yanahir's history written back down as I can." He turned his glowing eyes on Kaeritha. "I know Mistress Sherath gave you a good, solid grounding in history, Kaeritha. Didn't she ever mention Yanahir or the Cleaving to you?"

"Not that I can remember," Kaeritha said after several seconds of frowning thought. "She did describe *sarthnasikarmanthar* to us, but I think that was because some magi have stone-working talents which could be mistaken for it by people who don't know the difference and she wanted to be certain *we* did. She certainly never mentioned anything about 'cleft points,' though. And she didn't say anything about the elves having been 'created' either. Of course—" she twitched a shrug and grinned "—Mistress Sherath tended to concentrate on *Norfressan* history, Wencit. That's quite ancient enough for most people, you know."

"Oh, dear." Wencit rubbed a hand over his eyes, and as their glow disappeared behind his hand, he looked every year of his unthinkable age for just an instant. Then he lowered his hand and smiled crookedly. "Let this be a lesson to you, my friends. Never assume that just because something was once common knowledge it must be still."

"I'm thinking it's likely you're after having a bit more opportunity for that than such as we do," Bahzell said dryly, and Wencit chuckled.

"No doubt," he agreed, then shook himself. "All right. Basically, Yanahir was curious about how the different Races of Man came into existence—or, to be more precise, about how the differences *between* them arose—and he decided to find out."

"But weren't they always different?" Vaijon asked, brow creased in confusion.

"No." Wencit shook his head firmly. "I'm not privy to all of the techniques Yanahir used in his investigations. Remember, he'd studied directly under Ottovar, and many of his techniques had been lost long before even the Fall. I do know some wizards are actually capable of traveling through time, though there aren't many who can do it, thank Orr. And only a madman would do so willingly, given that one can only travel backwards, not forward, and that a careless act on the wizard's part would be entirely capable of . . . um, *uncreating* the time from which he came." He grimaced. "But Yanahir had developed some of the best scrying spells of his time to assist Ottovar in the First Wizard Wars. He might have used some variant of those, and whatever he did, those of his contemporaries who were privy to his studies accepted his findings unequivocally."

"And those findings were?" Brandark asked, and his eyes were almost as bright as Wencit's with the knowledge-hunger at his core.

"Originally, there was only a single Race of Man," Wencit said simply. "Humans."

"But that's—" Vaijon began, then stopped.

"But that's ridiculous," Wencit finished for him, and shrugged. "No doubt it seems that way, but Yanahir insisted the evidence was there. According to his studies, the three 'original' Races of Man had all diverged from one another during what he called 'the Cleaving,' when the 'cleft points' that distinguish them drove them apart. As support, he pointed to the emergence of the elves. For that matter, we've had evidence of our own to support the same theory in the halflings. All the tales and histories agree that there *were* no halflings until after the Fall, and I can personally attest to that fact."

"So what were the cleft points?" Kaeritha asked.

"Well, for the dwarves, it was *sarthnasikarmanthar*. The occasional human had possessed the same talent, though in much weaker form, before the Cleaving. According to Yanahir, people with the talent—or the potential for it—were drawn to one another, and gradually, as they interbred, it grew stronger and stronger in their descendants. I said earlier that it's a talent, not true wizardry. Brandark found that difficult to accept, I believe, and now that I've had a chance to think about Yanahir's theories a bit, I'm not sure he was entirely wrong to doubt it. In a sense, it *is* wizardry, but a very specialized sort. It's almost like wild wizardry in that respect, and, like wild wizardry, it produced certain physical changes—" his hand flicked up, indicating his burning eyes "—in the people who possessed it.

"The most obvious one, of course, was their shorter stature, but there were others. Their life spans increased considerably, but their fertility declined. And there were no dwarvish wizards. Yanahir's conclusion was that *sarthnasikarmanthar* or the potential for it somehow desensitizes its possessors to the rest of what wizards call the magic field. Since they can't even perceive it aside from its manifestation in stone and ores, none of them can ever develop the techniques to manipulate it."

"And the hradani?" Brandark demanded.

"Oh, yes. The hradani." Wencit smiled sadly. "Do any of you know where the word 'hradani' comes from?" His listeners shook their heads. "It's a shortened version of the original word '*hradahnahin*,' which came in turn from the Old Kontovaran '*hra*,' which meant 'calm,' and '*danahai*,' which meant 'foxlike.'"

"Calm?" Brandark repeated very carefully. "Did you say *calm*?"

"I did. And before the Fall, it was exactly the right word." He looked at the two hradani. "I know your people's tales of what the Carnadosans did to you during the Wizard Wars, Bahzell, Brandark. But even the darkest of them don't tell it all. For thousands upon thousands of years in Kontovar, the hradahnahin were considered the calmest, sanest of all the Races of Man."

"I don't believe it," Brandark said flatly. "I *can't* believe it!"

"I'm not surprised," Wencit told him. "How could you, given the curse the Fall left your people? But it's true nonetheless. Your people were always bigger, stronger, tougher than the other Races of Man, but there was no such thing as the Rage, and your lives were only a very little longer than those of humans."

"What happened?" Bahzell asked very quietly, and Wencit sighed.

"Yanahir found the cleft point for your people in something much more subtle than *sarthnasikarmanthar*, Bahzell. It wasn't something the hradahnahin *did*; it was something they *were*, and it explained their strength and size and how rapidly they recovered from injuries. Unlike humans or dwarves—or elves and half-elves, for that matter—your ancestors were directly attuned to the magic field. They were *linked* to it, drawing upon it for their strength and vitality, and it gave them a sort of harmony which showed in a calm demeanor, an almost deliberate approach to any question or problem.

"But when the Dark Lords needed shock troops, all they saw was your people's strength and toughness. You made ideal soldiers— or would have, if you'd been willing to serve them. And if they'd been able to control you. So they developed the spells to let them do just that."

A memory of ancient anguish—and, perhaps, of shame—twisted the old wizard's face, and he looked away for a long moment while tension crackled in the tunnel.

"We tried to stop them," he said finally, his voice very soft. "The White Council tried, Bahzell. I swear it. But we were too late, and the Carnadosans . . . They took *insane* chances with the art. They reached down deep inside your ancestors and they twisted and they *ripped* and they—"

He broke off, then turned to look Bahzell and Brandark squarely in the eye.

"We shielded as many of the hradahnahin as we could, but we couldn't protect enough of them. And those we couldn't protect, or who fell into Carnadosan hands as the war turned against us, were changed. The Dark Lords inflicted the Rage upon them, and at the same time, they strengthened that link to the energy field so that their slave soldiers would be even harder to kill, would recover even more quickly from their wounds so they could be thrown at the Gryphon Guard again and again. That's why your lives are longer than they were . . . and the same changes are also the reason your people became so much less fertile than humans."

He stopped speaking, and despite the sound of hooves and wagon wheels echoing in the tunnel, an odd sort of silence enveloped his listeners. Bahzell and Brandark stared at one another, stunned by what they'd just heard, and then Bahzell felt another pair of eyes upon him. He turned and met Kaeritha's dark blue gaze, saw the understanding and sympathy in it, and felt her reach out to rest one hand lightly on his shoulder. He reached up and covered it with his own hand, then looked back at Wencit.

"Well, that's worth knowing," he said, vaguely surprised by how normal his own voice sounded. "And I'm thinking it's yet another reason for my folk to not be trusting any wizards—with one exception, maybe." He grinned crookedly at Wencit and deliberately changed the subject. Or, rather, returned to an earlier one. "But you were saying as how the elves were 'created' after the First Wizard Wars?"

"Hm?" Wencit twitched his shoulders. "Oh. Yes, I was." He rubbed an eyebrow, marshaling his thoughts and obviously grateful for Bahzell's question.

"The main difference between the elves and the races which came before them," he said after a moment, "is that they *chose* to become a separate race. You see, before Ottovar imposed the Strictures, there was a group of magic-users known as warlocks or witches. The main difference between them and what we call wizards today—or, more properly, *wand* wizards—was that a warlock didn't spend years in study and didn't evolve elaborate techniques for manipulating the energy about him. His approach to the art was much more . . . basic than that, because he saw it more clearly. In a sense, he was directly linked to the energy much as your ancestors were, Bahzell, but in a different way. It didn't *sustain* him; instead, he was able to manipulate and use it much as the stoneherds use *sarthnasikarmanthar*. The effects they could achieve were far less spectacular than a *sarthnasik* could produce, but they weren't limited to stone, and they'd been very useful as a sort of magical support troops for the wizard lords Ottovar had vanquished.

"Unfortunately, it was much more difficult to police warlocks than wand wizards, which posed a problem for Ottovar and Gwynytha's Strictures. It wasn't impossible, but it wouldn't have been easy, and, frankly, the use of their abilities came too easily to them. It was highly unlikely that they could have renounced their use even if they'd wanted to, but Ottovar and Gwynytha hadn't spent centuries fighting to impose some sort of restraint on the unbridled use of the art just to see that restraint destroyed within a generation or two. So they made a bargain with the warlocks. They created a spell—according to Yanahir, it was Gwynytha's work, and it must have been an incredible feat—which changed the warlocks' talent into something very like your own people's link to the magic field. The warlocks gave up sorcery . . . and in return, they received immortality." He smiled—a wry, bitter twist of the lips. "I don't think it was a bargain I would have made. Immortality would give me too long to remember what I'd given up to get it."

"But you're already—" Vaijon blurted, then clamped his jaw shut. Wencit looked at him, then smiled more naturally.

"Immortal, Vaijon?" He laughed. "Oh, no. Wild wizards live a long, long time, but we're not immortal. And the elves truly are, you know. They can be killed, and they *do* die, but unless they're murdered or die in battle or of a disease or in an accident they truly can live forever. Not that they do. In time, even immortality can become a curse, and eventually most of them *choose* to die.

"But—" he shook himself "—that's how the elves became the fourth Race of Man. I don't suppose—" his smile became a grin "—that I have to explain where the *half*-elves came from, do I?"

"No, I'm thinking we've all a fair enough grasp of how that's after working," Bahzell assured him dryly.

"Good. As for the halflings, they're obviously a true fifth race, but I have to admit that I'm not entirely certain what constitutes their 'cleft point.' I'm inclined to think it was simply the amount of raw wizardry their ancestors were exposed to. People too close to unshielded workings of the art can be . . . changed, and the Carnadosans often ignored their responsibility to shield others from the emanations of their spells. My best guess is that the halflings are descended from the servants and slaves of dark wizards who were sloppy about shielding . . . and I'd also guess that's where the magi come from, as well."

"Um." Brandark nodded slowly, eyes half closed as he considered all he'd just learned. "That's quite a lump of information, Wencit," he said finally, "not all of it exactly pleasant. But it does explain a few things I've wondered about in the past."

"But not the Purple Lords," Kaeritha put in. The others looked at her, and she shrugged. "Half-elves breed true, and they've existed almost as long as the elves themselves. Why aren't *they* considered the fifth race instead of the halflings? And why don't any other crossings between the races breed true?"

"Actually, half-elves only 'breed true' with elves or other half-elves," Wencit told her. "I sometimes think that's one reason the Purple Lords are so arrogant. Their ancestors deliberately chose to breed a new Race of Man, but none of the others have ever acknowledged them as such. *They* certainly think they should have been known as the 'fifth Race of Man,' but if they truly constitute a race at all, it's an artificial one. If they were to interbreed with humans or dwarves, they'd quickly disappear once more."

"They would?" Kaeritha sounded surprised, and he nodded.

"Certainly. Any of the Races of Man can interbreed with any of the others, Kerry. It happens more in Norfressa than it did in Kontovar—the Empire of the Axe is proof of that—but it happened even there upon occasion. Of course, there could be problems. For example, crosses between dwarves and elves tend to be very short-lived, and the offspring of human and hradani parents are sterile. For that matter, so are the children of elvish and hradani or elvish and dwarvish parents."

"Sterile, is it?" Bahzell rumbled.

"I'm afraid so," Wencit confirmed. "And where the human-hradani crossing is concerned, it may be just as well for the rest of the Races of Man!" Bahzell glanced at him quizzically, and Wencit laughed. "If they *weren't* sterile, Bahzell, they'd probably end up ruling the world."

"What?" Brandark pricked up his ears. "And why would that happen?"

"Just for starters, they live even longer than half-elves," Wencit said dryly, "and they normally inherit the best of both their parent stocks."

"'The best'?" Kaeritha repeated.

"Well, I think so," Wencit said. "They get the strength and toughness of their hradani parent, along with the hradani link to the magic field, but some of them also get the one thing which sets humans apart from all the other Races of Man."

"Which is?" Brandark asked.

"Wizardry, Brandark," Wencit said softly. "Ever since the days of Ottovar the Great, there hasn't been a single dwarvish, elvish, or hradani wizard. Every single one of us has been human . . . or at least half-human." He smiled again, sadly. "So you see, *we're* the ones to blame for the Fall, aren't we?"

CHAPTER FIFTEEN

The Dwarvenhame Tunnel measured ten leagues east to west, and it covered that distance in an arrow-straight line. The sheer scale of it was so overwhelming that the travelers were unable to find anything against which to set it in perspective, for it was more than their senses were designed to cope with.

Every so often, however, they came up against something which *forced* them to recognize its magnitude. Like the underground river which poured out of the northern side of the tunnel, fuming and roaring in its rough, craggy bed. Lantern light struck the white-lashed black of the buried water as it boiled and leapt beneath an arched stone bridge, and Bahzell stood for several long moments peering over the bridge's balustrade and feeling the fine, fresh spray on his cheeks.

There were other springs and streams, smaller but crystal clear and icy cold, and fascinating shifts and gradations in the tunnel's walls as it pierced different stone strata. Vertical air shafts flung round circles of daylight on the smooth stone floor at intervals, and Brandark drew up under one of them and threw his head as far back as it would go to peer up at the tiny blue circle of sky at its top. He stayed that way a long time, watching light bounce down the endless stone walls of the shaft, then shook himself and refused to look up any of the others they passed.

Bahzell started to twit him for it, then stopped himself, for he knew precisely what afflicted the normally insouciant Bloody Sword. Looking up and up and up that endless gullet had driven home how many hundreds of feet of stone and earth lay above them, and Brandark Brandarkson was ill-suited to imagining himself as no more than an ant.

Fortunately, they were far from the only people to use the tunnel. The winter conditions outside it had reduced through traffic enormously, but the tunnel itself offered destinations in plenty. The architects had provided for taverns, inns, and hostels along the way, and the tunnel opened out at intervals into vast, smooth-walled caverns, their roofs supported by fluted stone columns. The first the travelers reached housed little more than a place to stop and rest—a single inn, with attached stables, a remount string for Royal and Imperial dispatch riders, and room to draw freight wagons out of the main roadway to rest draft animals. The place looked cheerful enough, but it was still too early in their day to stop for the night, so they paused only to water and feed their animals, then pressed on.

The second cavern, however, housed an entire small town, and Bahzell and Brandark paused side by side in wide-eyed wonder as they saw it.

The stone walls were honeycombed with elaborately carved and embellished doors and windows that looked out over the cavern's bustling floor from what must be homes. The roadway split to pass on either side of the large fountain that splashed and danced at the center of the cave, and cheerful music and bright light spilled from the doorways of several inns. Other doors—much wider, most with stout locks and loading docks—were obviously warehouses; the rhythmic clang of a hammer sang from a smithy where a burly dwarf hammered out a replacement horseshoe for a waiting rider; and everywhere the two hradani looked, there were people.

It took them several seconds to realize there were actually far fewer people than they'd first thought. Perhaps it was the surprise of seeing so many in one place after so long in the wilderness which made the cavern seem filled to the bursting point, but Bahzell thought not. He suspected the answer was much simpler: that he and Brandark *knew* this thriving town was buried under countless tons of solid rock . . . and that none of its inhabitants cared. Or, perhaps even more daunting (if that was the word he wanted), that those inhabitants *liked* knowing all that ponderous weight lay above them like some impenetrable shield.

A dozen or so children, mixed dwarves and humans, raced past, shrieking with laughter as they jostled and fought in some sort of game played with a large, round ball, and hucksters at "open air" stalls shouted enticements at the newcomers to sample their wares. Five or six dwarves and as many humans grunted and heaved as they unloaded crates from a high-wheeled freight wagon at one of the loading docks. They paused to glance at the travelers, then returned to the job at hand, slinging the heavy crates onto wheeled dollies for others to roll off down the aisles of the warehouse. Lanterns hung everywhere, or so it seemed, throwing a clear light over the entire scene, and a cheerful bubble and froth of conversation, hammers, the chantey-like singing of the warehouse men, of harp music from the taverns and the chaffering of shoppers picking over potatoes, garlic, and apples at the grocers' stalls, filled their ears. Nothing could have been less like the dark, hushed habitations Bahzell had imagined whenever he thought of dwarves, and he grinned suddenly at his own naivety. He'd met Kilthandah-knarthas, after all, and traveled for weeks as part of his personal bodyguard, and the mere thought of Kilthan's sturdy, loud-voiced cheerfulness in a "dark, hushed" place was ludicrous.

They found quarters for the night at the Stone Dwarf Inn, whose landlord flatly refused to allow Kaeritha and Bahzell to pay for their lodgings. Nor would he allow Wencit to pay for his . . . although Bahzell suspected that the rates he charged the *rest* of their company more than compensated for his generosity. Not that the possibility particularly bothered the hradani. The Order of Tomanāk was paying for this trip, and all the cold nights they'd spent in the wilderness since Sharnā's abortive ambush attempt had saved its coffers more than enough to square accounts.

Still, the unaccustomed ease of the day's travel left both him and Brandark with unexpended energy, and they set out to explore the cavern with Kaeritha and Vaijon for company. Kaeritha had been here before and slipped easily into the role of guide, but it was all as new to Vaijon as to the hradani, and he stared around in frank curiosity.

At first, the inhabitants of the town—which they called Tunnel's End—stared back at the two hradani with equal curiosity and an edge of nervousness to which Bahzell had become entirely too well accustomed. Aside from his ears, Brandark might almost have escaped notice, but no one could possibly overlook Bahzell Bahnak-son or mistake him for a human. He'd stripped off his poncho to show his surcoat and left his great sword and arbalest at the Stone Dwarf, yet more than one person eyed him askance anyway, and he snorted with wry, bitter humor at the familiar sight of mothers chivying children out of his path.

"D'you think they're thinking as how I'd like to eat 'em raw, or should I be cooking them first?" he asked Kaeritha, and she looked up quickly at the mingled amusement, bitterness, and resignation in his voice.

"Some of them are certainly ready to expect the worst from any hradani," she replied after a moment, "but most of them—?" She shrugged. "I'd guess it's no more than an automatic reaction to something they've never seen before. I remember how we used to feel when I was a child and armed retainers rode through our village. It didn't matter whose colors they wore, or how peaceable they were. That first sight of them always sent a bolt of terror right through you, because they had swords and we didn't, and if they'd wanted to . . ." She closed her mouth, dark blue eyes grim, then shrugged again. "It's natural enough, I suppose. Which doesn't make it any easier for you, I'm sure."

She reached up to thump his armored shoulder gently, and he smiled at her.

"Aye, well, I suppose there's a bit of something to that," he said. "And truth to tell, it's no doubt as well for parents to be prudent. Better safe than sorry, as they say, and especially where children are concerned."

"No doubt," Kaeritha agreed, then cocked her head sideways at him. "And do *you* have any children, Bahzell?"

"Me? Children?" Bahzell looked down at her in surprise, then laughed. "Not a child—and not likely to have one, either, now that himself's been and drafted me as one of his blasted champions."

"The job *does* seem to eat up your time, doesn't it?" Kaeritha said with a chuckle.

"Aye, it does that. But would you mind my asking why you wondered such?"

"Oh, I don't know. The tone of your voice when you spoke about parents and prudence just now, I suppose. I think you'd make a good father, Bahzell."

"Ha! I've seen what Mother and Father've had to deal with, Kerry my girl, and I've no mind at all, at all, to put up with such myself. And especially not daughters."

"Oh?" Kaeritha's eyes glinted challengingly. "And is there something *inferior* about daughters, Milord Champion?"

"Nothing in this wide world, Milady Champion," he replied. "It's naught but that it's always seemed to me that daughters are after being the gods' revenge on a father, y'see." Kaeritha cocked an eyebrow, and he shrugged. "He's always all a-twitter lest his little girl be meeting someone just like *he* was as a lad, and not a bit of sleep does he get thinking of it," he explained with a slow smile.

"I . . . never quite thought of it that way." Kaeritha spoke very carefully, with the air of one suppressing a bubble of laughter. She cleared her throat, then went on in a determinedly normal tone. "But you do have nieces and nephews, I suppose, don't you?"

"Oh, aye. More than I'd care to be trying to count," he assured her. "Wencit's the right of it when he says my folk're after being less fertile than humans, but we live to be as much as two hundred, so we've time for big families even so. Father's past a hundred and twenty now, and my mother only a few years younger. Between them they've brought five sons and six daughters into the world, with nine of 'em still living and me the next to youngest of the lot. Last count, I was up to ten nephews and eight nieces, but my sister Maritha and my sister-in-law Thanis were both after being in the family way again, so I've no doubt the total's gone up since."

His voice had softened, and he smiled again, this time in memory. Kaeritha returned his smile, but there was an edge of old sorrow in her eyes.

"I'm glad for you," she said quietly. "My own brother and sister—" She twitched her shoulders and raised a cupped palm, then made a pouring motion. Bahzell nodded and laid one huge hand on her shoulder as he recalled the brief, bitter history she'd recounted in Axe Hallow. She touched his hand with her own for a moment, then inhaled sharply.

"But at least Tomanāk and Kontifrio saw fit to send me to Seldan and Marja," she said. "And thanks to them, I've got at least as many brothers and sisters as you do, and a whole crop of nieces and nephews of my own. It's a good thing, isn't it? Knowing the family is there, even if you can't be with them as much as you'd like?"

"Aye, it is that. And I'm thinking it's a good thing another way, too." Kaeritha looked a question at him, and he flicked his ears at a mother who was hurrying two children out of his path. "It's knowing how I'd feel were any of mine threatened as makes me patient with people like that," he told her.

"I can see that," she said, "but it's different for me. Partly, I think, because people don't tend to think of me as a 'threat,' I suppose, but even more as a reflection of my own childhood. Because Seldan and Marja gave me a family of my own, I *know* what my mother endured when Father's death left her alone with three children. And it was knowing that that sent me to Tomanāk in the first place, to try and make a difference for some other Kaeritha and her mother."

She brooded in silence for several seconds, then shook herself and looked around, as if taking her bearings.

"Ah! Here we are," she said. "I wanted to show you this place because I know the owners. One of their sons was with a trade caravan that ran into trouble in Rustum last year. He was hurt pretty badly and hauled off to be held for ransom, but the Order caught up with the raiders. I was headed this way on another matter, so I escorted him home afterwards and met his family." She smiled. "I think you'll like them. Come on."

She led the way through an arched doorway between spotless glass shop windows that seemed to glitter and dance in the lantern light. It took Bahzell a moment to realize that the sparkling radiance came from the neat rows of gems laid out on a background of black velvet like fire-hearted stars, and his ears twitched in surprise when he did realize it, for there were no protective iron bars. Nothing lay between those jewels and any potential thief but a fragile layer of glass, which suggested the shop's owner had a far stronger faith in the goodness and honesty of his fellow men than Bahzell did.

But perhaps the shop owner wasn't quite that foolish after all, he reflected. Large as Tunnel's End seemed after so long in the wilderness, the shopkeeper probably knew all of his neighbors by name. Worse, any stranger who tried a smash-and-grab would have only two ways to run—east, or west—and the Dwarvenhame Tunnel offered no convenient side roads or places to lie hidden while the pursuit thundered by.

The shop had been designed to accommodate humans as well as dwarves, and even Vaijon found it a comfortable fit. Bahzell, of course, did not, but then he'd found very few buildings which were a 'comfortable fit' for him since leaving Navahk, and he'd become almost accustomed to it. What he had not grown accustomed to was the sudden ticking sound which surrounded him—a quiet sound, almost hushed, that still managed to be somehow thunderous in the sheer multiplicity of its sources.

Clocks. Scores of clocks, of all shapes and sizes, ticked and tocked about him. Pendulums swung, ornate hands inched around illuminated faces, biting off precise intervals, and cuckoos hovered behind closed doors, poised to burst out and proclaim the hour. Nor were clocks all that ticked, for watches lay on their own beds of velvet in glass cases, and each produced its own tiny part of the all-encompassing harmony.

Bahzell and Brandark stared at all the moving hands, then grinned at one another in delight. They'd known what clocks and watches were long before leaving their homelands, and they'd seen several of each, since, but they'd never imagined seeing so many in one place. Nor had they been prepared for the artistry which had been invested in them or for the sheer fascination of watching the intricacy of their function in action, and Bahzell chuckled as he realized every one of them was set to precisely the same time. Despite his own lack of exposure to them, he doubted that even dwarves could make this many timepieces all keep exactly the same time, and his grin grew as he pictured the proprietor running around his premises every morning resetting his inventory.

"Yes? How can I hel— *Kaeritha!*"

The deep, pleasant voice pulled Bahzell back from his thoughts, and he turned as quickly as his cramped surroundings allowed. A dwarf, shorter even than Kilthan but with the full head of hair Kilthan lacked, came bustling from someplace in the back. The newcomer stood for a moment, beaming at Kaeritha, and then hurried forward and hopped up onto a footstool to throw his arms about her.

"Kerry! By the Stone, it's wonderful to see you again! Where have you *been*, girl? And what have you been eating? Not enough, whatever it was, I see! You're thin as a rail! Haynath will skin us both if you don't come home with me for supper!"

"It's good to see you again, Uthmar," Kaeritha replied, hugging him back, "and I'd love to have supper with you—if there's time. But I'm traveling with friends, this time, and our business is fairly urgent."

"Is it, now?" Uthmar leaned back to look up at her, eyes glinting golden in the lamplight as he smiled. "So urgent that *you* want to explain to Haynath that you didn't have time to join her for even one meal? Have you gotten *that* brave since last year?"

"No, but I *have* gotten cowardly enough to hide and let *you* explain it!" she said impishly, and he laughed a deep, booming laugh. He let her turn him, still laughing, to view the others, and his laughter stopped suddenly as he saw Bahzell and Brandark.

"My word!" he gasped. He stared at them for several seconds, then hopped down from the stool and walked over to them. He stood with his hands on his hips, leaning well back to peer up at them, then walked around Bahzell in a complete circle, muttering under his breath.

Bahzell shot a glance at Kaeritha and cocked his ears in question, but she only smiled in reply and shrugged, then folded her arms and watched Uthmar patiently. The dwarf came closer to Bahzell and reached up to stroke a mail sleeve, shook his head, and made a small clucking sound.

"Axeman work," he said. "Karamon of Belhadan, wasn't it?" He darted a sharp look up at Bahzell. "I'm right, aren't I? It *is* Karamon's work, isn't it?"

"Aye, I'm thinking Karamon was his name," Bahzell agreed. "A wee short fellow, like yourself, but with hair red as fire."

"Ha! I *knew* I was right!" Uthmar crowed, and tapped his prowlike nose. "I've one of the best eyes in Dwarvenhame, if I do say it myself, and Karamon does good work. Very good work. Not but that we couldn't've done better for you, Milord!"

"No doubt," Bahzell rumbled. He looked back across at Kaeritha, eyes twinkling with amusement, and she stepped forward to rest a hand on the dwarf's shoulder.

"Bahzell Bahnakson, be known to Uthmardanharknar, the proprietor of this shop, senior partner of the firm Uthmar and Sons, and husband to Haynathshirkan're'harknar, who happens to be the senior alderwoman of Tunnel's End . . . and an *excellent* cook. Uthmar, this is Bahzell Bahnakson, Prince of Hurgrum, and the newest champion of Tomanāk, and these are our companions, Brandark Brandarkson of Navahk, and Sir Vaijon of Almerhas."

"You!" Uthmar was pointing at Bahzell with a huge grin. "You! You're the one in the *song*, aren't you?"

"I—" Bahzell began, but the dwarf was already humming, and the Horse Stealer heard choking sounds from Vaijon and Kaeritha. The two humans glanced hurriedly away, looking anywhere but at the Horse Stealer, but Brandark only cocked his head, ears pitched forward in innocent attentiveness, as he listened to the melody of *The Lay of Bahzell Bloody Hand.* The glare Bahzell shot him should have reduced him to cinders on the spot, but he returned it with the bland smile of a man in whose mouth butter would refuse to melt.

"It *is* you, isn't it?" Uthmar demanded happily at last, and Bahzell gritted his teeth. But then he made himself smile and nodded.

"Aye, in a manner of speaking. Not but what you'd not want to be believing all you hear." He shot another glance at Brandark. "Like as not the sot who wrote it all down was drunk as a lord," he added.

"Oh, I don't care about *that*," Uthmar assured him, waving one hand airily. "Heavens, it's actually a pretty silly song, don't you think?" He sniffed. "The lines of the third stanza don't scan at *all* well, and that forced rhyme in the *fifth*—!"

He rolled his eyes, and Bahzell's ears flicked straight upright. His lips twitched for an instant, and then he laughed out loud.

"Oh, aye, a *very* silly song," he agreed enthusiastically, grinning wickedly at a Brandark whose studied innocence had just become a thing of the past.

"Yes, well, but the point was," Uthmar said, "that Silver Cavern sent word you'd likely be coming this way, and Clan Harkanath specifically said you've a line of credit."

"Did they now?" Bahzell watched the dwarf cautiously. He was only slightly surprised to hear Kilthan had sent word up the tunnel that he and Brandark were on the way, for Master Kresco had promised to pass that information on to the Silver Cavern dwarves via the relays. But he *was* a little surprised Kilthan had mentioned anything about lines of credit.

"Oh, they didn't tell just anyone," Uthmar assured him, "but my *sanitharlahnahk*—" He paused and frowned. "Um, that would be my wife's sister-in-law's second cousin on her father's side the way you'd say it, I think. Is that right, Kerry?" He looked questioningly at Kaeritha, and she shrugged.

"Uthmar, you know no one but a dwarf can possibly keep your clan and family relationships straight. If you say it's your wife's sister-in-law's second cousin, then that's what it is."

"Oh dear." Uthmar frowned for another moment, then shrugged. "At any rate, my *sanitharlahnahk* is married to Kilthandahknarthas' *sanhanikmah*." He looked at Bahzell as if that should mean something to him. The Horse Stealer glanced at Kaeritha, who shrugged again—helplessly—and then looked back down at Uthmar.

"And?" he said encouragingly.

"Why, that makes us almost brothers!" Uthmar exclaimed, waving both hands in the air. "That's why he asked me to take special care of you—and your friends, of course—if you should happen to stop off in Tunnel's End."

"Take care of us, is it? And just what were you having in mind in that regard?" Bahzell asked politely.

"Well, it's plain enough you're not in need of armor. Not—" Uthmar sniffed "—that I couldn't have fixed you up with some *much* superior to old Kara— But that's neither here nor there! You've adequate armor, and I'll assume you have weapons as well?" He looked expectantly up at the towering hradani, who nodded in confirmation. "I thought so. I thought so! But I'll wager there's one thing you *don't* have, Milord Champion, and that's a first-rate watch!"

"A watch?" Bahzell blinked. "And what in Tomanāk's name would such as I be needing with a watch?"

"*Everyone* needs a good watch, Milord!" Uthmar asserted. "If you've never had one, you can't *begin* to imagine how much more efficiently it lets you organize your day! Anyone who works to a schedule needs one, and especially mariners!"

"Mariners?" Brandark's ears cocked sharply. "Why do mariners need watches?"

"For navigation, Milord—for navigation!" Uthmar shook his head.

"A seaman must know precisely the right time to take his position sightings. That requires the finest chronometer he can get, and with all due modesty, there's not a finer timepiece in all Norfressa than the ones in this shop."

He waved an arm to indicate his ticking wares, and Brandark followed the gesture with intent eyes.

"Really?" he murmured.

"Assuredly, Milord. Most assuredly. And, of course, he'll need a good sextant, as well, and it just happens that Uthmar and Sons markets the finest Crystal Water Cavern optical instruments and sextants."

"I see."

Bahzell could almost feel his companion's palms beginning to itch, and he gave the Bloody Sword a stern glance, then looked back to Uthmar.

"It's honored I am that you should be thinking of us, but I'm thinking we'll do well enough without such, and it wouldn't do for us to be spending Duke Jashân's credit for aught we don't need, so—"

"Oh, but it isn't Duke *Jashân's* credit," Uthmar broke in. "It's Kilthan's."

"I beg your pardon?"

"I said it's Kilthan's. He set up a credit line for you himself."

"Did he, now?" Bahzell murmured, and his eyes began to twinkle.

"My, my. Wasn't that *kind* of old Kilthan," Brandark said.

"Now, now, lad. Let's not go coming all over grasping. I'm thinking Kilthan had more in mind than to be turning two greedy little boys loose in a candy store."

"Then he should have said so," Brandark argued. "I mean, he *does* know us, Bahzell. Do you think for one minute he doesn't know how telling us that would affect any self-respecting hradani?"

"Aye, like as not he does—or should. But that's not so much the point as—"

"Oh, come now, Bahzell," Kaeritha interrupted. "Brandark's completely correct. Anyone who's ever met the two of you—well, him, at least!—must have known what he'd be letting himself in for."

"Anyone who met *me*?" Brandark demanded in injured tones, and she laughed.

"Unless all those books we're lugging around belong to someone else named Brandark Brandarkson!" she shot back, and Brandark made a fencing master's gesture to indicate a touch.

"Now just the both of you be holding on—" Bahzell began, only to be interrupted yet again, this time by Uthmar.

"I really could make you a *very* nice price on one of my finest watches, Milord Champion. And perhaps one for your illustrious father? And a clock for your mother?"

Bahzell paused, mouth open, then closed it with a click. As Brandark had said, he *was* a hradani, and the hradani habit of returning home from uninvited visits with odds and ends which had somehow gotten into their pockets was a strong one. Of course, it went against all tradition to actually *pay* anyone for those odds and ends, but under the circumstances . . .

His eyes strayed back to the beautifully illuminated faces of the gold- and silver-cased watches, and he felt that centuries old acquisitiveness tingling in his bones.

"You were saying as how old Kilthan set up a credit line?" Uthmar nodded. "And what sort of limit was he after putting on it?"

"He didn't," Uthmar said with a wicked little smile of his own. "I can't imagine how he came to be so forgetful. But, there—he *is* getting on a bit in years, you know. Still, he's also a kinsman. Don't you think I owe it to him to teach him not to be guilty of such oversights in the future?"

"No doubt you do, no doubt you do," Bahzell murmured. He looked back up at Kaeritha, then glanced across at Brandark and grinned. "Now, then, Uthmar," he said, "just exactly how much were you saying these watches of yours were costing?"

CHAPTER SIXTEEN

A courier from Kilthandahknarthas was waiting late the next day when Bahzell and his companions finally emerged from the tunnel into the city of Mountain Heart.

Actually, they emerged not so much into as *through* Mountain Heart, for the city burrowed for over eight miles into the base of White Horn Mountain. Despite its size, Mountain Heart was one of Dwarvenhame's younger cities, having come into existence only after work began on the tunnel. The tunnel's construction had been a joint effort of all the other cities—each of which had, for all intents and purposes, been a totally independent city-state at the time—and Mountain Heart had been intended from the beginning to serve as Dwarvenhame's interface with the Empire of the Axe. Legally, the dwarvish province had actually been a part of the Empire for a little less than a century, but its cities had been an integral part of the Empire's economy for several hundred years, and its people had realized eventual union was inevitable. Still, dwarves seldom rushed into anything, especially when it involved formal relationships with nondwarves, and so they had eased into the new affiliation, and Mountain Heart had been part of that process.

The fact that all the older cities had cooperated in its founding had also led to a degree of interclan mixing which was virtually unheard of among dwarves outside the old Royal and Imperial borders. Dwarves were the most clannish of all the Races of Man. Although few of them shared the sort of arrogant belief in their own inevitable superiority which distinguished the Purple

Lords, they did keep very much to themselves, and that held true even in dealings with their own kind. Traditionally, a dwarf's city was also his kingdom, even more independent of one another than the half-elvish city-states of the south, and most dwarvish cities were populated almost exclusively by—or certainly completely dominated by—an alliance of no more than two or three great clans. Their familial structures were so extended and so intricately defined that nondwarves might have been excused from noticing that, but the *dwarves* knew, and each of their great clans tended to evolve its own distinct, often insular personality over the centuries.

Because of the peculiar alloy of its citizens, Mountain Heart had less of that insularity. It was also closer to the rest of the Empire physically, as well as in outlook, as part of its role as a buffer for the rest of Dwarvenhame. As such, it had a sizable year-round human population and routinely welcomed a far larger seasonal influx of human labor during the winter months than did Dwarvenhame's other cities, and it showed. The travelers had encountered a substantial leavening of humans throughout their trip through the tunnel; once they reached Mountain Heart, the proportion of humans to dwarves increased radically, and, like Belhadan, the fusion of more than one Race of Man had produced a distinct impact on the city's character and architecture.

Unlike its sister cities, Mountain Heart spilled well out beyond the mountain into which it was cut. Its permanent human population was more addicted to seeing the sky, and sturdy stone houses extended for several miles in all directions from the half-dozen entryways cut into the base of the White Horn. Yet as Bahzell emerged from the tunnel and started down the ramp which led up to it, he noticed something very odd about the open-air portion of the city. The first oddity was almost instantly obvious, for Mountain Heart's outer fortifications were almost rudimentary. No doubt they were adequate for routine security, and they could probably be held for at least a short time even against a serious attack, yet they offered far too little depth to permit any long-term defense against an enemy who meant business.

But the logic behind their design was apparent once he thought about it, especially after he noticed the second oddity. The outside portion of Mountain Heart contained *only* homes, with market squares, parks, and a few shops scattered here and there among them. There were none of the workshops and warehouses which were the heart of the city's economy, for all of those—along with at least three-quarters of its population—were buried deep inside the White Horn. And unlike the light fortifications covering the aboveground portion of the city, the gates and towers and bastions, the portcullises, dry moats, and loopholed galleries protecting any of the entries to *that* part of Mountain Heart were all but impenetrable. Only a desperate man would even consider voluntarily fighting dwarves underground, and assuming anyone were mad enough to try it here, he would pay a dreadful price just to break the outer defenses. Bahzell still didn't much care for the notion of living underground himself, but there certainly were some advantages to it.

Kilthandahknarthas' courier was (inevitably) a kinsman of his, although not even Kaeritha could figure out exactly how he and the young man, who introduced himself as Tharanalalknarthas, were related. It had something to do with three marriages, a stepson, and a pair of uncles, as nearly as Bahzell could sort it out, but it didn't really matter. Dwarves were used to foreigners' inability to grasp those fine distinctions, and the term "kinsman" was considered a perfectly polite alternative.

Whatever his relationship to Kilthan, Tharanal bore a marked family likeness to his clan head, and it seemed obvious he had deliberately chosen to pattern his own personality on Kilthan's. Despite his youth, he was already beginning to lose his hair, which only heightened the resemblance, and Bahzell and Brandark quickly became comfortable with him. It was also evident that he was very much in Kilthan's confidence, and he was able to bring them speedily up to date on the latest news. Nothing important ever happened in Norfressa without Kilthandahknarthas learning of it—usually sooner rather than later—but Bahzell was still impressed by Tharanal's knowledge, especially about relations between Hurgrum and Navahk.

"They've been going steadily into the chamber pot for the last six months," Tharanal said, squinting up at the clouds as his pony trotted along beside Brandark's horse. Dwarvenhame's roads were even better than those of the rest of the Empire, and despite the cold, damp afternoon's promise of fresh snow, they were clear, at least for the moment, which allowed the travelers to make excellent time.

"In fact," Tharanal continued, turning his head to smile grimly at Bahzell, "you could almost say they started heading that way about the time you and your friend decided to go traveling, Prince Bahzell."

The two hradani glanced at one another, and their mouths tightened. It was one thing to know war between their clans was inevitable, or even to anticipate it as the only way in which their people's lot could be improved. It was something very different to hear Tharanal's blunt confirmation of their fears, and Bahzell knew both of them were thinking of the men they knew—friends and family, as well as enemies—who might soon find themselves trying to slaughter one another in battle.

"I wouldn't say your beating that bastard Harnak within an inch of his life was the main cause for it, mind you," Tharanal went on. "Torframos knows both sides've been circling long enough, looking for their chance. But you struck a spark to the tinder, and no mistake. And it cost Navahk a pretty steep price, too."

"How so?" Bahzell cocked his ears in question.

"Well, let's just say Arvahl of Sondur was already a bit uneasy. From all accounts, it had more to do with the fact that what passes for a road net among Bloody Swords makes his city a natural target for a cross-country attack from Mazgau and Gorchcan, but Arvahl decided to believe the bards' version of what happened between you and Harnak."

"Are you saying Prince Arvahl's gone over to Hurgrum?" Brandark demanded in shocked tones.

"That he has," Tharanal said with obvious relish. Then he seemed to remember he was speaking to a Navahkan, for his expression went suddenly blank and he glanced back and forth between Bahzell and his friend.

"Phrobus!" Brandark said, then shook himself and smiled crookedly at Bahzell. "I knew Arvahl didn't care much for Churnazh, but you really *did* strike a spark if he could convince his nobles and captains to back him in an alliance with Horse Stealers!"

"With all due respect, Milord, I'd say Churnazh had as much to do with it as Prince Bahzell or even Prince Bahnak," Tharanal said diffidently. Brandark cocked an ear at him, and the dwarf shrugged. "I'm a merchant, not a prince, Milord, but if I tried to run my affairs the way Churnazh runs Navahk, I'd be out of business in a month. You won't need me to tell you what a nasty customer he is, of course, but it's obvious as the nose on your face that he's no match for Bahnak—or, for that matter, that the Bloody Swords as a whole are no match for the Horse Stealers, now that Bahnak's gotten them all pulling together. I wouldn't want to bring up rats and sinking ships, but anyone willing to look the truth in the eye can see that, barring direct demonic intervention, it'll be Churnazh's head that goes up on a pike when push finally comes to shove. And if *I* were a Bloody Sword prince who didn't want my head alongside his, I'd be looking for a way out, too."

"Does that mean Churnazh's alliance is about to come apart?" Vaijon asked, frowning intently as he followed the discussion and worked to relate it to what Bahzell and Brandark had already told him.

"I wouldn't go that far," Tharanal said, shaking his head. "Arvahl is not only smart enough to see which way the wind is blowing but—if you and Lord Brandark will forgive me, Prince Bahzell— weak-livered enough to want out of the draft. Most of the other Bloody Sword princes and chieftains will stand by Churnazh, I'm afraid. Not because they *want* to, you understand, but because they're hradani."

"And would you care to be explaining that last little bit, friend Tharanal?" Bahzell demanded. The dwarf glanced at him apprehensively, but the twinkle in the Horse Stealer's eye seemed to reassure him. Some.

"I only meant that they were . . . ah, *determined*, Prince Bahzell," he said with the air of a man choosing his words carefully.

"You mean they're stubborn as blocks of granite and too bloody-minded to see another way out," Brandark corrected him with a grim smile.

"It could certainly be put that way, yes, Milord."

"But wouldn't that change if the others knew about Sh—" Vaijon began, only to cut himself off in mid-word as Kaeritha shot him a sudden glance. Tharanal's ears perked up almost visibly at the interrupted remark, and he glanced speculatively at Vaijon, but no one offered further explanation, and he was far too courteous to press. Nonetheless, Bahzell felt certain Kilthan would hear about it as soon as his younger kinsman reported.

But that was all right with him. He'd intended to bring Kilthan fully up to date on his plans—such as they were—from the outset. Kilthan was no hradani, and he had no direct dealings with the Horse Stealers, but he was a canny man who had sources and contacts in the most unlikely places. If anyone outside Hurgrum itself could give Bahzell good advice, it was certainly Kilthan, and Bahzell was only too well aware of how much advice he needed. Now he withdrew into his own thoughts, listening to Brandark shift the conversation to other topics, and frowned as he pondered what Tharanal had already said.

It contained few surprises—except for Arvahl's sudden shift in allegiance. There had been occasional instances in the past in which this or that Horse Stealer or Bloody Sword leader allied with his

traditional enemies for momentary advantage, but they were rare.
More to the point, ever since it became obvious Bahnak intended to
bring the incessant bickering and warfare between the two clan
groups to an end once and for all, there had been absolutely no sign
of any wavering among the Bloody Sword princes and clan lords. As
Brandark had succinctly if unkindly implied, hradani could persist
with unbelievable stubbornness even in actions which they *knew* were
ultimately doomed. It wasn't simple stupidity, though there were times
Bahzell found himself unable to call it by any other name, so much
as a sort of elemental intractability. On the plus side, that same stubbornness meant that once a hradani swore loyalty to someone, he
tended to honor that oath. As Bahzell himself had told Tomanāk one
cold, windy night in the Empire of the Spear, when a hradani gave
his word, it meant something, and the very fact that any hradani had
survived the Fall and the flight to Norfressa was probably due to the
same dogged refusal to yield, however impossible the odds, that kept
Churnazh's allies loyal. But it did make for messy politics, since the
only way most hradani chieftains could admit defeat was with the
point of a sword pressed firmly to their throats. That was why it had
been obvious from the outset that the only way the northern hradani
would ever be united was by force.

And now it looked as if that force was about to be employed.
Bahzell glanced at Brandark and saw an echo of his own intro-
spection in his friend's eyes even as the Bloody Sword listened
with apparent concentration to Tharanal's description of the
market in gemstones. Bahzell's faith in their friendship was absolute, yet he knew that friendship would be harshly tested when
the inevitable happened. Brandark's father and both his brothers were trapped on Churnazh's side, and so was almost everyone else he'd ever known. He himself would be greeted with a
hefty degree of suspicion by Bahzell's fellow Horse Stealers, some
of whom would regard him as a turncoat and traitor, and if he
actually found himself forced to take up arms against other
Bloody Swords—

Bahzell shook his head. One thing at a time, he reminded himself.
They had to deal with Sharnā first. That, at least, should pose no
conflict of loyalties, and the revelation that Sharnā had established
a foothold in Churnazh's domain—and, for that matter, that
Churnazh's late, unlamented heir had been a party to it—might
just bring the approaching war to a much more rapid conclusion.
If Arvahl of Sondur could change sides over Harnak's rape of a
servant girl, Churnazh's alliances were likely to start leaking like
a sieve when the full story came out. Not even hradani stubbornness

would keep his allies loyal if they believed there was even a remote possibility that he'd known about Sharnā's activities in his realm. And even some of those who decided he hadn't known were likely to switch allegiances on the basis that any prince worthy of his crown *should* have known about them . . . and dealt with them.

Bahzell hoped so. He didn't want to see his friend caught between loyalties, and deep inside, he knew he didn't want to see the sort of war this one was likely to be.

It was going to be bloody, whatever happened, and the outcome would be of intense interest to all of their neighbors, as well. Neither the Horse Stealers nor the Bloody Swords were all that numerous compared to the populations of the human-dominated lands which bordered their own, but any army of hradani had an impact out of all proportion to its mere size. Anyone who had ever had the misfortune to encounter one knew that, and Bahzell was quite certain that no one outside the hradani homelands was going to be pleased by the prospect of any one ruler bringing all of them under one banner. If Bahzell were a Sothōii or an Esganian, *he* certainly wouldn't have been happy over it.

No, this promised to be a fundamental shift in the power and politics of northern Norfressa—one whose like was seen only once or twice in generations. For good or ill, the northern hradani were about to emerge as a single, unified entity unless someone—or something—from the outside prevented it. Was that Sharnā's true purpose in Navahk? To prevent that unity and keep the clans at one another's throats forever? Or did he want the unification to succeed . . . under *Churnazh* and his heirs rather than Bahnak? And if Sharnā succeeded in insinuating his pincers deeper and deeper into a united hradani empire, what would that mean for the hradani's neighbors? Or, ultimately, for all hradani everywhere? Tomanāk knew enough people among the other Races of Man were ready enough already to remember tales of the Fall and automatically associate all hradani with the Dark Gods. If Sharnā was able to blow the embers of that distrust and fear back into a blaze, even briefly, he might just manage to provoke the outside attacks which could finally destroy Bahzell's people.

From what Bahzell knew of him, Sharnā would probably find that almost as enjoyable as exerting control through Harnak would have been. At the very least, Demon Breath would seize any opportunity to destroy Bahnak and all he stood for. That made it personal, and Bahzell felt his lips trying to curl up and bare his teeth at the thought. No doubt a champion of Tomanāk shouldn't think in such terms, but he rather doubted his deity would hold it against him just this once.

And however Tomanāk might feel, it was time and past time for Sharnā Phrofro to discover that there were easier targets—and far safer prey—than Horse Stealer hradani.

CHAPTER SEVENTEEN

"Let's take a walk, Longshanks."

Bahzell looked up from his book and quirked an eyebrow. Kilthandahknarthas dihna'Harkanath stood in the doorway of the comfortable (if low-ceilinged) room the Horse Stealer had been assigned and propped his fists impatiently upon his hips.

"Well, come along!"

"Ah?" Bahzell closed his book on the index finger of his left hand and used his right to tug at the fob dangling from his breeches pocket. He pressed the crown of the handsome—and expensive—watch attached to the fob and squinted at the golden hands sweeping about its painted ivory face. "Why, it's naught but eleven of the morning," he remarked. "Sure and you seem in a tearing rush about something, Kilthan. Are you sure it can't be waiting while I'm after finishing my chapter?"

"No, it can't," the dwarf said tartly. His topaz eyes twinkled wryly as they rested on the watch, but then he shook himself and glared at his towering guest. "And we don't have all day, you know."

"And why not?" Bahzell asked pleasantly. "From all accounts, it's snowing fit to bury a mountain whole outside. That being so, I'm not so all-fired eager as all that to be on my way, and I've naught else planned for the day except this book. And truth to tell, I've not found *it* all that enthralling."

"Good! In that case you won't mind coming with me. And I'm still waiting."

The dwarf was barely half Bahzell's height but with shoulders as broad as he was tall. He was also bald as a polished brown egg, with brilliant eyes under bushy tufts of eyebrows, and a magnificent forked beard streamed down over his belt buckle. From conversations with some of the other members of Clan Harkanath, Bahzell had discovered that Kilthan was considerably older than he'd first assumed. In fact, the clan lord merchant-prince was well into his third century, although the massive muscles characteristic of his race were only now beginning to lose the hard suppleness of his youth. Despite the difference in their heights, Bahzell would not have been eager to face Kilthandahknarthas in battle even today, much less in his prime.

But for the last century and a half Kilthan's most deadly weapons had been trade wagons, merchant ships, letters of credit, and investment funds, not battle axes. He favored plain clothing—well tailored and of good, serviceable fabric, but without the silks or velvets or the jewels or gold bullion embroidery others might choose—and he scarcely looked the part of one of Norfressa's wealthiest men. In fact, he looked more like an irascible tutor, standing there with his fists on his hips. But that was only true until you saw his eyes. Those strange, topaz eyes from which a core of burnished steel looked out upon the world.

"And what's after being so Phrobus-taken important?" The Horse Stealer demanded . . . but he also marked his place and set his book aside with the air of a small boy obeying an order to wash up for supper before things got still worse.

"We need to talk—and I want to show you something. Come on with you now!"

Kilthan turned and stumped away, and Bahzell shrugged, climbed out of his chair, patted his belt out of long habit to be certain he had his dagger, and followed him.

Someone else was waiting in the passageway, and Bahzell smiled and held out his hand to another friend. Rianthus of Sindor was a human, once a major in the Royal and Imperial Army, who had risen to command the private army which protected Clan Harkanath's merchant empire outside the Empire of the Axe, and both Bahzell and Brandark had developed a deep respect for him during their time under his orders.

"Is he always after being like this?" Bahzell asked him, jerking his head at Kilthan as the two of them followed the dwarf down the passage.

"Like what?" Rianthus replied. "You mean pushy, pompous, and a little arrogant?"

A loud snort came back from ahead of them, and Bahzell grinned.

"Aye—except that I was thinking more of a *lot* arrogant."

"Only when he's awake," Rianthus assured him.

"I might as well be 'arrogant' with you lot," Kilthan said without turning his head. "After all, there's no point wasting anything else on you, since neither of you seem to notice anyone else until they kick you in the arse."

"Are you saying we're just a mite dense?" Bahzell asked innocently.

"I'm saying I've met boulders with more brains than either of you," Kilthan told him tartly, and Bahzell laughed.

"Here now! That's no way to be talking to a man as has gone and signed on with Tomanāk!"

"Ha! I've never met a champion of Tomanāk yet who didn't need a little boy with a lantern to lead him around anywhere but on a battlefield!" Kilthan shot back, and Bahzell laughed again.

Kilthan said no more, even when the Horse Stealer deliberately gave him a few fresh openings, and Bahzell shrugged. Kilthandahknarthas of Silver Cavern was accustomed to doing things his own way, and he wasn't the sort to waste his time or anyone else's on frivolous concerns. Whatever he wanted to discuss was probably important, and Bahzell was willing to let him get to it in his own good time.

In the meanwhile, the Horse Stealer and Rianthus chatted amiably, bringing one another up to date on all that had passed since Bahzell and Brandark had left Kilthan's employ in Riverside. The hradani enjoyed the conversation—it was good to catch up on the affairs of the men who had been his companions in arms—and the walk also gave him a chance to see a bit more of Silver Cavern than he had upon his arrival yesterday.

Unlike Mountain Heart, Silver Cavern had been built exclusively by and for dwarves. With the exception of a few thousand humans like Rianthus and his men, who had become almost adoptive members of one of the great clans, *only* dwarves lived in Silver Cavern, and there were none of the surface homes which had covered the approaches to Mountain Heart.

Silver Cavern was also the better part of five hundred years older than Mountain Heart, and much larger. The original silver veins from which the city took its name had played out within two centuries of its founding, but there were other ores under the East Wall Mountains. More importantly, perhaps, there were also at least two powerful subterranean rivers, and the Silver Cavern dwarves made full use of them.

The city proper sprawled over half a dozen main levels, and an entire host of secondary and tertiary ones meandered off on their own. Bahzell was privately certain no one had the least idea where all the tunnels, passages, and chambers went, and one excavation had run into a series of immense natural caverns. The cave system ran for scores of miles, and even now, forty years after its discovery, had yet to be fully explored. Wide avenues and squares were interspersed with the large, underground villas and palaces of Silver Cavern's nobility and wealthy over the city's first two or three levels. From there, housing ran downward—both in elevation and quality—through the well-to-do to the middle-class and skilled artisans, to the poorest laborers.

Oddly enough, those laborers seemed to cherish little resentment of the wealthy compared to other places Bahzell had visited since leaving Hurgrum. Not that dwarves weren't ambitious, for very few people were *more* ambitious. No doubt there was a great deal of not-too-deeply-buried envy in the stereotype of the greedy, avaricious dwarf cherished by many members of the other Races of Man. Like most stereotypes, it was a gross exaggeration in many respects, yet a remarkable percentage of the world's wealth *did* end up in dwarvish hands somehow. By the standards of peasants in places like Navahk or the Land of the Purple Lords, even the poorest of Silver Cavern's dwarves were unbelievably rich, but they didn't compare themselves to outlanders. They compared themselves to their own wealthy, and every single one of them aspired to amass the fortune which would let *him* move to the High Quarter.

But that was the point—and, no doubt, the reason for much of their reputed avarice. They wanted to acquire wealth and the things that went with it, and they both believed they could and were completely willing to work like a lake full of beavers to attain that goal. When others talked of how dwarves were eternally on the lookout for opportunities to squeeze another kormak out of someone, they were absolutely accurate. There were exceptions, of course, as there were in all things, but the average dwarf *was* constantly working, thinking, and looking for opportunities. As a people, they didn't waste time sitting around envying others; they got on with improving their own lots, or those of their children, at least, and they had two- or three-hundred-year life spans in which to do it.

Small wonder there was a sense of bustling energy about Silver Cavern, even in the winter, Bahzell mused, and at least there was always room for upward mobility—in every sense of the word.

The underground city was liberally supplied with spiral ramps and staircases between levels, and some busier, heavily traveled sections also boasted moving cars which Kilthan called "elevators" to move people even more efficiently. Now the dwarf led Bahzell and Rianthus down one of the more secluded stairs, winding steadily deeper and deeper into the living rock of the mountains. The stairwell was on the cramped side for Bahzell, and the risers' height had been planned for people with legs much shorter than his. His calves began to complain in fairly short order, but he told them sternly to leave him alone and concentrated on following his guide. If a man two centuries older than he could make this hike, then no power in the universe could have made Bahzell Bahnakson beg for a rest break!

He kept a careful eye on his surroundings, as much to take his attention off those increasingly insistent calf muscles as anything else. Like Mountain Heart and, to a lesser extent, Tunnel's End, Silver Cavern's walls and doorways and windows were as much excuses for artwork as functional. The dwarves' passion for stone and rock crystal showed in the loving execution of leaf patterns, birds, stars and moons, tiny gargoyle faces, and clouds which adorned walls and ceilings. Door posts were carved in the shapes of tree trunks, executed with such fidelity Bahzell could identify them from their bark, and window frames were covered in traceries of climbing ivy, roses, and morning glories.

Bahzell hadn't seen it, of course, but Tharanal had pointed out the peak beyond which the city's main reservoir lay as they approached Silver Cavern yesterday, and pipes from it fed not only public buildings and private dwellings but also the fountains which danced and splashed at major intersections. The springs and freshets which had been loosed in the course of the city's excavation had also been trained, and streams ran cheerfully down rough, natural-looking beds carefully inset into the smooth floors of passages and halls. Here and there, those streams ran together into deep pools where huge, exotic goldfish and carp nudged up against stepping stones or swam their slow, endless dances under the arches of delicate bridges.

Almost certainly, though, the thing which made the uppermost levels the most desirable was their gardens. Like other dwarvish cities, Silver Cavern maintained vast, commercially run farming operations in the surface areas surrounding it. Those outside gardens produced most of the food stored away in the city's vast storerooms and icehouses, but the same natural gift for stone which had wrought the city as a whole had also produced the Upper Quarter's gardens by opening deep shafts wide enough to admit not simply air, but sunlight, as well. Those shafts drove all the way to the tallest peaks of the mountains above Silver Cavern in order to make their upper ends as inaccessible as possible from outside, and they were guarded by steel-barred grates and incorporated hatches of solid steel which could be closed at need, for they were potential chinks in the city's defenses. But they were chinks the Silver Cavern dwarves accepted cheerfully, for the mirrors which controlled and spread the light that streamed down those shafts let them bring the greenery and freshness of the outer world into their underground homeland.

Yet wonderful as Bahzell found Silver Cavern, he recognized the city's less lovely side, as well. As Tharanal had led them towards it yesterday, he'd seen thick plumes of smoke—and other, more noxious vapors—rising from outlying ventilation shafts like the fumaroles of volcanos. The acrid bite of coal smoke had caught at the back of his throat, and he'd seen the great, dark streaks of soot that discolored the snow on the downwind sides of many of those vents. He hadn't immediately recognized the purpose of the pairs of gleaming metal rails which ran down long ramps and intricately braced trestle bridges from several dark openings in the mountainside. But then he'd seen the cars, piled high with slag and ash and other refuse, that ran down those rails on flanged wheels. Gravity pulled them downward—sometimes singly, and sometimes in short trains that had been chained together—but they trailed stout cables or hawsers behind them, so that some unseen engine buried within the mountain could winch them back up and inside after they deposited their contents in one of the monstrous waste dumps at the foot of the ramps. The rails ran past what Bahzell had thought at first were steep, natural hills between the dumps and the mountain proper. But as they drew nearer and the regularity of those snow covered slopes registered, he'd realized that entire centuries of refuse had been deposited there as the rails extended further and further from the city. Apparently the dwarves had taken pains to shape and contour their garbage heaps, and the older dumps actually bore well-grown groves of trees, but those "foothills" were still an appalling comment on the sheer amount of rubbish Silver Cavern had spewed forth over the centuries.

No doubt the waste dumps, and the smoke and soot, and all the other fumes, were inevitable by-products of the dwarves' industry, but even though they seemed to make tremendous efforts to minimize the impact, he'd found the sights and smells less than appealing. Not that he hadn't seen far worse in other places, and with far smaller justification. Navahk, for example, was a cesspit compared to the damage Silver Cavern had inflicted upon its surroundings, as were parts of Riverside and other human cities he'd seen, and *that* squalor had produced nothing but disease and misery.

He shook himself out of his thoughts as Kilthan stepped off the stairs at a landing and led him and Rianthus down a side passage. There were few decorations here. Instead, these walls—some slick with condensation from the steam drifting through ventilation ducts—bore painted notices in the blocky dwarvish alphabet. Bahzell's command of written dwarvish was limited, to say the least. He could make out bits and pieces here and there, but not enough to make much sense beyond the obvious fact that most of them were directions of one sort or another. The arrows painted under some of them would have suggested that even if he'd been unable to read a single word of them.

It was much warmer down here, and the air had taken on a sharp, metallic tang that seemed to coat his sinuses and throat. And he became aware of vibrations, as if the rock itself were purring roughly, like some monstrous cat. He glanced sharply at Rianthus, but the human only smiled and flapped a hand, urging him on after Kilthan. The dwarf had paused at a bend in the corridor, looking back and beckoning impatiently, and Bahzell shrugged and trotted forward to join him—then stopped in astonishment.

Kilthan had halted on a high catwalk that snaked along the wall of a passage as wide as the Dwarvenhame Tunnel. But where the tunnel had been quiet, almost hushed, with the semisomnolence of winter's declining traffic, *this* passage rumbled and thudded and thundered. More of those steel rails were spiked to its stone floor, and powerful draft horses hauled dozens of cars along them, heaped with an indescribable welter of freight. He saw pike shafts and battle axes piled in some of them like bundles of firewood. Others seemed to be filled with shimmering fish scales until he realized what he was actually seeing was the glitter of light off the steel rings of mail, and still others were filled with shovel blades, mattock heads, axe and hammer heads, and dozens of other metal tools. Flatcars carried more of the gleaming rails, followed by gangs with sledge-hammers and drills who clearly intended to extend the rail network still further somewhere far down the tunnel. More cars rumbled the other way, loaded with what looked like coal but wasn't, and knots of workmen flowed up and down the tunnel in either direction, as if Bahzell and his friends had arrived just in time for shift change.

The hradani stood staring down at the scene, awed by it yet wondering why Kilthan had brought him to see it. But then the dwarf poked him sharply in the ribs and jerked his head for Bahzell to follow him down the catwalk. It was too noisy for casual conversation. Not even Bahzell's powerful bass could have made itself easily heard, and the hradani opted to follow without questions. Hopefully, there would be a time for those—and answers—when the background racket had fallen to more endurable levels.

They walked down the catwalk for another fifteen minutes and passed three major cross tunnels before Kilthan turned into a small alcove, pulled open a heavy door, and waved the others through it. Bahzell had to squash himself down in an awkward crouch to clear the top of the opening, but he sighed in relief as the closing door muted the noise behind them. The lighting was much dimmer than it had been outside, but only until Kilthan opened a second door and ushered him into the most amazing sight yet.

The long, gallerylike chamber beyond the double doors was built in tiers, so that the dozens of dwarves seated in it all had a clear view through the huge window which made up its outer wall. That gave Bahzell space to stand fully upright once more, which would have been relief enough by itself, but the doors also acted as a sound baffle. No doubt that was so the dwarves in the chamber could hear one another without shouting, but his ears appreciated it anyway as he looked about him.

He had no idea what most of the people around him were doing, but he saw one of them bend over one of a bank of several bronze tubes (at least they looked like bronze) before her. The young woman flipped up a cover on the tube and blew down it, then spoke in firm clear tones. It would have looked ridiculous . . . if not for the fact that another voice, this one male, came back up the tube to her, clearly audible despite the background noise that came with it.

But however bizarre that might have seemed, Bahzell had little attention to pay it, for his eyes were fixed in wonder on the view through the windows which separated the gallery from the enormous cavern beyond them. He had never seen so much glass—or such clear glass—in one place, and he reached out to touch it as if to reassure himself that it truly existed. It was actually a double window, he realized after a moment, his thought processes slowed by the scene before him, and somehow that extra window muted the noise from its other side. And a good thing, too, he thought numbly. Without that muting effect, the people in this . . . this *control room* would have been deafened, for the racket beyond the glass must be far worse than the noise which had assaulted him on the catwalk down which they had come.

A wide river, its current diverted into square-cut stone channels, poured through the chamber beyond the windows to drive dozens of the largest waterwheels Bahzell had ever seen with steady, merciless force. Complex gears and shafting reached out from the wheels, transferring their power to machinery whose function, for the most part, the hradani was unable even to guess. But impressive as the wheels were, it was the steady, shuddering roar of enormous furnaces which dominated his impression of the scene. Despite the double windows and the thick stone wall separating him from them, the harsh, basso rumble of the forced-draft furnaces reached out to him, and he felt their power grumbling in his bones. Streams of fiery, lava-like slag spilled from openings in the furnaces' sides. More of those rail carts rolled steadily up to their tops, dumping crushed ore and what looked like already-burned coal into the hoppers which fed them. Kilthan stepped up beside him.

"That's coke mixed with the ore," the dwarf said quietly. "We used to use charcoal, but then we learned how to run coal through coking ovens." He smiled wryly. "A good thing, too. You may have noticed we have a lot more coal than trees down here."

Bahzell nodded, but his attention was on a huge iron cauldron or ladle as it tracked along an overhead rail, driven by the thumping waterwheels. It was enormous—twice his own height—and he swallowed as he watched molten metal seethe within it. He stared into that liquid, incandescent heart, and then flinched, despite all he could do, as a huge, fan-shaped billow of flame and sparks erupted from another vast piece of machinery.

"We're making steel, not iron, Bahzell," Kilthan told him, still quietly. "That—" he pointed at the bright shower of fury "—is from where we're blowing a stream of air through molten iron. Without going into details, let's just say it lets us produce steel by the ton . . . and more cheaply than we could produce wrought iron, as well."

Bahzell looked down at him, and the dwarf shrugged, then waved an arm at the scene beyond the window.

"We don't show this to just anyone. Not because it's arcane and complex—in fact, most of what you see out there is actually quite simple, once you break it down by task and function—but because it's the true heart of the Empire's economic dominance. We've spent centuries working out the most efficient ways to do the jobs you see going on out there, and after so long an investment, we've no interest in sharing our techniques with people like the Purple Lords." He paused, then frowned and shook his head. "No, let's be honest. Until we joined the Empire, we had no interest in sharing them with *anyone*. They were our secrets—the *dwarves'* secrets—and the source of our wealth and power. That was the true reason we were so hesitant about using nondwarvish labor."

Bahzell blinked down at him, overwhelmed and still confused. It seemed to take an inordinately long time for him to get his voice to work, but at least he cleared his throat and asked, "Were you after bringing all this from Kontovar after the Fall?"

"No." Kilthan stood beside him and gazed out the window with him, eyes distant. "Before the Fall, most of what we do here would have been done with wizardry, or at least with devices created and powered by wizardry. We had to start over, working our way up from the most basic concepts, to what you see out there. It's harder than it was in Kontovar—or the records seem to indicate that, at any rate—and we need enormous amounts of water power. There aren't too many sites where we can have that and proximity to coal for the coking ovens *and* to iron ore and copper ore and tin. Transportation is the biggest single bottleneck of our entire operation, but when all the elements combine properly, we can actually produce more steel and bronze in less time than anyone ever managed before the Fall."

"But why be showing *me* this?" Bahzell asked.

"Because of your father," Kilthan said simply.

"Ah?" The hradani turned to look down at him, and the dwarf met his eyes levelly.

"I was honored when you told me about Sharnā's meddling in Navahk and asked my advice on dealing with it, Bahzell, but we already knew about it." He snorted at the Horse Stealer's expression. "Of course we did! Of all the Dark Gods, Torframos probably hates Sharnā worst. He's none too fond of Fiendark, either, mind you, but Demon Breath prefers to hide his corruption underground, and Stone Beard doesn't like that. Stone and earth are *His* domain, and even if they weren't, no sane person wants Sharnā anywhere near him, whatever god he serves. We don't have any more details about the late, unlamented Harnak's friends than you do, but we have enough to know we want that infection crushed, and the people who opened the door for it with it," he finished grimly.

"Well enough," Bahzell said, nodding slowly after another moment of silence. "I can be seeing that much, but you were after mentioning my father, as well."

"I was." Kilthan agreed, gazing out at the blast furnaces and water wheels. "Dwarves are patient, Bahzell," he said. "But we're good haters, too. I think both those qualities come from the stone dust in our blood. And we're also Torframos' servants, so patience or not, what we'd really prefer is to offer you a Dwarvenhame army to go in and burn Navahk to the ground. Unfortunately, we can't. We don't have proof Sharná is even there, and the only way we could get it would be to go in and dig it up by force. But we need the proof *before* we act."

"Just slow down there a mite," Bahzell interrupted. "Who exactly might this 'we' be that you're after mentioning?"

"I can't—" Kilthan began, then paused. "Let me just put it this way," he went on after a moment. "There are those both here in Dwarvenhame and back in Axe Hallow who recognize the threat Sharná's worship poses and who, under other circumstances, would possess the power to do something about that threat. But there are problems.

"First, if we were to invade Navahk, no matter what the reason, it would be seen as a foreign incursion that might well rally all the Bloody Sword cities behind Churnazh.

"Second, and to be honest, the thought of fighting hradani doesn't really appeal to us—and especially not to those of us who know hradani best.

"Third, the confrontation between Churnazh and your father has reached a stage where any outside interference could have catastrophic, unpredictable consequences. We might crush Churnazh and then withdraw, leaving a vacuum for Prince Bahnak to expand into . . . but we might also 'taint' him in the eyes of his fellow hradani as a 'tool' for outside interests. In that case, we could eliminate Churnazh only to shatter your father's alliances and set *all* the clans at one another's throats. That would be bad enough for *your* people, but if your lands turn into an ongoing, endless civil war like the one in Ferenmoss, it could spill over onto any of your neighbors, as well.

"And fourth, we don't dare make a move that even *looks* like we're taking sides between Churnazh and your father because of the Sothōii."

Bahzell had nodded slowly in time with each of Kilthan's earlier points, but now he stopped and looked at the dwarf sharply.

"And just what would the Sothōii be having to do with all this?"

"They're worried," Kilthan replied simply. "Ever since they first claimed the Wind Plain, there's been raiding and warfare between your people and them, Bahzell. Surely you know that better than I!" The hradani nodded once more, and Kilthan shrugged. "The way they see it, only the fact that you've been fighting amongst yourselves just as long has prevented it from being any worse. They were anxious enough when your father began uniting the Horse

Stealers, but the idea that he may conquer and assimilate the Bloody Swords as well frightens them—badly."

"But we've scarcely bothered them at all, at all, since the first war with Navahk!"

"Of course you haven't. You've been preoccupied with Churnazh and his allies. But once Churnazh is gone and your father rules all the northern hradani, what will he do then? Troll Garth and the Ghoul Moor would block expansion to the southeast, and moving west or southwest would bring him into collision with the Border Kingdoms, which would bring the Empire in under the terms of our treaties with them. That leaves the north and northeast . . . which would bring him right up against the Wind Plain and the Sothōii, who just happen to be his own people's bitterest traditional enemy."

"That's daft, man! Oh, raids and counter-raids are one thing, but if we were ever actually *invading* the Wind Plain, the Sothōii would call in the Axemen quick as quick, and Father knows that as well as you or I!"

"I didn't say it was a rational fear," Kilthan said patiently. "But consider this. If—and I say *if*—Prince Bahnak did attempt a full-scale invasion, what would happen to anyone in its path before the Empire could respond to any Sothōii request for aid? The fact that any invasion would eventually turn into a slaughter for our combined forces—or, for that matter, the possibility that the windriders alone might beat it back—couldn't prevent your people from inflicting enormous damage before they were stopped."

"But we've no *reason* to!"

"I know that, and most of the King-Emperor's advisers know that. The Sothōii, unfortunately, *don't* appear to know it. At the moment, King Markhos is maintaining a wait-and-see attitude and hoping for the best. He's worried by the prospect of a unified hradani kingdom on his flank, but he's got the Escarpment as a barrier if worse comes to worst. And I think he also feels there's some potential for good in the possibility. For one thing, your Iron Axes may not have been raiding the Wind Plain, but some of the other Horse Stealer clans have shown less restraint, and your father hasn't been in a position to *make* them behave. I suspect Markhos feels having a single paramount hradani lord through whom he can negotiate with *all* the clans—or threaten them all, if he has to—could help put an end to that sort of thing.

"Unfortunately, he's not the only Sothōii with an interest in what happens. His own court is divided badly enough, but the situation is even worse in the West Riding. They're the ones closest to your folk, and the ones with the longest memories of what you and they have done to one another over the centuries. Baron Tellian *seems* to be taking his cue from King Markhos, but we can't be certain of that. And whatever Tellian may do, some of his district lords and minor lords are looking to their own flanks. Our information's become more spotty since winter closed the roads, but a good many of the West Riding's younger knights seem to be at least listening to Mathian Redhelm, the Lord Warden of Glanharrow, and *he's* an anti-hradani hothead if ever there was one. All of which means that if we were to intervene openly in Navahk, for any reason, and tilt the balance suddenly in your father's favor—" The dwarf shrugged.

"You're thinking they might be seeing no option but to nip in quick and nasty, before Father's gotten his feet under him, as it were," Bahzell said quietly.

"That's certainly one possibility. And another one is that someone like Mathian of Glanharrow might decide to act on his own and end up dragging the rest of the Kingdom with him, whatever Markhos and Tellian want. On the other hand, most of us—and I'm speaking now for Dwarvenhame in particular, not the Empire as a whole—feel your father's success would be in our interest, as well as his own. Ultimately, we think it would even be in the Sothōii's interest, although we don't expect all of them to see it that way immediately. You remember the first day we met, when I said your father sounded like a man who understood the business of ruling, not just looting?"

Bahzell nodded once more, and Kilthan flicked a hand in the air.

"Well, I still think that, and a man who understands ruling, and who can teach those who'll follow him to understand it, makes a *far* better neighbor than a snakepit of warring chieftains. Not only that, but anyone who knows anything at all about Bahnak knows he would never—ever—tolerate the worship of such as Sharnā in his domain. And that being the case, we want to support him."

"But not openly," Bahzell said slowly.

"Not openly. Not at once," Kilthan agreed. "But I can make arrangements through my factor in Daranfel to slip some shipments over the border to Durghazh come spring."

"Shipments of what?" Bahzell's voice was flat, and Kilthan waved at the seething activity beyond the control room window.

"Armor. Pikes. Halberds. Axes and swords and arbalests."

"And in return?"

"In return, you and he will root out Sharnā's activities in Navahk and wherever else you may find them in your lands. He'll pay us for the weapons when and as he can, and I assure you our price will be below the current market value of our wares. In addition, once he's defeated Churnazh, he will sign binding peace treaties with his neighbors—including the Sothōii. Some people might not place much faith in his word; I do, and so do my fellows on the Dwarvenhame Council. And in return for those treaties, Dwarvenhame will undertake, by equally formal treaty, to extend the same trade relationships to him as exist between us and other citizens of the Empire."

Bahzell inhaled sharply. That was a better offer than even the Border Kingdoms enjoyed. It amounted to the ability to trade with Axeman merchants without import or export duties of any sort. Prince Bahnak would not only have access to all the wonders Bahzell had seen since leaving home but also have that access at a considerably lower price than anyone else outside the Empire!

"That's a mighty tasty carrot, Kilthan," he said finally. "Speaking for myself alone, I've no choice but to call it a very tempting offer, but I've no authority to be speaking for anyone else."

"We realize that. We also realize that at this particular moment, your duty as a champion of Tomanāk takes precedence even over your duty to your father. We have no intention of putting you in the position of trying to pick and choose between those responsibilities, and we know you can't possibly answer for your father without even speaking to him. But we also know that if we can't trust a champion of Tomanāk to deliver a message for us, there's no one we *can* trust, and that your father trusts *you*. If we approached him openly or through some other intermediary, he would almost have to be suspicious. *We* certainly would be in his place. And while we might eventually convince him of our sincerity, it would take time we're very much afraid we may not have. So I was asked to explain this to you, because you know and, I hope, trust me. All we ask of you is that you carry our offer to your father and answer any questions he may have as honestly and completely as possible."

"Um." Bahzell nodded slowly, staring out through the control room windows once more while his mind turned over what Kilthan had just said. It had come at him completely without warning, but that didn't keep it from making sense, and his thoughts flipped back over his own earlier reflections on the monumental power shift looming in his homeland. He could readily believe the fears and suspicions Kilthan had described existed—especially on the part of the Sothōii—however daft *he* might think them to be. And he could see the logic behind Kilthan's offer. If he wanted to be crudely honest about it, he might as well call it Kilthan's *bribe*, he supposed, but it could equally well be called an astute act of statesmanship. What Kilthan offered, after all, would cost him, Dwarvenhame, and the Empire as a whole very little. In fact, all of those entities would undoubtedly make money off the transactions in the long term, if not quite as much as some of them might have with the import and export duties in place. And if the arrangement could bind Bahnak and his successors' interests to the Empire . . .

"All right," he said finally. "I'll take your message, Kilthan. Mind, I can't be promising Father will accept your offer, but I'll take it to him. And—" he looked back down at the dwarf "—for myself, I'll say I hope as how he accepts it."

"Thank you," Kilthan said solemnly, and held out his hand.

CHAPTER EIGHTEEN

"Gaack! That smells *horrible!*"

Vaijon jerked his head back from the steaming cup in Bahzell's hand, and the Horse Stealer laughed. His breath went up in a dense plume, the lower part shadowed by the dense firs sheltering their campsite while the upper part was struck to pale gold by the rising sun.

"Aye, I can't be disagreeing there, lad. But I heard you groaning when you rolled out this morning."

"Well, *you'd* groan, too, if you'd never been on those Phrobus-dam—" Vaijon began spiritedly after regarding the cup with obvious distaste for several seconds, then cut himself off. "Your muscles would ache, too, if you'd never been on skis before," he finished with a sort of plaintive dignity.

"No doubt," Bahzell agreed, nobly forbearing to mention that he had not, in fact, been on skis in over three years. For that matter, it had probably been longer than that for Brandark, for there was no place to practice cross-country skiing inside Navahk, and Brandark was a city boy. Somewhat to Bahzell's initial surprise, however, Kaeritha was as graceful on skis as she was on horseback. On further consideration, he'd wondered why he was surprised. He knew little about her birth land, but the Duchy of Moretz lay almost as far north as Hurgrum. A peasant girl growing up there might very well have learned to ski. And if she hadn't learned then, she'd obviously spent a fair amount of time in the northeastern provinces of the Empire, judging from her familiarity with them, and skis were commonly employed by people in that area.

"If you'd like," Kaeritha suggested now, "you could ride in the sled, Vaijon." The youngster turned his head, prepared to shoot her a glare, but she only smiled sympathetically. "Getting back into condition is hard enough on people who already have the skills. For a beginner, using an entirely new set of muscles, it's even harder."

"I know, Milady. It's just—" Again Vaijon broke off and looked back at the cup. He sniffed gingerly and grimaced as his nose confirmed that it still smelled just as bad. "It won't kill me, will it?" he demanded suspiciously.

"That it won't," Bahzell assured him.

"I'm not sure I'd mind if it *did*," the knight-probationer admitted, then grinned crookedly. "Oh, hand it to me, Milord! I'm just trying to put off the inevitable."

He took the cup with one hand, pinched his nose ostentatiously with the other, and poured the evil-smelling brew down his throat in one long, endless swallow.

"Gods! It tastes worse than it *smells!*" He gagged. He sat there for several seconds, with the expression of a man commanding the tea to remain down through sheer force of will, then grimaced and handed the cup back to Bahzell. "You're certain your people drink this all the time, Milord?"

"What? *My* folk?" Bahzell gave a long, rumbling chuckle. "Lad, there's not a hradani born would drink something like that—" he jerked his head at the pot still steaming on their small fire "—if he was having any choice at all, at all!"

"But you said—" Vaijon began indignantly, only to be interrupted by Brandark.

"What he *said*, Vaijon, was that East Wall mountaineers, reindeer hunters, and skiers drink it to relax muscle cramps. He never said *hradani* drink it."

"I see." Vaijon gave his superior a rather grim look, but the corners of his mouth twitched, and there was the hint of a twinkle in his eyes.

"Well, I had to be getting it down you somehow," Bahzell told him. "And it worked, didn't it?"

"Remind me not to buy any horses or land from you, Milord," Vaijon replied, and pushed himself to his feet with a stifled groan. He stood for a moment, then tried an experimental deep knee bend.

"You'll need a bit longer than that for the tea to be helping," Bahzell said as he abandoned the experiment with a groan which wasn't at all stifled. "Just move about a bit. Give those muscles a chance to be loosening up while the rest of us strike camp."

"I can help," Vaijon protested.

"Don't be silly," Kaeritha said. "It's not as if you were still lazing around in your sleep sack, Vaijon! In fact, we can probably do the job faster without you, at least until you start moving better than you are now."

Vaijon grimaced, but he also nodded in agreement. He began pacing up and down in the shallower snow in the lee of the fir trees, very slowly at first, and Bahzell, Brandark, and Kaeritha went about the task of breaking camp with practiced efficiency.

They were several days south of Dwarvenhame, almost into Daranfel. Their party was much smaller, for Bahzell had left the Belhadan chapter's men in Dwarvenhame as he'd told Sir Charrow he would, and Wencit had left them to continue on across the Wind Plain on business of his own. Bahzell had been surprised by the wizard's departure, since he'd assumed Wencit intended to help deal with Sharnā, but he hadn't argued. Wencit of Rūm went where he chose, when he chose, and he knew his own business best. Besides, this was Bahzell's responsibility, and given the Strictures of Ottovar's ban on Wencit's use of wizardry on an enemy unless that enemy first used wizardry against *him*, he would have been little more than a welcome adviser.

The one thing Bahzell truly regretted about leaving the others behind was that he'd had to leave the wagons with them. He wasn't about to admit to his companions that he'd grown accustomed to all the little luxuries tucked away within those wagons—especially not when a loudly complaining Brandark had been forced to leave his precious books with Kilthan, as well—but he was willing to confess the truth to himself. They were still far better provided for than he and Brandark had been when they fled Navahk, for they'd brought one light sled along, loaded with provisions, emergency fuel and tools, one large tent, and their sleeping sacks. He and Brandark took turns towing the sled, and although Kaeritha and Vaijon had protested that they should take their turns, as well, they'd stopped objecting by the second day. Neither could begin to match a hradani's endurance—a fact they were forced to admit as they watched Bahzell and Brandark slog along with the sled for hour after hour.

They'd made only fair time by hradani standards—they could have been even further south by now if Vaijon had been an experienced skier—but Bahzell was content. They'd crossed the entire Duchy of Barandir lengthwise since leaving Silver Cavern, and they should reach Durghazh, the closest Horse Stealer city, within another week at most, even with Vaijon slowing them.

He grinned at the thought and watched the young man from the corner of his eye. Vaijon was moving more easily now, with a slightly surprised expression as the tea began to work, and Bahzell hid a snort of amusement. He'd never really considered the source of his own people's endurance and rapid healing until Wencit explained them. It was simply the way his folk were, an inevitable fact of life. In fact, he hadn't realized the other Races didn't share those advantages until he set out on his wanderings the year before, and he found himself with somewhat mixed feelings about them now. The fact that hradani owed so much of their physical toughness to the Carnadosans was scarcely a palatable thought, but he had to admit it had its positive aspects. As he and Brandark had just informed Vaijon, hradani never drank the tea he'd fed the youngster, because unlike humans, hradani almost never woke up stiff-muscled and aching. Even a few hours of rest were enough to restore them completely under all but the most severe conditions . . . which was a very helpful thing when his calves and thighs had forgotten just how demanding cross-country skis were.

He watched Kaeritha stow her rolled sleeping sack on the sled and admired the way the rising sun struck red fire on the few strands of dark hair which had escaped her braid. She made a striking picture with her shortswords at her side and her breath haloing her head in mist and her eyes intent on her task, and he felt a sudden rush of love. There was nothing romantic in it, although he certainly wasn't blind to her attractiveness. She had a severe beauty in the clear, cold morning, like an heirloom blade, and she moved with the grace of one who had trained for years in a combat technique based on speed and absolute balance, but she was in fact the sister he'd called her at their first meeting.

She looked up, as if she felt his gaze, and smiled at him, and he saw the same awareness of him in the dark blue eyes which briefly met his. Then she turned back to the task at hand, taking another sleeping sack from Brandark and stowing it beside her own. And as she and the Bloody Sword worked together, Bahzell realized something it suddenly seemed he'd always known yet never consciously considered before.

They were *all* brothers and sisters, he and Kaeritha and Brandark and Vaijon. How it had started, what had brought them together, and any difficulties some of them might have experienced along the way—he glanced at Vaijon and smiled at the thought—no longer mattered. They *belonged* here in this cold, icy morning, and the daunting task which lay before them was the proper one for them to confront, and for just that one moment, a great, golden light seemed to stream through Bahzell Bahnakson's soul. It shook him like a mighty wind, yet there was a gentleness to its fierce power, and a sense of rightness so perfect it was inevitable. In that moment, he was aware not only of how much he loved his companions but of how fragile they were. Of how fragile *all* of them were, even himself, and of how terribly it would hurt to lose any of them. He saw the stark price of love more clearly in that instant than he ever had before. Not as the chink in his armor he had once feared it might prove. No doubt an enemy *would* be quick to exploit it if there was a way to turn it against him, but that was almost inconsequential beside the other price.

The price of loss. The knowledge that, in the end, he must lose *anyone* he loved, for only elves were immortal, and even elves died. Yet it wasn't a depressing awareness, for the pain he would feel if he lost his loved ones was the other side of how much joy he took from their company. He could avoid the pain only by renouncing the joy and the trust and the knowledge that he was not alone, and building that sort of armor around his core would simply be a different sort of death.

That stabbing moment of recognition was too intense to last . . . or to forget. It shivered through him, passing like a silent storm of light, and settled into memory like some exquisite, jewel-winged insect preserved forever in amber. It would always be there, ready for him to draw it forth like a talisman against the dark, and he knew he would treasure it forever.

"Ho, Longshanks!"

He blinked and looked up just in time to see the tight roll of his own sleeping sack fly at him. His hands shot up in pure reflex, catching it just before it would have hit him in the chest, and he glowered at Brandark.

"I'm thinking it's a mite risky to be coming all over frisky so early in the morning, little man," he rumbled. "I'm not full awake yet, y'see, and I might be doing something you'd regret."

"Promises, promises!" Brandark said airily. "Besides, I'm not worried. Kerry will protect me."

"Oh no Kerry won't," Kaeritha said primly.

"You won't?" Brandark stared at her hurt-eyed, voice plaintive, and she laughed.

"No, I won't," she told him. "In fact—"

Her hand flicked, and the snowball neither Bahzell nor Brandark had seen caught the Bloody Sword squarely on the tip of his prominent nose. He squawked in surprise and stepped back, arms windmilling for balance, and then landed flat on the seat of his breeches in the snow while Kaeritha crowed with laughter.

"I see boys will be boys!" she chortled. "And let that be a lesson to you, Brandark Brandarkso—*awwk!*"

Her laughter broke off as Vaijon hit her with a snowball of his own, and then, suddenly, the air was thick with flying white spheres. Bahzell never figured out who hit *him* with the first one, and it didn't really matter. Under the circumstances, anyone made a perfectly acceptable target, and he hurled himself into the fray with a deep, rumbling laugh.

They were quite late getting back on the trail that morning.

CHAPTER NINETEEN

Hurgrum was smaller than Bahzell remembered.

He'd expected that, but even so he was surprised by how *much* smaller it seemed. It was half again the size of Navahk, and Prince Bahnak and his father had razed its worst slums and done their best to straighten out the street grid. They'd installed a rudimentary sewer system (which put Hurgrum ahead of most hradani towns, not just Navahk); imposed bloodthirsty regulations to prevent fires, discourage the construction of fresh slums, and govern the disposal of garbage; and required all new construction to be of brick or stone, not the ramshackle wooden structures which burned in winter with dreary regularity. By any hradani standard, Hurgrum was a thriving metropolis; by the standards of the lands Bahzell had seen since leaving home, it was no more than a largish provincial town. All of its citizens and all the inhabitants of the surrounding territory over which it held sway added together would scarcely have matched the population of anything worthy of being called a "city" in the Empire of the Axe.

Yet even through his surprise, Bahzell felt nothing but respect for his father. Whatever its shortcomings, Hurgrum looked like a *town*—and a civilized one—because it was. Bahzell's father and grandfather had accomplished that much, and it had been a monumental task for people so little removed from barbarism. And looking upon the fruits of their efforts, Bahzell Bahnakson had no doubt at all his father would complete the other task at which he had labored so long and bring the incessant feuds and small-scale wars of the northern hradani to an end at last.

He paused atop the hill, gazing down at the city in which he had been born, and the rest of his enlarged party halted with him. The day was almost balmy, with a temperature several degrees above freezing and the familiar wet, melting scent of an early—*very* early—northern spring. He was too accustomed to his homeland's weather to be fooled, of course. There were weeks of snow left, but not so many as there had been, and for now he savored the wind that plucked at his hair and ears like playful hands. There was a vitality in that breeze, the promise of life stirring drowsily beneath its blanket of snow, rousing to check the time and then settling back with a comfortable sigh to enjoy one last, short nap.

He glanced to his left and smiled as he watched Kaeritha push back the hood of her poncho and raise her face to the late morning sun. The honor guard which Prince Hûralk of Durghazh had assigned to see him and his companions safely to Hurgrum also watched her, and Bahzell's lips twitched as he noted the uneasiness in their eyes. Hûralk was the lord of Clan Broken Spear, but though the Broken Spears were Horse Stealers, they were considerably more "traditional" than Clan Iron Axe. They were also more xenophobic, seeing no need to waste courtesy on strangers unless there was some specific reason not to cut their throats and be done with it. Prince Bahnak had been able to quench the worst of their xenophobia, but Durghazh remained distrustful of all outsiders, and the fact that Kaeritha was not only a stranger but a woman *and* a trained warrior had been hard for Hûralk to deal with. Only the fact that she was also Bahzell's companion (and he knew some of the Broken Spears suspected—very privately; they wanted to keep their teeth—that she was a bit more than that) had won her anything like acceptance, and Hûralk's younger warriors continued to regard her as a distinctly unnatural being.

Brandark had been another source of unhappiness. By now all the northern hradani knew the tale of Bahzell's flight from Navahk and that Brandark had accompanied him for friendship's sake despite the traditional enmity between their cities and their rulers. But Brandark *was* a Bloody Sword. In fact, he was a Raven Talon, a member of Churnazh's own clan. Of course, it was well known that Churnazh had slaughtered his way to the clan leadership at the same time he'd seized the crown of Navahk, but even so Brandark's mere presence on the brink of what everyone expected to be the final war against the Bloody Swords had struck some of Hûralk's followers as a bad idea. Indeed, Hûralk had quietly suggested to Bahzell that he might, perhaps, want to leave his "friend" behind in Durghazh. He had assured Bahzell that Brandark would be treated with the utmost respect and comfortably housed, but the implication had been clear enough. Obviously Hûralk felt that, however close their friendship, Brandark's natural loyalties to his city and clan were likely to suck him into becoming a Navahkan spy if he got close enough to Bahnak's inner councils.

Bahzell had declined the offer, equally quietly, and without mentioning it to anyone else, but firmly. He was only his father's fourth son, and sixty years younger than Hûralk into the bargain, but Durghazh's prince had paled just a bit at the look in his eyes, and the offer had not been repeated. Nonetheless, Bahzell suspected their "escort" had orders to keep a particularly close eye on Brandark, and he knew the Bloody Sword suspected the same. He could tell by the exquisitely polite way in which Brandark had needled Yrothgar, the escort's commander, from the moment they left Durghazh. No doubt it was just as well that Yrothgar was an urbane sort himself—for a Broken Spear, at least—and had chosen to take it in stride, but Bahzell recognized the sharp, genuine edge in Brandark's humor. His friend would have pushed and prodded at the escort commander whoever that commander might have been, with no regard whatsoever for the consequences. It was precisely the same way he'd twisted Churnazh's nose in satiric verse before he fled Navahk, and anyone who made the mistake of thinking for one moment that he wasn't poised on a hair trigger behind his smiling facade, with one hand already halfway to his sword, would never make another mistake again.

And finally, there was Vaijon. In many ways, Hûralk seemed to have found the young knight-probationer the easiest of Bahzell's companions to swallow. He wasn't a woman, he wasn't a Bloody Sword, and thanks to his earlier experience with Bahzell, he was no longer an overdressed, arrogantly conceited popinjay, either. Unfortunately, he *was* a knight of Tomanāk. Kaeritha was too, of course, but in her case the fact that she was a woman warrior constituted such a shocking breach of traditional proprieties that her membership in a militant religious order was little more than an afterthought. Where Vaijon was concerned, however, that membership loomed up in the foreground, more important even than the fact that he was a human in an area in which humans were virtually never seen except on the backs of Sothōii war horses and coursers.

Like Bahzell's own clan, the Broken Spears had little use for any gods, whether of the Light or Dark. They might fear, hate, and despise the Dark Gods, but they placed no particular trust in those of the Light, either. After all, *no* gods had done them any favors over the last twelve hundred years, and virtually any hradani would have hooted with laughter at the very thought that any deity might choose to do one for them now.

The fact that Bahzell had sworn Sword Oath to Tomanāk was bad enough, but at least he was hradani. Presumably he'd looked before he leapt, and even if he hadn't, his common sense would probably come to his rescue before he did anything *too* foolish in the name of religion. But how could anyone trust a human to show the same restraint? Especially one as young as Vaijon? There was no way to predict how someone with his brain softened by religion might react under the wrong circumstances, and so despite the fact that they rather liked him, Hûralk's guards kept a wary eye on *him*, as well.

In fact, Bahzell thought with a snort of inner laughter, the escort had been so busy "keeping an eye" on his companions that none of them had had any time left over to pass more than a handful of words with *him* during the entire journey. But that journey was almost over now, and he felt his spirits rise with every step as he churned back into motion through the muddy, slushy snow.

"Hmpf! Took you long enough to be making it home, didn't it just? And not a letter did your mother and I have in all that time, either! Can you be giving me one good reason I shouldn't be coming down off this throne to kick your hairy backside for you?"

Bahnak Karathson, Prince of Hurgrum and Lord of Clan Iron Axe of the Horse Stealer hradani, had a voice even deeper than his son's. He was three inches shorter than Bahzell, but his words rumbled up out of an enormous chest, and his mobile ears pressed close to his gray-streaked hair as he glowered down at his offspring from the dais on which his throne sat. Bahzell and his companions stood in the Great Hall of Bahnak's palace. The Great Hall would have been appropriate enough as a town hall in most cities of the Empire, but few of those would have been illuminated with the traditional, barbaric spill of torchlight or had such huge, heavily armed guardsmen lounging against the walls and grinning as they watched their prince greet his wandering son's return.

"Not a reason in the world," Bahzell admitted cheerfully. Then he paused and cocked his head thoughtfully. "Other than to be pointing out my hairy backside is wearing armor as might be a bit hard on your toe, that is."

"Oh, might it, now?" Bahnak glared, but the corner of his mouth twitched. "And while we're speaking of armor, could you be so very kind as to be telling me what you think you're doing in *those* colors? It was bad enough to hear as how you'd been after fooling about with wizards—even a 'white' one!—but it was in my mind that I'd at least taught you better than to be mixing in the business of gods and demons and such!"

"Aye, you did that," Bahzell agreed. "But what's a man to do when a god decides as how he wants him? I tried not listening, and that didn't work. Then I tried outrunning him, and *that* didn't work. And in the end, a demon tried to eat me and then himself was after turning up in the flesh to bid me join up, as it were, and not a bit of good at all did it do to be telling him no then. Besides, I'd asked his aid, and he'd given it, so what else was I to do?"

"Hmpf! Not much, I suppose, if you'd asked such of him in the first place," his father growled. "And now I think on it, no one as knew you's ever said you were smart, now have they?" Bahzell grinned as Brandark smothered a laugh behind him. "And stupid or no, I'm thinking the color becomes you," Bahnak went on with a slow smile of his own. "Contrasts with your eyes, it does."

"Thank you, Father," Bahzell said with exquisite politeness. "It's pleased I am that you approve."

"I'll not go quite that far—not yet," Bahnak replied, and the hint of steel in the words promised that he meant it. "And Krashnark only knows how it's likely to affect the war. But it's more important that you're after being home, I suppose."

He spoke grudgingly, but even as he did he rose from his carved wooden throne and came down the three steps to the floor of the Great Hall to throw his arms about his son. He hugged him fiercely, hard enough to break the back of any lesser man, and his eyes glowed. Bahzell returned his embrace for endless seconds, and then Bahnak clapped him on the back once with both hands and stepped back.

"Well!" he said, his voice just the slightest bit husky, "your mother's wishful to see you too, and you've some brothers and sisters and nieces and nephews somewhere about the place, as well. We've a deal to talk over, you and I," he went on, letting his eyes move briefly over Brandark, Kaeritha, and Vaijon, "but no doubt we'll get to that in time, and I'm not so brave as to be putting matters of state in front of your mother's orders. So come along— you and your friends—" he added, gathering up Bahzell's unlikely companions with a sweep of his hand, "and let's be getting all the hugging and sniffling over with first."

CHAPTER TWENTY

"So that's the way of it, hey?"

A huge fire crackled on the immense hearth at one end of the drafty dining room as Prince Bahnak leaned back in his chair at the head of the table. There had been a time when Bahzell would have noticed neither the drafts nor the thin wisps of smoke which escaped the chimney to add their tiny contributions to the soot blackening the overhead beams, but he'd met rather more efficient means of heating since then. Not that such small considerations as cold fingers and toes or a little smoke mattered in the least beside the opportunity to see his father once again raising an enormous tankard of ale to gaze thoughtfully at him over the rim.

Bahzell's oldest brother, Barodahn, sat to Bahnak's left, facing Bahzell across the table. Barodahn was a bare half-inch shorter than Bahzell and twenty-five years older. Despite the difference in their ages, they had always been close, but Barodahn was a taciturn sort. Although he shared their father's aspirations to drag their people out of barbarism and had always taken greater pleasure than Bahzell in scholarly pursuits, he was far more like the Horse Stealer ideal, outwardly at least. A long-ago sword had left him with a scarred, grim-looking visage, and he had to feel very close to someone before he decided to open his mouth. Even then, he seldom used two words if one would suffice, but he was their father's senior field commander, and when he gave an order, the hardiest warrior jumped to obey. Bahzell's other brothers were absent—carrying their father's instructions to some of his allies, no doubt—and three of his sisters sat with his mother (much closer to the fire) chatting with his companions.

His mother had her embroidery frame before her, taking advantage of the light to set beautiful stitches, and warm memories flowed over Bahzell as he watched her skillful hands. His grandfather, Prince Karath, had been appalled when his heir chose Arthanal Farlachsdaughter as his bride. She was a Horse Stealer, true, and a first cousin of the Prince of Mazgau, but Clan Iron Axe and her own War Hammer Clan were scarcely friends, and she was a slender, delicate young woman (for a hradani). Karath and his own wife had produced only three children in an eighty-six-year marriage, and he'd nursed serious doubts over how many grandchildren a frail young thing like Arthanal could be expected to bear.

Worse, she had a reputation as a shy girl who was actually *bookish*—not exactly the sort of consort who would be a political asset to a ruling prince's efforts to unite a warrior people. Karath had done his utmost to prevent such a clearly unsuitable union, but for the first time in Karath's memory, his son's intransigence had matched his own. Bahnak had been attentive, polite, and willing to admit at least some of his father's points; he'd also been as unyielding as granite, and, against his better judgment, Karath had accepted that an estrangement from his heir would be even more disastrous than a sickly War Hammer daughter-in-law.

But Prince Bahnak's lady had made liars of her father-in-law's fears. True, she chose to remain in the background, but her apparent shyness actually stemmed from a calm self-assurance which knew her strengths lay in less public areas and saw no need to thrust herself forward. She was an astute observer and analyst, and if she was "bookish," it was only because she shared the same thirst for learning that filled Bahnak, although in her case it was the love of knowledge for its own sake while Bahnak hungered for it as the one thing which could raise his people from barbarism. Despite his initial reservations, Prince Karath soon found himself listening very carefully to her advice, and however fragile she might *look*, she was far, far from frail. The arrival of his first sturdy, *noisy* grandson put that particular concern to rest quite nicely, and the way the marriage also turned her War Hammer kinsmen from enemies into allies also dawned quickly on him. The old man was never noted for changing his mind easily, but Arthanal was a special case. He soon came to dote upon her, and his son's willingness to defy his own wishes to wed such a treasure only strengthened his faith in Bahnak's judgment.

Even today, few people realized how heavily Bahnak depended upon her. She was not only his collaborator, analyst, and closest strategic adviser, but also his balance wheel, the steadying influence which helped restrain his occasional bursts of excessive enthusiasm for a given project or stratagem, as well as the center about which his entire family orbited. And if she still chose to remain in the background, she had encouraged her daughters to follow their hearts and make their own decisions. Halah and Adalah, the youngest of them, were made very much in her mold, but Marglyth and Maritha, the two older girls, had thrown themselves into Bahnak's projects as boldly as any of her sons.

Sharkah, Bahzell's middle sister, was the odd one out, for she had no taste for politics and less for scholarship. What she *was* interested in was the martial arts, and she'd fastened on Kaeritha like a limpet. Bahzell had little doubt Kaeritha's example was going to be the final straw that broke the back of his father's insistence that political considerations made it impossible for Sharkah to pursue a warrior's vocation. Not that his insistence wouldn't have crumpled eventually, given his wife's calm assumption that her daughter—as herself—would do whatever she chose to do.

At the moment, Marglyth and Maritha were elsewhere—no doubt, Bahzell thought, analyzing the initial response to his own return—but Sharkah, Halah, and Adalah helped Arthanal entertain his friends while he and his father talked and Barodahn listened.

"We'd Farmah's and Tala's word for the first bit of your . . . um, *disagreement* with Harnak, of course," Bahnak went on, flicking his ears to where the girl Bahzell had rescued from Harnak sat with Sharkah, talking very shyly to Vaijon while Bahzell's sister chattered nonstop at Kaeritha, "and we've heard the song for the rest."

"Song?" Bahzell let his own tankard clunk back onto the table and looked at his father suspiciously. "And what song would that have been?"

"I think they're after calling it *The Lay of Bahzell Bloody-Hand* or some such foolishness," his father said, with a glance at Barodahn for confirmation. Bahzell's brother nodded, and Bahnak looked back at him. "Why? I thought it a bit pompous, myself, and the third verse doesn't scan at all, but it's not so bad a song as all that. In fact, most folk seem to find it a bit catchy. I can have old Thorfa sing it for you if you've not heard it," he offered.

He started to raise his hand to catch his court bard's eye, but Bahzell caught his wrist with a bit more haste than courtesy, and he looked at his son in surprise.

"It's a kindly thought, Da," Bahzell said through gritted teeth, "but I'm thinking I *have* heard the one you mean a time or two. And if it's all the same to you, I'd sooner not be hearing it again just now. It might seem a bit prideful, you know."

"Well, as you will," Bahnak agreed, sitting back once more, and Bahzell's teeth ground harder as he saw the faintest twinkle in the backs of his father's eyes. It was all he could do not to turn and glare at Brandark, but the gesture might be misconstrued by one of Prince Bahnak's guards, with potentially lethal consequences for the Bloody Sword. Not, Bahzell thought darkly, that lethal consequences for Brandark didn't hold a certain wistful attraction just at the moment.

"Mother likes it," Barodahn offered suddenly.

"Aye, she does that," Bahnak confirmed, and this time the twinkle was pronounced. "You should see her coming all misty-eyed with pride whenever Thorfa's after playing it." His ears flicked impishly, and, despite himself, Bahzell chuckled. "Would your friend yonder have been having anything to do with it?" Bahnak inquired, gesturing slightly in Brandark's direction, and Bahzell sighed.

"Aye. The little man's no singing voice at all, at all, but he's a damnable hand for setting songs you'd sooner see die an early death to tunes no one can forget."

"And a bit of a wit to him, too, I'd say," Bahnak agreed. He stretched out his legs, crossed his ankles, and regarded his son from under thoughtful brows. "I'll tell you true, boy. I was none too pleased to be hearing as how one of my sons had been after taking up with a Bloody Sword. Come to that, I was even less pleased when the first tales of you and Harnak started coming in. I hadn't thought you totally daft when I sent you to Navahk, but damned I was if I could be seeing any other answer for your mixing in the whole affair. She was naught but a serving wench, when all was said, and there you were, throwing over your hostage bond and like to be after starting the war all over again before I'd had time to make all ready for it—and losing your head into the bargain! Oh, aye, boy. I was ready enough to skin you out and salt you down my own self, if it so chanced Churnazh missed you . . . until Farmah and Tala reached Hurgrum with the true tale."

He fell silent, left hand playing with the golden chain he wore to mark his rank while his right held his tankard. He took another long, slow swallow, then shook his head.

"But once I'd had time to be looking it over from all angles, as it were, it came to me that you'd done well, lad," he said very quietly. "Not too smartly, perhaps, but you made me proud you were after being my son."

Bahzell met his father's gaze steadily, but his eyes burned. Those two sentences meant more to him than all the other praise of a lifetime, and he knew his father and brother saw it in his face, for they looked away and gave him time to compose himself.

"Well," he said finally, "I did remember as how you'd always said a man looks after his own in this world, and lucky he is if he can do it. I'd not thought it through then, but it came to me that perhaps 'his own' was after taking in just a bit more people than I'd first supposed you meant."

"It was that," Bahnak agreed with a slow smile, "but it's not so very wise to be letting those as wish you ill realize that it does, now is it?"

"No. No, I can be seeing that, especially for someone as sits on a throne—or likely will one day," Bahzell added with a glance at Barodahn.

"Aye." His father sipped more ale, and his eyes were somber when he lowered the tankard once more. He set it very precisely on the table and propped his right elbow on the arm of his chair while he leaned his chin into his palm. His ears shifted in slow thought, and he frowned.

"Truth to tell, Bahzell, and glad as I am to be having Farmah as another daughter, it's the other part of Harnak's doings as makes me most uneasy. Is it certain you are of your facts, lad? It's not that I'm inclined to be doubtful of your word, but I'd not want to be making charges as later turn out false. That's one way to be losing the faith of your own allies and warriors quick as quick, and it's a mistake I've so far managed not to make. I'd sooner not be starting now."

"Aye, Father. I'm certain," Bahzell said heavily. "I saw the Scorpion with my own two eyes when Harnak and I were blade-to-blade, and I heard its scream as he died." His voice was harsh, and his father and brother shuddered at whatever they saw in his eyes. "Even if I'd not seen it then, I'd've known later," he went on after a moment. "There's sides to being a champion of Tomanāk as are hard to put into words, but since I took Sword Oath to himself I've . . . *sensed* things, I suppose, as I'd never've guessed were there to be sensed before, and I had the handling of Harnak's sword after his death." This time it was *Bahzell* who shuddered, and he closed his eyes briefly.

"Sharnā's there, Father. Whether Churnazh is after knowing he is—that's another matter. But Demon Breath's there, right enough . . . and though I'm too far from it to be certain of it just this minute, I've more than a suspicion that once I've come close enough to his lair, I'll scent it like a hound on a blood trail. There's a stink to Sharnā's work as no one could mistake who's ever smelled it."

"I'll not lie to you, Bahzell," Bahnak said after another long, thoughtful moment. "All this talk of gods and demons and wizards and such—it's enough to make a man come all over bilious." He spoke almost lightly, but his tone fooled neither of his sons. "I've a war to fight—the biggest of my life, or of any of ours—and not a one at all of any of my plans considered such as that. If I had my own way in it, I'd be closing my eyes and ears and letting Light and Dark see to their own coils while *I* got on with the taking of Churnazh's head once and for all. But—"

He sighed, then shrugged and looked wryly at his youngest son.

"You do have a way with you, don't you just, Bahzell?" He chuckled. "I remember the first day you ever discovered a river, and the muddy, soaked-rat mess of you when Barodahn fetched you up off the bottom. I was set to take the hide right off you for the fright you'd given your mother—aye, and me, too! And do you know why I didn't?"

"No," Bahzell said. "My memory's not so clear as all that. I know I'd *expected* you to thrash me within an inch of my life. Aye, and it was in my mind I had it coming, as well. But aside from that—?" He shrugged and raised his own tankard.

"The reason I didn't thrash you was that you looked me right in the eye, and you said, 'I'd not've fallen in if you'd've told me it was there, Da. And I'd not've sunk if you'd've taught me how to swim. And I'll have you know I'd almost figured it out for my own self when Barry fetched me out, so if you'll just be getting on with the thrashing, I'd like to go back and try again.'"

Bahnak shook his head with a chuckle, and Bahzell choked on ale as his father's words brought the entire scene back to him. He sputtered for several seconds while Bahnak pounded him helpfully on the back, then shook his finger at his father.

"Aye, I *do* remember, now that you've recalled it to me. And damned if you didn't take me right back down and throw me in all over again!"

"Well, it was what you'd asked for," Bahnak said with a slow grin. "And you'd been almost right, you know. You *were* starting to catch the knack of it. We only had to be fishing you out three or four more times, and I don't suppose you'd swallowed more than half the river before you managed to stay on *top* of the water for a change."

"Oh, I'd think he'd drunk a bit more than half, Da," Barodahn put in in the melodious tenor that always sounded so odd from one of Bahnak's mountainous sons.

"Aye?" Bahnak cocked his head thoughtfully, then shrugged. "Well, perhaps you've the right of it, son. But the point, Bahzell—" he looked back at his younger son and his eyes narrowed "—is that though you've always had a way of leaping into the deep end of anything that comes your way, more often than not you've your priorities straight before you do. I'll not say you've reasoned them out, exactly, and it may be those of us watching from the bank don't *know* you have them straight, but in the end you're after coming out on top of the water, not blowing bubbles from the riverbed."

He reached forward to recover his tankard, then leaned back in his chair once more, eyes still on his son.

"I've never met a demon, or a wizard, or a god," he said quietly, "and I'm not wishful to. But you *have* met 'em, and for all I may twit you, and for all you're still not so old as all that for one of our folk, I've a lively faith in your judgment in most things. It cuts against the grain to be having aught to do with such unchancy things, but if Tomanāk is after being a good enough captain for you to be swearing loyalty to, then that's good enough for me. And if you—and your friends—" a nod of his head indicated Vaijon, Brandark, and Kaeritha "—are having business with Sharnā in Churnazh's back pasture, well, maybe there are some things important enough to be risking my own plans over."

"Then you'll not stand in our way?"

"Stand in your way? No, I'll not do that. And I've no doubt at all, at all, that you'll be finding quite a few of the younger lads ready enough to be going with you."

"Hurthang, for one," Barodahn said. Bahnak glanced at him, then nodded.

"Aye, he's one," the prince allowed, and twitched his ears at the far end of the table. "He's asked for Farmah's hand, for all she's more than a bit young for that yet, and she's accepted," he explained to Bahzell. "And since you were after being so hasty as to take Harnak's head before Hurthang could see to taking his privates with a dull blade, I've no doubt he'll be expecting you to be letting him have some of Sharnā's other scum for forfeit. And I'd think Gharnal would be another, being as how it'll offer a chance to be killing Bloody Swords. But they'll not be alone, and *I'll* not be trying to stop them, either." He grinned suddenly. "Come to that, I might just egg 'em on a bit. It wouldn't hurt a thing for your friend Kilthan to be knowing as I did, now would it? And truth to tell, whatever I may think of the 'good' gods, I'm not so feeble-witted yet that I'll stomach such as Sharnā."

"I'd thought you'd see it that way, Da," Bahzell said, "but it's a weight off my mind to hear you say it, and it's grateful I am."

"Ah, don't be thanking me!" Bahnak waved his left hand. "I've nasty, selfish motives of my own. Besides, it's naught but the river all over. Say what I will, you'll be going, for you've always been that way. And these days I've no right to be telling you nay, for you're a man grown, and you've sworn your sword to another's service."

A flicker of hurt leapt into Bahzell's eyes, but his father shook his head quickly.

"No, lad," he said gently, reaching out to squeeze his son's shoulder. "I meant no complaint, and I know your heart will be here with us, always. But you've taken on a man's duties, and if the choice you made might not have been mine, why, I wasn't there, and you were. You'll always be my son, and you'll always have my love, and my sword will always be here to help and guard you at need. But *your* sword is Tomanāk's to command now, not mine, and I know it."

"Thank you for understanding that, Father," Bahzell said very quietly. "Thank you very much."

"Hmpf!" Bahnak snorted, then leaned back once more and grinned at both his sons as he raised his tankard in lazy salute to his youngest. "I was young once myself, boy! Or were you thinking a man as wasn't soft-headed with youth, or feeble-witted, or crazy, or maybe a bit of all three, would be daft enough to take on the chore of uniting *hradani?*"

CHAPTER TWENTY-ONE

Pipe smoke hung heavy among the overhead beams as Bahzell, Kaeritha, and Vaijon leaned over the map of Navahk. It wasn't as good as the ones Prince Bahnak had ordered made of his own lands and those of his allies, since Prince Churnazh would have taken the presence of Horse Stealer survey crews unkindly. But it was better than the vast majority of maps the Navahkans themselves might possess, and Brandark had smiled with pleasure when he saw it. Now he sat opposite Bahzell and Kaeritha, flanked by Gharnal and Hurthang, most senior of the young warriors who'd chosen to join Bahzell's effort to deal with Sharna's contamination. Another fifty-two Horse Stealers crowded around the table, peering over shoulders while they nursed carved pipes and foamy mugs of ale.

They'd been joined by a single hradani woman: Bahzell's sister, Marglyth, who sat beside Kaeritha. Eleven inches shorter than Bahzell, Marglyth bore a strong resemblance to her mother, with the same slender gracefulness. Only a year younger than Barodahn, she had a husband and twin sons of her own, the younger named for his Uncle Bahzell . . . none of which prevented her from serving as Prince Bahnak's Chief Justiciar.

Vaijon had seemed surprised that Hurgrum's senior magistrate was a woman, but only because he still failed to understand how deeply the Rage had cut into hradani souls. Even in Hurgrum, no woman could hold a crown in her own right among a warrior people whose ruler, by tradition, must be prepared to meet challengers personally. That didn't mean they couldn't exercise powerful authority in other ways, however, and most hradani judges and diplomats were women for the simple reason that their immunity to the Rage meant it could not affect their judgments.

What was unusual about Hurgrum, however, was that women comprised half the members of the Prince's Council. Most hradani rulers had at least one or two women on their councils, and any clan lord (as distinct from princes) *always* listened with enormous respect to the advice of his clan's matriarch. But Bahnak's decision to make ten of his twenty-one privy councilors women was yet another unheard of innovation . . . and yet another which had paid powerful dividends. In fact, Marglyth was not only his Chief Justiciar but his First Councilor, and he relied on her political advice almost as heavily as he did on her mother's—or as he relied on Barodahn's advice in military matters. One of Bahnak's greatest strengths was that he had sufficient confidence in himself to take advantage of the advice of others, and his children had been trained to think for themselves just as he did.

In this case, however, Marglyth was present because, in addition to her councilor's and judicial duties, she also headed Hurgrum's espionage service. As such, she probably knew more about events in Churnazh's court even than Brandark.

The huge map room in which they had met had been designed as a place for Bahnak and his senior officers to confer while planning strategy, which meant it had been built to scale for Horse Stealers and had been intended to house fairly large numbers of them, but it still seemed unreasonably packed. On the other hand, few of the people in it cared very much. This was the first time all of them had been gathered in one spot, and, as a security measure, Bahzell had refused to brief anyone until all were assembled. It wasn't that he was especially distrustful of anyone in his father's court, but Sharnā was the patron of assassins and deceit as well as demons, and his minions' ability to ferret out secrets was renowned. But the volunteers were all here now, and every eye was intent as Brandark tapped the map with the tip of a dagger.

"There," he said, using the dagger to trace a rough triangle in the heavily wooded hills southwest of Navahk. "This section down here—right on the border with Arthnar. I've never been near the area myself, but this is the general direction the rumors say Harnak liked to 'go hunting' in."

"Hunting, hey?" Gharnal rumbled. He gazed at the map, then raised his eyes to Bahzell. "I can't say as how rumors about hunting trips fill me with confidence, Bahzell."

"Can't you, then?" Bahzell sat back, propping his crossed forearms on the table before him, and looked at Gharnal thoughtfully. Gharnal Uthmâgson was his and Marglyth's foster brother, and the three of them had been the closest of friends from childhood. Unlike Hurthang, who was his fourth cousin, Gharnal was about as distantly related to Bahzell (by blood) as a man could be and remain a member of the same clan, but he'd been raised as Bahnak's son after his own father was killed in a border clash with Navahk. At barely six feet ten, he was short for a Horse Stealer, but he compensated with a barrel-like chest and enormous shoulders and arms, and he'd distinguished himself in Hurgrum's last war against the Bloody Swords. Unfortunately, one reason he'd done so was the Rage-like passion of his hatred for Bloody Swords in general and Talon Claws in particular, and Bahzell knew he'd managed to tolerate Brandark's presence with a sheathed sword—so far—only because the Navahkan was Bahzell's sword brother.

"No, I can't," Gharnal replied without so much as a glance at Brandark. "We're after speaking of sending nigh on three-score warriors into Bloody Sword territory in the middle of winter. Aye, and when we're still officially at peace with the bast—scum!" He glanced at Marglyth and Kaeritha and hastily substituted another word for the one he'd started to use, but then he went on with undiminished forcefulness. "If it's all the same to you, I'm wishful to be having something just a mite more certain than rumors of *hunting trips* to guide 'em by when we do."

Brandark started to speak but closed his mouth when Bahzell stepped on his toe under the table. The Bloody Sword had exhibited unusually diplomatic behavior during the six days it had taken for Bahnak to pass the word that Bahzell needed volunteers and for those volunteers to assemble. It didn't come naturally to him, and he'd managed it only because the iron rules of hradani hospitality cut both ways. Just as Gharnal could not offer him open discourtesy while he was Bahzell's guest, so it was incumbent upon Brandark to refrain from provoking his hosts by openly insulting *them*. But that was more easily said than done, and Bahzell knew his friend's temper was growing dangerously short. He opened his own mouth, but Hurthang spoke before he could.

"Hisht, now, Gharnal!" At a mere seven-two, Hurthang was, if possible, even stronger than Bahzell. His weapon of choice was a battleaxe: a two-hand, daggered great-axe, the weapon from which Clan Iron Axe had taken its name centuries ago. Similar to the dwarvish axes still used by the Royal and Imperial Army's elite Brothers of the Axe, Hurthang carried it slung across his back even now. But whereas the Axe Brothers used it two-handed, Hurthang used it with one, and he could do things with it which no dwarf had ever even dreamed of.

Now he looked at Gharnal with a crooked smile and shook his head. If his voice was less deep and rumbling than Gharnal's it was still stronger and more resonant than any human voice, and he had at least as much reason to hate Navahk as Gharnal did. He hadn't lost a father, but he *had* lost two brothers . . . which didn't even mention what Harnak had done to Farmah. In some lands, Farmah would have been considered forever soiled, as if what Harnak had done were somehow *her* fault. Hradani didn't see things that way, but they did believe in justice and vengeance, and Hurthang wanted those things for his betrothed. He wanted them badly, and with Harnak dead, the only place he could get them was from Harnak's kin. That was the reason he'd hurried to answer Bahzell's call, and everyone knew it. Which meant that when *he* was prepared to accept that there were other, equally important considerations, even Gharnal had to listen. He was also four years older than Bahzell and one of Barodahn's junior captains, with an easy air of authority. And he *wasn't* Gharnal's foster brother. However much Gharnal might accept Bahzell's authority, that childhood relationship colored their thoughts and reactions. That meant that in many ways Hurthang could speak much more pointedly to Gharnal than Bahzell or Marglyth without raising the specter of injured feelings and potential friction.

"Unless you've some better clue to guide us," he went on, "then I'm thinking you should be keeping your mouth shut—or busy with an ale mug!—till we've had the hearing of whatever it is Brandark here has to say."

The grin which accompanied his words defused their sting, helped by the rumbling chuckles from the men standing around the table. For an instant it looked as if Gharnal might take umbrage anyway, but then he shook his head with an unwilling chuckle of his own. He still didn't look at Brandark, but he flicked his ears in assent.

"Aye, you've the right of it," he told Hurthang, and glanced at Bahzell. "I'll just be taking Hurthang's advice," he said in oblique apology, reaching for his mug, and Bahzell nodded back, then made a small gesture for Brandark to continue.

"As I say," the Bloody Sword began afresh, tapping the map once more and speaking—almost—as if no one had interrupted, "this is one area where the rumors say Harnak liked to hunt. But he never took any other members of Churnazh's court—except for

Lord Yarthag, who's as sick a bastard as ever Harnak was—with him. And unlike the other areas in which he sometimes hunted, he *did* take a picked group of his own guard with him. They were always the same ones, and every one of them was a clanless man loyal only to him." He looked up at Bahzell. "I recognized two of them when he and his men caught up with us down south," he added quietly.

"Ah." Bahzell folded his ears close in understanding and heard a soft rustle go through the Horse Stealers at Brandark's indirect reminder that, unlike any of them, *he* had been there when Bahzell fought a living avatar of Sharnā sword-to-sword. Even Gharnal nodded, his distaste for Brandark at least temporarily muted.

"Would there be anything more 'rumor' could be telling us?" Bahzell asked after a moment, and Brandark shrugged.

"I don't know, really. Harnak liked to tell stories about taking enemies off into the woods to 'play' with, and I know for a fact that he often *did* take people from his father's dungeons—or sometimes right off the street—and come back without them. And he was always certain they were unarmed and bound before he went anywhere with them."

Brandark's lip curled, and the Horse Stealers growled contemptuously. Any one of them would have agreed that the only truly good enemy was a dead one, but they had nothing but disdain for a so-called warrior who tortured helpless foes for pleasure.

"We've been hearing the same rumors," Marglyth put in, her rich contralto voice thoughtful. She reached out and rubbed the tip of her own finger over the area Brandark had indicated. "I'd not heard where it was he took them, though—or that Yarthag was after going with him, Lord Brandark—but now that you've said it, I'm thinking a few things have just come clear for me."

"Such as?" Bahzell asked.

"Well—" His sister frowned, right hand caressing the small golden balance scale she wore on a chain about her neck to mark her justiciar's office. "This Yarthag is after being one of Churnazh's favorites, and from all accounts, he and Harnak were close as close before Harnak's . . . difficulties." She smiled at Bahzell. "But the thing we'd never been able to puzzle out was just where he'd come from. It was as if he'd sprung up out of the ground one day, with no one at all, at all, knowing who he was or why Churnazh should be showing him such favor.

"The best we could be making out was that Yarthag had been Churnazh's spy—aye, and maybe a bit of an assassin—in the old prince's household." Bahzell's eyes narrowed and his ears flattened at the word "assassin," and she nodded. "Whatever it was he'd done, Churnazh was after rewarding him well enough, for he stripped the old House of Harkand's head of his lordship and bestowed it on Yarthag."

"I remember Father talking about that when he was among people he trusted," Brandark confirmed. "The other old families didn't much care for it, but that was before you people took Churnazh down a peg. At that point, he could still ride roughshod over opposition, and anyone who complained openly about what happened to Harkand—or about Yarthag's sudden precedence— tended to lose his head."

"True enough," Marglyth agreed. "But the thing that's stuck in my mind about him, and especially since Harnak's fall, is how good the man's proved himself at shifting sides without losing *his* head. Apparently he was after betraying the old prince to Churnazh, and after that, he spent his time sucking up to Harnak. It's common knowledge he'd made his choice to back Harnak against the rest of Churnazh's sons, and all our sources agreed as how he and Chalghaz were at dagger-drawing over it."

Bahzell nodded. Chalghaz had been Harnak's next younger brother, which had made them rivals for their father's favor . . . and his crown. That could all too easily have led to fatalities, under the rules of Navahkan politics, but with Harnak dead, Chalghaz was his father's undisputed heir. For now, at least. Arsham Churnazhson was next in line, but he was also illegitimate. Known as "the Bastard," he was popular with the army, yet few of his father's courtiers would have supported him. Although he was no paragon of virtue, he came far closer to it than his father or brothers, and he chose to spend as much time as possible in the field rather than watching his relatives' abuse of power in Navahk. As for Chalak, Churnazh's fourth son, only desperation could make him an acceptable candidate for the throne. Known behind his back as "Tallow Brain," Chalak was a plotter whose intrigues were both endless and boundlessly inept.

"But now that Harnak's gone," Marglyth went on, "Yarthag's changed his tune. As nearly as I can be telling, he's grown as close to Chalghaz as ever he was to Harnak, and in record time."

She paused, looking at her brother with one ear cocked, and Bahzell nodded. It had to have been record time, given that Chalghaz had been the peace hostage Churnazh had exchanged with Bahnak for Bahzell himself. The Navahkan princeling had been sent home when Bahzell "violated" his hostage bond, but that still meant Yarthag had been given no more than five or six months to suck up to him since his return.

"I'd been wondering how it was a man as could shift and dodge so well wasn't after being prince himself by now," Marglyth continued after a moment, "but if Sharnā's poked a finger into Navahk's pie, it's in my mind that the answer's plain enough."

"You're probably right," Kaeritha put in. "Sharnā's followers always prefer to work from behind the throne. People have a tendency to look much more carefully at princes and kings than at faceless advisers, and that extra layer of insulation makes it easier to hide their connections to the Scorpion."

"Like as not you and Marglyth have the right of it," Bahzell mused. "Still and all, I'd like to be hearing the rest of what Brandark has to tell."

"I don't know that I have much more," the Bloody Sword replied. "As Marglyth says, there's always gossip about scum like Harnak. But there *were* rumors—whispers, really—that he did more than just kill the people he took into the woods with him. No one wanted to say exactly what he *did* do, you understand, and I always assumed they were hinting at torture and such. But given that we know he was involved with Sharnā's church, it could just be that torture was the least of what his victims had to worry about."

"That's true enough," Kaeritha said grimly, and Gharnal turned his head to cock a questioning eyebrow—and both ears—at her. "Not that torture wouldn't be bad enough, given the sort of 'games' Sharnā and his filth enjoy," she told Bahzell's foster brother in a voice of frozen steel. "I've seen what they leave behind. They like flaying knives, and they know how to use them. They can keep a victim alive for hours—even days—as part of their demon summonings, and their high 'holy days' involve ceremonial cannibalism. Preferably raw, while the 'meal' is still alive . . . and while Sharnā himself devours its soul." She gave a death's-head smile. "They call it 'The Feast of Sharing.'"

Bahzell heard someone gag behind him, and Gharnal blanched. Young or not, all his volunteers had seen the agony and butchery of war, but what Kaeritha had described went far beyond that. Not that any of them doubted her. In an odd sort of way, she'd found the quickest acceptance of any of Bahzell's companions once the Horse Stealers saw her working out. Sothōii war maids didn't wear armor, and her two-sword technique wasn't identical to the one they employed, but it was close enough to make Horse Stealers who'd actually run up against war maids wince in memory. That had sufficed to erase most of the doubts over the propriety of teaching women to be warriors, and her cheerful willingness to take on any one of them on the practice field had done the rest. As she had discovered sparring with Bahzell, she lacked the stature to meet a hradani—and especially a *Horse Stealer* hradani—on truly equal terms, despite her formidable size and strength for a human woman. But as *Bahzell* had discovered in those same sparring bouts, any hradani who approached her with anything but the utmost respect (and wariness) soon found himself flat on his back with her sword at his throat. Aside from Hurthang, not a single one of them had been able to best her in his initial bout with her, and that despite having watched her trounce his fellows ahead of him. Things changed once they grew used to her style, but even then she faced the bruises, sprains, and potential broken limbs of training against warriors twenty percent taller than she with absolute fearlessness . . . and still gave as good as she got despite her smaller size. The fact that (short ears aside) she was extremely good looking hadn't hurt either, Bahzell suspected, though none of the men who'd joined him would ever be rash enough to say so where she could hear them. And their innate respect for women was undoubtedly another factor.

Brandark, of course, suffered from the stigma of being a Bloody Sword, but at least he was a hradani. The Horse Stealers had a good notion of who he was and what his motives were—even the ones like Gharnal who hated him. But Vaijon was decidedly the odd man out. He was neither fish nor fowl: a stranger who was neither a hradani nor a woman, who had so far mastered only an extremely limited hradani vocabulary, and whose accent and mannerisms struck his hosts as . . . effete. His devotion to Bahzell was a point in his favor, and Bahzell was devoutly thankful his kinsmen had never met the old Vaijon, but they still regarded him with wariness. And, Bahzell suspected, with a certain hidden contempt. Tall and powerful as Vaijon was for a human, he looked like a callow stripling among Horse Stealers, which only emphasized his extreme youth, and the edge of surprise that a *woman* could trounce them—which had shocked them into accepting Kaeritha—didn't apply in his case.

Fortunately, Vaijon seemed to be handling it well—better, for example, than Brandark was. It was almost as though the young knight-probationer had decided his hosts' derision was another aspect of his penance for his own earlier contempt for the notion of a hradani champion of Tomanāk. Which was fine, as far as it went, but Bahzell fervently hoped no one got around to pushing him too far. Vaijon might be reformed in many ways, but there were limits, and once someone stepped beyond them . . .

The Horse Stealer decided—again—not to think about that. Or

about Brandark's losing *his* temper. It seemed Tomanāk had neglected to mention more aspects of this champion business than he'd realized, and keeping the peace among this group ranked high on the list.

"All right, then," he said now, shaking loose from his thoughts, "it sounds to me as if the place we're hunting is after being somewhere in here." He tapped the same area Brandark had indicated. "All that's needful now is to go in and find it."

"And just how were you thinking to do that?" Hurthang asked quizzically. "It's a small enough space on a map, Bahzell, but I'm thinking you might be finding it just a *mite* bigger than that slogging about in snow and avoiding Churnazh's patrols!"

"Aye, it is," Bahzell agreed, "but I've a notion that I need only get close enough to the spot to be feeling it up here." This time he tapped his temple, and Hurthang's ears flicked skeptically.

"Feel it, is it? I'd not like to sound like a man as doubts your word, Bahzell, but that's one 'notion' as I'd like a bit more explanation of."

"I'll not blame you for that, but it's not something as I can truly explain." Bahzell frowned, rubbing his chin with one hand. "It's something that's come on me since I swore Sword Oath to himself," he went on after a moment. "Like the sword here."

He touched the huge sword leaning up against the table beside him, and one or two hands twitched as if their owners wanted to make signs of warding. He'd demonstrated his ability to summon the sword to prove his champion status. Most of his volunteers had been impressed, but many had remained skeptical, so he'd laid the blade down and invited any who wished to try to pick it up. Several of them—including Hurthang—had accepted the challenge . . . and almost ruptured themselves straining to lift it. When he'd picked it up effortlessly and extended it to Kaeritha, who took it from him easily, even the most doubtful had been forced to conclude that he truly was a champion of Tomanāk.

What they still didn't know was why, after twelve centuries, Tomanāk should suddenly decide he gave a copper kormak for what happened to hradani, but that was less important for the moment than the news that Sharnā was at work among the Navahkans. Whatever Tomanāk might or might not want of them, they knew only too well what *Sharnā* desired, and they had no intention of letting him have it. For his part, Bahzell knew there was one other point he had not as yet mentioned that would be much more important to them than even Sharnā's plans . . . once he got around to telling them about it. But he hadn't found quite the right time to bring it up. It was as though something—or, he thought darkly, some*one*—was holding him back until exactly the right moment.

"Aye, well, I can be *seeing* the sword, Bahzell," Hurthang said almost apologetically, "but this other business—this notion of 'feeling' things—" He twitched his shoulders in a shrug, and Bahzell smiled bleakly.

"It wasn't so very easy for *me* to be accepting, so I'll not say I'm surprised to hear as how others find it a mite difficult. Yet it's true enough. Kerry?" He looked at Kaeritha for support, and she frowned down into her own ale.

"Bahzell's probably right, Hurthang," she said finally. "No two champions are precisely alike, and none of us do things exactly the same way. This particular task was laid on Bahzell, and I have no idea just how he'll be guided or helped—or *if* he'll be guided or helped—in its completion, and there are limits on the knowledge we can be given, as well. I suppose the best way to put it is that Tomanāk can usually *confirm* things for us, but He won't reach down and lead us by the hand when we're trying to figure them out in the first place. That's our job, not His, and as a rule, I think that's how it ought to be. He's forging us to be His blades and to think and act for ourselves, after all, not to be His helpless suppliants . . . or slaves."

She paused, and Hurthang nodded slowly. However little use most hradani might have for deities, that, at least, was an outlook they understood. Their own harsh lives taught them to stand on their own, and the one thing for which every hradani felt contempt was weakness. Among their folk, *physical* strength could be taken almost for granted, but *internal* strength was another matter . . . and a much more important one.

"In my own case," Kaeritha went on, "it's something I *see*, like an aura or a light that guides me once I come close enough. For Bahzell, it would probably be something else, and I wouldn't presume to try to put it into words for him. But if he says he'll 'feel' something, then I'd have to say he will. When the time comes."

"Umph." Hurthang shoved himself back in his chair, scratching his nose, then shrugged once more. "All right, then, Bahzell. I suppose I've done dafter things in my time than follow a man as says he'll 'feel' the enemy when he gets close enough to 'em. Not that I can be calling any of them to mind just now, you understand, but if you'll be giving me a few days to think, I've no doubt at least one will be coming to me."

"No doubt," Bahzell agreed politely, and laughter rumbled about the map room. But then it died as one of the others spoke up in a voice which held no humor at all.

"Well, aye, I'd have to be agreeing with Hurthang so far as Sharná's concerned," he said, "but as for this business of other gods and demons and such—!"

Bahzell turned to look at the speaker, but the young man refused to look away. Instead, he met Bahzell's eyes and shook his head with dogged hradani stubbornness.

"It's grateful I am to you for warning us what's toward, and no mistake. Aye, and that Tomanāk will help kick Sharná's arse out of our business, as well. But I'm thinking as how he's his own reasons for wanting Demon Breath gone, and meaning no disrespect, Bahzell, I'm not so very inclined to be welcoming Scale Balancer in in his place."

No one spoke up in agreement, but Bahzell felt it in the others' silence.

"I'll not speak a word against your own choice," the critic went on, "but this I'll tell you plain, I've seen no reason at all, at all, to be welcoming *any* god in as *my* lord and master, and it just might be that one reason Tomanāk's so all-fired eager to help us is to be changing our minds about that. But the fact is there's not a one among all the 'Gods of Light' whose been after doing a single damned thing for hradani since the Fall."

He fell silent, and someone coughed into a fist behind him. The silence hovered tensely, and Bahzell looked around the gathered members of his clan with level eyes. Then he nodded slowly, and stood. The two men closest behind him had to step back to make room, and he heard someone curse as a boot heel came down on an unsuspecting toe, but he didn't even turn to look. He simply reached down for his sword, the symbol of his champion's status, and held it up, hilt uppermost, and the crowd parted before him like water before a ship's prow as he made his way to the hearth. He put his back to the mantle, feeling the fire's heat on his back and calves, and faced them all, still holding his sword before him.

"I do be hearing you, Chavâk," he said then, addressing the young warrior who had spoken as formally as a chieftain in a clan's great conclave, "and you've my respect for speaking your mind plain and unvarnished. Aye, and so far as that goes, it wasn't so very long ago I'd've been saying the selfsame things. Come to that, I *did* say 'em, and a mite louder than you just have, when himself and I first stood face-to-face."

"And how did he answer you?" Chavâk asked.

"He didn't," Bahzell said simply. "Not then, for he'd seen plain enough as how it would take something stronger than words to be changing a hradani's mind." He smiled faintly. "We've a way of being on the stubborn side, from time to time, or so I've heard tell."

He twitched his ears, and several members of his audience chuckled. But then his own smile faded, and he went on quietly.

"Well, he found something stronger. Leastways, I'm thinking as how most folk might be seeing a demon in that wise. But there was a bribe he could have been offering me long before that, a secret he might've told, if it so happened he'd been minded to buy my oath. But himself wouldn't bribe me, Chavâk. He won't be bribing you either, come to that, yet I'm thinking there's something you should know—something himself gave me as a gift, with neither price nor strings attached—that all hradani should be knowing, Horse Stealer and Bloody Sword alike."

He smiled briefly at Brandark, surrounded by his hereditary enemies as he sat still by the map table, and then drew a deep breath.

"You see, lads, there was a reason himself was after choosing a hradani champion after twelve hundred mortal long years. Come to that, I've no doubt there are more things than one as he has it in mind for me to do, but telling you what himself told *me* is the task as will mean the most to all our folk, for it's about the Rage."

Sudden silence slammed down. The tiniest crackle of the hearth fire and the sigh of wind across the roof carried clearly in the stillness, and Bahzell smiled crookedly in bitter understanding.

"We're all knowing who we've to thank for the Rage," he told them, his deep voice sweeping over them like a quiet sea, "but there's something we none of us ever knew until himself told Brandark and me the truth. When the dark wizards in Kontovar set the Rage on us to make us fight and die for them, their spell went into the bone and blood of us. For twelve long centuries we've passed it, father to son to grandson to great-grandson, and it's the Rage as truly makes the other Races of Man hate and fear us. But the Rage we have now, it's not the one as the scum who gave it to us meant us to have."

Still no one spoke, but he saw ears rising and foreheads furrowing as his audience wondered where he meant to go, and he raised his sword higher.

"I swear this to you upon this sword," he said, and he didn't raise his voice, yet it carried like thunder to them all, and his eyes flashed. "The old Rage exists yet, and will for years to come, but it's after changing at last. When we call the Rage to us—when we summon it rather than let it be taking us against our will—then *we* control *it*."

Most of the others looked confused, but he saw the start of understanding—and a wild, burning fire of hope—on some of the faces gazing back at him, and he nodded.

"Tomanāk himself has said it. The Rage can take and master us against our will only if we let it, but we can be taking *it*—aye, and *using* it—as we will and need from this day on. Not as a curse that makes animals and less of us, but as a tool, a weapon as answers to our hand and our will and makes us *more* than we are! That's the reason himself was after claiming a hradani champion—to be telling all hradani that after twelve hundred years, our fate lies in *our* hands again at last, and not the hands of the Phrobus-taken wizards who cursed us all!"

He stopped speaking, and the silence was deafening. No one spoke, as if each of them feared it was all a dream which his own voice might break, taking away the fleeting hope that the impossible might somehow be true. But then, at last, Hurthang Tharakson rose slowly. The others flowed aside to give him room, and he walked very slowly down the length of the map room to stand facing Bahzell.

"Is it true?" he whispered. "D'you swear to me it's *true*, Bahzell?"

"I do that," Bahzell told him quietly. "By my life, by my father's honor, by the clan blood we share, and by the Sword of Tomanāk Itself."

Hurthang stared at him, his face white and strained, and then steel whispered on leather as he took his axe from his back. He held it for a long, still moment, and then he knelt at his cousin's feet, laid the axe before him on the floor, and bent his head.

"Then Chavâk is wrong, and I see indeed why Tomanāk was seeking you, Bahzell Bahnakson," he said, the words deeply formal despite the emotion that choked his voice, "and I owe you more than ever man could hope to repay. For first you saved my Farmah's life, and then you sent her here for me to meet and love, and then you slew the black-hearted bastard who hurt her, and now you've bidden me join you to take vengeance on the like of him, and for that alone would I owe you my life. But for this—" He drew a deep, shuddering breath. "For telling my people *this*, I owe you more than life, and I beg that you will be taking me as your *charkanahd*, in the ancient way of our folk."

Someone drew a hissing breath. The oath of *charkanahd* was the most solemn any hradani could swear. Some foreign scholars, who thought the ancient word was purely hradani, translated it simply

as "armsman," but they were wrong. Other scholars, more familiar with the dead languages of fallen Kontovar, could have told them
that it meant literally "death sworn," but only the hradani still
remembered what it had once implied. What it *still* implied and
meant to them.

Hurthang had just offered Bahzell all he was—all he could *ever*
be. Not simply his service, and not even simply his sword in battle.
Those things came with the oath of *charkanahd*, but they were the
easy part, the reason "scholars" who knew no better used "armsman"
as its equivalent. True *charkanahd* cut far deeper, for it superseded
all other oaths, all other loyalties. It renounced *any* other claim
upon the loyalty of the man who swore it, and he gave his liege
lord his very life. More than that, he gave his lord the moment of
his own death—the right and power to choose the place and time
at which he would lay down the life which no longer belonged to
him, without question or hesitation.

But Bahzell only rested a hand gently on his cousin's bowed head
and shook his own.

"No, Hurthang," he said softly. "You're not owing me a single
thing, for whatever I did, I did because I chose to, and because I
couldn't just be turning away and pretending I didn't know what
was needful to do, and I've no need for *charkanahd*. But I *do* need
sword brothers, and if *I* can't be taking your oath, I know someone as can."

Hurthang looked up, and his eyes went huge, for a corona of
blue brilliance crackled about Bahzell. It clung to him, outlining
him in azure lightning, and his voice was no longer his alone. There
was another timbre to it, deeper even than his own, and powerful, like the beat of heavy cavalry charging through a battle dawn.
All around the map room, men sank to their knees before the
majesty flowing out of him, and even as they knelt, they knew it
was not truly Bahzell Bahnakson they beheld. Or, rather, that it
was not *solely* him. And as that realization ran through them, they
also realized that all he had told them—about Sharnā, about his
own ability to sense the Dark God's lair and seek it out, and above
all about the Rage—was true. Bone-deep, unquestionably true. As
Hurthang, they recognized in that instant the enormity of the gift
Bahzell—and Tomanāk—had given them. Of the vast change which
had come into their lives, and the fact that nothing would ever be
the same again.

"I'm thinking I see another reason himself was sending me here
now," Bahzell said, still in that voice which was his and yet was
not. "I'll not take your oaths for myself, Sword Brothers, but it's

in my mind that any chapter of Tomanāk's Order has to be starting somewhere." He smiled, and a ripple of laughter like joyous
trumpets seemed to shiver and dance behind his words. "No doubt
there's many a fine lord will be a mite upset when he learns as
how himself's been and created an entire *chapter* of blood-thirsty
barbarian hradani, Brothers, but they'd best be getting over it as
quick as ever they can, for I've the strangest notion there's worse
to come for 'em than that!"

Laughter answered him from the kneeling warriors, breathless
and yet somehow reverent, and he looked out over them.

"Will you swear Sword Oath to Tomanāk, as his warriors and
members of his Order, Brothers?" he asked, and steel whispered
and sang throughout the map room as every Horse Stealer warrior in it drew sword or axe and held it up before him.

CHAPTER TWENTY-TWO

"Somehow, I don't think your father quite had it in mind for you to swear in an entire chapter of the Order," Brandark said with a lurking smile. He spoke quietly, in small puffs of breath steam, as he and Bahzell lay under the low branches of a fir thicket. Fifty-four other hradani—and two humans—lay hidden about them, but any observer might have been excused for not realizing it. Even Brandark had been unsettled by the discovery of how easily half a hundred huge Horse Stealers had simply disappeared into the snow-struck woods. Granted, the foggy morning's gloomy overcast helped, yet it still seemed impossible. But, then, he'd never been part of a Horse Stealer raiding party on the Wind Plain, either.

"I'd not be so very sure of that, little man," Bahzell murmured back absently, eyes scanning the silent trees. "He's a canny one, my da, and it's in my mind he'd've seen it coming before ever he gave me leave to ask for volunteers. Besides, this way he's after getting credit as the first 'patron' of the Order amongst hradani if things go well, without risking the blame if it should happen they work out badly. Come to that, he's seen it set up so the Order won't be being 'his,' and that's no small thing if I'm to get the rest of our folk to believe himself is neutral and the Order's more than just a tool of Hurgrum."

"Really?" Brandark reached under the hood of the white smock which he, like every other member of the raiding party wore, to rub his truncated ear, then grimaced. "You're probably right," he acknowledged. "He's a deep one, your father, and somehow I've got the feeling he never does anything for a single reason."

"Which is the very reason he'll soon be after sitting on Chur-nazh's throne," Bahzell agreed equably. "But—"

He chopped off abruptly, and Brandark reached for his sword as he squirmed around to look in the same direction. But it was only Urach, Hurthang's chosen scout, skiing quickly and quietly back towards them out of the fog. He looked around searchingly, and Bahzell raised one hand in a small wave. Tiny as it was, the gesture caught Urach's attention, and he moved quickly towards Bahzell and Brandark.

"Well?" Bahzell asked quietly, and Urach grimaced.

"It's as Lord Brandark said, Bahz— Milord. There's a road of some sort up ahead. It's not after being much of one—more of a trail, really—but there's tracks enough to mark its course plain. Not many. I'm thinking it's naught but a pair of horses—not more than three, at the most—and they were only after going the one way. They've not come back yet. And as for the trail itself, it winds off to the north a bit, and it's twisty as a Bloody Sword's mind. Ah, no offense, Lord Brandark!"

"None taken," Brandark said dryly. Urach eyed him doubtfully, then ducked his head with a grin.

"Any road, Milord, it's after creeping about like a snake with the ague, and it clings to low ground like a leech. I've not scouted much along it, but if you were to be asking me, I'd have to say as how who-ever planned it wasn't wishful for anyone to be seeing him use it."

"Um." Bahzell rubbed his chin, then nodded. "Well enough, Urach—and well done, too. It's grateful I'd be if you'd tell the same to Hurthang—he's over yonder, by that dead oak—and fetch him back to me here when you've done."

"Aye, Milord!" Urach hastened off, and Brandark cocked a sardonic eyebrow.

"'Bahz— *Milord*', is it? My! What formality for a batch of unwashed Horse Stealers! Does Tomanāk know about this sudden elevation of yours?"

"I'm wondering how you'd look with your mouth stuffed full of snow?" Bahzell murmured thoughtfully. "Like as not you'd be *quieter*, anyway."

"My, my, my. We *are* feeling touchy, aren't we?" Brandark needled, but Bahzell only grinned.

"It's in my mind they'll get over it soon enough, little man. But just this minute, they're still not that all-fired sure just what it is they've let themselves in for. So if it makes a lad like Urach feel a bit more proper to be calling me 'Milord' for a bit, I'm thinking I can stand the embarrassment."

"No doubt. But you *do* realize you've made me even more of the odd man out, don't you?" Brandark demanded. Bahzell eyed him quizzically, and he sighed. "I was already a Bloody Sword—which, if you'll recall, isn't exactly the safest thing to be around a murderous lot of Horse Stealers—but at least I had company, since Vaijon and Kerry weren't what you might call Horse Stealers themselves. But then you had to go and swear the lot of them into the Order of Tomanāk, which Vaijon and Kerry *are* members of. Which just happens to leave me as the sole participant in this little expedition who *isn't* one of Scale Balancer's hearty minions."

"D'you know, I believe you've a point there. But don't let it be bothering you. Just you be keeping close, and we'll look after you right and tight anyway. Why, you'll be safer than if you were after lying in your mother's arms."

Brandark opened his mouth to reply, then shut it with a click as Hurthang slid under the firs beside them and jerked his head back the way Urach had come.

"Tracks, hey?" he said softly. "Now what would you be thinking could bring honest folk out into the middle of these gods-forsaken woods *this* time of year, Bahzell?"

"What? Not 'Milord'?" Brandark jibed. Hurthang darted him a quick look, then chuckled and reached across Bahzell to punch the Bloody Sword on the shoulder.

"I can see why himself here is after being so attached to you, little man. You're enough to be keeping any man humble, aren't you just?"

"I try," Brandark admitted. "It's a hard task, mind you, but someone has to do it. And at least Bahzell gives me plenty of material to work with."

"Now that'll be enough out of the both of you," Bahzell said austerely as Hurthang smothered a laugh. "We've more important things to be thinking on here."

"Aye, that's true enough," Hurthang agreed. "But given the rumors Brandark was after sharing with us, I've little doubt as how Urach's trail will be taking us where it is we're wishful to go." He narrowed his eyes at Bahzell. "Have you felt anything yet?"

"No, not yet. Or, that's to say I don't *think* I've felt aught—other than a bit of nervous flutter, as you might say. Still and all, I'm thinking you're right enough, and it's grateful I'll be if you'll take your section up ahead there. I'll follow along on your heels, and Gharnal's lot can watch our backs."

"Fair enough." Hurthang nodded and squirmed back out into the open, waving for the other thirteen men of his section to join him. White-smocked Horse Stealers appeared suddenly, blending out of the most improbable bits and pieces of concealment, and all fourteen of them pushed off in a quiet hiss of skis.

Bahzell let them get perhaps fifty yards ahead, then crawled out of his own cover. Brandark followed, and Vaijon and Kaeritha joined them in short order. The humans looked weary, but they'd managed to keep up, and Bahzell knew they'd earned the admiration of his Horse Stealers in the process. His people took their own endurance for granted, but they knew other races didn't share it . . . and that however tired Vaijon or Kaeritha might have become—however hard they'd panted, or however soaked with sweat their faces had been— the humans had matched them league for league.

Fortunately, Bahzell had slowed the pace once they reached the wooded area Brandark had identified as their likely hunting ground. Haste was the enemy of stealth, and at the moment caution was more important than speed could ever have been. The peace treaty between Horse Stealers and Bloody Swords still held—technically, at least. But even though hradani tended to be surprisingly proper sticklers for things like formal declarations of war, they were also masters of the occasional preemptive raid, and unlike many people, they had no objection to launching those raids in winter. Which meant Churnazh *had* to be keeping a closer watch than usual for Horse Stealer trespassers in his realm . . . and that didn't even consider anything Sharnā's lot might be up to. The fact that slowing down had allowed his human friends to catch their breath was a useful bonus, but Bahzell's real purpose had been to avoid blundering into some sentry or trap his enemies might have set.

The rest of his section joined him, and he waved them forward, he and his friends moving off on Hurthang's heels at the center of their loose formation. Behind them, Gharnal began beckoning for his own people to form up, and Bahzell let automatic, trained reactions carry him along while he half-closed his eyes and concentrated.

He hadn't been entirely honest with Hurthang. Or, more precisely, he'd understated his own speculations to be on the cautious side. Privately, he was convinced he *was* picking up a faint, unpleasant sensation, almost like something stirring in the dark, from the north. Now his head turned, nostrils flaring as if to scent the air, and his lips drew back from his teeth in a snarl he wasn't even aware of, for the sensation was stronger than it had been, and strengthening by the moment.

"D'you think as how Sharnā's lot can be sensing us as well as we can sense them?" he asked Kaeritha quietly, and she shrugged.

"I don't know. I suppose Demon Breath has the equivalent of his own champions, but I've no idea at all what capabilities they might have." She frowned, arcing away from Bahzell to pass on the far side of a tree and then coming back, and shrugged. "I know *our* champions have wandered into ambushes from time to time. It doesn't happen often, but it does happen. As far as I know, though, it's usually when they don't expect trouble." She grimaced. "I suppose no one *could* be ambushed in the proper sense of the word if they *were* 'expecting trouble,' of course, but that wasn't what I meant."

"What you were meaning was that the champions in question weren't after trying to sense their enemies because they'd been given no *other* reason to think as how they might be there," Bahzell said, and she nodded.

"Exactly. And that being the case, I've always assumed we can do the same thing to the other side under similar conditions. Of course, Sharnā may well have told them we were coming. He did try to ambush us in the Empire, after all."

"Aye." It was Bahzell's turn to grimace. "Well, the best we can do is all we can be doing, and we'll just have to be hoping it's enough."

He looked up, beckoned, and another of his men hurried forward.

"Aye, B— Milord?"

"Take yourself on ahead there, Torlahn. Tell Hurthang I'm after being certain now. There's a pocket of pus and nastiness up ahead, and I'm wishful he should go slow and easy, for they may've guessed we're coming."

Torlahn nodded and pushed off with his ski poles. He faded quickly into the fog, and Brandark looked around with a jaundiced eye.

"I don't want to sound as if I'm complaining," he observed, "but it's just occurred to me that fifty-eight men—well, fifty-*seven* men and one woman—could find themselves just a bit outnumbered by a nest of demon-worshiping filth on its own ground."

"That just occurred to you *now*?" Vaijon asked in a hoarse whisper, surveying the same woods, and shook his head in disbelief.

"I'm a city boy," Brandark replied with dignity, "not a Horse Stealer. *I'm* not the expert on raids and sneaking about in the woods." He sniffed and jabbed one of his ski poles at Bahzell. "*That's* the management for this little operation, my boy."

"And a good thing, too," Bahzell rumbled, "for the two of you are after carrying on like little old ladies in a brothel! We're after trying to *sneak up* on 'em, as even this Bloody Sword knows, and I'd take it kindly if the both of you would be keeping your jaws still for just a bit. And as for being outnumbered, well, I'm doubtful somehow that Sharnā and his lot would be wanting to keep a lot of men under arms out here. Even a Bloody Sword might spot such as that—though I'll grant you he'd need to be walking right into 'em before he stopped chattering long enough to be taking notice!"

"There's no need to be *rude*," Brandark said with even more dignity. He and Vaijon exchanged slightly strained grins, and then the two of them concentrated on moving as smoothly and silently as possible.

That sick sense of something putrid and vile grew stronger and stronger as Bahzell concentrated upon it. The chaffering with Brandark had distracted him from it for a few moments, but now it was back and worse than ever, and his ears flattened under his hood. He glanced at Kaeritha and made a small gesture for her to retain her position at the center of his section, then pushed ahead to overtake Hurthang. He wasn't certain why it suddenly seemed so urgent for him to do that, but he didn't question the feeling, either.

One of Hurthang's men saw him and hissed a warning that brought the entire section to a halt. Hurthang himself loomed up out of the fog, eyebrows arched and ears cocked as Bahzell caught up with him. Bahzell started to speak, then swayed, gagging as a carrion reek seemed to catch at the back of his throat like filthy hands. He caught himself on his ski poles and shook his head violently, then spat into the snow.

"What?" Hurthang asked, his voice little more than a rumbling thread.

"We're close," Bahzell said equally quietly. "What's ahead?"

"Not a lot," Hurthang replied. "A clearing of sorts, and a valley. It's an ugly place, too. I'd not set foot in it under other circumstances, and that I'll tell you plain, Bahzell."

"And why not?"

"That's more than I can say, to speak truth. Maybe it's naught but the fact that I know what it is we're hunting. That's cause enough for any man to be feeling a bit hesitant, I'd guess. And it's after being the sort of nasty, narrow, twisting place I hate. In fact, it's narrow enough I'd almost think as how the tracks up and vanish right into a hillside to look at it, but it must be there's a way around it on the far side as we just aren't able to see from here."

"I'd not count on that," Bahzell said grimly, for a sudden stab of certainty had gone through him like a knife the instant his cousin mentioned a hillside. "There's no way around that hill, Hurthang. The bastards are after being *inside* it."

"Inside?" Hurthang sounded dubious, and Bahzell nodded.

"Aye. Kilthan had the right of it when he said as how Sharnā's lot hide themselves underground, and I can be feeling some kind of trickery even from here."

"*Wizardry?*" Hurthang hissed, but Bahzell shook his head quickly.

"No, not that, but like it. I'm thinking it's a bit of Sharnā himself, spread out so as to be tricking minds and eyes to keep us from seeing what's really there. And I'd not be surprised if it's the real reason the place is after looking 'ugly' to you, too. He'd not want to encourage folk to come right in on his . . . people."

"Then just how is it we're supposed to be getting at them?"

"Well, as to that, it's surprised I'll be if Kerry and I betwixt us can't convince that little bit of Sharnā to be moving aside," Bahzell replied, and bared his teeth in a vicious grin. "Old Demon Breath's scared to death of himself, and I'm thinking that when a pair of champions come calling all unannounced, and bring himself along with 'em when they knock on the door, that door will be after opening."

Hurthang looked less than totally convinced, but he nodded and waved his men into concealment to wait while Bahzell went back for Kaeritha and the rest of the party. Then the two champions, accompanied only by Vaijon, Brandark, and Hurthang, moved to the very edge of the woods and peered out into the foggy late morning light.

As Hurthang had said, the woods gave way to a narrow valley between brooding hills. The tracks they'd followed this far snaked out into that valley, looking somehow furtive and lost, and seemed to vanish straight into a rough, almost vertical hillside. But the scene didn't look quite the same to all of them, and Bahzell heard Kaeritha—and Vaijon—suck in sharp breaths even as the hillside began to waver like wind-struck water to his own vision. Details were hard to make out, but his jaw clenched as he caught the likeness of a huge scorpion carved out of the rock above an arched opening that was somehow . . . wrong. He couldn't put his finger on exactly what made that arch look subtly perverted and diseased. After all, how *could* a simple opening in the stone look "perverted"? The concept made no sense, and yet that was the only word which fitted that obscene, waiting mouth under the protective claws of the scorpion.

"What is it?" Hurthang asked quickly as he caught his cousin's expression.

"What we came for," Bahzell replied grimly. He tore his eyes from the rippling hillside to scan the other slopes, looking for any sign of guard posts or sentries. There were none, and he supposed that made sense. Even knowing exactly what they sought, neither Hurthang nor Brandark could see a thing but blank stone. Coupled with the sense of aversion Hurthang had felt for the entire valley—and which Bahzell felt, as well, when he let himself—that offered Sharnā's followers almost perfect concealment, and posting sentries would actually be more likely to attract attention, not less.

But Bahzell knew what was hidden there, and his belly tightened as he sensed a dark, malevolent presence inside that hill. Not Sharnā himself, though there was a trace of the dark god present. No one who'd ever sensed him could mistake that skin-crawling shudder of pure evil for anything else. But there was something more, another presence, infinitely weaker than Sharnā's potential power but enormously stronger than any mortal creature. He glanced at Kaeritha and Vaijon, and their expressions showed they sensed it, too. But they looked perplexed, uncertain as to just what it was they felt, for unlike him, they had never faced one of Sharnā's greater demons.

He drew a deep breath, then sank back into the cover of the forest edge and waved his friends in close.

"All right, then," he said softly. "We've found what we came for, but I'm thinking we've a real fight on our hands." He darted a sharp glance at Kaeritha and Vaijon. "The two of you are after sensing something else in there, too, aren't you, now?"

"Yes," Kaeritha said shortly, and Vaijon nodded.

"Well, I've sensed its like before—and so have you, Brandark." He flicked a look at his friend. "In the Shipwood."

"Phrobus!" Brandark whispered. "D'you mean there's a bloody *demon* in there?!"

"And why not? Sharnā *is* after being their patron, and as Kerry said naught but a moment ago, *he's* after knowing we're coming, whatever the bastards inside that hill may know or guess."

"A demon?" Hurthang shook his head. "That sounds like being just a mite much for our lads to handle, Bahzell."

"Aye, it does that. And I'll not say I'm looking forward to it myself," Bahzell admitted. "Still and all, it's a pleasure I've had before, and if I'm not all aquiver with eagerness, at least I've another champion to back me this time. You and the lads be leaving the demon to Kerry and me, Hurthang. There'll be enough others in yonder for you lot to be dealing with."

"Are you sure about this?" Kaeritha asked quietly. "I mean, you're the only one of us who's actually ever faced a demon, but I've always heard the worst possible place to take one on is underground."

"I've no doubt of that at all, at all," Bahzell said grimly, "and I'll tell you true, it was footwork as much as bladework got me off whole last time. But more even than that, it was himself. He was with me when I was needing him worst, and I've no doubt at all as how he'll be with both of us—with *all* of us—" he amended, waving one hand to encompass their entire party "—this time, as well."

"I don't either," Vaijon said, and smiled suddenly at the two champions. "And if He *is* with us, what more do we need?"

"Oh, I'd say a bit of courage, a good sword, some muscle, and more than one man's fair share of luck," Bahzell said judiciously, with a smile of his own. "Still and all, you've put your hand on the meat of it, Vaijon. And all we need or no, it's a damned sight more than anyone on t'*other* side is likely to be having!"

He paused a moment, looking around the circle of his friends' faces, seeing his own fear—and he *was* afraid, he admitted—and determination in their expressions, then nodded. No man could ask for better companions. He would take his chances with Tomanāk and these people any day.

"All right, then," he said. "Here's what I'm thinking to do. . . ."

CHAPTER TWENTY-THREE

Prince Chalghaz, heir apparent to the throne of Navahk, tried to hide the crawling terror which simmered somewhere deep down inside his pulsing excitement. Until last autumn, he had never so much as suspected this buried sanctuary existed—and if he *had* known, he would have been as eager as anyone else to see it rooted out and destroyed. But not now. Now his fate had become inextricably bound up with its survival, and he still didn't understand exactly how that had happened.

It was Yarthag's doing. He was certain of that much, and he wondered if Yarthag had . . . *done* something to him to bring it about. It was certainly possible, and neither Yarthag nor Tharnatus, the human priest who presided over this enclave, would have hesitated a moment to use any tool at their disposal. Yet in his moments of self-honesty (of which he subjected himself to as few as possible), Chalghaz knew it wouldn't have taken much, for Sharnā's support offered him so many things he desperately craved.

The sensual pleasures of the Demon Lord's unspeakable worship appealed strongly to the debauched part of him, of course. Where was the point in possessing power if it did not permit a man to do as he wished? That was a lesson his father had taught him well, although the things Chalghaz enjoyed were best kept hidden—especially among hradani—however much power he held. But a man had to have companions (which was ever so much nicer a word than "procurers") in the pursuit of passion, and it was that need which had given Yarthag's influence its first toehold with Chalghaz, especially after the endless months he'd spent at Bahnak's disgustingly

248

respectable court. He'd plunged deep into the enjoyment of the flesh as soon as he was released from that bondage, and Yarthag had always seemed to be there, guiding him and constantly introducing him to new and different drugs or more . . . sophisticated delights. In a sense, he supposed, it had been only a small step from those pleasures to these.

Yet heady as they were, and deeply as the dark and twisted parts of him rejoiced in the blood-sweet rites of Sharnā, it was the Scorpion's *power* he valued most. As Sharnā had supported Harnak, now He supported Chalghaz, and for the same reasons. Chalghaz knew Tharnatus saw him only as one of Sharnā's pincers, sunk deep into the heart of Navahk and thus into all Bloody Swords, and that bothered him no more than it had bothered his brother. Whatever Sharnā desired of him in return for the throne and power, Chalghaz would give willingly, for his secret deity would protect and shield him against all enemies, even that bastard Bahnak and his cursed armies.

Of course, there were moments when he remembered how Sharnā had *not* protected Harnak against Bahnak's *son*, but Tharnatus had explained that. Harnak had displeased the Scorpion by trying to keep Farmah for himself rather than bringing her here so that the whole body of His worshipers might have partaken of her. That was the reason He had permitted Bahzell to interrupt Harnak before he could kill the slut. But He'd also given Harnak the opportunity to avenge himself and regain His favor, and it was the ineffectualness of Harnak's weak efforts to slay Bahzell even with the mighty weapon Sharnā had put into his hand which explained his final downfall.

And besides, as Tharnatus had said reasonably, if Harnak had not fallen, then how could Chalghaz, who was such a better choice, have supplanted him as Navahk's heir?

Unlike his brother Chalak, Chalghaz was wise enough to see the sophistry hidden in that argument . . . and the warning. For if Harnak had been discarded as unsuitable, then *Chalghaz* could be thrown aside in turn if *he* became unsuitable. But he had no fear of that. The approaching war with Bahnak had pushed Tharnatus and his deity into moving more rapidly than they'd planned. It was painfully obvious that Churnazh, whose armies had been smashed so easily three years past and whose alliances had already been shaken by what had passed between Harnak and Bahzell, could never defeat Bahnak and his Horse Stealers. The desertion of Arvahl of Sondur had been a serious blow, but even without it, Hurgrum had already proven what she could do to the best Navahk could field against her. No, Churnazh couldn't match Bahnak in the field. Nor, for that matter, could *Chalghaz* have matched him . . . under normal circumstances.

But circumstances weren't going to be normal, for Tharnatus had devised a plan to shatter the *Horse Stealer* alliance, instead of the Bloody Swords'. Best of all, it would require Churnazh's death, which would put Chalghaz on the throne at exactly the right time to take credit for the Bloody Swords' inevitable victory. Just six months ago, Chalghaz had been resigned to spending his life in the shadow of his older brother; now, within weeks, *he* would rule Navahk, and within months, all of the northern hradani.

And all it had required was the sacrifice of one nobly born maiden to summon one of Sharnā's demons to do their bidding. Well, that and a second sacrifice when the time came to actually launch the creature against Churnazh's palace to rend and destroy every living thing in its path until it reached the prince himself.

Chalghaz smiled dreamily, watching the sweet smoke curl up from Tharnatus' censer as the priest circled the gore-encrusted altar stone at the heart of the sanctuary. He had attended the first sacrifice, as he would also be required to attend the second, for it was necessary for the demon to know him as one of its summoners so that he might emerge unscathed from the impending carnage, but he'd found that duty no hardship. Indeed, he looked forward eagerly to the second ritual, and his soul shuddered in ecstasy every time he recalled the night of summoning. In a way, the terror he felt whenever he thought of the demon and recalled the raw power of hate and destruction they had bound to their will—remembered the dark rage which had burned against *them*, as well, as the monster recognized who had enslaved it—only made the razor edges of that pleasure still sweeter. But even more than the memory or anticipation of the rites still to come, it was contemplation of Tharnatus' elegantly simple plan which made him smile. He knew as well as the priest that even his closest followers would turn upon him in the blink of an eye if they ever suspected he'd given his allegiance to the Scorpion, but Tharnatus had turned that source of apprehension into the key to success.

The demon would be unleashed against Churnazh, and Churnazh was Bahnak of Hurgrum's foe. It would be sent forth within weeks of the start of the campaign season, which would be the most propitious time—from Bahnak's viewpoint—for Churnazh to die and the Bloody Swords' alliances to be thrown into confusion. And when the new prince of Navahk, weeping as he knelt in the blood of his slaughtered father and brothers, cried out in grief-filled rage to accuse Bahnak of sending that creature of darkness to smite his foes, who would question it? And so *Bahnak* would be labeled a secret worshiper of Sharnā, and the very people—Horse Stealer, as well as Bloody Sword—who would have turned upon Chalghaz would turn upon Bahnak, instead.

And yet . . . There was something else at work here. Chalghaz didn't know what, yet he was oddly certain that Tharnatus and Yarthag had another reason to send the demon forth. It was almost as if they faced some time pressure about which they had told him nothing, as if there were some reason they had to unleash the demon and brand Bahnak with responsibility for it *now*. He couldn't object to moving quickly, since it would only put his own backside on the throne sooner, but the uncomfortable sense of not knowing everything his allies intended gnawed at the back of his brain like rats at a sack of grain while he watched Tharnatus kneel to press his forehead against the altar.

Then the priest rose, spreading his arms in benediction as he looked out over his congregation. Most of the eighty-odd people in the chapel never left the sanctuary, for its hidden secrecy was its true defense, and the comings and goings of so many might well have been remarked. That was true at all times, but especially now, when tracks showed so damnably clearly in the snow that covered everything. It was also the reason Chalghaz, Yarthag, and Thulghar Salahkson, the head of Yarthag's personal guard and the only man he truly trusted, were the only outsiders present. But as he had for the actual summoning of the demon who waited, hissing and snarling in the warded chamber beyond the chapel, Chalghaz had to be here today, for this was the service which would actually loose the demon to do its work of slaughter.

"My brothers," Tharnatus intoned, his voice deep and resonant for a human's, "the Scorpion welcomes you, for this day we take a momentous step and set one of His own upon the throne of Navahk! And from Navahk, our brother Chalghaz shall reach out to rule all the Bloody Sword clans, and the Horse Stealers, as well, and he shall forge of them a weapon which will sweep beyond his present borders with fire and the sword. Not in twelve hundred years has this world seen the power of the massed clans of the hradani, and no one will stand against them when our brother strikes, for the Scorpion shall ride with him, and his enemies will be as straw in the furnace before him!"

A rumble of dark agreement went up from the gathered worshipers, almost all of them hradani. They had not forgotten the dark and terrible things their enslaved people had done in the Fall of Kontovar, but unlike the vast majority of their folk, they didn't care. No, that was wrong. They *did* care . . . but only because they hungered to do the same dark, terrible things *themselves*, and the fact that doing them would confirm all the hatred the other Races of Man felt for their people meant less than nothing to them.

"Very well," Tharnatus said, and nodded to the four burly hradani who waited by the side door. They bowed to him, opened the door, and slipped through it, and Chalghaz felt his nerves tighten with hungry anticipation as he heard the hopeless, sobbing pleas of the sacrificial victim echoing through the doorway. Metal rang as the cell door beyond it was unlocked and thrown wide, and the pleas became louder and more frantic as the sacrifice was dragged down the short passageway. And then—

"TOMANĀK!"

Chalghaz jerked as if an arbalest bolt had struck him squarely in the back as the sudden, basso rumble of that hated name beat in on him. No voice, not even a hradani's, could thunder so! It wasn't a voice; it was an earthquake, an avalanche crunching over everything in its path, and he wheeled towards the sanctuary's entrance in shock.

"Tomanāk! *Tomanāk!*" Other voices screamed the same terrifying war cry, and Chalghaz heard Tharnatus curse vilely while other members of the congregation cried out in confusion as great as the prince's own.

Bahzell Bahnakson leapt across the threshold of Sharnā's hidden fortress just as the first startled warrior spilled out of the guardroom inside the arch. He had no idea why no one had spotted his Horse Stealers as they crept soundlessly up on the entrance. His people were masters at such things, yet there was precious little cover out there, and he'd expected to be seen at any moment. But they hadn't been. It was almost as if the men who should have been watching for him had been distracted, concentrating on something else instead of their duty. Not that he intended to complain.

His clansmen had looked at him with wondering eyes as they neared the hillside. The hidden entrance and its guardian scorpion had become clearer and clearer to him as he drew near, yet still none of them saw a thing. He'd felt the noisome, clinging stench of Sharnā's power reaching out to blind and baffle them, and he'd stepped directly in front of the arch, his sword in his hands, and concentrated all his mind and will upon his god.

And then he had called upon Tomanāk. Called upon him as his champions should, when the moment for battle came and they summoned him as their captain. And as his bullthroated bellow echoed from the valley walls, the power which had baffled his men went out like a tempest-snuffed candle, and he heard their exclamations as they, too, saw what he had seen from the start.

That had been enough. Kaeritha and Vaijon had echoed his war cry even as he drove forward, and behind them three-score Horse Stealer hradani had taken up the cry. The deep, deadly music of their voices had thundered into the hillside like hurricane-driven surf, and the newest chapter of the Order of Tomanāk had charged into battle on its leaders' heels.

That first, gawking guard barely had time to get his sword up—not that it did him any good. Bahzell's blade crashed down in a two-hand stroke that sheared clear through his own right at the quillons and carried on to split his helm and the skull within it, and bright blue fire flashed as the champion's blade bit home. More of the same fire washed about Bahzell, gilding his massive frame in swirling flame, and the other guards rushing to meet him cried out in terror of the light the Dark hated and feared above all others.

Nor did that light cling to Bahzell alone, for Kaeritha charged at his right hand and Vaijon charged at his left, a compact, deadly wedge leading the attack, and *all* of them glittered like bright blue stars in the maw of darkness. Some of the guards fled deeper into the hillside, wailing in terror. Others tried to stand and fight, but they stood no chance against two champions of Tomanāk and a warrior of Vaijon's caliber. Steel crunched and bit, bone shattered, screams died in wet, horrible gurgles, and then Bahzell and his companions were through the antechamber and charging onward to find their foes.

"—dozens of 'em! *Scores!*" the guardsman blurted as he flung himself at Tharnatus' feet. "They came through the arch like the shield wasn't even there! They—!"

"*Silence!*" Tharnatus' hand cracked viciously across his face, but the priest's own fear was evident to Chalghaz, and the crown prince understood it only too well.

The shouting and clash of steel cascaded towards the chapel, growing louder and more deadly sounding with every second. The Church had mustered a force of trained warriors to guard the sanctuary. Some were human, and even a handful of dwarves had been smuggled in, but most were locally recruited Bloody Swords. Yet there were less than a hundred of them, for the sanctuary could house only so many men and much of its space had been taken up by other functions. The crash and fury of combat told Chalghaz that more and more of them were joining the fray, but it was also clear they were merely slowing the attackers, not stopping them. Fortunately, whoever was assaulting the sanctuary was too unfamiliar with its serpentine architecture to pick the shortest path to the chapel . . . not that they didn't seem to be doing just fine with the longer way around. On the other hand, their unfamiliarity might offer him a chance to escape with his life. If he could fade away, slip past them down the side passages—

"Get your arms, Brothers!" Tharnatus cried to the rest of the congregation. "The Scorpion is with us yet, but I must have time! Buy me only a few moments, and we shall drink our enemies' blood still!"

Chalghaz stared at the priest, then stabbed a glance at Yarthag. The Navahkan lord was pale, his ears plastered tight to his skull, but understanding flashed in his eyes as they met Tharnatus', as if he, at least, knew what the priest was talking about. More importantly, as if he believed Tharnatus spoke the truth.

That was the deciding factor, and Chalghaz abandoned his plan to creep away and drew his own sword.

"You heard, Tharnatus!" he bellowed. "So come on, you whoresons!"

The warren of tunnels and side passages hampered Bahzell's advance badly. Not because it was confining—it had been built for Bloody Sword hradani, which meant the tunnels had almost enough headroom even for Horse Stealers—but because he had no idea of its layout. He knew the direction he must go to reach the core of corruption which lurked at the heart of this lair, but none of the tunnels led straight towards it.

And there were other problems—like far more guards than he had expected to meet. Not all were Bloody Swords, either, and human and dwarvish blood, as well as that of other hradani, steamed on his blade as he cut his way forward. At least the tunnels limited the number of foes who could face him at any one time, but the side passages gave opportunities for enemies to slip around his peoples' flanks and hit them from the sides. He heard the crash of steel behind him, but he also heard the thunder of his warriors' war cries as they bellowed Tomanāk's name and hewed their foes into ruin. He knew too much of battle to think only the enemy were falling in this brutal, close-quarters fight, but his people had two enormous advantages. They served the God of War, whose strength supported them . . . and they knew the truth about the Rage.

Every one of the Horse Stealers—and Brandark—had given himself to the Rage, summoning its exaltation and strength and deadly concentration. Most hradani feared the Rage, and many fought desperately to keep it from taking control in battle. Bahzell's Horse Stealers did not, and unlike the handful of Bloody Swords who they met after the Rage had taken them, the Horse Stealers were completely in control of themselves. They used the Rage—they *rode* the Rage—and it carried them forward in a storm of gory steel.

And at the very head of them, the spear point thrusting into the sanctuary's vitals, was Bahzell Bahnakson, with Vaijon of Almerhas, Kaeritha Seldansdaughter, and Brandark Brandarkson advancing at his side and covering his flanks.

Kaeritha was unable to tap the power of the Rage, and she seemed little more than a schoolgirl against her towering enemies, but she glittered like blue ice in the light of Tomanāk, and her twin swords were scythes. She was splashed with other peoples' blood to the elbows, and a cut on her cheek bled freely, yet she spun through her foes like a tornado edged in tempered steel.

Vaijon was taller, bigger, stronger—only a human, perhaps, but nearly a match for a Bloody Sword in size and strength. His longsword was the same gem-encrusted weapon he had carried for his disastrous trial at arms against Bahzell, and its steel no longer gleamed, for it was coated in blood. He moved like a hunting panther, weaving back and forth, using his shield as yet another weapon as he covered Bahzell's left flank and hacked down any enemy unfortunate enough to cross his path.

Brandark came behind his friends. He was no coward, but neither was he a fool, and he knew what that glittering blue corona was. He had no doubt that it afforded the others at least some protection against whatever deviltry Sharnā might have prepared to defend his sanctuary, but none of it had decided to cling to *him*. That being so, he was prepared to let them take the lead while he watched their backs . . . and in this interlocking web of tunnels, their backs needed watching. He followed directly behind Bahzell, closing the open side of their wedge and turning it almost into a diamond, with Hurthang and his section battling hard to keep up as the champions and knight-probationer carved their way deeper and deeper into the bowels of the hill.

"Here they come, Sharnā take them!" someone shouted, and Chalghaz Churnazhson spat a curse of his own. A straggling knot of guards staggered backwards, trying to fight even as they gave ground, and Chalghaz spat another curse as he realized who the giant at the attackers' head must be. *First Harnak, and now me,* he thought, and waved the reinforcements from the chapel forward.

Bahzell staggered as a fresh surge of bodies hurled itself at him. Someone got through with a stroke that rang on his helmet like an anvil, and someone else got a gash in behind the greave on his right calf, but the shock of the blow and the pain of the wound were distant things. They couldn't pierce the armor of his Rage, and he bellowed Tomanāk's name as he threw himself forward once more and the deadly sweeps of his blade harvested limbs and heads in gory profusion.

To his right, Kaeritha cried out as a mace smashed through her guard. It came down like a sledgehammer, impossible to block or deflect, and crashed into the side of her helmet. It struck obliquely, at just enough of an angle to rebound without shattering her skull or snapping her neck, but she went down bonelessly, instantly unconscious.

Her enemy bellowed in triumph and raised his mace to finish her, but his bellow died in a wet, rasping gurgle as Brandark leapt forward, eyes blazing with the Rage's icy flame, and drove two feet of steel through his throat. Another attacker came at Brandark, and his blade hissed down. It bit into the outside of his foe's exposed knee, and the wounded hradani screamed. His own stroke went wide as he flailed for balance, trying to remain upright, and Brandark's blade came up in a deadly, economical backhand that split his jaw and rammed through the roof of his mouth into his brain.

Someone shouted his name, and he darted a glance back just in time to see Gharnal cut down the guardsman who had crept up behind him. Bahzell's foster brother grinned wildly and threw up his blood-soaked sword in salute, all trace of distrust vanished.

"Go on with you, man!" the Horse Stealer shouted. "I'll watch over Kerry!"

Brandark nodded back curtly and moved forward once more, hurrying to catch up with Bahzell and Vaijon.

The tunnel was wider here. The guards had fallen back farther and faster than Chalghaz had hoped they would, and his rush from the chapel hadn't gotten here in time to dam the enemy up further back. Now more of the attackers shouldered forward, at least half of them armed with the dreadful axes Hurgrum's warriors continued to favor, as the melee spread out. At least there were only two of the glittering blue figures left. He had no idea what had happened to the third the panicked guards had reported. He spared a brief moment to hope whatever it was had been fatal, but a moment was all he had, for he had somehow found himself in the front ranks of the defenders. He hadn't planned on that, and he felt his belly tighten in fear. Yet he was no coward, and if he wasn't the warrior his half-brother Arsham was, he was no slouch with a blade, either.

"*Sharnā!*" he shouted, and crossed blades with his first enemy.

The Horse Stealer came in ferociously, and he was both stronger and had a longer reach. But he was also badly wounded, with blood pumping down his side from a brutal rent in his scale armor. He moved almost like someone in the grip of the Rage, except that his eyes were clear, without the berserker haze the Rage produced, but his injury slowed him. Even so, he almost did for the crown prince with his first attack. Chalghaz managed—barely—to parry the blow and riposted savagely. Their blades flashed and rang, crashing together again and again, and then Chalghaz twisted his wrist and lunged with all his strength, and the Horse Stealer went down as the Bloody Sword's longsword drove through the base of his throat in a shower of blood.

Chalghaz whirled to face the next Horse Stealer, but the man didn't attack instantly. Instead, a gore-smeared blade flipped up in mocking salute, and a voice that never came from a Horse Stealer cut cold and taunting through the clangor of the fight.

"How nice to see you again, Your Highness," Brandark Brandarkson said, and unleashed his first lightning stroke.

High Priest Tharnatus knelt beside an iron door sealed with the Scorpion of Sharnā. The evening's intended sacrifice lay beside him on the stone floor, eyes glazing in death, and the thick, red flood of her blood pooled about his knees and soaked into his ceremonial robes. His hands were slimed in blood as well, tracing signs on the door as he muttered prayers and exhortations. It was never safe to move this quickly, but he had no choice. The roar and tumult had been faint when he began his task; now he heard them all too clearly, and he knew how little time he had before the enemy was upon him.

He finished the last prayer and wiped sweat from his forehead, smearing his victim's blood across it. It had been a pity to use her up so quickly, a corner of his brain thought, but there would be many more where she came from if his followers could just defeat this attack and he could recast his plans. And for that to happen—

He drew a deep breath, unlocked the iron door, and pulled it open.

Bahzell cut down yet another guard. From the corner of his eye, he saw Brandark dueling viciously with an elegantly clad Bloody Sword, and even the fraction of his attention he could spare to think about such things recognized the cold, cruel efficiency with which his friend fought. There was something special about that confrontation, but Bahzell had no time to worry about what it was, for more guardsmen were coming at him with the frenzy of despair.

He met their attack in a clangor of steel. There were three of them, but it didn't matter. He took the one in the middle with his first blow, using his reach advantage to kill the man before any of the three were in range to strike at *him*, then cut to his left and brought a looping backhand whistling back to his right. The three bodies hit the floor in the same heartbeat, and he whirled to meet whoever was coming behind them.

But what came behind them wasn't more guards, and he heard cries of fear, coming from his Horse Stealers this time, as they saw what it was.

He didn't blame them. It didn't look much like the only other demon he'd ever seen. That one had been a hideous blend of insect, spider, and lizard; this one came forward on a hundred segmented, flickering legs, mandibles and fangs clashing. At least its body was no more than four or five feet in diameter, unlike the other demon he'd fought, but it made up for it by being much, much longer. He couldn't even see the full length of its body as it came slithering down the tunnel, and its claw-footed legs carried it forward like some unstoppable juggernaut. A blind, bulbous head armored in bony plates quested this way and that, seeking its prey, and one of Sharnā's own guards bellowed in terror as his movement attracted it. The head lashed forward, belying its blindness, and the mandibles shot out. They fastened on their hapless victim, jerking him in close, and the fangs parted to show a vile-smelling maw studded with cruel, barbed hooks to draw its prey inward. The guard screamed and fought, lashing out with his sword, but his scream became a high, endless shriek as he was thrust living into that barbed maw.

The other Horse Stealers wavered, despite the Rage which had carried them so far, but Bahzell heard Hurthang's booming voice quelling their panic. And at least he and Kaeritha had warned them it was coming. They knew a demon was champion's work—that there was no shame in leaving it to him and Kaeritha—and they concentrated on keeping the rest of the guards out of the fight.

Not that the sanctuary's denizens had any desire to force their way *into* that battle. Bahzell sensed them streaming aside, literally crawling over one another in their desperation to stay clear of the demon, but he paid them no heed, for they were utterly unimportant now. All that mattered was the demon.

He took a step to the side, eyes fixed on his opponent, and opened his mouth as he flicked a glance at the blue-lit figure beside him. But the words he'd meant to say stayed unspoken as he realized the warrior beside him wasn't Kaeritha.

It was Vaijon, and the young knight-probationer's face was pale as the raw, stinking power of the demon assaulted him. It was like a sword, an invisible blade that drove deep into the heart and mind of whoever faced it, and Bahzell knew it well. He had felt it before, on the night he swore himself to Tomanāk's service, and he'd never meant for Vaijon to face its like. He'd planned to fight the creature with Kaeritha by his side, for Vaijon was too young for this, too untried. But even as he started to order the knight back, he knew it would be useless. Vaijon looked frightened and physically ill with the corruption beating at him, yet there was no retreat in his eyes.

Bahzell ripped his attention back to the demon, seeking some vulnerable spot—*any* vulnerable spot!—while it finished devouring its first victim. Well, that was one vulnerability. It was stupid enough to waste time dealing with tidbits one at a time instead of charging forward to crush and rend its opponents. Not that slothfulness looked like all that terrible a weakness. The thing truly was like some enormous, slime-streaked centipede, and its body was covered in hard, horn-like armor.

"The belly, Bahzell." Vaijon's almost conversational voice carried through the hideous cacophony of battle with unnatural clarity. "We've got to get at its belly."

"Belly, is it?" the Horse Stealer muttered. Vaijon might well be right, but just how did a man go *about* getting at a centipede's belly in a tunnel without being swallowed on his way past?

There didn't seem to be a good answer to that, and he was still looking for one when the thing became aware of him. Its first victim had disappeared down its maw, and its head swiveled, pointing at Bahzell. Mandibles clashed, clacking together like snapping tree trunks, and spittle drooled from its fangs. And then it heaved itself forward, with a deceptive speed which looked far slower than it truly was.

Its front end reared up, brushing the roof of the passage. The movement exposed its thorax, but only briefly, and then it lashed down like an earthquake.

Bahzell darted aside, grateful that he and his men had at least reached a wider spot which gave him room to dodge. The blunt head slammed the floor with an ear shattering clash, and stone shards flew as the mandibles drove into it, but Bahzell spun on his toes like a dancer, sword whining, and the demon lurched with a high-pitched, grunting squeal as he sheared away two of its legs. It flinched back, twisting with pain, but however much it might have hurt, the wound was minor, the damage only superficial. It had scores of legs, and it coiled around, trying to reach him once more.

The head darted at him again, and this time he had less room to dodge, for the bulk of the demon itself filled much of the tunnel. Legs clawed and writhed, reaching for him even as the head struck, and he heard Vaijon screaming Tomanāk's name as he hacked and slashed at the creature from the far side. But the demon ignored the young knight. It had been commanded to deal with any champions of Tomanāk first, and it flowed after Bahzell like some dark, unstoppable tide.

The Horse Stealer backed further, then grunted as his spine rammed into the wall. The head loomed above him once more, and this time there was no room at all to dodge.

"*Tomanāk!*" He bellowed the war cry and lunged forward desperately, his sword at full extension. The steel was edged in blue flame, and the demon shrieked as Bahzell drove home against the side of its head. Bony armor hissed like ice in a furnace as that dread blade struck, and Bahzell sank it to the hilt with one mighty thrust.

But his thrust was off-center, and it missed the brain, driving lengthwise down the armored, massively muscled barrel of the demon's body. The monster shrieked again as it whipped away from him . . . and his blade went with it. One of the virtues of that sword was that he would never drop it or lose his hold upon it in battle, yet that meant little here. The demon couldn't wrench it out of his hands, but neither could *he* draw it back out of the monster's body—not without better leverage than he had. And so the whipping head took him with it, clinging to his hilt. It flailed about, shaking him like a rat, and he had no choice but to release the weapon intentionally before the creature battered him to death against the passage walls without even realizing what it was doing.

He landed on his knees, directly in front of it once more, and he heard Brandark and Hurthang and Gharnal shouting his name in horror as the demon heaved up before him yet again. He was weaponless, but he didn't even reach for the dagger at his belt. It would have been useless against such a foe, but that wasn't why he left it alone.

"The belly, is it?" he bellowed up at the demon, and his lips drew back to bare his teeth in a snarl. "Come on, then, you bastard! Let's be having you!"

He remained on his knees, but he pounded his breastplate with his fists, mocking the creature, daring it to attack him.

"*Come on!*" he screamed again . . . and it did.

The head struck, mandibles gaping wide, and this time Bahzell didn't try to dodge. He reached out instead, his hands striking with the speed and power and deadly precision of the Rage. They closed on the saw-toothed mandibles like steel clamps, one on each side, and Bahzell threw all four hundred-odd pounds of his brawny, heavy-boned body to his right. His left leg straightened, thrusting at the floor while he pivoted on his right knee, giving still more power to his desperate heave, and the demon squealed in shock as he literally twisted the front of its huge body to one side.

"*Now, Vaijon!*" he bellowed, every muscle locked as he held it there.

It was impossible. No one could possibly have pinned that multiton carcass even for a second. But Bahzell Bahnakson did it, with the strength of his own Rage and the power of his god as it snapped and crackled within him. Not even he could hold it for more than an instant, but an instant was all he needed, for in that brief flicker of time, Vaijon of Almerhas struck like the very Sword of the War God. The full length of his blade drove through the demon's thinner, weaker ventral armor, and it shrieked like a soul in hell. For one more fraction of a second it froze, and then its head snapped up with a bone-breaking violence not even a god-touched Horse Stealer hradani could resist.

Bahzell and Vaijon flew away like discarded toys, bouncing in opposite directions, and the howling fury of the demon's agony hammered a dozen more warriors to their knees. It screamed again and again, battering its head back and forth, shattering the stone of the passage's walls and roof even as it splintered its own armor against them. Ichor splashed and steamed, and Bahzell shook his head groggily and heaved himself back to his knees as the monster's own death struggle completed what Vaijon had begun.

It took over five minutes for the thing to die, and Bahzell left it to it and crawled over to Vaijon. The young knight lay unconscious, and unless Bahzell was badly mistaken, his right arm was broken again—this time in at least three places. But he was alive, and Bahzell gathered his head into his lap and leaned back against the tunnel wall, feeling every aching, battered muscle of his own body complain, to watch the demon sag slowly down in death. Even then unnatural vitality sent quivers and twitches through its enormous body, but they were only the last flickers of a life which was already fled.

By the time it stopped thrashing madly, the last of Sharnā's guardsmen had been killed or battered into surrender. Gharnal's bloody left arm hung limp at his side, and Hurthang had lost the little finger off his right hand, but the two of them were still going concerns, and, together with Brandark, they saw to it that none of Sharnā's worshipers who were still breathing got their throats cut. Not because any of them had given oath to Tomanāk, but because live witnesses would be far more useful than a few more lopped-off heads which couldn't confirm what had happened here.

At least eight Horse Stealers lay scattered among the dead. Others were wounded, and Bahzell knew there must be still more of them—dead and wounded alike—strewn along the tunnels down which they'd fought. But they'd accomplished what they'd come for, he thought, and looked up as young Chavâk, the warrior who'd seen no reason to "replace" Sharnā with Tomanāk, came striding up a side passage. Two more Horse Stealers trotted along behind him, and all three of them bore minor wounds to go with their bloody weapons. But Chavâk bore something else, as well; an unconscious body in richly embroidered, blood sodden robes.

"I was thinking as how you might be wanting this one alive," he grunted, and dumped his burden at Bahzell's feet.

Bahzell stretched out his right leg without rising or disturbing Vaijon's head in his lap, and dug a toe under the body's shoulder. He jerked his foot up, flipping it over onto its back, and a cold, hungry light flickered in his eyes as he recognized the amulet of a high priest of Sharnā on the chain about its neck.

"Aye," he said softly, one hand resting on Vaijon's forehead, and looked up at his young kinsman. "Oh, aye, Chavâk, I do that."

CHAPTER TWENTY-FOUR

The last of the captured guardsmen were dragged in under Hurthang's watchful eye, searched for weapons, and securely bound. There weren't many, and those who survived were beaten men in every sense of the word. They knew the penalty which awaited those who lent themselves to the service of the Dark Gods, especially among hradani, and they sat white-faced and silent. The only good thing about their situation was that Bahnak disliked torture even when the law prescribed it. That wouldn't save them from the full rigor of the punishment prescribed by hradani law, but at least the Prince of Hurgrum wouldn't make their deaths still worse out of personal vengeance.

Bahzell had no choice but to leave the details to Hurthang, for he himself had the wounded to care for. He wasn't happy about Kaeritha, for the blow her helmet had turned had left her stunned and unfocused. She seemed a bit vague about where she was or who Bahzell might be, but aside from that she appeared unhurt. And however concerned he might be, there was little he could do for her—or, for that matter, Vaijon—immediately, in light of how many others had taken life-threatening wounds. He was forced to turn his healing ability to those most in need of it, and he had little time in which to do it. They couldn't be certain *none* of Sharná's worshipers had escaped, and if a Bloody Sword hradani informed one of Prince Churnazh's army posts that a company of Horse Stealers was wandering about in his territory it was unlikely any questions would be asked until after the invaders had been dealt with. Should any of Bahzell's kinsmen survive the experience,

263

the Bloody Sword who'd called in the army would probably face some rather pointed inquiries of his own, but it was unlikely there would *be* any survivors. Which meant Bahzell couldn't afford the dazed, disoriented euphoria which healing all of their injured people would have plunged him into, so walking wounded would simply have to look after themselves until he could be certain they'd made a clean getaway.

And then there were the warriors not even a champion of Tomanāk could heal. Of the fifty-four Horse Stealers who'd sworn Sword Oath and followed Bahzell on the raid, seventeen had died. Nine more who would have joined them would live because of Bahzell's aid, but seventeen, all of them kinsmen, remained a grievous total.

Hurthang also saw to organizing their withdrawal while Bahzell dealt with the wounded, but he was aided by Brandark and Gharnal. None of these Horse Stealers would ever again look upon Brandark with suspicion, not even Gharnal Uthmâgson. Or, perhaps, *especially* not Gharnal Uthmâgson. Gharnal had watched Brandark deal with Crown Prince Chalghaz, and it was Gharnal who found him a sack to put Chalghaz's head in afterward. He offered it without a word of apology for his earlier distrust, but Brandark understood the gesture . . . and the warrior's arm clasp which had come with it.

Yet however much they might want to avoid bothering Bahzell with details, none of the others knew what to do about the sanctuary itself. All of them sensed the palpable miasma of evil which clung to its tunnels, though some were more sensitive to it than others. But even the least sensitive recognized the malevolence of the hideous mosaics which adorned its walls, and no one could mistake the clotted blood which crusted the altar or the atrocious instruments of torture hanging on the "chapel's" walls.

"Begging your pardon, Bahzell," Hurthang said finally, shaking Bahzell gently to recall him from the daze into which healing so many near-fatal wounds had sent him, "but it's time we were going."

"Ah?" Bahzell's head jerked up, and he blinked. He stared at his cousin for several seconds, then shook himself. "Aye. Aye, you've the right of it there." He reached out and clapped Hurthang on the shoulder, then stretched enormously. "My sword—?" He blinked again and looked around, then grinned sheepishly as he felt the familiar weight on his back where he'd put it after healing the last of the seriously wounded.

"Aye, you've *your* sword, right enough," Hurthang allowed, "but we've no least idea where Vaijon's has gotten to. We've looked high and low, and not a sign of it can we find."

"It wasn't after being stuck in yonder beastie?" Bahzell asked in surprise, jerking a thumb back in the direction of the tunnel where the demon lay.

"That it wasn't, and it's a puzzle to me where else it could be. I saw him stick it in the thing my own self, but unless it's buried under its carcass somewhere—?"

He shrugged and Bahzell frowned. His own memory was less than crystal clear, yet he felt certain he'd seen the gems that studded Vaijon's sword hilt flashing against the demon's hide in the torchlight well after the creature was dead. He started to turn back down the tunnel himself, then stopped. Hurthang was right about the need to leave, and if he said the others had searched for the sword, there was no reason to believe Bahzell would somehow spot something they'd missed. Especially through the befuddling aftereffect of so much healing.

"Have you told Vaijon?" he asked instead, and Hurthang nodded. "Aye, I told the lad. Mind, I think that arm of his is after hurting a deal worse than he's wishful to let us guess, but his mind's clear enough, and he said as how we should leave it be." Bahzell raised an eyebrow, and Hurthang chuckled. "He says as how he's willing enough to be trading even a fancy bit like that for his first demon."

"Is he now?" It was Bahzell's turn to chuckle. "All right, then. Are the others ready to be gone?"

"Aye. I've the worst hurt—and our dead—in the sleds, with teams told off to pull 'em, and I've bid Vaijon and Kerry ride as well. They're neither one fit to be staying on their skis. I've seen to all that right and tight enough, but I've no idea at all, at all, what we should be doing about this place—" Hurthang waved at the tunnels "—before we go."

"We do what you'd do with any wound gone bad," Bahzell said grimly. "There's enough barrels of oil and brandy down in their storerooms. Set the lads to breaking them open, and see to it that that filthy 'chapel' of theirs is after being well doused."

"If you say to," Hurthang agreed in a dubious tone. "But I'm none so sure that'll be enough, Bahzell. This place is solid stone and earth; I'd not think any fire we can set with all we have to work with could finish the stink I'm smelling."

"It'll not be that sort of fire," Bahzell told him. Hurthang glanced at him frowningly and started to ask another question, then shrugged. After what he'd already seen, he supposed this was as good a time as any to start taking a few things on faith, so he simply turned away and began bellowing fresh orders.

✦ ✦ ✦

"We're ready," Brandark said, and Bahzell looked up from where he knelt beside Kaeritha's sled. She looked a bit better, and she seemed to know who *he* was, at least, yet he wished he had the time to heal her properly. But that would have to wait, and he nodded to his friend and rose.

"I understand you and Chalghaz were after having a little disagreement," he rumbled quietly.

"I suppose you could say we had a pointed discussion," Brandark agreed with a crooked smile, and nodded to the ominously stained cloth sack lashed to one of the equipment sleds. "I'm afraid I had to chop a little logic there at the end, but I don't think he'll be raising any more objections to my reasoning. Or anything else, come to that."

"Such a nasty temper for such a wee little fellow as yourself," Bahzell said mournfully, and Brandark laughed. Then he sobered.

"We've poured out every flammable liquid we could find, just as you told us to," he said. "I don't doubt it'll make an impressive bonfire, but that's an awful big—and solid—complex in there, Bahzell. I'm afraid we won't do much more than singe it a bit, and I'll be honest with you. For all I've thrown in with your lot, I'm still a Bloody Sword, and I'm downright afraid of what has to be lingering on in there. I wouldn't want any of my kinsmen—or anyone else, for that matter—to wander into it unawares."

"Don't you be worrying your head about it, little man," Bahzell told him softly, and turned away. He left the sleds and his companions behind him, walking back out of the woods into the narrow valley, and faced the opening. No one had told him what to do or how to do it, yet he felt only absolute assurance as he stopped before it. He didn't draw his sword this time. He only stared into that black bore, feeling the sewer stench of its evil eddying about him, and raised his hands. He held them out at shoulder height, like a priest delivering a blessing, and closed his eyes.

"All right, Tomanāk," he murmured. "You've been with me this far. Now let's be going that one last league together, you and I."

He reopened his eyes and glared up at the carved scorpion above the archway.

"*Burn!*" he commanded, and the single soft word soared up into the heavens like a storm. He didn't raise his voice, but every person watching heard him, and the terrible power of that quiet command echoed in their bones like thunder.

For just one instant, nothing happened at all, and then a gout of smoke and flame and an eye-tearing blue radiance blasted from the arch like a volcano vomiting its guts into the sky. The stormfront of light and heat rolled right over Bahzell, swallowing him up in an instant, and his companions cried out in horror as he vanished within it. Half a dozen ran forward, as if they thought they could somehow dash into that seething inferno and pull him out, but the heat beat them back, and they stopped helplessly.

And then Bahzell Bahnakson walked out of the firestorm, his expression calm, almost tranquil. He nodded to the would-be rescuers who crouched where the heat had stopped them, and they fell in behind him with huge eyes. They followed him back to the others, while the flames beating out of the hillside behind them roared like a huge forge—or like one of Silver Cavern's blast furnaces. There was no possible way for Bahzell to have set off such a holocaust. There was insufficient fuel to feed that seething fury, and even if there had been, there was too little draft to sustain it. But that didn't matter, and more than one Horse Stealer jumped as the stone above the arch cracked in the dreadful heat. The scorpion broke loose and plunged into the column of fire to shatter into a thousand pieces, and Bahzell strapped on his skis without speaking. Then he gathered up his ski poles and looked calmly at Hurthang and Gharnal.

"Let's be going home, Sword Brothers," he said quietly.

CHAPTER TWENTY-FIVE

The trip back to Hurgrum took several more days than the outward journey had. The need to transport their wounded (and their dead) would have slowed them anyway, but the real problem was their prisoners. There were only thirteen of them, including Tharnatus, but every one of them knew he was a dead man when he finally reached Hurgrum. The Horse Stealers kept them bound at all times and still had to guard each of them like hawks. Even so, one of them managed to saw through the ropes binding his legs with a sharp-edged stone he'd acquired somewhere and made a break for it late on the second day. The light was none too good, but he made less than seventy-five yards before an arbalest bolt tore through him. Unlike their own dead, the Horse Stealers let him lie where he had fallen for the scavengers, and none of his erstwhile companions uttered a word of complaint.

Once Bahzell was certain he and his followers had gotten away cleanly, he took time out to see to Vaijon and Kaeritha properly. On examination, it was obvious Kaeritha was recovering on her own. Aside from an atrocious headache, a few fresh cuts, including one which was going to leave yet another scar on her cheek, and some spectacular bruises, her only lingering difficulty was her right eye's reluctance to focus properly, and she waved off Bahzell's offer to heal her.

"I'm not so fragile as all that! Besides, Tomanāk would get irritated if I ran around asking Him to take care of every little ache and pain for me."

"If you're certain about it, then," Bahzell said, and she nodded, then winced and pressed a hand to her temple.

"I'm certain. Mind you, I won't complain if you order me to ride in the sled for another day or two."

"So that's the way of it! You're thinking as how you've an excuse to lie about like a lady to the manor born while we're towing your lazy carcass back to Hurgrum, hey?"

"Of course," she replied smugly, and curled up like a cat under the thick rug covering the sled. "Wake me when we get there," she said with an elaborate yawn, and he laughed, patted her shoulder, and turned his attention to Vaijon.

He found the knight-probationer sitting up and practicing his Hurgrumese with the three Horse Stealers who had been taking it in turns to tow his sled. His accent was still atrocious, and the hradani were teasing him unmercifully about it. The old Vaijon would no doubt have felt mortally insulted—especially when his accent turned the Hurgrumese for "mud" into something much more organic—but the new one only laughed along with them, and Bahzell watched appreciatively for several seconds before he interrupted.

"It's sorry I am to be breaking in on this serious-minded language lesson," he said finally, "but I'm thinking as how the youngster here might be wishful to have his arm healed. Unless, of course, he's some objection to my 'wasting' healing on such minor bumps and sprains like her ladyship yonder?"

He twitched his head at Kaeritha as he spoke, and the lump under the rug stirred.

"I heard that!" it warned him. "And you'll pay for it the next time I get your hairy backside in a training salle, Milord Champion!"

Vaijon laughed and shook his head.

"I've no objection at all, Milord. I hope this isn't going to get *too* habit forming, though. Somehow you always seem to be patching up broken arms for me."

"Do I, then?" Bahzell said with a smile, dropping down to sit beside him and ease the splinted arm out of its sling. "Well, I'm thinking I might just be done with such as that, lad, for it's in my mind you won't be after needing any more of 'em broken." He paused and looked Vaijon squarely in the eye. "And speaking of arms, and in case I wasn't after saying it at the time, Sir Vaijon," he said quietly, "it's grateful I am for your aid and the strength of your arm. You did well, and your courage was all that Sir Charrow—aye, or Tomanāk himself—could have been asking of you."

Vaijon blushed fiery red, but the hradani who'd teased him earlier murmured agreement and approval. The young man blushed even darker and looked around as if searching frantically for some other topic of discussion, and Bahzell took pity on him.

"Now let's be looking at this arm of yours," he said briskly. "And as you're a special friend and all, I'll not be charging you more than half my normal surgeon's bill."

Bahzell sent Gharnal ahead with a complete report for his father while the rest of his party was still a full day out of Hurgrum. He wasn't at all surprised when messengers from Prince Bahnak appeared early the next day with a request which stopped just short of an order to be as inconspicuous as possible when they entered the city. With that in mind, he timed their travel so that night had fallen by the time they reached Hurgrum. The weather had turned bitterly cold again in one of the sudden, seesaw weather shifts which usually marked the end of winter in that part of Norfressa, and the plunging temperatures had driven virtually everyone inside with the sunset, so their late arrival allowed them to reach the palace without attracting any attention.

Bahnak himself, with Barodahn and Thankhar, Bahzell's next older brother, awaited them, and the prince threw his arms around his youngest son in a crushing hug.

"I'd not guessed all you were off to face when I bid you farewell, boy," he said quietly, "and it's glad I am to see you home hale and whole." He broke the hug, then stood back and eyed Bahzell critically. "Gharnal was after giving me all the juicy details you'd seen fit to be leaving out of your own letter. For example, you'd not mentioned a word at all, at all, about fighting demons in *your* report."

"Well, as to that, it was Vaijon did the thing in," Bahzell replied with a shrug.

"Aye, Gharnal said as much. But it's just as happy I'd be if you could see your way to avoiding such little affairs in the future. Not—" Bahnak raised a deprecatory hand "—that I'm after *complaining*, mind, and I'm sure you'll know your own business best. But like as not your mother'll be just a mite upset if demons or devils or such were to be biting pieces out of you after all the time she spent bearing and raising you. Mothers are like that, you know, and I'd sooner she wasn't after taking it out on me."

"I'll be bearing that in mind," Bahzell assured him with a grin. But then the grin faded, and he turned back to the door through which he'd entered. His companions were quietly carrying in stiff, blanket-wrapped bodies, and he shook his head.

"I was after losing the best part of a third of my men, Father," he said quietly.

"From all Gharnal said, it's lucky you were to lose so few," Bahnak said, equally quietly, and Barodahn and Thankhar nodded agreement. "I've not told their families yet," the prince went on after a moment. "I'd no idea how you and your brothers—" he nodded to the rest of the raiding party, not his other sons "—would be feeling such should be handled. And, truth to tell, I'd a few other motives of my own." He waited until Bahzell turned to look at him once more, then smiled humorlessly.

"What you've done needed doing, and no mistake, but I'm thinking it's likely to be like kicking a hornets' nest when word of it's after getting out. And it *will* get out. Come to that, I suppose it *should* be gotten out, and the sooner the better, but the other princes will all be having their own reasons to think the worst of my involvement—especially when they hear as how Chalghaz was after getting caught up in it. And since all that's the case, I'd take it kindly if you and Hurthang and perhaps your friends Kaeritha and Brandark would be sitting down with Marglyth and me to thrash out just how we'd best go about letting that word out."

Rumors of the raiders' return began circulating with the dawn, and they grew more extreme with each generation of whispers. No one outside Bahnak's immediate family and the warriors who'd actually carried out the raid knew that Bahzell's volunteers, to the man, had sworn their swords to Tomanāk's service. As far as that was concerned, only a handful of people had the least idea what the raid itself had been about.

The least fantastic explanation bandied about was that Bahnak had dispatched a party to burn several Navahkan frontier posts without issuing a formal declaration of war. No one was quite certain why he should have done such a thing, although the darker tales suggested it had been intended as the first step in a complex strategy designed to push Churnazh into counterattacking. The idea, apparently, was that Bahnak would deny his men had ever set foot in Navahk and brand Churnazh's claims as lies intended to justify *Churnazh's* "unprovoked" aggression against *him*. That was bad enough, but there were even rumors the prince had ordered a sneak attack on Navahk itself, guided by Bahzell (who'd put the knowledge of the city he'd gained while a hostage there to good effect), for the express purpose of murdering Churnazh and his sons in their beds. Exactly how less than three score Horse Stealers could have carried out such a mission in an entire city full of Bloody Swords was left to the imagination of the audience.

In many respects, the rumors' possibility or impossibility meant very little. While many Hurgrumese were shocked by the notion that their prince might have so violated custom as to open hostilities without first declaring his intention to, they were delighted by the reports that he'd done so *successfully*. On the other hand, most of the ambassadors to his court could scarcely have cared less whether or not the attack—whatever it had been—had succeeded. Those who served Churnazh and his allies were furious that Bahnak had violated their peace treaties without first bidding Churnazh proper defiance, and those of Bahnak's allies were equally furious that he should have done so without first warning them. After all, such actions could well drag their princes into a war right alongside him, and he hadn't even discussed it with them. That sort of high-handed action would not sit well with any hradani warlord, and the arrogance of it might very well destroy his newborn union of Horse Stealers at the very outset.

Claims, protests, rumors and counterrumors flew that morning as friendly and hostile envoys alike worked themselves into something very like a frenzy. But what not one of those ambassadors suspected was that Bahnak himself had taken great care to ensure that they heard the juiciest possible versions of events from his own agents.

Bahzell had looked at his father in disbelief when he admitted responsibility for spreading the tales, but Bahnak had only smiled crookedly.

"Well, of course I did, boy—and a great help Marglyth was, too."

"But *why*, Father?"

"The word was bound to be getting out, whatever we did or didn't do," Bahzell's sister explained patiently, "and there's going to be some as aren't likely to accept the truth whatever happens. Some will have reasons of their own not to be taking Father's word *officially*, no matter what they might be thinking in their own minds, for they're after serving Churnazh and his allies."

She paused until Bahzell nodded his understanding, then shrugged.

"So when Father and I discussed it, it came to me that the greater the difference betwixt what they were thinking had happened and what they later learned had *truly* happened, the better all 'round. The more accusations—aye, and the wilder—Churnazh's lot can be sucked into making, the sharper the truth will bite them back when it's after coming out. And the greater the shock when Father proves Demon Breath's doings in Navahk, the more likely it is the most of the ambassadors will be believing him."

Bahzell turned to give his father a very hard look indeed, and Bahnak shrugged.

"Aye, aye. I know what you're after thinking, boy. Here's the old man again, dipping his finger into the pie and scheming how best he can make use of it. But politics are politics, and whether you'll have it or no, this Order of Tomanāk you're after creating's such as to pitchfork you right out amongst 'em. I'll not deny it's in my own mind to wring every advantage I can from the affair, but just you be thinking about it from your own side. You say you've no mind to see your Order made political or to have any of our folk— Horse Stealer or Bloody Sword—thinking as how your swords are after being in *my* pocket. Well, I'll not say your wrong. In fact, I'll say you've my total agreement, and the politics of it are the least important reason why. But if you're meaning to convince the other princes of your Order's independence, then you'd best be starting down that path right now. That mean's you've no choice but to be hitting 'em square betwixt the eyes with it, and it may be you've noticed as how it takes a heavy hammer to drive *any* notion through a hradani's skull!"

"I see." Bahzell rubbed his chin, then shook his head. "It's thankful I am for your consideration, Da," he said with exquisite propriety, "and grateful you're after being so concerned for the Order's future. But it's in my mind himself will be finding his own road to make our status clear."

"No doubt, no doubt," his father said, patting him on the shoulder with another smile. "But it's a father's duty to be looking out for his son and helping him on in any way he can, and it's glad I am this little opportunity was falling in my way, as it were."

Bahzell regarded him for another long, thoughtful moment, then sighed deeply and looked back at his sister.

"And did you manage that other thing I was asking for?"

"I did," she replied. "I can't tell you for certain sure that no one *else* will be throwing his name out, mind, but I've seen to it as how Brandark's not been mentioned at all, at all, in any of *our* 'rumors.'"

"Good," Bahzell said softly, and hugged her briefly in thanks. The members of his fledgling chapter knew the importance of Brandark's part in their mission, but they also knew how vital it was that Churnazh not learn of it. Brandark's father and his allies among the old families of Navahk were too powerful for Churnazh to risk alienating when he stood on the brink of a war for survival, but if the Navahkan learned Brandark had not only helped the raiders locate Sharnā's sanctuary but personally killed the heir to the throne, he would have no choice but to move against Brandark the Elder anyway.

"All right, then," his father said much more seriously. "Are you and your lads ready, Bahzell?"

"We are that," Bahzell said grimly, and Bahnak nodded.

"In that case, boy, let's be about it."

CHAPTER TWENTY-SIX

The Great Hall was packed. Only the space directly in front of the dais had been kept clear by Bahnak's household guards. The rest of the hall was filled by ambassadors and envoys—almost all of them women, each accompanied by the single, heavily armed armsman to whom law and tradition entitled her—and the mutter and rumble of agitated voices sounded like a fretful sea.

But the surflike sounds stilled with dramatic suddenness as a door was thrown open and Bahnak Karathson, Prince of Hurgrum and Lord of Clan Iron Axe of the Horse Stealer hradani, stalked through it. Three of his children followed him—Crown Prince Barodahn and his eldest daughter Lady Marglyth directly behind him, and Prince Thankhar, his next to youngest son, bringing up the rear like an armsman—and a dropped pin would have sounded like a thunderbolt in the silence their appearance evoked. Bahnak carried only his dagger, but both of his sons were armed and armored. Barodahn carried the daggered axe of his clan's traditionalists upon his back, and Thankhar's hand was hooked nonchalantly into his belt, inches from the hilt of his longsword.

Bahnak seemed unaffected either by the stillness which greeted his appearance or by the dignitaries and envoys who crowded his hall. To look at him, no one would have guessed the rumors frothing about Hurgrum claimed his alliance was about to collapse in ruin because of his own rash actions. In fact, he seemed so unaware of this morning's importance that he hadn't even bothered to dress for the occasion. He wore a serviceable but plain jerkin over a woolen shirt that was warm and comfortable but darned in two

275

places, and his boots could have used a shinier coat of polish. A moderately prosperous farmer might have dressed equally well, and some of the newcomers to his court made the serious mistake of assuming only a yokel would appear on such a morning in such garments. Those who knew him better, however, drew a very different message from his appearance. Bahnak had always made a point of dressing plainly, but he dressed *this* plainly only on days when he planned to execute some particularly telling stroke.

Now he seated himself on his throne, with Marglyth to his left and Barodahn to his right, and faced the crowd of dignitaries. He scanned them thoughtfully, then leaned back, folded his hands across his belly, and crossed his ankles.

"Well," his deep voice rumbled mildly in the stillness, "I suppose we'd best be getting on with it. Jahnkah?"

"Yes, Your Highness." The old man who served as Bahnak's majordomo and chamberlain had been one of the most feared warriors of Clan Iron Axe in his prime, and he retained the broad shoulders and powerful arms of his youth. He also used a cut-down halberd rather than the white staff chamberlains carried in most Norfressan courts, and its iron-shod heel rang like a hammered anvil as he thumped it on the floor.

"Hail His Highness Prince Bahnak!" he intoned in a voice trained on a hundred battlefields. "Let those who seek justice and judgment draw nigh!"

There was a moment of silence, and then a short (for a hradani), richly clad, barrel-chested man shouldered through the crowd. Mutters of anger followed his rude progress, but he ignored them to plant his fists on his hips and glare at Bahnak.

"Phrobus take 'justice and judgment'!" he snapped. "I want to know what in Fiendark's name you mean by attacking my prince's territory!"

Jahnkah swelled with rage, but Bahnak raised one hand in an almost bored gesture before the chamberlain could speak. Then he returned his raised hand languidly to its companion, clasped across his middle, and looked down his nose at the belligerent figure before him. Alone among the princes of the northern hradani, Churnazh of Navahk was represented exclusively by male ambassadors. There were several reasons for that, not the least being that his personal habits meant very few women would willingly have served him in any capacity, much less as his ambassador. Almost as importantly, however, he trusted no one from outside his inner circle for sensitive missions. Halâshu Shakurson had been chosen as his envoy to Hurgrum because that was the single most important diplomatic post Churnazh had to fill, and Halâshu had been one of his closest lieutenants from the day then-General Churnazh slaughtered his way to Navahk's throne.

Over the years, Halâshu had served his master zealously but with limited results. It wasn't entirely his fault. Almost anyone would have been over-matched by Bahnak Karathson and his daughter Marglyth; the fact that Halâshu was of less than stellar intelligence only made the match even more unequal. Still worse, from his viewpoint, Churnazh equated strength with repression. Halâshu was no genius, but neither was he an outright fool, and he'd realized early on that Bahnak was a dangerous opponent. Churnazh, however—constitutionally incapable of recognizing the strength of anyone less brutal than himself—had brushed off Halâshu's warnings until it was too late.

Now that Churnazh's decision to ignore those warnings had landed him in a disastrous position, it was Halâshu's unenviable duty to buy as much time as he could before the inevitable final war. That had been a hard enough task even before the clash between Bahzell and Harnak, but it had become far worse since. Harnak's idiocy (and the patently false version of the affair which Churnazh had concocted as Navahk's official position) had put Halâshu in an intolerable diplomatic bind, and he'd grown more and more short-tempered as the winter dragged by. Now he hovered on the very brink of the Rage, and the armsmen of the envoys nearest to him kept hands close to their hilts.

"Attack your prince's territory, is it?" Bahnak rumbled at last in mild surprise. "And what would be causing you to think I'd done any such thing, Lord Halâshu?"

"Don't play games with me, Bahnak!" Halâshu waved an angry hand at the crowded hall. "Everyone knows your son Bahzell is back in Hurgrum! And everyone *also* knows that, not content with assaulting and half-killing Crown Prince Harnak in violation of his hostage bond, he's led a raid by *your* men on Navahkan territory in clear violation of the treaties between you and my prince! I'll leave it to your allies to decide whether or not they want to follow anyone who authorizes such aggression without even consulting them, but your son's actions are another matter. This new outrage makes him twice an outlaw, and on behalf of Prince Churnazh of Navahk, I demand he be surrendered to face our justice!"

"Well, now. That's after being quite a mouthful so early in the morning, isn't it just?" Bahnak replied, and looked at Marglyth. "Would you be knowing of any treaties we've had the breaking of?" She shook her head with a small smile, and he glanced at Barodahn.

"And you, Barodahn. You wouldn't've been authorizing any raids on those bast—I mean on our esteemed Navahkan neighbors without asking me, would you now?" Barodahn shook his head in turn, and Bahnak turned back to the purple-faced Halâshu and shrugged. "Well, there you have it, Milord Ambassador. I'm afraid you're after being misinformed. Was there something else I could be doing for you this morning?"

"*Damn* you!" Halâshu hissed. One hand dropped to his dagger, and he started to step forward, only to stop as Thankhar took a single stride to his left and faced him. Like all Bahnak's sons, Thankhar towered well over seven feet in height. *Un*like Halâshu, he wore mail, and his right hand rested lightly on the hilt of his sword. For just an instant it looked as if Halâshu's Rage would take him forward anyway, but it didn't. Instead, he stood absolutely motionless for several fulminating seconds, and then made his fingers unclench from the dagger. He inhaled deeply and glared at Bahnak.

"You can play all the word games you like," he grated, "but everyone in this room has heard the same stories I have. You and your murdering son have played fast and loose with our treaties since they day they were signed, and you've gotten away with it so far only because your son is as cowardly as he is treacherous! If he hadn't run for his life like a mongrel cur, we would have proven it was he who raped that girl and half-killed Prince Harnak for trying to stop him! But he's back now, and up to his old tricks—no doubt cutting the throats of our sentries while they sleep in time of peace! Well, this time he's gone too far—and so have you!"

"Raped—?" Bahnak began in a puzzled voice. Then his expression cleared. "Oh! You're meaning those foolish lies you and Churnazh were after spreading after Bahzell sent Farmah to me for safety! Well, it's sorry I am to have to tell you this, Halâshu, but Farmah herself is ready enough to tell what happened to her, and I'm thinking her tale won't be so very close to yours."

"Of course not! No doubt you've paid the wench enough!" Halâshu shot back, but his voice was weaker, despite his anger. He'd had no choice but to parrot the line Churnazh had adopted, ridiculous as everyone knew it to be, but he had no desire at all to hear Farmah tell her side of what had really happened.

"Aye, no doubt I have," Bahnak agreed soothingly, like a man humoring a lunatic. But then he smiled. "On the other hand, and speaking of sons and all, I was wondering if you could be telling us just where Crown Prince Harnak has taken himself to? It's been some months now since I've heard a thing at all about him." His smile vanished suddenly, and all levity disappeared. "I'm hoping his health hasn't been taking a turn for the worse," he finished in a voice of cold iron, and Halâshu flinched.

He licked his lips and darted nervous eyes around the room, but not even the other Bloody Sword envoys would return his look. No one in Navahk had received any official word of Harnak's fate . . . but they knew, for *The Lay of Bahzell Bloody-Hand* was highly popular in certain circles. No one was foolish enough to sing it where Churnazh might hear of it, but it had been enough to get Chalghaz named crown prince in Harnak's place.

Halâshu opened his mouth once more, but Bahnak had toyed with him long enough. The Navahkan had been trapped by his own untenable position into making exactly the accusations Bahnak had wanted someone to make. Now the Prince of Hurgrum came to his feet, uncoiling from his false pose of relaxation like a serpent, and glared at the hapless ambassador.

"So my son's a coward and a murderer, is he?" His voice rumbled and echoed in the hall. To his credit, Halâshu stood his ground, but his ears pressed tight to his head and his shoulders tightened. "No doubt that's the tale *Churnazh* would be wanting told," Bahnak went on witheringly, "but the truth's after being just a bit different, isn't it now?"

He looked away from Halâshu, sweeping all the envoys with his eyes, and this time it was he who propped his fists on his hips.

"There you stand, every one of you, half ready to be believing the lies scum like *this* is after telling," he said, jerking his head contemptuously at Halâshu. "How many of you are thinking his tales about Bahzell and Harnak have any truth at all, at all, in them?" he demanded. No one spoke, and he snorted. "Aye, so I thought. Yet let the same lying pile of hog dung tell you as how I've sent men to attack Churnazh in time of peace, and it's another tale, is it?" Still no one spoke, and he raised his voice. "*Is it?*" he barked.

"With all due respect, Your Highness, it is," someone said. The crowd parted, and another ambassador stepped to the front. Silver-haired Lady Entarath of Halk was a Bloody Sword, and her city-state was allied to Navahk, but she eyed Halâshu with undisguised contempt before she turned back to Bahnak.

"The matter of your son and Crown Prince Harnak lies solely between you and Prince Churnazh," she told him calmly. "Prince Bahzell was outlawed by Churnazh for breaking hostage bond. Under the letter of our law and traditions, that means his life is forfeit to Churnazh. Yet as you are quite well aware, given the . . . dispute concerning his actions, my own prince, and those of the other cities allied to him, have declined to support Churnazh's demands that Prince Bahzell be surrendered to him. But be that as it may, Your Highness, the reports of Horse Stealer attacks on Navahkan territory do not come from Lord Halâshu alone. My own sources report the same thing to me, and they, too, insist that Prince Bahzell led the attack in your name."

The hall was still and quiet. Lady Entarath was a very different proposition from Halâshu. Halk was allied with Navahk because it was a Bloody Sword city, not because its people held any love for Churnazh, and Entarath had served as ambassador to Hurgrum for Prince Thalahk, her present prince's father, for decades. She was a senior member of the hradani diplomatic corps and widely respected, even among Horse Stealers, and her calm, deliberate tone carried far more weight than Halâshu's half-hysterical posturing.

"Because those reports are so wide spread," she went on, "I now ask you formally, in the name of Prince Ranthar of Halk, whether or not they are true. Have you in fact attacked Navahk without declaration of war? Or is it possible such an attack was made *without* your authorization? And if so, was that attack led by Prince Bahzell?"

Bahnak gazed down at her, then looked out across the hall once more. He let the silence linger for a long, tingling moment, then returned his gaze to Entarath.

"In answer to your question, Milady," he said with grave courtesy, "neither I, nor any warrior under my command, nor yet any warrior of mine acting without my leave or let, has attacked the army or people of Navahk."

A rippling sigh of relief went up from half the envoys, to be answered by a buzz of disbelief from the other half, but Bahnak raised his hand.

"Nonetheless," he went on, "Horse Stealer warriors *were* after crossing into Navahk last week . . . and my son Bahzell *was* at their head."

Shocked silence fell at the admission. It lay upon the hall like a fog bank for endless seconds, and then Halâshu broke it.

"But you said—!" he began furiously.

"I *said* as how no warrior under my command was after attacking that scum-eating, fornicating, base-born bastard *you* call prince!" Bahnak snapped "And no more did they! Nor was it me who had the sending of them into Navahk!"

He nodded curtly to a guard, and the man reopened the door through which he and his children had entered the hall. The movement drew every eye, and a chorus of gasps echoed as Bahzell walked through it, followed by his cousin Hurthang, his foster brother Gharnal, and half a dozen other Horse Stealers. Every one of them wore a green surcoat over a chain or scale hauberk, and the seamstresses of Bahnak's household had stayed up late embroidering the sword and mace of Tomanāk onto each of them. That should have been enough to make any one of the envoys gasp in surprise, but it hardly even registered at first, for two humans— one a golden-haired young man and the other a raven-haired woman—in the same surcoats accompanied them . . . and so did perhaps a dozen prisoners, most of whom were clearly Bloody Swords.

Bahzell led the way, hands tucked unthreateningly into his belt, but the envoys and armsmen in his path began backing away the instant they saw his eyes. Even Halâshu stepped back, swallowing hard, as he found himself face-to-face with the man he'd just finished accusing of rape, cowardice, and treachery. Only Lady Entarath and her armsman stood their ground, and Bahzell nodded courteously to her as his followers and their prisoners flowed forward into the space his mere presence had cleared for them.

"These are the men—some of them, at least—as you've heard so many tales about," Prince Bahnak said quietly, seating himself once more upon his throne. "And though it's proud I am to call them Horse Stealers, aye, and warriors of Clan Iron Axe, they're no longer mine to command, for they've sworn their swords to another . . . as my son has." He turned to look at Halâshu with an expression of withering contempt. "I've no doubt at all, at all, you'll recognize the symbols of Tomanāk, Milord Ambassador. So perhaps you'd be so very kind as to be repeating now the tale you and your 'prince' have been after telling for nigh on six months? It's interested I'll be to hear you accuse a champion of Tomanāk of rape and murder and cowardice to his face!"

"Champion?" The word came out of Halâshu half-strangled, and the same ripple of shock ran through everyone else. "Are you— D'you mean to stand there and claim your son is a champion of Tomanāk?"

"He does that," Bahzell rumbled. Halâshu's eyes jerked back to him, and Bahnak's youngest son smiled thinly. "And would you care to be telling me just what it is you've been saying of me?" he invited.

"I—" Halâshu swallowed, then shook himself. "What I've said or your father's said about that doesn't matter," he shot back gamely. "What does matter is that he's just admitted he sent you to attack Navahk after telling everyone he'd done no such thing!"

"You've the ears of a hradani," Bahzell replied in tones of profound disgust, "but it's clear they've done you no good at all, at all, for if you'd used them, you'd know he'd 'admitted' nothing of the sort. Father wasn't after sending us *anywhere*, you stupid bugger. *Tomanāk* sent us, as members of his Order, and not to be attacking Navahk."

He nodded to Hurthang, and his cousin jerked a prisoner roughly forward. Tharnatus still wore the blood-soaked robe in which he had been captured, and he cried out as Hurthang shoved him to his knees. But the Horse Stealer ignored his cry and gripped his hair, jerking his head up, and then ripped the throat of his robe wide to show the gleaming, gem-studded scorpion he wore about his neck.

Half a dozen voices cried out in horror, and Lady Entarath stepped back at last. Her right hand signed the crescent moon of Lillinara, and her lips worked as if to spit upon the floor. She jerked her eyes from Tharnatus to Bahzell, and the Horse Stealer nodded in grave answer to the question he saw in them. She stared at him a moment longer, and then she bent her head—not in submission, but in recognition—and touched her armsman's mailed sleeve. The two of them stepped back into the crowd behind them, and Bahzell raised his eyes to sweep the entire hall.

"I'm thinking as how you all know whose sign *that* is," he rumbled, "and it was to deal with those as follow it that Tomanāk was after sending us into Navahk."

"A-Are you—? D'you mean—?" Halāshu sputtered furiously. He was white-faced with shock, but for the first time his outrage seemed completely genuine. "Are you accusing my prince of worshiping *Sharnā*?" he managed at last.

"Accuse Churnazh?" Bahzell met his infuriated stare levelly while the rest of the envoys listened in hushed anticipation. "No. No, I'll not lay that on Churnazh." A deep, soft sigh greeted his answer, but Bahzell wasn't done. "But this I will be saying, Lord Halāshu— your precious Harnak *was* after worshiping Demon Breath, and it was in Sharnā's service he fell to my own sword." Halāshu jerked as if he'd been struck, and Bahzell smiled coldly. "And as for the rest of Churnazh's family—"

He nodded again, this time to Gharnal, and his foster brother stepped forward. He untied the cloth sack he carried and upended it, and the solid, meaty thud as Crown Prince Chalghaz's severed head hit the floor echoed in the stunned silence.

"I'll not call Churnazh demon-worshiper," Bahzell said softly into that silence, "but I *will* be saying he's not been so very careful as he might have about his sons' doings, has he now?"

Halâshu's eyes bulged as he stared at the head of his prince's heir. Two of Churnazh's sons had fallen to Bahzell Bahnakson now, and his teeth grated with his own hate, as well as the anticipation of how Navahk's ruler would react. The other envoys were at least equally shocked, but they were also confused. Halâshu had no more idea than they of what had actually happened, but he already saw where this disastrous morning was headed. Whatever Churnazh might or might not have known, the accusation that his two eldest sons had *both* worshiped Sharnâ would devastate his alliances. But there was only one way that accusation could be refuted, and the Navahkan envoy shook himself and wrenched his eyes away from Chalghaz's head.

"So *you* say!" he spat at Bahzell, and wheeled to glare at Bahnak. "And you—*you* say it! But I see no proof. I see only the head of another murdered prince of Navahk!"

"And what of that other lot?" an envoy from one of the other Horse Stealer princes called out. "Or would you be saying *they're* not after being 'proof,' either?"

"I don't know anything about them," Halâshu shot back, turning to glare at the woman who'd spoken, "and neither do you! Perhaps they truly do—did—worship Sharnâ, and perhaps they didn't. Anyone can be forced to wear a fancy bedgown, Milady, just as anyone can be forced to wear a fancy necklace. I won't say they are or aren't what they seem—but neither will I say *he* is!" He waved his hand at Bahzell in a choppy gesture. "I see *Horse Stealers* wearing the colors of Tomanâk and claiming *Bloody Swords* worship Sharnâ. Well, why the Phrobus should we take *their* word for it?"

"Are you after calling me a liar, then?" Bahzell asked in a voice whose mildness deceived no one, but Halâshu only flicked a sneer at him, secure in his ambassador's inviolability. He felt the attitudes of the other envoys shifting as his argument registered, and he moved to drive his momentary advantage home.

"I'm saying I see no reason to accept your unsupported word that my folk are blood-drinking, flesh-eating, demon-worshiping monsters," he said flatly. "It would certainly be *convenient* for you Horse Stealers if we were, now wouldn't it?"

"Maybe it would, and maybe it wouldn't," Bahzell replied coldly, "but I've not said any such thing. *Some* of your folk, aye, and we've the proof of that right here." He waved at the prisoners. "But all of 'em? No. Whatever the feelings between Horse Stealer and Bloody Sword, I'm after knowing as well as you that most of your folk are decent enough, and few among 'em would wallow in such filth as that. Not even Churnazh, if only because he's after knowing exactly how his allies would turn on him if ever he did."

Several envoys murmured agreement, and Halâshu's jaw clenched as the small opinion swing in his favor swung back the other way. Bahzell's refusal to accuse Churnazh of sharing his sons' perversions was a telling blow. If all this *had* been some ploy by Bahnak to discredit his enemy, Bahzell would have done exactly the opposite, and Halâshu knew it. But he also knew the Horse Stealers didn't have to accuse Churnazh personally. The mere fact that Sharnā had gained a hold in Navahk—and upon two successive heirs to the throne, at that!—would shake the Bloody Sword alliances to their foundations. He felt a sick, sinking certainty that Bahzell was telling the truth, or a part of it, at least, yet he dared not admit it.

"How *kind* of you to omit Prince Churnazh from your lies!" he sneered instead. "Of course, you didn't accuse either of his sons until after they were safely dead, either, now did you? It's hard for a dead man to defend himself, isn't it, *Prince* Bahzell?"

"So it is," Bahzell agreed. "Of course, it's also a mite hard to be taking a man alive when he's been given a cursed sword as opens a gate to Sharnā himself, now isn't it, Milord Ambassador?"

"So *you* say!" Halâshu spat. "But why should we believe you? You say you're a champion of *Tomanāk*, too, don't you?" He turned to the assembled envoys and threw up his arms in appeal. "A champion of Tomanāk? A *hradani* champion? I ask you all, my lords and ladies—why in the names of all the gods should we believe *that*? Oh, I'll admit it's a bold stroke! What *better* way to discredit my prince than to murder his sons and then accuse them of having worshiped the Demon Lord? And who better to make the accusation than a 'champion of Tomanāk'? But there hasn't been a hradani champion in over *twelve centuries!* Who among us would be fool enough to claim someone like *Bahzell Bahnakson* as such?"

"*I* would," a voice like a mountain avalanche said. It shook the entire hall, and Halâshu spun about and his mouth dropped open as he saw the speaker.

Tomanāk Orfro stood beside Bahzell. It was impossible, of course. There was no room in that crowded hall for a ten-foot-tall deity, and yet there was. In some way every person there knew he or she would never be able to explain, Prince Bahnak's hall remained exactly the same size and yet expanded enormously. There was room in it for *anything*, and the god's presence swept through it like a storm. The prisoners his Order had brought back from Navahk wailed in terror, thrashing wildly against their bonds as the Dark Gods' most deadly foe appeared before them. The guards tightened their grips upon them, but before they could do more Tomanāk glanced once at the captives, and their wails were cut off as if by an axe. They stood petrified, eyes bulging in horror, and the smile he gave them was colder than the steel of his blade.

Then he looked away from them. His gaze—no longer crushing and silencing, but no less potent—swept the envoys and, throughout the hall, men fell to their knees and women sank in deep curtseys before the power which had appeared among them.

But not everyone knelt. Halâshu of Navahk stood almost like the prisoners, too frozen to move and, as the others knelt, Bahnak himself rose once more from his throne. He stood with his daughter at his side and his older sons behind him, and Tomanāk glanced at Bahzell with a smile.

"It runs in the family, I see," he said wryly, and eyes brightened throughout the hall at the laughter which flickered in his voice.

"Aye, I suppose it does," Bahzell agreed. "We're after being a mite on the stubborn side, the lot of us."

"The lot of you, indeed," Tomanāk said, looking at the ambassadors. "I hope you won't take this wrongly, Bahzell, but it seemed to me as if the argument could go on for at least a week. Under the circumstances, I thought perhaps I could speed things up a bit."

"Did you, then?" Bahzell murmured. He let his own eyes sweep the stunned envoys, and a small smile hovered on his lips. "D'you know, I'm thinking as how you might just have done that thing."

"I intended to. Of course, with hradani it's hard to be certain you've gotten through," Tomanāk observed, and this time half a dozen of the people in the hall surprised themselves by laughing with him.

"That's better," he told them, then looked back down at Bahzell. "You've done well," he said. "It's not often that even one of my champions creates a whole new chapter of the Order singlehanded and then leads them to such victory in their very first battle. You've exceeded expectations yet again, Bahzell. That seems to be a habit of yours."

"I'm sure that's flattering," Bahzell said dryly, "but I'd not say as how I was after doing it 'singlehanded.' You'll be knowing even better than I the quality of the lads who followed me—and I'd not call the help of another champion naught."

"No, you wouldn't. And neither would I, though some might attempt to in your place. I stand corrected."

Tomanāk nodded gravely. Then he turned to Halâshu, and his expression became stern. "I trust, Ambassador, that your doubts as to my champion's honesty have now been resolved? Do you take *my* word that he is, indeed, my champion, and that whatever *you* may think, *I* know all of these—" a hand waved at the warriors who'd followed Bahzell into Navahk and now knelt in wonder as they gazed at their deity "—as my own?"

"Y-Y-Y—" Halâshu swallowed hard. "Yes, Sir," he choked out finally.

"Good." Tomanâk made a shooing gesture with one index finger, and Halâshu fell back instantly into the crowd and went to his own knees. The War God folded his arms, regarding them all for several moments, and a strange, breathless hush seemed to hover somewhere at the bases of their throats.

"Halâshu was correct about one thing, you know," Tomanâk told them at last, and now that boulder-shattering voice was gentle. "Neither I nor any other God of Light have had a hradani champion since the Fall of Kontovar. It wasn't because we no longer cared for you, nor had we abandoned you, however hard your lot had become. But the damage which had been done to you by the Dark Gods and their servants was too terrible. We had been unable to prevent it, and your ancestors—"

He sighed, and his brown eyes shone with a sorrow too deep for tears—one so deep only a god could know it.

"Your ancestors could not forgive our failure," he said softly, "and how could we blame them? If we could have prevented it, we would have, but as Bahzell here could tell you, we may act only through our followers in your world. The Dark won an enormous victory in the Fall, and not the least of their triumphs was the hatred and suspicion which have divided your people not simply from the other Races of Man, but also from us.

"But the damage you suffered can be healed, and those divisions need not remain forever, and *that*, my children, is why the time has come for me to choose a hradani champion once again. Bahzell and the chapter of my Order he has established here among you have much to tell you and teach you. I will leave that task to him and to those he chooses to help him with it, but I tell you now—all of you—that my Order welcomes *all* hradani. Horse Stealer, Bloody Sword, Broken Bone and Wild Wash . . . any hradani who keeps my Code and honors the Light will be as welcome among my Blades as any human or dwarf or elf. The time has come for you to stand once more in the Light, and you will find that the terrible years your people have spent in the shadows have given you strengths and abilities the other Races will someday need sorely."

"But—"

The single word came out of Halâshu, and Tomanāk looked at the Navahkan once more. There was no judgment or condemnation in the god's eyes, yet they cut Halâshu off like a knife blade, and sweat beaded the envoy's face as all the endless times he and his prince had violated Tomanāk's code flickered in his brain.

"But you wonder if my choice of Bahzell—and his willingness to accept the burden of serving as my champion—mean I have chosen sides between Navahk and Hurgrum?" the god asked quietly, and somehow Halâshu found the strength to nod.

"I am the Judge of Princes, Halâshu of Navahk, and my courtroom is the field of battle. My decision will be rendered there, not here. I did not appear before you for that purpose, and neither my Order nor my champions will take part in any fighting between your prince and Hurgrum's." The god gazed out at all the envoys. "More, I here confirm what Bahzell has told you: Churnazh of Navahk had no knowledge of his sons' actions or of Sharnā's presence in his realm. If you would oppose him, oppose him for reasons other than that. If you would support him, then do not hold the crimes of others against him. You are not slaves, and we of the Light do not seek such. You must make your own decisions in this, as you must decide what god—if any—you will follow."

Halâshu nodded again, a bit more naturally, and Tomanāk looked at Bahzell.

"I know how stubborn you can be. Will you obey my wishes in this respect?"

"Aye," Bahzell replied. "I'll not say I like it, but I'll do as you wish. Besides—" he grinned suddenly "—it's not as if there aren't after being Horse Stealers enough to deal with the likes of Navahk without me!"

"I suppose that's the most gracious promise I can hope for." Tomanāk sighed so mournfully that, once again, the envoys surprised themselves with a ripple of laughter. The god smiled at them, then glanced at Kaeritha and beckoned her forward.

"Did you think I would forget to greet *you*, Kerry?" he asked teasingly.

"No." She smiled. "I just assumed you needed to concentrate on Bahzell first. I've noticed that getting ideas through to him requires a certain amount of effort."

"Even from a god," Tomanāk agreed. "Ask him someday to tell you about how long I had to pester him before he even realized who was trying to get his attention."

"I will," she promised.

"Good. For now, though, and in answer to the question in your mind, yes. You're doing exactly what you ought to be doing."

"I am?" She blinked. "Well, that's reassuring. Now if *I* only knew what I'm doing, everything would be perfect."

"Don't worry. It will come to you. And now—" the god turned to where the members of the newest chapter of his Order knelt "—there's only one more detail to be dealt with. Come here, Vaijon."

The golden haired knight-probationer jerked as if somehow had just touched a particularly sensitive portion of his anatomy with a well-heated poker. His head flew up, his expression one of mingled delight and fear, and he rose. He walked across the floor through a hush that was once more total to stand between Bahzell and Kaeritha, gazing up at his deity's face, and Tomanāk smiled.

"I have something of yours," he told him. Vaijon's eyebrows rose in surprise, and then the god reached out a hand and plucked a sword out of the air as casually as a mortal might have reached into a pocket. He held it up, turning it so that the gems set into its hilt and guard glittered, and astonished recognition flickered in Vaijon's eyes.

"I believe you left this in a demon," Tomanāk said.

"I—" Vaijon looked up at him, then nodded. "I suppose I did," he said.

"A pretty toy," Tomanāk observed, "but the steel is sound enough under all the fancywork. One simply has to look close enough to see it, wouldn't you say, Vaijon?" The young man nodded slowly, never looking away from the god's face. Every person in the hall knew the words meant far more than they seemed to, but only Bahzell and Vaijon knew what that something more was.

"Yes," Tomanāk went on judiciously, "I think you understand that now. Just as you understand that a blade that looks a bit rough and unpolished—" he flicked a grin at Bahzell "—can bite deeper and truer than the most beautiful one ever forged. And just as you've learned to understand that—" he returned his eyes to Vaijon "—I've tested the steel in you, Vaijon of Almerhas. It took a while to see past the gems and decoration, but there's a fine blade underneath all that gaudiness . . . one I would be pleased to call my own."

He reached down and handed Vaijon's sword not to him, but to Kaeritha. Vaijon's eyes flickered in confusion for a moment, but then Tomanāk reached back over his shoulder to draw his own sword and extend the hilt to him.

"Will you swear Sword Oath to me as my champion, Vaijon?" he asked, and Vaijon sucked in deeply. His eyes clung to that plain, wire-bound hilt, and he started to shake his head—not in rejection, but with a profound sense of his unworthiness. But a hand on his shoulder stopped him, and he turned his head to see Bahzell's smile.

"It's not a thing as any man feels worthy of, lad," he said softly.

"No, it's not," Tomanāk confirmed, "and the more worthy of it he is, the less worthy he *feels*. But you *are* worthy, Vaijon. Will you serve me?"

"I will," Vaijon whispered, and laid his hand upon the hilt of his god's sword.

Blue light crackled about his fingers as he touched it, and prominences of the same light ran up his arm to dance and seethe about his head like a crown of fire. The same blue radiance danced above Bahzell and Kaeritha, flickering in a web of power that linked both champions to the champion to be and to their deity, and Tomanāk's deep voice echoed in the silence of Prince Bahnak's hall.

"Do you, Vaijon of Almerhas, swear fealty to me?"

"I do." Vaijon's voice had taken on an echo of the War God's, and there was no more doubt, no more hesitation in it.

"Will you honor and keep my Code? Will you bear true service to the Powers of Light, heeding the commands of your own heart and mind and striving always against the Dark as they require, even unto death?"

"I will."

"Do you swear by my Sword and your own to render compassion to those in need, justice to those you may be set to command, loyalty to those you choose to serve, and punishment to those who knowingly serve the Dark?"

"I do."

"Then I accept your oath, Vaijon of Almerhas, and bid you take up your blade once more. Bear it well in the cause to which you have been called."

There was a moment, like a pause in the breath of infinity—one Bahzell remembered well from a windy night in the Shipwood when *he* had sworn that oath—and then Tomanāk drew back his sword and Vaijon blinked like a man awaking from sleep. He drew a deep, lung-filling breath and smiled up at his god, and Kaeritha stepped up beside him and extended the sword Tomanāk had handed her. He took it from her and, as he touched it, Bahzell saw the same spark in him he had seen in Kaeritha from the first—the flicker of Tomanāk's reflected presence burning like some secret coal at the young man's heart. He reached out, embracing the War God's newest champion, and Tomanāk smiled down at them all.

"Remarkable," he said, drawing his champions' eyes back to him. He shook his head. "It isn't often one of my champions has the opportunity to swear Sword Oath with even one other champion present, and here I am with three. And the three of you," he told them, "are quite possibly the stubbornest trio of mortals I've come across in millennia. If you think you had a hard time with Vaijon, Bahzell, you should hunt up Dame Chaerwyn and let her tell you what *she* went through with Kerry!"

"I wasn't *that* bad, Milord!" Kaeritha protested. "Was I?"

"Worse," Tomanāk assured her. "*Much* worse. But the best ones usually are."

"Are they, now?" Bahzell asked.

"Of course there are, Bahzell," Tomanāk said. "That's why I feel confident I'll be finding *lots* of them among your folk in the future."

And he vanished.

CHAPTER TWENTY-SEVEN

Brandark Brandarkson leaned back on the weathered wooden bench with a mug of beer and basked in the first real sunlight in almost a week. The cold, wet rains of a northern spring were no stranger to him, but that didn't mean he enjoyed them, and he savored the clean, mellow taste of the beer as he soaked up the warmth. His bench was in an angle of the wall around the exercise field of the fortified manor Prince Bahnak had deeded to the fledgling Hurgrum Chapter of the Order of Tomanāk. The sharp bend shielded him from the breeze—still unpleasantly biting—while he enjoyed the sun and the first, shy flowers of spring poking through the muddy grass, and his balalaika lay beside him, weighting down the pad on which he'd been jotting potential lyrics.

He took another long swallow. The chill damp in the air only contrasted with the sun's warmth and made it even more welcome, and he luxuriated in sensual enjoyment. Yet his joy was less than complete, for the same sun had cleared most of the snow from the roads. The short northern campaigning season was almost upon them—would be, as soon as the mud dried a bit and the spring planting was in—and he felt time passing like the ticking of his pocket watch in the back of his brain while he watched the members of the newest chapter of the Order of Tomanāk at drill.

There were more of them than there had been. Fresh recruits had trickled in steadily—most Horse Stealers, but with a prickly, defensive Bloody Sword tucked away among them here and there—ever since the dramatic scene in Bahnak's hall. The word that Tomanāk Himself had appeared had spread like wildfire, and the

291

response had been astounding, especially for hradani. Their centuries-long distrust of all gods should have made them react as young Chavâk had: with suspicion and doubt. And if the truth was known, Brandark suspected, many *had* reacted in exactly that fashion. But a significant number had not, and even Churnazh had been forced to give his blessings to the creation of the new chapter. He hadn't wanted to. The grudging wording of his proclamation made *that* perfectly plain! Yet he'd had no choice but to grant any of his warriors who wished to join it leave to do so—not after the Order's very first act had been to rescue his own realm from the influence of the Dark Gods. And especially not after Bahzell had proclaimed Tomanâk's news about the Rage.

Now over eighty warriors were out in the exercise field, squelching around the brown, sodden turf while wooden training weapons whacked and thwacked with bruising enthusiasm. Even from here he could hear occasional grunts of anguish as blows got through on practice armor, and Vaijon had two or three of the younger members off to one side, demonstrating a pass they'd never seen before. Despite his foreboding over the rapidly approaching war, Brandark smiled into his beer as he noted how intently the youngsters listened. It was amazing how having the War God Himself turn up to declare a man a champion could raise his stock, he thought wryly.

Someone walked around the corner into his sheltered nook and he turned his head, then rose with a smile, flourishing his beer as he bowed gracefully to Marglyth.

"Good morning, Milady," he said, and she smiled back at him.

"And good morning to you, Lord Brandark." She dropped a tiny curtsey in response to his bow. "And now you can just sit back down before I'm after kicking you somewhere as you wouldn't like," she suggested, and he laughed.

"Ah, you Horse Stealers are so . . . *uncomplicated*," he said, waving her down to sit beside him, and it was her turn to laugh.

"I suppose we are that," she agreed. But then her smile faded as she turned her head to watch the field. Her sister Sharkah was out there, working with Kaeritha, and Marglyth's eyes were worried as she watched them. Kaeritha wasn't teaching Sharkah her own style. Unlike Marglyth, who was as close to petite as any Horse Stealer was ever likely to come, Sharkah favored her father and brothers. She stood close to seven feet tall, and if she was built on slimmer lines, without her male siblings' massive thews, she was also faster. Kaeritha had her training with a bastard sword, and her progress was so excellent that Marglyth felt certain Sharkah had convinced one of their brothers—probably Thankar—to give her a little surreptitious training even before Bahnak relaxed his edict. Kaeritha had not yet moved beyond the most basic moves while she worked to build up the girl's muscle mass, and Sharkah was still awkward. But she was much less awkward than any of her brothers had been at the same *official* stage in their training, and her determination was almost frightening.

"Worried, Marglyth?" Brandark asked gently. She glanced quickly at him, expression guarded, then relaxed as she saw the understanding in his eyes.

"I am that. Mind, it's not because I've any objection to her doing as she chooses. Come to that, I've been telling Da for two years now that he'd be wiser to see to her training himself before she was after sneaking off to learn it on her own. It's only that she's so . . . focused. I've this dream comes to me these nights that she's like to be running off half-trained to do something truly stupid when once the war ever starts."

"She *does* rather remind you of her youngest brother, doesn't she?" Brandark murmured, and Marglyth chuckled.

"Aye, she does. And as you'll be knowing as well as I, there was never a day in his life Bahzell Bahnakson looked before he leapt!"

"Actually, I don't think I can agree with that—not really," Brandark said much more seriously, and Marglyth raised an eyebrow. "He's not a patient man, your brother, but I don't really think of him as hasty. It's more a matter of knowing his own mind. Or knowing *himself*, maybe." The Bloody Sword frowned, trying to find exactly the right words. "It's not that he doesn't think about the consequences of what he does, Marglyth; it's just that he *accepts* those consequences, whatever they may be, if that sense of responsibility tells him he should do it anyway." He shook his head.

"Bahzell is probably the least complicated man I know, once you figure out what's truly important to him, but he's also the stubbornest. It's like this business about the Rage. Tomanāk told him to tell all hradani, and damn me if he didn't—right on the brink of a flaming war!" Brandark shook his head again, gazing out across the field at his friend. "Somehow I suspect your father would have preferred for him to wait to tell Churnazh and his lot about that until after the fighting was over."

"He would that," Marglyth agreed. "But Bahzell was after insisting it had to be *now*, before the fighting. He said Tomanāk hadn't told him to be doing it at the most convenient time for *us*. I was thinking Da was like to burst a blood vessel, but then he just threw up his hands and went stalking out of the room." She chuckled. "Truth to tell, I'm thinking he was a mite pleased about it, once his temper'd cooled."

"He would be," Brandark said dryly. "But that's my point. Bahzell loves his father dearly, but even if he'd expected Prince Bahnak to be furious—and to *stay* that way—he still would have done exactly the same thing because it was his *job* to do it. I may not accuse him of being very smart, but he *is* a bit on the determined side."

"Aye, and Sharkah's another chip from the same boneheaded boulder!" Marglyth said tartly, then sighed. "I could wish as how she'd be just a *bit* less mulish than he. After all, she's the better part of ten years' advantage on him, and she could have been learning *some* discretion in that long! But it's useless telling myself there's hope she'll change this late in the day."

"Probably not. On the other hand, Kerry's as well aware of that as you are, and she gave her as stern a lecture as I've ever heard before she agreed to train her." Brandark laughed again. "The funny thing is, Sharkah is a good fifteen years older than Kerry is, but in terms of experience—!" He shrugged, and Marglyth nodded.

"Aye. It's hard to remind myself sometimes that humans are only like to live seventy or eighty years. It must give them a dreadful need to be out and doing early."

"I don't think they really see it that way," Brandark said thoughtfully. "That they're shorter on time than we are, I mean. All other things being equal, they're inclined to let their children grow up faster than we let ours, I think, but then, they have more of them than we do. If Kerry's childhood had been less ugly, she'd probably have stayed in her home village and had at least four or five children by now. Probably more."

"What?" Marglyth blinked at her. "But if Sharkah's being—" She broke off and did some rapid math. "Why, she's not a day past thirty-two!" she said in half-shocked tones, for a hradani girl seldom married before her late twenties and it was extremely rare for her to bear her *first* child before thirty.

"No, she isn't." Brandark took another swallow of beer and nodded towards the practice field. "She's little more than a girl, by our standards, but do you see her deferring to any of the lads out there?" Marglyth shook her head, and he shrugged. "That's what I mean about them growing up faster. That 'girl' has been a belted knight of Tomanāk—and a champion—since she was twenty-four. What were you doing at that age?"

"Mooning after my favorite tutor," Marglyth admitted with a smile.

"And Sharkah?"

"*Avoiding* my favorite tutor. In fact, she was after avoiding *every* tutor, if the truth be told. I did mention as how she was just a *mite* like Bahzell, didn't I?"

"Yes, I believe you did. But that difference in the rate at which we expect our children to grow up is why she listens to every word Kerry says." He shrugged. "I doubt it even crosses her mind to think about Kerry's age, because what she's *hearing* is Kerry's *experience*. So when Kerry delivered her lecture, Sharkah listened, believe me."

"And what would that lecture have been about?"

"The most important part was a solemn promise from Sharkah that she'll stay home and tend to her training until *Kerry* decides she's ready. It was a precondition of Kerry's agreeing to train her at all, and then Bahzell came along and made her swear to obey *all* the Order's trainers."

"Are you saying he's admitted her to the Order?" Marglyth blinked in surprise, but Brandark shook his head.

"No. Not that he'd tell her no if she wanted to join it. But even if she did, he wouldn't let her take Sword Oath until she'd completed her initial training to the Order's satisfaction. I think the training itself is a testing process. It's grueling enough that no one who's survived it can cherish any illusions about what swearing obedience to a military order entails."

Marglyth nodded, but her eyes were on Brandark, not the field, and her expression was thoughtful. The Bloody Sword didn't seem to notice at once, but then her silence drew his own attention back from the field and he cocked his ears at her.

"You're after knowing a lot about the Order, aren't you?" she asked.

"Well, thanks to your brother I've been hanging about with it one way and another for the better part of four months," Brandark said wryly. "I suppose I've learned a little about it along the way."

"Aye, so you have. And I'm hoping you'll not take this wrongly, but why is it that *you* haven't joined it?" Brandark cocked his head, and Marglyth hurried on. "What I'm meaning to say is, you've been going along with Bahzell and watching his back wherever the Order took *him*, and from all I've had the hearing of, there's not a knight of Tomanāk at all as has done more."

"Um." Brandark reached for his balalaika and picked out soft, plaintive notes while he considered her question. She watched his maimed left hand chording around the missing fingers and waited patiently for more than a full minute. Then he shrugged. "Tomanāk's not the right god," he said simply.

"Excuse me?" Marglyth blinked, and he laughed.

"Oh, I *respect* Him, and I certainly agree with what He seems to have in mind. But the deity I've always felt closest to is Chesmirsa. Unfortunately, as you may've noticed, I lack the voice of a true bard. And despite the success of my little ditty about Bahzell, I'm actually a pretty terrible poet, as well." He said it so lightly most people might have been fooled into missing the sad longing which lurked behind the words. Marglyth wasn't one of them, but she respected him too much to show it, and so she simply nodded.

"Bahzell and I actually met Chesmirsa, you know," Brandark went on, and the lingering sorrow vanished as his eyes glowed. "It was . . . . I don't begin to have the *words* for what it was like, Marglyth. The most wonderful night of my life—the night I truly realized for the first time how much magic there is in the world. Not just what wizards and gods can do, but in here." He tapped his chest. "Inside *us*. She showed me that, and even when She told me I would never be a bard, She promised She would always be with me. That I would always be at least partly Hers."

He fell silent once more, fingers caressing his instrument, and Marglyth sat very still, listening to the wistful, yearning beauty he coaxed from it. Then he inhaled deeply.

"At any rate, she told me then that I was 'too much Her brother's to be fully Hers. At the time, I assumed she was speaking of Tomanāk, and perhaps she was, in part. But somehow—" He frowned, then shook his head. "Somehow that's not . . . quite . . . right. There's something more to it. I just haven't figured out what."

"But they've every one of them accepted you as one of their own," Marglyth said.

"That they have—even if I *am* a Bloody Sword. But that's between *us*. Between them and me, not Tomanāk and me."

"So will you be staying with us, then? After the war, I mean?"

"After the war," Brandark murmured, and the balalaika's soft notes were suddenly dark and discordant. He gazed back out over the exercise field, but Marglyth doubted that he actually saw it, and he shook his head slowly, his eyes sad.

"I don't know," he said finally. "I just don't know. You've made me as welcome as Bahzell himself—not just the Order, but your family, as well—but I'm *not* a Horse Stealer. I'm a Bloody Sword, and when the fighting starts, my father and my brothers and my cousins will be on the other side. I can't fight for a bastard like Churnazh, but they haven't got a choice. So the only way to avoid the risk of finding myself facing one of them across a sword is to not fight *against* Churnazh, either. Yet I can't just walk away. I have to *be* here, to know what's happening. So the only place I truly have is with the Order, because Tomanāk Himself has ordered them to remain neutral. But afterward?"

He took his gaze from the exercise field and looked at her levelly.

"I love your brother, Marglyth," he said in a quiet voice. "I won't tell *him* that, but I imagine he knows. And I respect and admire your father. I agree with what he wants for our people—all our people, not just you Horse Stealers—and he's the only alternative I see to an unending succession of Churnazes. But if Prince Bahnak wins the war, then my people have to lose it, and however justified I was not to fight alongside them, some of them will never forget—or forgive—the fact that I didn't. And I don't think I can stay here if that's the case. As much as I hate what Churnazh has made of my clan and my city, I'm still Raven Talon, and I'm still Navahkan, and I don't think I can handle being this close to them and . . . estranged. Do you understand that?"

"Aye, Brandark." She reached out and laid a hand gently on his elbow, and her eyes were soft. "Aye, I can be seeing that, and so will Bahzell, I'm thinking. But do you be remembering this, Brandark Brandarkson. Raven Talon you may be, and Bloody Sword, aye, and even Navahkan, but you're ours now, too, and you've brothers and sisters here in Hurgrum. You go on, if you've a need to, but never be forgetting us, for we'll not forget you, whatever chances."

CHAPTER TWENTY-EIGHT

"And I'm after telling *you* that it won't work!"

Hurthang Tharakson slammed a massive fist on the table and glared at his cousin. Other conversations paused as the tankards on the table danced and clattered, and the other members of the chapter broke off their own discussions and turned to watch Hurthang and Bahzell match glares. They sat across from each other in the main hall of the Hurgrum chapter's new chapter house, and their expressions were not cheerful.

"And a useless thing it is to be telling me it won't, too, and no mistake," Bahzell rumbled back in only slightly milder tones. "There's too much Horse Stealer and not enough Tomanāk in your head yet, Hurthang! It's not a matter of will it or won't it, but how best to be *making* it work!"

"You're daft, man! Stark, staring mad! You're talking Bloody Swords—and Raven Talons to boot!" Hurthang snapped, then had the grace to look embarrassed. He glanced around the big room quickly and heaved a sigh of relief. None of the novice members were present, and Prince Bahnak had asked Brandark to join him to discuss Marglyth's spies' latest information from Navahk. Which was undoubtedly just as well, he reflected, only to have his attention drawn back to Bahzell as his cousin snorted magnificently.

"Fiendark seize me, but the man's been after figuring out a part of it, anyway! Aye, it *is* Bloody Swords I'm talking of right enough, you rock-pated lump of gristle, and not just Raven Talons! There's Dire Claws and Stone Daggers—aye, and Bone Fists, too! And if you're thinking *I'm* daft, then I can't but wonder where you'd left those hairy ears of yours when himself was amongst us!"

Hurthang glowered. Bahzell's last sentence had hit home, but it was clear he didn't want it to have, and he *was* Bahzell's cousin, with a determination to match. He gathered himself once more, shoulders hunching, and leaned forward into the argument once more.

"But—" he began, only to be cut off by a mild tenor.

"You're not going to win, Hurthang," it remarked, and he turned his head sharply. Vaijon gave him a crooked smile and shrugged. "You're a stubborn man, but not as stubborn as Bahzell," Tomanāk's newest champion told him. "*No one* else is that hardheaded. Besides, this time he's right. The Order must be open to any who feel the call to serve the War God . . . wherever they come from."

"But—" Hurthang tried again, and Vaijon laughed.

"Give it up," he advised, not unkindly. His Hurgrumese had gotten much better, but he still had to revert to Axeman to make his points most clearly, and here and there other members of the fledgling chapter leaned towards friends to translate.

"Trust me," he went on, "it'll be easier that way. Tomanāk has a way of making His points, especially to people who only continue to argue out of sheer bloody-mindedness. And the stubborner you get, the more . . . interesting the lesson is when it finally arrives. Believe me, I speak from painful personal experience. You can't possibly be more upset by this than I was at the notion of accepting *any* hradani as a member of the Order, and look where *I* wound up!"

He waved a hand at the hall about them, and a rumble of laughter answered the gesture. Hurthang glowered at him for another instant, but the wicked smile Vaijon gave him was too much to resist, and his own lips quirked as the worst of his fury faded.

"Aye, well, it's all very well to be making us laugh, Vaijon," he said much more calmly, "but you've yet to answer my worries. I've no doubt at all, at all, that Himself means for us to be doing just as you say—aye, and Bahzell, too, even if he *is* stubborn as a pasture full of mules! But there's a war coming, and it's coming on fast. And whatever you may be thinking, or me—or even Bahzell!— there no way to be *knowing* as how everyone as says he's been called by the Sword God truly has. D'you think for a moment the likes of Churnazh or Halâshu would be turning up their noses at the thought of slipping their spies inside Uncle Bahnak's court by *pretending* to join the Order?"

"I don't know," Vaijon admitted. He walked across to sit at the same table, and Bahzell leaned back comfortably, content to leave the main burden of the argument to the human. "Of course, right this minute I don't believe we're talking about any 'spies,' either," Vaijon went on thoughtfully, lifting the beer pitcher to pour a mug of his own. "You've met all of the Bloody Sword recruits, Hurthang. D'*you* think any of them are lying about their desire to join the Order?"

"As to that, no," Hurthang admitted grudgingly. "But they're naught but the first wave, I'm thinking. Aye, and we've not let any of 'em swear Sword Oath, yet, either."

Vaijon shook his head, conceding the point. Of course, they hadn't yet sworn any of the other *Horse Stealer* recruits to full membership in the Order, either. Irregular as Bahzell's attitude towards rules might be in most respects, he was determined to get the Hurgrum chapter properly organized. In part, Vaijon suspected, that was because he expected it to be greeted with profound reservations, even by its sister chapters (when they discovered its existence), and so he wanted to be certain every procedural concern had been covered. More importantly, however, he was determined to be as certain as possible that all of its members had true vocations for the Order, and so he had insisted each new member must serve a minimum of a three-month novice period before he—or she—would be permitted to swear Sword Oath and become a probationer of the Order.

Unfortunately, that same delay had given some of the original Horse Stealer members—particularly Gharnal—time for some of the awe of Tomanāk's visitation to work its way through their system. It wasn't that they felt any less reverence, but as they got further away in time from the direct impact of His presence, the old Horse Stealer-Bloody Sword rivalry had reasserted itself. In less than two months, the first Bloody Sword recruits would have completed their novitiates and be eligible to swear Sword Oath, and Hurthang wasn't the only Horse Stealer who worried about what would happen then.

"No, we haven't let them swear Sword Oath." Vaijon spoke evenly, holding Hurthang's eyes with his own. "But I was under the impression that that was to give *them* time to be certain of their vocations, not as a way to show our distrust of them."

Hurthang flushed darkly, and his ears folded halfway down against his skull. He opened his mouth quickly, then shut it again and grabbed up his beer, instead. He took a long, deep pull, and Vaijon went on in a more soothing tone.

"It's not that I don't understand your concerns, Hurthang. I do.

But Bahzell is right about who the Order must accept, and I'd be inclined to think anyone would hesitate to offer Sword Oath if they meant to break it, given that Tomanāk appeared in person to acknowledge us as His own. I mean, Halâshu, at least, knows that's exactly what happened, and if he's managed to convince Churnazh of the truth, then I'd think neither of them would want to risk angering the God. They've got enough problems already, the way this war is shaping up, without turning His favor against them. And whatever *they* might want, I'd think finding someone who would come here at their orders and personally foreswear himself would be even harder."

"Umph." It was Hurthang's turn to lean back, and he rubbed his jaw. "Aye," he admitted at last, grudgingly, "it could be there's something in that. Tomanāk knows you're like as not right about Halâshu, any road. But Churnazh, now . . . Churnazh is after being another pot of stew. He's one as might just decide he's in so deep he's naught to worry about in making it deeper, if you take my meaning."

"So I've gathered; that's why I said I didn't *know* what he might do." Vaijon sipped beer, then lowered the mug and looked Hurthang in the eye once more. "But I *do* know it's awfully hard to lie to a champion of Tomanāk . . . and that *I* wouldn't want to be the one who swore Sword Oath falsely!"

A rustle of agreement ran around the hall, and Hurthang's ears cocked. He darted a glance at Bahzell, but Bahzell only smiled and flicked the fingers of a raised hand at Vaijon, explicitly resigning the conversation to him. Hurthang's eyes narrowed, but then he nodded slightly. Ever since Tomanāk had taken Vaijon's oath, Bahzell had persistently if unobtrusively thrown the young man deeper and deeper into the organization of the new chapter. And it was taking some throwing, Hurthang reflected. The fact that all of its original members had actually seen their deity accept Vaijon's champion's oath lent his opinions a weight he himself had not yet recognized, but it was obvious he was uncomfortable at putting himself forward. Not unsure about his responsibilities or his own relationship to Tomanāk, but cautious lest anyone think he was taking too much upon himself—especially as one of the only two humans in Hurgrum.

"So you're saying we should be having them swear Sword Oath as soon as ever they ask to join us here?" Hurthang asked finally.

"No. Bahzell's right about that, too, especially since this is the first hradani chapter. Any recruits have to be given time to train with us and see all that's involved—and be certain of their own minds—before they make binding commitments. But I think we'd

certainly be justified in asking them to state all of their reasons
for coming here before the chapter's full brethren . . . and under
oath of truth to Tomanāk."

"Oath to Tomanāk, is it?" Hurthang murmured, and it was his
turn to smile crookedly. Even those with the least use for the Gods
of Light hesitated to swear falsely by Tomanāk's name. The War
God didn't like people who did that, and rumor credited him with
a tendency to let them get killed the next time the opportunity
arose.

"That's not such a bad idea at all, Hurthang," Bahzell put in after
a moment. "Though it might be best all 'round if it wasn't *me* as
took their oaths." Hurthang looked at him, and he shrugged. "Come
what may, I'm still Father's son, and if it should happen as we *did*
have someone Churnazh wanted put in amongst us as a spy, why,
I've no doubt at all he'd feel all over justified lying to *me* about
it, oath or no."

"I suppose," Hurthang grumbled, and then turned a baleful look
back on Vaijon. "Bahzell's the right of it there," he told the young
human. "Say what we will, there's some as would never believe we
weren't after being Uncle Bahnak's men if Bahzell were taking their
oaths. But that means it would have to be you."

"Me?" Vaijon sat up straighter, eyebrows arching, and Hurthang
shrugged.

"We're talking of hradani here, Vaijon, and a good fourth part
of 'em Bloody Swords," he explained with exaggerated patience. "And
we've just allowed as how Bahzell can't be swearing them in. Well,
no more can I, for I'm close enough kin to him to make me suspect, as well, and the same for Gharnal—assuming he could be
keeping his sword sheathed long enough for a Bloody Sword as
wasn't already a member of the Order to be saying two words in
a row to him! And that, my lad, is leaving us you and Kerry, and
would you be so very kind as to tell me just how you think a
Bloody Sword would be after reacting to a *woman* warrior as wants
his oath?"

"I don't really see the problem," Vaijon said after a few seconds'
thought. This time Hurthang's eyebrows went up in surprise, and
Vaijon shrugged. "I'm sure they'd have reservations about her as
a *warrior*, but as you just pointed out yourself, we *are* talking about
hradani. And just who do you people use to administer most of
your oaths or judge cases at law?"

"You're right enough there, lad," Bahzell said before his cousin
could reply, "but I'm thinking you've missed Hurthang's point. Our
women are after being judges and lawyers, aye, and ambassadors

and councilors, as well. But they've never been war leaders—not even amongst us Iron Axes—and there's likely not a dozen Bloody Swords in all the world as would even consider giving Oath to Tomanāk to such."

"Then they'd better not tell *me* about it," Vaijon said ominously. "If Kerry's not good enough for them, then—"

"You've been amongst hradani too long, Vaijon!" Hurthang interrupted with a laugh. "There's ways to settle things without swords, and I'm sure that once you've done explaining matters to 'em all right and proper there's not a one of 'em would question Kerry's right to be here. Aye, and if they were to be so inclined, she'd not need the likes of you—or me!—to be trimming out their ears for coin purses her own self." Vaijon blushed, then grinned, and Hurthang shrugged. "But the point is, until they've met her, there's not a one of them would be realizing what she truly is—or believing it, any road. So unless you're minded to cut 'em into collops and be done with it, you'd best make allowances for their prejudices when you're after asking them to swear that first oath."

"It doesn't have to be you or Bahzell," Vaijon protested. "It could be Harkhar or Aerich or Shalach or—"

"Good lads, all of them, and all of 'em hradani," Bahzell agreed for Hurthang. "But not a one of them a champion, and that's after leaving us with only one choice . . . Milord Champion."

Vaijon closed the mouth he'd just reopened and glared at Bahzell. Then he sighed.

"All right," he agreed. "I'll do it."

Prince Bahnak Karathson opened the waterproof leather tube the mud-spattered courier had handed him and removed the message inside it. His senior officers stepped back to give him room, and the mutter of conversation died into a respectful silence. As Bahnak, most of them had recognized the signet of his third son, Tormach, in the wax sealing the tube, and the letter itself was written in Tormach's hand, as if he'd been unwilling to trust it to a secretary. And as Bahnak ran his eye down the neatly written lines, he could see why that was.

He finished the message and let it roll back up again, then held it in his right hand, tapping it against his left palm as he gazed down at the map. He felt the officers behind him, their eyes on his back, and he could almost taste their tension. All of them were Horse Stealers, and half were his own Iron Axes. But the others were from every major Horse Stealer clan, and they'd had less time to learn his ways than his own Hurgrumese and their closest allies.

On the other hand, every one of them knew his methods had produced smashing victories in the last war. Even if the traditionalists among them might cherish private doubts about those methods, no one was going to disparage them openly.

He smiled crookedly at the thought, remembering days when he'd been forced to bellow at the top of his formidable lungs to get even his own clan to listen to his "radical" ideas. He could still recall the first time his father had introduced the concept of maps as weapons of war and the way the conservatives had howled, and his own tactical and command structure innovations had been far more sweeping than that . . . in the sense of being visible to all, at least. Actually, he'd always believed Karath's use of maps and his insistence on detailed, prebattle planning had been the turning point, even though it had been too subtle for most of his warriors to recognize it as such.

His eyes found the city of Durghazh to Hurgrum's north. Tormach's dispatch confirmed, among other things, that the last clandestine supply train had come in from Daranfel, and Bahnak wondered once again just how Kilthandahknarthas had managed to bribe Haraldahn IV of Daranfel to let his shipments through. Just getting them there must have been bad enough, given spring mud and the state of the roads in most of the Border Kingdoms. Indeed, there *were* no roads across the Daranfel frontier to Durghaz, and Tormach had been forced to break the heavy wagon loads down into something mules could pack for that nightmare journey. But like most lands with hradani neighbors, Daranfel was far from fond of them. The thought of shipping *anything*, especially weapons, to Bahnak, should have thrown the entire Daranfel court into a tizzy.

Assuming, of course, that King Haraldahn knew anything about it, Bahnak thought once more. The Daranfelian monarch actively disliked and distrusted hradani—not, unfortunately, without reason. From all accounts, he disliked Horse Stealers *less* than he disliked Bloody Swords, but he made no great distinction between them, and few merchants would risk alienating the ruling monarch of even a small country. On the other hand, Kilthan of Silver Cavern wasn't just any merchant . . . and no doubt things would be much simpler all around if he'd simply forgotten to mention his activities to Haraldahn. For that matter, Haraldahn himself might have wanted it that way!

But the exact means by which Kilthan had achieved delivery meant less at the moment than the fact that he'd succeeded in doing it. The forges of Silver Cavern had provided Bahnak with armor, halberds, swords, and axes enough to completely reequip his entire clan's warriors—the better part of ten thousand men. And as they were issued their dwarf-forged steel breastplates and chain haubergeons they had been able to pass their scale and splint armor on to their allies. There might have been some muttering among the other contingents at "making do" with "hand me downs," but any which might have arisen was muted, for all of them knew that Clan Iron Axe's warriors would bear the brunt of the fighting. Besides, the "hand me downs" were far superior to anything most of the other clans had been able to provide their own people in the first place.

They were as ready as they were going to get, Bahnak thought while his mind turned over the rest of Tormach's message. A courier from one of Marglyth's Navahkan spies had staggered into Durghaz, half dead of exhaustion, with word that Churnazh had just executed Halâshu and two more of his closest advisers. That message should have been delivered directly to Marglyth here, but Churnazh had decided to smother the countryside between Navahk and Hurgrum with patrols. Indeed, from all accounts, the courier to Tormach must have needed Norfram's own luck just to reach Durghaz. But even though it had been delayed, the report suggested several interesting possibilities.

Most obviously, Churnazh was in even more trouble than Bahnak had yet allowed himself to believe. Tomanāk's appearance in Hurgrum and the creation of the first chapter of his Order—again in Hurgrum—under the leadership of one of Bahnak's sons had been enough to rock Churnazh's alliances. Confirmation that Sharnā had managed to gain a toehold in Navahk had been another shock and, even with Tomanāk's personal assurance that Churnazh himself had known nothing about it, had dealt those alliances yet another blow. And Bahzell's insistence on announcing the truth about the Rage to all hradani—despite, Bahnak thought with a mental grimace, his father's *strenuous* objections—had left all hradani, Horse Stealer and Bloody Sword alike, enormously in Tomanāk's debt . . . and bestowed tremendous prestige upon His Order. And despite Bahnak's reservations about the timing of the announcement, it had also redounded to his own credit as the prince in whose lands the Order had first established itself. All of which had left Churnazh's position severely battered.

Nor had the erosion of the Navahkan's power base stopped there. Most observers had long since decided Navahk was totally outclassed by its Hurgrumese opponents, and the rumors that someone from outside the lands of the hradani was providing Bahnak with arms and armor had only underscored the difference in their capabilities. Arvahl of Sondur had been the first to change sides, but there were rumbles of disaffection coming from many of Churnazh's other allies. One or two had actually gotten as far as opening clandestine contact with Marglyth. Indeed, a part of Bahnak was tempted to sit back and wait to see how many more of Navahk's allies would fall into his lap without a fight, and the execution of a man like Halâshu, who'd been with Churnazh for so many years, only strengthened the temptation. Always assuming the report was accurate.

Bahnak rather suspected it was. Halâshu wasn't—hadn't been—a genius, but unlike Churnazh, he'd seen Tomanâk with his own eyes, actually *spoken* to Him. Under the circumstances, it was entirely possible he'd decided it would be suicidal for Navahk to fight Hurgrum. Even if the gods weren't *officially* on Bahnak's side, they obviously liked him more than they cared for Churnazh. Whether Halâshu had simply made the mistake of urging that view too strongly or gone the fatal step further into fomenting some sort of coup hardly mattered compared to the fact that Churnazh had felt compelled to make an example of one of his oldest lieutenants.

But however great the temptation to let Churnazh self-destruct, Bahnak dared not give in to it. The Bloody Swords were off-balance now, divided and led by a ruler who had been grievously weakened. But if Bahnak gave them long enough, someone would get a dagger into Churnazh's back, and he couldn't have that. However neatly it might solve one set of problems, it was all too likely to leave him with another, worse set, because whoever replaced Churnazh would almost have to be in a stronger position than the current Prince of Navahk. He could hardly be in a *weaker* one, after all!

No, Bahnak couldn't stand by and wait for someone *else* to topple Churnazh. He had to move *now* if he meant to end the eternal, bickering warfare between Bloody Sword and Horse Stealer once and for all. And, he admitted to himself, if he wanted to put a true crown on his own head and his sons' heads.

"The roads, Gurlahn?" he asked without looking up. He hadn't raised his voice, but it sounded thunderous as it broke the waiting silence, and Gurlahn Karathson, his only living brother, cleared his throat.

"Clear, at last report," he replied. Gurlahn had lost his left leg at the knee fifteen years before. Unable to take the field effectively thereafter, he'd become his brother's chief of staff, and he flipped through a pad of notes.

"There's no snow left," he said. "The scouts are after reporting the direct road from Hurgrum to Navahk is still naught but water and mud, but the plain between Gorchcan and Sondur is better. We'll not make wonderful speed however we go about it, but at least we've no cavalry to be worrying with."

"Um." Bahnak nodded, still gazing at the map. "And the Escarpment?"

Some of his officers looked at one another at that, but Gurlahn showed no surprise. The Escarpment—the stupendous stone wall where the Wind Plain heaved its mass up from the lowlands—was the traditional barrier between the Sothōii and the Horse Stealers. It was nearly vertical along its vast length, and close to a thousand feet high. There were very few routes by which cavalry could ascend or descend the Escarpment, and the upper ends of most of them had been heavily fortified by the Sothōii. Sufficiently determined infantry could make the climb in quite a few more places, and over the centuries, the Horse Stealers had found virtually all of them.

"From all accounts, the spring thaw's just now getting started atop the Wind Plain," Gurlahn said. "The most of the routes up and down the Escarpment are after being pretty well neck-deep in run-off the now, and should be for some weeks to come."

"Um," Bahnak grunted again. He sensed the speculation his question had stirred, but he ignored it. Whatever his officers might think, he had absolutely no interest in climbing the Escarpment to attack the Sothōii. There hadn't been a large-scale Horse Stealer attack on the Wind Plain in the better part of twenty years, and he had disallowed even small raids by his own Iron Axes for the past ten. Unfortunately, he'd been less successful at convincing his fellow Horse Stealer clan lords to share his restraint. Bahnak himself wanted only peaceful relations with the Sothōii, for he had worries enough amongst his own people, but he couldn't be positive the Sothōii realized that. Still, as long as the Escarpment remained impassable, he could feel fairly confident about the security of his own rear while he dealt with Churnazh. He hoped.

But that consideration added still more point to his urge to move quickly, and Gurlahn's report on the state of the roads promised him at least a short term advantage if he could seize it. Unlike Horse Stealers, Bloody Swords were close enough to human-sized to make decent heavy cavalry, and they tried to use their mounted men to offset the larger stature and greater strength of the Horse Stealer infantry. But Horse Stealers on foot would be more mobile in mud conditions than cavalry mounts.

"All right, then," he said, and drew a deep breath as he turned to look at Barodahn and Tharak Morchanson, his two senior field commanders. "Barodahn, I'll want you and your lads on the road to Gorchcan by dawn. You know what needs doing from there."

"Aye, Da," Barodahn agreed gravely, and Bahnak turned to Hurthang's father.

"I've another job for you, Tharak. One without so much glory— to be starting out, maybe—but just as important. I'll want your lads to start wading through the mud straight for Navahk. From all reports—" he waved at the pins stuck into the map "—old Churnazh has his main force massed against a direct attack, likely enough because that's what we were after doing to him *last* time. He's a flank guard out against Sondur, but he looks to be expecting the main attack from here, and it's your job to *keep* him thinking that. Hit him hard, and drive him if you've the chance, but so long as you're keeping him looking your way and not peeping over his right shoulder at Barry, you've done your part."

"Aye, Milord." Tharak nodded, and Bahnak smiled with sudden warmth, for there was no resentment in Tharak's level reply. Like the other officers in this room—even the ones from clans other than Iron Axe—Tharak knew *victory* was what truly mattered. He would play his role and play it well, even if the glory was going to go to someone else's flanking movement, and how many hradani princes could expect that of their captains?

"It's long enough we've been waiting on this, lads," he said simply, his eyes sweeping over *all* of his officers. "My father—aye, and most of *your* fathers, too, come to that—worked their whole lives for this day. Now it's come 'round at last, and I know there's not a one of you as isn't feeling it. But remember this, all of you. Bloody Swords or no, it's our own kind we're fighting, and I'll have no massacres." He gave Uralahk Gahrnason a particularly stern look, for the Plains Bear Clan general from Gorchcan had something of a reputation for transforming bothersome prisoners into good enemies, but Uralahk only nodded without reservation.

"Churnazh I want alive, if we can be taking him so, though I'll settle for his head at need," Bahnak went on, "and his surviving sons, as well. The same is after holding for any of the other princes, too, and I'll have the head myself of any man who's not after letting Lord Brandark of Navahk or any of his kin surrender, should it happen they so choose. And I'll be expecting you to take prisoners amongst Churnazh's regulars, as well, for it's not by their own choice the most of 'em are fighting us in the first place. But see to it that all your men are after knowing the colors and emblems of his personal guard. They're every one of 'em where they *chose* to be, and you'll know as well as I what he and they have been after doing to their own folk all these years. We'll give quarter where it's asked for by any decent fighting man, but for those as served that dung-eating, black-hearted bastard of their own will—"

He held out one hand, palm down before him, and slowly clenched it into a fist. It was the same gesture a judge used in a hradani court to pronounce sentence of death, and a soft, hungry snarl rippled around the room as he smiled coldly.

CHAPTER TWENTY-NINE

"Are you certain of your information?"

Sir Mathian Redhelm, Lord Warden of Glanharrow, leaned forward in his chair, and his hazel eyes were hard as he gazed at his "guest." Mathian was of only moderate height for his people, with shoulders whose narrowness his tailors tried manfully, if not with great success, to hide. He was young for a man in his position, having inherited the lordship of Glanharrow only seven years before after his father's unexpected death. He looked a great deal like the late Sir Gardián, and, like his sire, he had quickly established a reputation as a lord of great energy. But, also like his father, he was given to impulse and improvisation.

Most Sothōii were at least a little on the impulsive side, if the truth be known, but Sir Gardian had been more so than most. He'd been known for generosity and frequent acts of kindness, but also for having Fiendark's own temper. The punishments he levied on those brought before his judgment on his bad days had been legendary, and his tendency to make snap decisions would have brought anyone with less vigor quickly to ruin. But Gardian had always thrown himself body and soul into all he did, and his fierce energy and enthusiasm had allowed him to recover from most of his mistakes relatively unscathed. He'd wasted a tremendous amount of effort battering through problems a little forethought might have avoided along the way, but that had been his style.

And it had also been what killed him when he went galloping off after a party of hradani raiders with only six knights in attendance. In his defense, the hradani in question had made off with five of his prized studs and a dozen brood mares, and among the Sothōii horse lords thefts of that severity were not only a heavy economic loss but insults which could be washed out only by blood. Yet for all that, Gardian had been a seasoned warrior who should have known better than to let fury lure him into such a fatal mistake.

The fact that he hadn't had made Sir Mathian Lord Warden of Glanharrow at only nineteen years of age. That, unfortunately, was just old enough for him to assume his titles in his own name, without a regent to hold him in check, and he was his father all over again . . . but with far less experience. Worse, Sir Gardian's death had left him with a towering hatred for all hradani. Even he knew it was temper and lack of forethought which had led his father to his death, but if the accursed hradani hadn't raided Glanharrow's herds, none of that would have mattered. Sothōii distrust and hatred for hradani ran deep after centuries of mutual raiding and bursts of bitter, merciless war, but Mathian's burned hotter and much, much deeper than most. Things had been remarkably peaceful along the Escarpment for the past five or six years, but he didn't care, and he had quietly gathered quite a following among some of the other young knights.

All of which made his "guest" even more remarkable, for he was a hradani.

"And when have I been other than certain of anything before I was bringing it to you?" the hradani demanded, speaking Sothōii with a strong Hurgrumese accent. Had Mathian been more familiar with the differences between hradani clans he might have reflected that his guest was on the short side for a Horse Stealer. Not that it would have mattered to him. As far as he was concerned, all hradani were the same, and the world would be a far better place with none of them in it.

"No doubt," an older knight put in. "But I'm sure you can see why the accuracy—"

"Peace, Festian!" Mathian turned to glare impatiently at the older man, who clamped his jaw tight. Sir Festian Wrathson commanded Glanharrow's mounted scouts and skirmishers. He was also twice Mathian's age and more, and he'd seen more battlefields than Mathian had formal dinners. And unlike the unblooded young whelp who held Glanharrow in fief from Baron Tellian, Festian *did* know the difference between the hradani clans, and he felt quite sure that the fellow in front of them was no more a Horse Stealer than *he* was, whatever accent he might ape.

Mathian glared at him a moment longer, until he was certain

Festian wouldn't interrupt again, and then turned back to the hradani.

"You were saying?"

"I was saying as how Bahnak will be after marching on Churnazh within the week," the hradani replied. "And he'll be taking all of his men with him, too, for whoever wins this one will end up lording it over all the clans."

Sir Festian didn't care at all for the glitter in the spy's eyes, but Mathian didn't seem to notice it. Perhaps that was because of the sudden fire blazing in his own eyes.

"I don't suppose you've brought any proof of this, have you?" he made himself ask, and the hradani hooted with derisive laughter.

"Oh, aye! I thought as how I'd just be bringing along a copy of Bahnak's secret dispatches so as to have something to lend his guardsmen for light reading when they caught me!"

Mathian's jowls flushed, but he only nodded. He gazed at the hradani for a moment longer, then raised one hand and flicked it at the door.

"My steward will pay you," he said curtly, and turned to stare into the fire hissing on the hearth.

The hradani grinned sardonically at his back, swept a mocking bow to Sir Festian and Sir Haladhan, and left. Silence lingered in his wake for several minutes, and then Mathian turned back from the fire and looked at Haladhan.

"What do you think?" he asked.

"I think the same as you," Haladhan replied. "This may be the last opportunity we'll have before it's too late!"

Haladhan's deep voice was even lower than usual, throbbing with passionate enthusiasm, and Festian hid a mental grimace. He had no doubt of the accuracy of Haladhan's first sentence. The young knight was Mathian's first cousin, but if he ever had two kormaks to rub together it would be the first time he did. He was far more handsome than his wealthy cousin, and much more muscular, but if Mathian had declared the sun would rise in the west tomorrow, Haladhan would have said the same thing . . . only louder. Which made it all the more unfortunate that Mathian had promoted Haladhan to the rank of Marshal of Glanharrow, his senior field commander.

"True. True . . . perhaps," Mathian murmured. He raised his right hand to rub his jaw, and the ruby signet of the Lord Wardens of Glanharrow flashed like blood in the candlelight. "But if it is an opportunity, it will have to be acted upon quickly," he mused.

"Milord," Festian began, "before we do anything, wouldn't it be wise to—"

"I'm *thinking*, Festian!" Mathian said, and the older knight clamped his jaw once more, wishing—not for the first time—that Sir Gardian hadn't gotten himself killed so idiotically. No one had ever accused Gardian of thinking things through, but at least he'd occasionally been known to listen to advice if someone shouted it loudly enough!

"How many men could we assemble?" Mathian went on after a moment, directing the question at Haladhan.

"I'm not certain," his cousin said. He scratched the tip of his nose. "I suppose it would depend on the condition of the roads. It's still a mess out there, especially—" he darted a sharp glance at Mathian "—north of Glanharrow."

"True enough," Mathian grunted. "We'll just have to see how many of the minor lords we can get messengers to."

"I think—" Haladhan began, but Festian interrupted him.

"Forgive me, Milord," he said very firmly, "but should I understand that you actually contemplate moving against the hradani on the basis of this spy's information?"

"And why should I not?" Mathian demanded, looking down his nose at the older knight.

Because we've had peace with them for over five years and you're about to change *that, you young idiot!* Festian thought. *And just because you've been fortunate enough never to fight a real war against them doesn't mean that those of us who* have *fought them are looking forward to it!* But he couldn't say that, of course.

"Milord, you are Lord Warden of Glanharrow," he said instead, "and I am your sworn man, as I was your father's. But this is a very serious step you contemplate. At the very least, you should discuss it with Sir Kelthys. And Baron Tellian must be informed."

"Of course I shall inform Baron Tellian!" Mathian said sharply. "But as you yourself say, I *am* Lord Warden here. As such, I have every right in the absence of direct orders from Baron Tellian to call up the levies of Glanharrow on my own authority in time of emergency, do I not?"

He glared at Festian, obviously waiting for an answer, and the older knight sighed.

"You are, and you do, Milord," he said. *Of course, "emergency" is supposed to mean that someone else has launched an unprovoked attack upon you, you fool. But you do have the right . . . and I don't have the authority to forbid it.*

"Good!" Mathian snorted, but then he went on in a slightly less sharp tone. "As for Sir Kelthys, however, you're quite right. Please dispatch a messenger to ask him to join us here as quickly as possible."

He nodded dismissal, and Festian rose, fighting another surge of anger. He was no page to be sent scurrying about on errands, and he suspected that one reason he was being dispatched was to let Mathian and Haladhan put their heads together unhampered by his presence. Yet there was no courteous way to avoid obeying, and so he only bowed sharply and left.

He stalked down the castle hall, and those he met took one look at his face and stepped quickly aside. He knew they were doing it, but he didn't really care—not when those two young idiots were bent on what could only lead to disaster. Mathian had spent his life paying far too much attention to ballads and not enough to serious history. His mind was full of banners and gallant charges, and he'd managed to forget that Horse Stealers under the current Prince of Hurgrum's grandfather had sacked Glanharrow Castle itself and burned it to the ground. But at least he'd agreed to talk it over with Kelthys first. Festian tried to cling to that, for it was the sole positive aspect of the evening so far.

Sir Kelthys Lancebearer was a second cousin of Baron Tellian. Born a third son, he'd been a landless man, but one whose skill at arms—both in personal combat and as a strategist—had won great renown. He'd spent fifteen years commanding Sothōii cavalry forces attached to the Royal and Imperial Army, and he'd returned to the Kingdom a wealthy man. When Baron Tellian "suggested" Mathian bestow the manor of Deep Water upon Kelthys, the Lord Warden of Glanharrow had had little choice but to agree. And in fairness to the Baron, the transaction had worked out quite well.

Deep Water wasn't the largest of Glanharrow's holdings, and the manor had fallen into decay under its previous master. Under Sir Kelthys' careful husbandry, however, it had once again become a prosperous and productive steading whose rents enriched Mathian's coffers, and few lords of Mathian's rank had ever been blessed with a vassal with Kelthys' experience and skill. Indeed, Festian rather suspected Tellian had pushed the arrangement expressly to insure that Mathian had an older and wiser head to ride herd upon him. Yet Festian was also positive a certain rancor lurked under the surface pleasantries of Mathian's relations with Kelthys. Part of it was understandable enough. Given Mathian's comparative youth and lack of military experience, the younger man was bound to feel uncomfortable under the eye of a subordinate who was a proven veteran. But there was more to it than that, more even than Kelthys' relationship to Baron Tellian, for Kelthys was also a wind rider ... and Mathian was not.

Festian knew how that rankled the younger man. The gods knew *he* had always longed to be a wind rider, but the coursers chose whom they would, and no power on earth could make them accept any rider against their will. Mathian knew that as well as anyone, yet that didn't keep him from resenting his vassal's good fortune.

But at least he'd agreed to summon Kelthys. Whatever his other feelings, he had to know how valuable Kelthys' advice and opinions could be, and Festian prayed silently to any god who might be listening that Mathian would have the wit to listen to them.

Marglyth Bahnaksdaughter tied the sash on her robe and tried to ignore the big, empty bed behind her as she dragged a brush ruthlessly through her hair. Her husband Jarthûhl was away with the army, commanding a battalion under her brother Barodahn in the flank attack curling up from Sondur to close on Navahk like a steel trap. The southern Bloody Swords had been driven back and held there by one wing of Prince Bahnak's army, commanded by Uralahk of Gorchan, but Churnazh had managed to concentrate almost two thirds of his total fighting power to face the decisive thrust. He and his senior officers were battling desperately, only too well aware of what awaited them if they lost, and this time they had avoided their worst mistakes of the last war. Rather than charge out to fling themselves headlong upon their foes as they had then, they'd chosen to mount stubborn defensive actions, fighting for every ridge line and runoff-swollen stream. They were still losing ground steadily, but they'd slowed their attackers' progress to a crawl. Bahnak's advance was at least two weeks behind his original timetable, and his casualties had been higher than he'd hoped. Lower than he had *feared*, perhaps, but heavy enough to bring pain and loss to all too many Horse Stealer families.

But just this moment, her fear was not for Jarthûhl's safety, or her father's, or any of her brothers'. It was for their *absence*, and it cut deep into her. Jarthûhl had always taken a quiet pride in the way she stood second in authority only to her father in Hurgrum. Over the years, she'd grown accustomed to using him as a sounding board—much as her father often used her—when decisions had to be made, and he had always been there, quiet but supportive, when she needed him. Now he wasn't, and she felt his absence like a wound. For the first time in many years, she felt frail and alone in the face of responsibility, and she longed for the comforting embrace of his arms.

She yanked the brush through her hair one last time, then tossed it onto the dressing table with a clatter. That would have to do, she told herself, and rose, then looked at the servant hovering in the doorway.

"It's grateful I'd be if you'd tell the courier I'll see him in the Council Chamber," she said, and no one would have guessed from her voice how frightened she was.

Princess Arthanal was already waiting in the Council Chamber when Marglyth arrived. Arthanal had no official role on the Council, yet Marglyth knew how often her advice had been pivotal to Bahnak's important decisions, and a tiny part of the weight crushing down on her own shoulders seemed to ease under her mother's encouraging smile. She walked around the table to sit in her proper place as First Councilor, then looked up, heart suddenly racing, as the door opened once more. But it wasn't the courier—not yet—and her pulse eased slightly once more as the guards passed Bahzell and Hurthang into the chamber.

"Thank you for coming," she said, softly but from the heart. Bahzell only shrugged, then hugged her and stepped back against the wall behind her chair like an armsman behind his lord, and Hurthang joined him. Technically, the two of them had no more business here than Arthanal did, but Marglyth knew she would need advice, and it would have been impossible for her to summon a regular meeting of the Council in time. Even if it hadn't been the middle of the night, almost all of the Council's male members were at the front with Bahnak, and the other female members were scattered about Hurgrum trying to see to their absent fellows' duties as well as their own. Besides, this was one of the burdens that came with acting as First Councilor. In her father's absence, it was Marglyth's job to govern Hurgrum . . . and until she knew the full message the courier carried, there was no point in trying to assemble a quorum, anyway.

Someone else rapped on the door, and she made herself sit back in her chair as an exhausted, mud-spattered Horse Stealer was ushered in. He went down on one knee between the open ends of the U-shaped table, and she swallowed.

"Don't be crawling around on your knees, man!" she said tartly. "Get yourself up and say your say."

"Aye, Milady." The courier stood and reached into his pouch. The hastiness with which he had been dispatched was obvious, for the grubby piece of paper he produced hadn't been put into a message tube for safekeeping. In fact, it hadn't even been properly sealed, only folded into a screw. He held it out to Marglyth, and she was pleased to see that her hands didn't even quiver as she took it.

"Thank you," she said courteously, and straightened the tightly folded paper. The hand in which it was written was difficult to read, but not difficult enough, and she felt her ears fold tight to her head as she ran her eyes down the scrawled message.

"Would you be knowing what this says?" she asked, raising her eyes to the courier, and he nodded.

"Aye, Milady. Captain Garuth feared it might be lost, seeing as how he'd no time to seal it up proper. He was wishful to be sure I'd be able to be answer any questions should that happen."

"I see." She gazed at him for another long moment. "And your own estimate of the numbers would be?" she asked finally.

"Captain Garuth's the right of it, Milady. There's after being a thousand of them in the vanguard alone if there's one, and likely more following on behind."

"I see," she repeated. Then she drew a deep breath and nodded to him. "You've my thanks once again. It's grateful I'd be if you'd leave us to think on this—" she twitched the written note slightly "—for a bit. Tell the guards I'm wishful to have you wrap yourself around a good, hot meal."

The courier nodded, bowed, and withdrew, and Marglyth turned to her family. Her carefully calm expression wavered for just a moment as the door closed behind the messenger, but she forced it back under control.

"Garuth," Hurthang said softly. "He's after commanding the picket watching the Gullet if I recall aright."

"You do that," Marglyth confirmed grimly. She crushed the note in her fist and looked straight at Bahzell. "The Sothōii are coming," she said simply.

"Tomanāk!" Hurthang muttered, but Bahzell said nothing. He only looked back at his sister, and in the back of his brain he heard Kilthan's voice once more, describing the Sothōii's fear of a unified hradani realm. Well, if they wanted to prevent that, they'd chosen the right moment, he thought grimly. Bahnak had left five hundred men—a single battalion—to garrison Hurgrum itself, backed up by a half-strength City Guard. The other Horse Stealer cities were similarly vulnerable, for every warrior the massed clans had been able to scrape up had been thrown at Churnazh. His father had wanted to smash Churnazh as quickly as possible—partly in the hope that his allies, seeing how utterly he had been crushed, would surrender without further combat, and partly in order to free up the troops to guard his flank against just such an attack. But the Sothōii had managed to assemble their strength more rapidly than Bahnak had thought possible.

"They're coming down the Gullet?" he asked finally, and Marglyth nodded. Well, that made sense, too. Winter hung on late atop the Wind Plain, and the snow in its northern reaches and up near Hope's Bane Glacier was only now melting. The mighty Spear River was in full flood, but so were all the other, smaller streams which tumbled down the Escarpment, which meant most of the traditional routes from the high plateau to the lowlands remained flooded and impassable.

But not the Gullet. That long, narrow, tortuously winding crack stretched clear up the side of the plateau. Little wider than fifty paces in places, most of its length was protected from heavy snow accumulations. Once it had been the bed of the northernmost tributary of the Hangnysti River, but some long ago cataclysm had twisted and buckled the western edge of the Wind Plain, diverting the river further north and heaving up a steep shoulder of tilted rock to form an effective wall across the upper end of the Gullet and divert even the spring floods from it. The Gullet had never been flooded out in living memory, but it was also a difficult path. Most people's cavalry would have found it utterly impassable, and even the Sothōii's war horses and coursers would require over two days to make the descent. That was the main reason it had been used far more often by *hradani* raiding parties, and even now he couldn't completely shake off a sense of surprise that the Sothōii had chosen to attempt it.

Unfortunately, they had . . . and the Gullet's lower end was less than twenty-five leagues from Hurgrum's walls. If a Sothōii column debouched from it, it could sweep right through the heart of Prince Bahnak's realm—and there would be no warriors to stop it. Sothōii armies had penetrated that far before, if not in the last two or three generations, and each time the devastation had been terrible. Even as he smashed Churnazh's army to bits, Bahnak might find his own lands being put to fire and the sword behind him.

"How far into the Gullet have they come?" Arthanal asked in her quiet voice.

"They haven't—not before Garuth was after getting his message off," Marglyth replied. "He'd stationed watchers ten leagues out across the Wind Plain to spy out threats. As of this morning, they'd not started down. In fact, they'd not yet reached within five leagues of his main position."

"And how many men would he be having with him?" Bahzell asked.

"Not enough," Hurthang answered grimly for his sister. "He was never intended for aught but a forward scout. It's surprised I'd be if he's more than forty."

"But the Sothōii can't be after knowing that yet," Marglyth pointed out.

"Aye, and the Gullet's no bad place for a handful to be trying to slow an army, either," Bahzell murmured. He leaned back, rubbing his jaw while his ears moved slowly back and forth in thought. He didn't know Garuth as well as he knew some of his father's other officers, but the man he remembered was a thoughtful, canny commander. He wouldn't need anyone to tell him his job, and he'd know every trick there was to convince the enemy he had more men than he did. But if the Sothōii had decided to move in strength, he would never be able to stop them, however defensible the Gullet might be.

"—reinforcements?" He shook himself as he realized his mother was speaking and looked at Marglyth.

"We've none to send, Mother," his sister said flatly. "Oh, we've the battalion here in the city, but they'd not stop a serious attack. Slow it, perhaps, but not stop it. No," she shook her head, "we'll be needing them worse where they are when the Sothōii are after getting here."

"Marglyth's the right of it there," Hurthang agreed unhappily. "Not that one battalion's going to be doing us all that much good, even from behind a wall."

"Aye, that's true enough," Bahzell heard himself say. "But it's in my mind there might just be a better answer nor that, when all's said."

"It's hard put I'd be to think of a *worse* one!" his cousin said with a hard crack of laughter. But then Bahzell's expression registered, and he cocked his head at him. "D'you mean to be saying you've truly thought of something?" he demanded.

"Well, I'll not say it's the best thought the gods were ever giving a man, but it's better than naught," Bahzell told him. Then he turned back to his sister. "You'd best be getting a courier of your own off, Marglyth. Tell Garhuth he's to do all that ever he can to slow the Sothōii, but I want no pitched battles. He's to feel free to skirmish if he must, but he's not to be doing anything as would prove how weak he is. Tell him I'm wanting him no further down the Gullet than Charhan's Despair before noon tomorrow."

"And why would we be telling him that?" Hurthang asked.

"Because betwixt now and then, you and Gharnal and I are going

to be after force marching the entire Order to Charhan's Despair,"
Bahzell told him flatly.

"But Himself was saying—" Hurthang began.

"Himself was after saying we were to take no part in the fighting between Horse Stealer and Bloody Sword," Bahzell interrupted,
"and no more will we. But he said naught at all, at all, about our
fighting Sothōii, my lad!"

"But we've no more than six score blades, even counting all the
novices," Hurthang pointed out. "You'll not stop four or five thousand Sothōii with such as that, Gullet or no. And that's even assuming as you can be getting them there that quick!"

"Oh, I'll get 'em there all right and tight," Bahzell agreed in a
grim, hammered-iron voice. "And whether we can be stopping the
bastards or not, we've no option but to try. We've done naught to
be provoking a Sothōii attack—we've not even raided their herds
in the better part of five years, now—and I'm thinking himself
might not feel so kindly towards those as make undeclared war
against folk as haven't been hurting them in the least. That being
so, we've little choice but to take the Order out to argue the point
and show them the error of their ways, like."

"And they'll still be riding us into the mud, come what may,"
Hurthang argued.

"Maybe they will, and maybe they won't," Bahzell replied. "But
they'll not do it without getting hurt themselves, and they'll not
do it all in a minute, either. It's surprised indeed I'd be if we couldn't
be buying at least two or three more days' time, and it's possible
whoever's in command on the other side will take it into his head
to be taking his horsemen home if we can. He'll not know how
the battle is going against Churnazh, so he'll have no idea how soon
Father can be shifting troops around to be hitting *him*. And it's
mortal early in the year, Hurthang. I've no notion of just what
conditions may be up atop the Wind Plain, but I'll lay odds as how
they're worse up yonder than they are down here. Aye, and come
to that, I'm thinking Garuth may have been overestimating the odds
just a bit, as well. I've no doubt at all, at all, he was after seeing
the numbers he reported, but like as not there's not nearly so many
behind them as he was thinking."

"And just how might you be figuring that out?" Hurthang asked
skeptically.

"These lads will all be out of the West Riding, and most likely
from the local garrisons, at that," Bahzell said positively, remembering what Kilthan had told him about the Sothōii kingdom's
divisions over how to react to the hradani "threat."

"There's not been time for more to be mobilized—or to've been reaching the Gullet if they had—with the roads being what they must up yonder," he went on. "So whoever the fellow in command may be, he'll know as well as we do as how he's operating on a boot lace. He'll not want to be meeting four or five thousand Iron Axes and as many more warriors from each of the other clans in the open. No," Bahzell shook his head. "His whole notion is to be getting in and out quick, and maybe to be holding the bottom of the Gullet until reinforcements can be reaching him."

"Mph." It was Hurthang's turn to rub his chin. He considered Bahzell's argument carefully, but then, reluctantly, shook his head.

"I'll not fault your logic about mobilizations and what t'other side's after thinking, Bahzell, but that's mostly because it's damned I'll be if I can see a single reason why his notion shouldn't be working. I'll grant you we can like as not hold 'em for a day or two, but three?" He shook his head again. "Hard enough for two, lad; three would be taking miracle workers, not warriors! And even if we're after managing three—aye, or even four—it won't be enough. They'll ride right over us, throw out scouts to be certain sure there aren't any of our armies anywhere near 'em, then fan out, and they'll take their torches with 'em, curse it!"

"I'm thinking Hurthang is right, Bahzell," Marglyth said with quiet hopelessness. "All you'd be doing would be to throw your own men away alongside Garuth's."

"Maybe so," Bahzell said stubbornly, "but there's one point you and Hurthang are both after missing—one thing about our lads as is different from Garuth and his picket."

His cousin and his sister looked at him blankly, but he saw his mother nodding slowly. Arthanal's expression was still worried, but there was a glimmer of hope in her eyes, and he nodded back to her.

"Garuth is after fighting under the colors of Hurgrum," he said quietly. "*Our* lads will be under a different banner, Hurthang. Now, it may be the man commanding those horsemen won't be minded to see it so, but there's a whole world's difference between riding down bloodthirsty hradani raiders and slaughtering a chapter of the Order of Tomanāk as only wants to protect women and children and old folk. I've no doubt they picked a man as won't shed any tears at all for the killing of *hradani*, but angering the entire Order of Tomanāk—now *that's* a horse of another color, Hurthang!"

"Assuming as how they're minded to *believe* we're a chapter of the Order, it may be you've a point," his cousin admitted. "But what if they're not?"

"Then we'll be no deader in the Gullet than we would be in the ruins of Hurgrum," Bahzell told him grimly.

CHAPTER THIRTY

"*Well?*" Sir Mathian spat the one-word question at Festian.

"I warned you this route was more difficult than it looked on a map, Milord," Festian replied in a tart, stinging tone. The scout commander's eyes flashed, but he had himself under control. Which didn't mean he intended to suffer Mathian's tantrums. Not in the field, where Mathian's so far negligible exploits certainly hadn't earned him the right to tongue-lash a man who'd served his own apprenticeship under Pargan the Great.

Mathian's face darkened, but then he made himself draw a deep breath as the older knight's reply fanned his ill temper afresh. The fact that Festian had, in fact, argued against the expedition—and specifically against sending it down the Gullet—from the first didn't help . . . and neither did the fact that Mathian knew he *needed* the scout commander. Unlike Mathian, Festian had fought in the Gullet before. But Fiendark take it, this was the *only* way Mathian could get at the Phrobus-damned hradani, and if he meant to attack at all, it had to be *now*, while that bastard Bahnak had all his troops off slaughtering his fellow barbarians elsewhere.

"Very well. You warned me," he said. "Yet however well taken your warning may have been, we're *here* now. And that being the case, I need your report on what we face."

"As you say, Milord." Festian removed his open-faced cavalry helm and tucked it into the crook of his left arm. Like Mathian and Haladhan, he wore a steel cuirass over boiled leather armor, not the chain or plate knights would have worn in other lands. Aside from the wind riders, almost all Sothōii cavalry, nobles and armsmen alike, were light or medium horse whose forte was mobility and speed. In open terrain, their fast, slashing attacks and lethal skill with the horsebow made them deadly foes, but the Gullet would deny them virtually all their normal advantages. They couldn't fight on horseback in its cramped confines, and their light armor would be of limited value against Horse Stealer hradani on foot. Not that Mathian seemed aware of it.

Festian took a moment to survey the expedition's commander, and a mental lip curled. Despite his inherited position as Warden of the Glanharrow District, this was the first opportunity Mathian had found actually to command any sizable body of troops in the field, and if there were two mistakes he hadn't made, Festian couldn't think of what they might be. *He always was a pain in the arse,* he thought. *No wonder the coursers wouldn't take him! Now if only there were some way I could be rid of him!*

But there wasn't. And so Festian was out here, a third of the way down the Escarpment, with his weary horse mud to the belly, under the orders of a vengeance-driven fool who'd never grown up . . . and thought he was Torren Sword Arm reborn.

"The Gullet may not be flooded, Milord," he said, "but the mud's hock deep in places. In fact, it's *mostly* mud—where it isn't solid rock or piled up boulders so steep even a wind rider would have to dismount." Mathian's eye flashed at the mention of wind riders. His glance darted to where Sir Kelthys sat comfortably in the saddle, and Festian hid a smile of satisfaction. "On top of that, the hradani knew we were coming. My lead scouts are a third of the way down, and they've already reported at least a dozen spots where the enemy used mud or rock slides to block the main path."

"But we can get through them, correct?" That was Sir Haladhan, and Festian glanced at him coldly.

"We can, Lord Marshal. We'll have to clear the trail—especially if we mean to get *horses* through, which I presume we do—and some of my men are already working on that, but it's going to take more like three days than two to get all the way down."

Haladhan's eyes flashed at the pointed comment about horses and he opened his mouth angrily, but Sir Kelthys interrupted him before he could speak.

"That may be true, Festian," the wind rider said thoughtfully, "but the fact that they're trying to block the Gullet may actually be good news."

The others all turned to look at him, and he shrugged with a smile. It was a cheerful enough smile, but there was iron behind it, and Mathian knew it. He also knew that the combination of

Kelthys' experience and his kinship to Baron Tellian made him someone he had to listen to very carefully. Particularly since he'd already overridden Kelthys' advice against mounting this expedition in the first place.

"Good news, Sir Kelthys?" he asked now. "In what way?"

Kelthys smiled again. Unlike his companions, he wore full plate, and Mathian's bay raised its head as the older knight's courser stepped up alongside it. At sixteen hands, Mathian's gelding was tall for a Sothōii war horse, but it looked like a pony beside the courser. Sir Kelthys' mount stood just under twenty-one hands—almost seven feet—at the withers, and its coat was midnight black. In the years he'd served under Pargan the Great, Festian had seen horses in other lands which approached coursers in size, but none could compare in any other way. Coursers had none of the ponderous, muscle-bound massiveness that characterized the chargers of heavy foreign knights and made them look so clumsy and unwieldy. Aside from their size, Mathian's gelding and the courser might have been the same breed, and the same promise of explosive speed lurked in their deep chests and long, powerful legs.

But no one who'd ever met a courser would mistake it for a "horse." Oh, physically, perhaps, aside from the size, but not in any other way, and Festian found himself bending his neck in a courteous bow as the courser's eyes met his. There was an intelligence in those eyes at odds with all other horses—even the magnificent war horses his people bred and, upon rare occasion, sold for princely sums to foreigners. Legend said that Tomanāk and Toragan had worked as one to create the coursers. From Toragan had come the beauty and the grace, and the wild, unconquerable freedom of their nature, and from Tomanāk had come the courage and the fiery spirit which would face any challenge, any danger, at their chosen companions' sides. And after the gods had created the coursers, they had given them into the keeping of the Sothōii, with the command to protect and nurture them and never—ever—to let them fall into the hands of others.

Festian had no way to test the legends, but he believed them. Who *but* a god could have given grace and power such perfect expression? And who but a god could have given them their speed—the magnificent speed no other creature could match, and the endurance to trample the sun itself under their hooves?

He shook himself, breaking free of the spell coursers always cast upon him, and made himself listen as Kelthys responded to Mathian's question with one of his own.

"So far your scouts haven't actually seen a single hradani, have they, Sir Festian?"

"No, Milord," Festian replied, with none of the rancor he felt when Mathian or Haladhan threw out one of their arrogant questions, and Kelthys nodded.

"That sounds remarkably unlike them," he pointed out to Mathian. "As Sir Festian says, the Gullet is always a difficult passage, especially for horsemen, and the hradani know that as well as we do. Under the circumstances, I would expect them to pick one of the more defensible positions and hold it against us. Yet if our lead scouts are a third of the way down the trail, then they've already passed at least two places were a protracted stand might have been made." He shrugged. "Coupled with their efforts to block the trail, that would seem to me to indicate that they lack the strength to mount a credible defense even with the advantages the Gullet offers them. Of course, it also means we must be alert to the possibility of more . . . energetic blocking efforts on their part. If memory serves me, there are several places where a properly contrived mud or rock slide could easily bury half a mounted troop."

"Um." Mathian sounded struck by Kelthys' analysis, and Haladhan beamed as if he'd thought it up on his own. Festian merely looked thoughtful, but behind the mask of his expression, he had to admit he could find no fault in Kelthys' reasoning.

"You may well be right, Milord," he said, "and I hope you are—about the numbers, at least. But you're also right about the possibility of their using slides against us, especially as we get closer to the halfway point. The ground's worst of all in that stretch, and even without help from the hradani we'd have to be on the watch for slides this time of year. Which only reinforces what I said before, Milord Mathian," he added. "If it's as Sir Kelthys says, we may have to go even slower, which means it could take us as much as *four* days to get our lead elements down."

He looked at Kelthys, not Mathian, as he spoke, and the other knight nodded ever so slightly back to him. Unfortunately, the Lord Warden had made his determination to drive this attack home—and his refusal to listen to objections—abundantly clear.

"If it takes four days, then it takes four days," he said now, and gave Festian a cool look. "No doubt your men require your guidance, Sir Festian. Don't let us detain you."

"Of course not, Milord," Festian replied through gritted teeth, and turned his horse back down the Gullet.

❖   ❖   ❖

Shod hooves clattered on bare stone, but Bahzell Bahnakson hardly noticed. His attention was on the banner—a crimson axe on a field of black—that still flew above the crude fort called Charhan's Despair. For all his confident words in Hurgrum, he had been far from certain Garuth would be able to obey his orders. Now, as a dozen hradani jogged towards him from the rough-piled stone walls, he knew the Horse Stealer captain had.

He handed the lead rope of his own mule to one of Garuth's men, then stood back, breathing deeply. His calf and thigh muscles seemed to quiver, as though his feet still rose and fell in the ground-devouring lope of the Horse Stealers, and he squatted in a series of deep knee bends to ease the sensation as he watched the rest of the column move past him. The chapter's twenty novice Bloody Swords staggered drunkenly as they covered the last few yards. They were far more exhausted than their Horse Stealer brethren—although, he noted with a certain smugness, even the other Horse Stealers looked tireder than his fellow Iron Axes—but that was understandable enough. The Bloody Swords might have the same inherent endurance, but they lacked the *training*. They were small enough to ride horses, and so their muscles hadn't been built up by a lifetime spent learning to outrun cavalry on their own two feet. The twenty-odd leagues from Hurgrum to the foot of the Gullet had been a brutal ordeal for them . . . and not a lot better for the Horse Stealers, Bahzell admitted privately. It would have been bad enough under ideal conditions; with the rudimentary roads covered in mud and the need to cut cross-country in several places, it had been infinitely worse.

At least they'd been able to make things a bit easier on themselves. Not even Horse Stealers wanted to run sixty miles in armor if they could help it, and so they had loaded their personal equipment on mules. Each hradani had started out with two of them. By now their gear was on the second and the poor beasts drooped with exhaustion, but they raised their heads as they realized the pounding journey was drawing to a close at last. Some of Bahzell's warriors were already unfastening packs to get at their armor and weapons. Others had sagged down to rest, but Hurthang was chivvying them back to their feet and pointing them at their own mules. Bahzell was relieved to see him handling the Bloody Swords exactly as if they were Horse Stealers. Apparently running sixty miles with him in eleven hours and then climbing halfway up the Gullet in six more was enough to erase even the stigma of being born a Bloody Sword.

More hooves clattered, and he looked up as Brandark, Kaeritha, and Vaijon rode up the last, steep bit of the trail. The two humans looked wan and drawn, and hardened riders though they might be, all three of them undoubtedly felt as if someone had beaten them with flails. Vaijon had looked a little doubtful, as if he thought he was being made the butt of someone's joke, when Bahzell insisted that each of them start with a string of four horses. Now he knew better, and he bit back a groan as he slid down from the saddle. Kaeritha and Brandark stayed where they were, and Bahzell grinned. From Kaeritha's expression, she had no intention of ungluing herself from that saddle until she *knew* she was someplace where she wouldn't have to climb back into it again.

"Are we here?" Vaijon croaked.

"We are that," Bahzell agreed, and jerked a thumb at the crudely built fortifications. "Charhan's Despair," he said.

"Why is it called that?" Kaeritha asked.

"According to the tales, Charhan was a Horse Stealer clan lord when first the Sothōii wandered into these parts. They weren't so very fond of our folk even then, I reckon, for they were after doing their level best to kill us all, but they'd much the same problems as now, for there weren't so many ways we could be getting at one another. Well, to be making a long story short, the Sothōii threw an attack down the Gullet. There were too many for Charhan to be stopping them in the open, so it was here he made his stand. You should ask old Thorfa to sing you the tale if you're wishful to hear it. It's chock full of all manner of heroic deeds, but even Thorfa will tell you as how they're all made up by them as wasn't there to see."

He fell silent, watching the last of the column come up, and Vaijon frowned.

"But why is it called 'Charhan's *Despair*'?" he asked.

"Um?" Bahzell turned back to him, ears cocked

"I asked why it's called 'Charhan's *Despair*,'" he repeated, and this time Bahzell smiled grimly.

"I said it was here he made his stand, Vaijon," he said quietly. "I never said as how he *stopped* 'em, for he didn't. They rode right over him, and over all his men, and when they'd reached the bottom of the Gullet, why they rode right over the *rest* of his clan, as well. That's why it's naught but a legend amongst us, you see, for there wasn't a one of his people at all, at all, as lived to tell what truly happened."

CHAPTER THIRTY-ONE

"*What* banner did you say?"

Sir Festian stared at the muddy, sweat-soaked scout in disbelief, but the man only shook his head stubbornly.

"I saw what I saw, Sir."

"But—" Festian began, then stopped. Yarran was a good man, one of his best. If he said he'd seen something, then he'd seen it . . . however impossible it seemed.

The scout commander chewed on that unpalatable thought for several seconds, then dismounted and handed his reins to an aide.

"Show me," he ordered, and Yarran nodded and led the way down the trail.

At fifty-six, Festian was getting long in the tooth for this sort of thing. His wind wasn't what it had been, and the joints were getting a bit stiffer of late. But he forced himself to keep up with Yarran and smiled crookedly as their riding boots scraped on rock or sucked in mud. *Scouting on foot's not exactly the sort of job* any *Sothōii relishes,* he thought. *I think most of us would mount up to go take a piss . . . assuming we could get the horse into the privy with us!*

He almost laughed at the thought, then scolded himself for letting his attention wander this close to the enemy. He shook his head, concentrating on making as little noise as possible as Yarran led the way around another bend. Then the scout's hand waved urgently, and the two of them slipped off the trail and into the cover of one of the many boulder piles the long-vanished river had heaped up in the bends of the Gullet.

"There," Yarran said quietly, and Festian felt his eyebrows rise as he followed the scout's pointing index finger to the crude fortification.

Not surprising they stopped here, was his first thought. *The trail widens out enough to let us deploy more strength, but then it pinches in . . . and they're right atop that nasty slope.* He tried to remember what the hradani called the place. He knew it had a name—enough skirmishes and battles had been fought here to make him *that* familiar with it—but he couldn't recall it. Something's Despair, wasn't it?

He brushed the thought aside and sat back on his haunches in the concealment of a large boulder, rubbing at a patch of dried mud on his cuirass, and stared at the banner flying above the roughly built walls. Not the crimson-on-black axe of Hurgrum, but dark forest green, bearing a crossed sword and mace in gold.

So Yarran was right. But what the Phrobus is the Order of Tomanāk doing here? And Order or no, those are damned well hradani on the wall below it!

He grimaced, then nodded to Yarran.

"All right. Keep an eye on them, and I'll send a few more men down to watch your back and act as runners. Don't go getting yourself into any fights, but if those bastards do anything—anything at all except sit right where they are—you get word back up the Gullet fast. Right?"

"Yes, Sir."

"Good!" Festian patted the scout's shoulder and turned to scramble back up the trail.

"The Order of Tomanāk? Your man's mad—or drunk!" Sir Mathian declared.

"He's neither, Milord," Festian said tightly, "and I saw the banner myself—with these." He indicated his own eyes with a sharp, angry gesture. "Whoever or whatever is *under* it, that's Tomanāk's banner down there!"

Mathian recoiled as he finally recognized the fury boiling behind Festian's masklike expression. The two of them stood face to face under an awning one of Mathian's aides had managed to rig between two boulders while clouds of gnats swarmed in the humid afternoon sunlight. A nice, cool breeze blew across the Gullet at right angles, but the steep walls kept any breath of it from reaching them. The barren crevice was like a steamy oven, just the sort of place to exact the maximum discomfort from a man's armor, and the Lord Warden's red face was soaked with sweat.

"All right, Festian. I believe you, of course," he said, much more placatingly than he'd intended to. "But it just seems so . . . so *impossible.*"

"Indeed, Milord," Haladhan put in. "One would have thought even hradani would hesitate to profane the symbols of Tomanâk. Surely even they wouldn't willingly risk turning the War God's favor against them in their next battle!"

"Pah!" Mathian spat on the ground. "Hradani are animals! I doubt even the gods know what they would or wouldn't do. We should ride right over the scum, not waste time worrying over what savages like them *think!*" He spat again, then added, "*If* they think— which I doubt!"

Festian opened his mouth, his eyes bleak, but Sir Kelthys' raised hand stopped him before he spoke. It was just as well, he reflected a moment later. He himself might not *like* hradani, but he'd fought enough of them to respect them. They had guts and skill, and, by their own lights, they fought with honor. Indeed, at this particular moment, he would much rather be under the command of a hradani than what he actually had.

"Your pardon, Milord," Kelthys said in his quiet way.

"Yes, Sir Kelthys?"

"I believe Sir Haladhan has made a valid point, Milord. Whatever else they may be, hradani are warriors. And while it has been my own observation that they show no great reverence for any god, whether of the Light or the Dark, neither do they go out of their way to *antagonize* the gods. Especially not the Sword God."

"Are you actually suggesting that the Order of Tomanâk is waiting for us down there?" Mathian couldn't keep the incredulity out of his voice, but Kelthys only shrugged instead of taking offense.

"All I'm suggesting is that we face something unusual. It's always possible this is, indeed, no more than another ploy to delay us. On the other hand, there just might be something more to it. Under the circumstances, I believe we should determine what we actually face before acting hastily. If I recall correctly, that position can hold no more than two hundred men. Does that sound about correct, Sir Festian?"

"Aye. You might get as many as three hundred in there if you pounded 'em in with a hammer, but they'd be dead meat for high-angle archery. It's no more than a wall of piled up rocks, with no overhead cover."

"As I thought," Kelthys murmured, and turned back to Mathian. "We have the better part of four thousand men, Milord, all of them as well trained as archers as for melee. If we're forced to fight for that position, our losses will be heavy, but the enemy can't hold for long against our numbers. That being so, I see no harm in sending forward a messenger under a flag of truce to discover what the presence of Tomanāk's banner actually means. Even if it is only a ploy, the extra time we expend will be minimal."

"I suppose there's something to that," Mathian agreed finally, although his expression remained manifestly unhappy. He glared at the ground for a moment, then beckoned to his cousin. "Come with me, Haladhan. I want to consider any message we might send those bastards very carefully."

Haladhan nodded, and the two of them stumped off. For a moment, Festian thought Kelthys was going to follow them, but the wind rider only watched them go with a faint smile. Then he looked back at Festian, and the scout commander realized that it was the first time the two of them had actually been alone together.

"Tell me, Sir Festian," Kelthys' expression remained as pleasant as ever, but his quiet voice bit like a lash, "just what the *hell* you thought you were doing letting that idiot run off to war without even telling Baron Tellian about it?"

Festian flinched from the anger in the wind rider's voice, but then he shook his head sharply.

"He *did* send word, Milord. He—" He broke off at the look in Kelthys' eyes. "Do you mean he *didn't?* But he told me himself he was going to! Surely not even—"

He cut himself off again, abruptly, before he said something one of Mathian's household knights had no business saying, and Kelthys sighed.

"I'm afraid he would, Festian," he said, the anger vanished from his voice.

"But how do you know he didn't?"

"Festian, Festian! Did you think my cousin just *happened* to decide one afternoon that it would be nice to have me at Deep Water so I could visit regularly for picnics? He's worried about Mathian ever since Sir Gardian's death, and he wanted me to keep an eye on him. Which I have for the last two years. And for which service—" he grimaced "—the good Baron Warden of the West Riding owes me a *monumental* return favor."

Festian simply stared at him, and the wind rider chuckled as if against his will at the scout commander's expression. Then he stepped closer to Festian, "coincidentally" hiding Festian's face from anyone else until the older knight got it back under control and keeping his own expression casual as he spoke with quiet urgency.

"It's been obvious for at least ten years that the Horse Stealers and Bloody Swords were going to settle their disputes one way or another at last. Tellian has sent regular dispatches to Sothfalas to keep King Markhos and his ministers apprised of the situation, and the court has been sharply divided on how to proceed. One faction wants to stand back and let events take their course, hoping Bahnak truly will manage to civilize the barbarians. Another faction shares Sir Mathian's view; it wants to strike now, while the hradani are busy with one another, and burn them out root and branch. Yet another wants us to aid Bahnak's *opponent*, in order to keep the pot boiling and the hradani fighting amongst themselves, rather than bothering us, for as long as possible. And a fourth is stuck out in the middle between the extremes, with no clear idea of *what* we ought to do. Are you with me so far?"

He darted a sharp look at Festian, and the knight nodded.

"Good. Well, Tellian's been worried about Mathian for some time, and when he discovered that he and Haladhan had been quietly discussing certain 'contingencies' with the younger and more hotheaded of the minor lords here in Glanharrow and across the district line in Tharkonswald, he got even more worried. Hence my arrival at Deep Water. Mind you, I truly was looking for somewhere to settle down, and Deep Water is a lovely little place, but the real reason was to get me close enough to Mathian that I could keep an eye on him and hopefully induce him to include me in his discussions. Tellian wanted private reports from me to tell him whether or not there was a legitimate reason for him to summon Mathian to Balthar for some pointed inquiries into just what he was up to."

One of Mathian's aides walked past, and Kelthys broke off until the man was out of earshot, then resumed.

"Well, Mathian decided to include me, but apparently he was more careful in what he said to *me* than what he said to the other minor lords. I knew he hated hradani, and I knew he had spies among them. I even knew he contemplated some sort of action against them, but I had no idea his plans had progressed so far, and I never expected anything like *this*. Once he actually started to move, I judged my best course was to allow myself to be convinced to go along with him so that I could learn what his plans were, and it worked. He still hasn't taken me as fully into his confidence as Haladhan and some of the others, but at least I got close enough to learn that he plans to dispatch a messenger to Tellian only *after* he's committed us to open war against the hradani."

"But that's *treason!*"

"No it's not—quite," Kelthys said dryly. "As he's said, he has the authority as Lord Warden to summon the knights and armsmen of Glanharrow on his own authority if he judges an emergency to exist. And as far as the delay in informing his own immediate liege of his actions, he will undoubtedly argue that until the situation had clarified, there was no point in sending messengers as far as Balthar. Of course, by the time the 'situation clarifies,' he'll have us at war, but that's exactly what he wants." Festian blinked, and Kelthys sighed. "That's what this is all *about*, Festian! He wants to force us to smash the hradani before they unite under a single leader who might actually be able to threaten the Kingdom. He sees it as his gods-given duty—something that will both let him avenge his father's death and emerge as the hero of our people."

"*Phrobus*," Festian whispered, and Kelthys nodded.

"Exactly. Which is why, my friend, you and I have to delay the young lunatic as long as we possibly can. I sent my wind brother Karral off to Balthar to alert Tellian as soon as Mathian summoned me to Glanharrow. He should be there by now. In fact, Tellian's response—if not Tellian himself—should be on the way back. But unless they were already prepared to move almost instantly, not even coursers could get anyone here before tomorrow evening. So between then and now, it's up to you and me."

CHAPTER THIRTY-TWO

Bahzell stood atop the wall and watched the small group of men emerge from the boulder field that choked the sharp bend in the Gullet and start down the trail on foot. A white flag hung limp from a lance shaft above them, but from the way they moved, they were none too sure anyone in Charhan's Despair knew what a white flag meant.

He smiled grimly at the thought. The sun was moving steadily farther into the west, and shadows were beginning to envelop the Gullet. The sinuous passage was narrow and deep, and the narrower switchbacks and bottlenecks were already in twilight, while the wider spots were like golden beads of light strung on a chain of shade. Like the shade which covered the boulders behind the truce party . . . and hid the archers he had no doubt at all were lurking there.

Well, that was all right with him. He'd sent Garuth and his picket on down the Gullet in order to make this purely a matter of the Order and the Sothōii, but he still had over a hundred heavy crossbows and arbalests of his own tucked away inside the rough fort. He could get no more than forty of them onto the front wall at any one time, perhaps, but that would be more than enough to skewer the Sothōii messengers the instant anyone put an arrow into *him*.

Not that he had any particular desire to see *anyone* skewered. He glanced at his companions. Hurthang stood at his left, wearing the surcoat of the Order and carrying its banner while Vaijon stood at his right. Hradani being hradani, there had been some fairly

335

heated debate over precisely who should accompany him. Gharnal, in particular, had argued that Hurthang had no business out there, since, as the chapter's second in command, it would be up to him to take over if something happened to Bahzell. Kaeritha had been scarcely less vociferous in her insistence that she should go with him instead of Vaijon. Everyone had been able to see the value of including a human in any truce party which hoped to convince the Sothōii they truly were the Order of Tomanāk, but *she* was the senior champion present. As such, it was she who should take the risk beside Bahzell.

"I've no doubt you've the right of it and all," Bahzell had told her finally, "but we're talking of *Sothōii* here, Kerry! I've troubles enough without trying to be cramming a belted knight as is also a *woman* down their craws!"

She'd subsided at that, and her acquiescence had left Gharnal with little choice but to do the same, yet Bahzell wasn't fooled. Assuming they all lived through this, both of them would find their own ways to get even with him, probably sooner rather than later.

He smiled again, less grimly, at the thought, and nodded to his companions.

"Let's be going," he said quietly, and started down to meet the enemy.

Gods, that's the biggest hradani I've ever seen in my life! Sir Festian squinted into the westering sun and managed not to stare at the giant advancing towards him, but it was hard. He had to be at least seven and a half feet tall, and he looked like a mountain in armor. In very *good* armor, Festian noted suddenly—better than he'd ever seen on a hradani . . . or, for that matter, on most Sothōii nobles. And it had clearly been made specifically to fit its wearer, not cobbled together or looted from someone else.

He was still turning that over in his mind when Haladhan hissed beside him.

"Toragan! That's a *man* over there!" Sir Mathian's cousin gasped.

For an instant, the significance of the remark failed to register, but then Festian's eyes snapped around to look where Haladhan was pointing. Like the Lord Warden, Haladhan refused to apply the word "man" to anyone other than another human, although he might make a few grudging exceptions for certain dwarves. Festian considered that pointlessly stupid, but his own astonishment overwhelmed the familiar flash of disgust as he saw the richly dressed, golden-haired young human with the elaborately plumed helm.

Well, he thought wryly, *whatever Mathian might have thought before he sent us out here, this certainly isn't your typical bunch of hradani!*

The Sothōii were close enough for Bahzell to see their faces now. There were six of them, although four were obviously armsmen, not knights or nobles, and his impassive expression hid a mental smile of glee as he saw them trying not to stare at Vaijon. At his insistence, Vaijon had brought along the pick of his wardrobe, and while that might now be only a shadow of what it once had been, it remained impressive. His embroidered surcoat glittered, sunlight flashing off its gold and silver bullion thread; the tall plumes of his helmet nodded as he walked; and the gems adorning his sword hilt seemed to flame with an inner light all their own.

Come to think on it, it just might be they do *have a light of their own*, a corner of his mind reflected. *It is* after being a champion's *blade, now isn't it just?*

That thought carried him the last few paces forward, and he stopped three yards short of the burly young man in the center of the Sothōii delegation. The hard-eyed youngster was unusually heavy-set and broad for his people, but like most Sothōii men, he stood only a little over six feet tall, a few inches shorter than Vaijon and *much* shorter than Bahzell or Hurthang. He had the fair complexion common to most of his people, although his hair was dark, not the more usual blond or red, and his face was set in rigid lines of contempt as he surveyed Bahzell and his companions.

"And a good afternoon to you," Bahzell rumbled, breaking the silence before it could stretch out too far.

"I am Sir Haladhan Deepcrag, cousin and Marshal of Mathian Redhelm, Lord Warden of Glanharrow," the burly young knight declared haughtily. His voice was abrupt and harsh, with a cutting edge which made the fingers of Bahzell's sword hand tingle. "Who are you, and by what right do you block our path?"

The older knight standing to Haladhan's left winced visibly. Bahzell glanced at him, then tilted his head, ears cocked, to consider Haladhan as he might have examined some new species of bug. He let the silence drag out once more, watching the young Sothōii's flush darken, then replied in deliberately calm tones.

"Why, as to that, Sir Haladhan Deepcrag, I'm called Bahzell Bahnakson, and if we're to speak of blocked paths, it's in my mind to be wondering just why it is you and your lot seem so all-fired anxious to be creeping down the Gullet in the first place." He showed strong, white teeth in what could have been called a smile.

"I'm thinking there's just a mite many of you for a social call, and surely your Lord Warden wouldn't be so ill-mannered as to be coming to dinner without sending word ahead, now would he?"

"Sir Mathian is not answerable to such as *you!*" Haladhan spat. "He comes and goes as he will!"

"Does he, now?" Bahzell rounded his eyes and let his ears stand straight up. "Why, we've something in common, then, for so do I, as well." His expression hardened suddenly, and his voice deepened. "And just this moment, where I'm willing to be going is right here," he rumbled, and pointed at the ground on which he stood.

"Indeed?" Haladhan glanced about, then curled his lip. "If that's what you wish, I'm sure Sir Mathian can accommodate you. It looks a little stony for graves, but no doubt the buzzards will be glad for the feast!"

"No doubt," Bahzell said. "But I'm thinking you might be thinking hard and long before you've the making of a mistake your Lord Warden will be a long time regretting. I'm not so certain at all, at all, that Tomanak will be pleased to be hearing as how he went and slaughtered an entire chapter of himself's Order."

"*You?*" Haladhan stared at Bahzell, then uttered a short, contemptuous laugh.

"Aye, myself," Bahzell agreed, and swept his hand to include Hurthang and Vaijon. "And my sword brothers, of course."

"You can't bluff *us*, hradani!" Haladhan spat. "I don't know where you found *this* traitor," he sneered at Vaijon, "but you're no more the Order of Tomanak than I am!"

"Now that's where you're wrong, friend," Bahzell said softly, "and you'd best take me seriously. Aye, we're hradani right enough, the most of us—and Horse Stealers, for the most part, too. But we're also after being the Order of Tomanak, sword sworn to him when he was after appearing himself in Hurgrum this month past."

"Nonsense!" Haladhan shot back, but there was just the tiniest edge of uncertainty in his tone.

"I'd ask you not to be questioning my word, truce flag or no." Bahzell's voice was mild enough, but his eyes weren't, and Haladhan shifted uneasily and stepped back a half pace without even realizing it. "I've no doubt you're finding that a mite hard to be taking in, yet it's true enough. And it's as a champion of Tomanak I stand here, Sir Haladhan, to ask you and your Lord Warden by what right you're after bringing war and destruction to those as haven't attacked you . . . and who you've not declared war upon, either."

"I don't bel—" Haladhan began, then stopped. "You claim to be a champion of Tomanāk," he went on in a slightly less caustic tone. "I . . . find that difficult to believe. And even if it were true, you have no right to question Sir Mathian's actions."

"I'm having every right there is," Bahzell told him flatly. "Both as a hradani, who's after seeing a hostile army marching against his folk; and as a son of Prince Bahnak of Hurgrum, who's a duty to guard his people; and most of all, as a champion of Tomanāk sworn to protect the weak and the helpless from those as think there's *honor* in murdering women and children while their own warriors are away."

Haladhan flushed, and his eyes fell for the first time. But he shook the moment off and summoned up a fresh glare.

"That sounds very fine, hradani, but Sothōii women and children have been murdered by hradani in their time!"

"So they have, and if you're minded to be keeping the slaughter going, you're a fool," Bahzell said dispassionately.

"Oh, no." Haladhan's voice was cold. "We have no intention at all of keeping the slaughter *going*. We mean to end it, once and for all!"

"Ah?" Bahzell cocked his head, eyes cold. "So this is what the Sothōii are after coming to, is it now? A pack of cowards and murderers—brave enough to be burning down farms and towns and butchering them as can't fight back, but only when those as might have protected them are safe out of their way!"

"How *dare* you talk to—" Haladhan began furiously, but Bahzell slashed a hand through the air, cutting him short.

"It's not after sounding so pretty put that way, is it now?" he asked softly. "It may be you'd not thought of it in just those words, Sir Haladhan Deepcrag, but just you be thinking on them now, for that's the truth of it. You may not believe me a champion of Tomanāk, but be that how it may, just you be asking yourself what Tomanāk would be saying to such as you and your precious Lord Warden are having in mind to do here."

"I—" Haladhan stopped himself, glaring at Bahzell, then spat on the ground. "*That* for you—and for Tomanāk, too!" he snarled. "'Women and children,' is it? Well, nits make lice, *hradani*, and we've suffered your kind too long as it is!"

"I see." Bahzell gazed down at the furious young knight, then swept his companions with his eyes. "Hear me now, all of you," he said finally, his deep voice flat, "for I'll say this only the once. The lot of you can be turning around and marching back up the Gullet, and no harm done. Or you can be staying right where you are, and again, no harm done. But you'll not go another furlong down this trail without you come through *us*, and whether you're minded to admit it or no, we *are* the Order of Tomanāk. I've no doubt you can kill us all, for we're but his servants, and mortal enough, the lot of us. But you'll not find it so easy as you may be thinking, and himself—and the *rest* of the Order—won't be so very pleased to hear as how you've done it. Go back and show you've the sense to turn around, Sir Haladhan . . . or come ahead and see how many of your own will be dying with us."

He turned and stalked back to Charhan's Despair without another word.

"Well *that* was a masterpiece of diplomacy," Brandark remarked as Bahzell climbed down the inside of the wall. The Horse Stealer cocked an ear at him, and he shrugged. "Your voice does tend to carry, Bahzell. Tell me, do you think there was any incentive to slaughter us that you *didn't* give him?"

"As to that, I doubt he'd any need of incentive *I* might have been giving him," Bahzell replied. "And it was plain enough he'd no interest at all, at all, in talking his way to anything else. But he's not after being the commander of those lads, either, and he wasn't alone. I'm thinking as how that older fellow will be one as makes sure whoever *is* in command is after getting the whole tale. But if they're so set on slaughtering hradani they're minded to take on the Order to do it, then there's not an argument in all the world that I could be making as would stop them, now is there?"

"I suppose not," Brandark admitted. He stood gazing out over the wall, rubbing the tip of his cropped ear while the sun sank still lower and the shadows deepened. "I *do* wish I could hear how their commander reacts to your version of diplomacy when he hears it, though," he said finally.

"Those *bastards!* Those thieving, murderous, lying, Phrobus-*damned* bastards!" Sir Mathian slammed his gauntleted fist against the hilt of his sabre, and his face was twisted with rage. "How *dare* they threaten me—us!"

Sir Festian glanced sideways at Sir Kelthys. The facts in Haladhan's version of the parley had been accurate enough, but the marshal had allowed contempt and hatred to color his report. In his turn, Festian had tried to soften the more vitriolic of Haladhan's remarks. He'd had to proceed carefully, though, and while he was confident he'd recounted the entire conversation accurately, he hadn't been at all sure Mathian had bothered to listen to him.

Now he was sure the Lord Warden hadn't. He knew the signs,

and his stomach tightened as he watched Mathian working himself up into a towering fury.

"I'll kill them all!" he shouted. "I'll kill every murderous one of the bastards, and then I'll burn their stinking towns to the ground! I'll—"

"A moment, Milord." Kelthys' voice was so calm that Mathian's mouth snapped shut in astonishment. He wheeled to face the wind rider, interrupted in mid-tirade, and Kelthys shrugged. "I understand your anger, Milord, just as I understand why you wish to insure the hradani are never able to threaten the Kingdom. But even so, I think it behooves us to at least consider the possibility that this Bahzell is telling the truth."

"The *truth?* You think a hradani could be telling the *truth* when he claims to be a champion of *Tomanāk?*"

"I think all things are possible—theoretically, at least, Milord," Kelthys said serenely. "The priests and philosophers would have us believe so, at any rate. Some are more probable than others, no doubt, and I must confess that, as you, I find the thought of a hradani champion less likely than most. But I also doubt that many men would make such a claim falsely. If Tomanāk failed to punish them directly for it, no doubt His Order would do so as soon as it heard."

"The whoreson is lying to stop us from hitting his godsdamned kind while their warriors are away," Mathian said flatly. "Phrobus, Kelthys! He's got no more than two hundred warriors down there. He knows he can't stop us from killing all of them any time we choose to, so *of course* he's lying! It's a bluff, and nothing more!"

"With all due respect, Milord, I don't think it is," Kelthys said, and now his voice was flat . . . and loud enough for the other officers clustered around to hear. "I believe we should at least consider the possibility that he's telling us the truth. At the very least, we should not risk arousing the justified anger of the Order of Tomanāk—to which, I remind you, the King's own brother Yurokhas has sworn Sword Oath—without first consulting with Baron Tellian, in whose name we are acting."

Mathian stared at the wind rider, his face bone white, and Festian held his breath. The Lord Warden of Glanharrow ground his teeth, and then he spat on the ground.

"I thought you a *man*, Kelthys!" he snarled.

"At least I am not a boy driven by his own unheeding passion," Kelthys replied, and his own tone was like a slap in the face. Mathian's hand darted to his sabre, and steel scraped, but

Festian's hand snapped out and caught his wrist before he could draw it.

"Calmly, Milord! *Calmly!*" he said urgently. "This is neither the time nor the place for us to begin killing our own!"

Rage quivered in every sinew of Mathian's body, and muscles ridged like iron lumps along his jawline as he glared at the wind rider.

"Very well, Kelthys," he ground out finally. "You've given your *advice*. Now stand aside. Those of us who aren't puling cowards have work to do."

"I think not, Milord," Kelthys said softly, and watched Mathian's eyes flare. "You are our Lord Warden. In time of emergency and in defense of the realm, you may command us to do your will, and any disobedience on our part is high treason. But, Milord, there *is* no threat to the realm. We stand not upon its borders, but halfway down the Escarpment. Tomanāk or no, the hradani who face us cannot possibly fight their way through us to invade the Wind Plain, and if it is treason for us to disobey you in time of invasion, it is also treason for *you* to use the forces which you command solely by right of the fealty you have sworn to Baron Tellian and, through him, to the King himself, to invade *another* realm."

"Treason?" Mathian whispered. "You *dare* to accuse me of *treason?*"

"Not yet, Milord," Kelthys replied gravely. "However, if you—or any of these other lords who follow you—continue on this course, then, yes. Treason is an ugly word, but the only one which will apply."

"*Curse* you!" Mathian snapped, and whirled to Haladhan. "I want his head for mutiny in the face of the enemy!" he screamed.

"Milord, I—" Haladhan began, and then stopped as a sabre whispered from its sheath. He turned to Kelthys, hand dropping to his own hilt, but it was not the wind rider who had drawn. One of the lords from the Tharkonswald District had stepped in front of Kelthys and stood facing Mathian with the back edge of his naked blade resting on his right shoulder. Another sabre was drawn, and another. In the space of less than a minute, almost half the minor lords who'd followed Mathian had formed a circle around Kelthys with weapons ready. No one said a word, but there was no need to.

Mathian stared at them, seeing his plan crumble, and something worse than rage boiled within him.

"So," he said, his voice cold and empty. "There are that many traitors among you, are there? Very well. Go. Go, all of you! *Go!*"

His voice was no longer cold or empty, and he spat again. "Take this other cursed traitor with you, and may Krahana lick his bones! I'll deal with him—and *all* of you—later! But for now, I command those of you who still know your duty to summon your men! We've got a nest of hradani to kill!"

CHAPTER THIRTY-THREE

"It seems they've decided."

Brandark's tone was dust-dry, and Bahzell nodded grimly as he peered up the Gullet. There was little to see as yet, but the Sothōii were making no effort to disguise their intentions. Horses could make their way through this boulder-strewn stretch of the Gullet only two or three abreast, and the footing was treacherous at the best of times. That meant any sort of cavalry attack was out of the question, but the narrow cleft's steep walls acted like a funnel, bringing them the sounds of booted feet fumbling across rocky, uneven ground and the jingling sound of weapons harnesses or the occasional scrape and ring of steel on stone.

"Aye, but they'll be coming in afoot, not mounted, and they've lost some sun," the Horse Stealer said after a moment, turning to look back over his shoulder. The Gullet bent sharply south to the west of Charhan's Despair, and its walls rose high; now the sun lay directly atop the western edge. The rude fort sat atop a low rise in the Gullet's stony floor which had once formed the waterfall lip of a broad pool when the Hangnysti ran through it, and the late afternoon sunlight spilled heavily down over it. But east and west of it, darkness was claiming the Gullet quickly.

"They've no more than an hour or so of daylight left," he went on. "Once it's gone, they'll not be able to use their bows so well."

"Oh, only an hour? Well that's a relief!" Brandark replied. "All we have to do is hold several thousand Sothōii warriors off for an hour—an hour while they *do* have the light for arrow fire, mind you—and everything will be fine. I'm *so* glad you told me!"

Bahzell grinned at him, then turned to check the rest of his men. All the hradani had brought shields, and now all those not directly behind the front wall of Charhan's Despair were crouched with those shields raised above them. Not all of the shields were the same size and shape, which prevented them from building one of the tortoises an Axeman army might have erected against plunging arrows, but most were large enough to offer at least the men who bore them fairly good cover. Kaeritha hadn't brought one, but Hurthang crouched beside her, and the oversized shield he held was big enough to protect them both. As Bahzell looked at him, his cousin glanced up from some unheard conversation with Kaeritha, grinned at him, and raised his axe in a one-handed salute.

"All right, then, lads," Bahzell said quietly, speaking to the Horse Stealers who waited on their knees, arbalests ready, behind the fort's front wall. There were eighty-two of them, as many as he could cram into the dead ground behind the wall, in two ranks, with the first on the firing step. They looked back at him, and their eyes were as calm as his own—calm with the serenity of hradani who had summoned the Rage—as he showed his teeth. "You'll be after shooting uphill and into shadow if you fire the instant you're seeing a target," he reminded them. "So just you be patient, and wait for the word. We'll be letting them reach the flat, where you'll have good light, and start up to us. Right?"

Heads nodded, and he checked the quarrel on the string of his own arbalest. Unlike most of their companions, he and Vaijon stood upright, gazing out over the wall. As the defenders' commander, Bahzell needed to see what was happening, and he and Vaijon had the best armor of anyone in the fort. Even a wind rider's great bow would have a difficult time driving a shaft through it, and the wall itself offered them fair protection. Chest-high on Bahzell, it was tall enough that only Vaijon's plumed helm showed above it, and the human cocked his head as bugles began to sound.

Sir Festian swore a long and bitter oath in the privacy of his own mind as he followed Mathian and Haladhan down the shadow-choked Gullet. For a moment, he'd thought Sir Kelthys' defiance might actually stop the Lord Warden, but it was clear now that nothing short of armed force could have deterred Mathian. And even if Kelthys had shaken half of Mathian's adherents into holding their own men back, there'd never been any hope he could convince them actually to turn upon the Lord Warden of Glanharrow.

And if the young bastard is determined to do this gods-damned, stupid thing, then I have no choice but to follow him, Phrobus fly away with him! Whatever else he may be, he is my sworn liege.

"All right," Mathian snapped to the men about him. They looked uncomfortable dismounted, as if they didn't know quite how infantry formations were put together. Most had left their lances behind, but a few souls, more inventive than others, had cut their lance shafts short to make them into light spears, which at least gave them a bit more reach than their sabres would.

This isn't their kind of fight, Mathian thought, *but that hardly matters. Not with the numbers we've got.* His lip curled as he looked once more at the hradani "fort." *It's nothing but a heap of rocks, like something a gang of children might make playing at siege engineering! Let the bastards think it'll save them!*

"They're only hradani, lads," he went on. "The archers'll keep their heads down till we reach their Phrobus-damned rock pile, and then we'll swarm 'em! The bastards may be big, but we outnumber them ten to one, so remember—*don't* go for one of them by yourself! Take 'em two or three to one, and we'll be done in time for dinner!"

A few cheers answered his ringing declaration, but only a few, and most of those from younger men who had never fought hradani. The others simply waited, expressions grim, determined enough, but also aware of what they faced, and Festian gritted his teeth with the rest of them.

Bad enough to fight the buggers from the back of a horse, but this—!

The thought was still flickering through his mind when the bugles sounded and the first flight of arrows hissed into the air.

"Heads down!" Bahzell shouted as a storm of arrows soared upward. They rose from the boulder field, now all but invisible in the shadows, but their lethal tips flashed golden as they arced into the sunlight and came driving down upon the fort like black death fletched in crimson and green. The sound of their flight was like nothing else on earth—a rustling, whistling *hiss* of a sound, like a million enraged serpents—and then they struck. Steel arrowheads rattled like driven sleet as they thudded home, burying themselves in shields or skipping off helmets or stone in showers of sparks. Here and there one of them licked past a shield and drove through chain or scale mail, and men cursed or shouted in pain. But only a very few of them actually struck flesh.

Four hit Bahzell, ricocheting from his breastplate and the fine-knit links of his dwarvish mail, and he bared his teeth in a hungry grin as the bugles sounded a second time. The deep-throated bellow of male voices rose like thunder in the confines of the Gullet, and the first Sothōii warriors charged out of the shadows behind their war cries. More arrows slashed down, deluging the fort to cover the charge, but the archers couldn't arc their fire steeply enough to drop it into the dead zone directly behind the wall, and he glanced one last time at the other crossbowmen.

"Ready, lads!" he bellowed, and leveled his arbalest across the uneven parapet as the others rose to their feet on the firing step with him.

Mathian of Glanharrow knew better than to lead the attack in person. That wasn't a commander in chief's task, and so he'd let Haladhan take the lead. But he had rejected the argument that he should stay in the rear. He'd let himself be talked into taking a place in the eighth rank, with Sir Festian at his right hand and his banner bearer at his left, but that was as far as he would go, for this was a battle he refused to be denied.

And so it was that he burst into the sunlight, screaming his own war cry and waving his sabre like a madman as the fourth arrow flight screamed overhead. He saw the shafts sleet down across the fort, and his heart rejoiced, for surely *nothing* could live under the merciless beating of that steel-pointed blizzard!

But something could, and his eyes went wide as two score and more of hradani rose behind the wall. They moved almost calmly, without hurry, ignoring the arrows screaming past them, and every one of them leveled a steel-bowed arbalest across the parapet. Mathian's front ranks were on the up-slope to the fort now, their charge slowing, and there was something dreadful about the deliberation with which the hradani took aim. He saw one of them go down, an arrow sticking out of what had been his right eye, but only their heads and shoulders were exposed to his own archers. Worse, the sunlight lanced directly into his men's eyes. They could see well enough for unaimed plunging fire, but picking out a specific target was all but impossible. And then a voice like thunder bellowed a command he heard clearly even through his warriors' battle cries.

"Loose!"

Whhhhunnnng!

Forty-two steel bow staves, the lightest of them easily a four hundred-pound pull, straightened as one. The heavy bolts were short and stubby compared to the arrows raining down on the fort from above, but they smashed out in flat, ruler-straight lines, and the range was barely fifty yards. They drove through cuirasses with contemptuous ease, and the light Sothōii shields were useless against them. Shrieks of agony broke the deep-sea surge of war cries, and men went down in heaps. Many simply fell over others who'd gone down in front of them, but at such short range a single quarrel could drive clean through two or even three men, and they wreaked terrible havoc.

And then the first batch of hradani stepped back and a second row took their place. Forty-one more arbalests came down, and Mathian heard the terror in his own voice as he screamed the Glanharrow war cry. But there was nowhere to go. The rush of his own men carried him forward, and he felt his testicles trying to crawl up into his body as he ran straight ahead.

Whhhhunnnng!

At least two hundred men were down—dead, wounded, or simply fallen over someone who'd been hit in front of them—and their formation, loose to start with compared to the tight intervals they would have kept mounted, came apart. They were no longer an army; they were a mob, and their own archers had to cease fire as they neared the enemy. But they were still charging forward, and there were still almost two thousand of them, and the only obstacle in their path was that ragged heap of rocks across the Gullet.

The second group of crossbowmen stepped back, and Bahzell tossed his arbalest to one of them. His blade snapped out of its scabbard, and the first group of bowmen, arbalests exchanged for swords and axes, leapt back up onto the step their fellows had abandoned. The front of the Sothōii attack was barely thirty feet away, and he felt the exaltation of the Rage take him like a lover, dancing down his nerves like lightning.

"Tomanāk! *Tomanāk!*"

He bellowed his war cry, and it came back like brazen thunder from six score throats.

Mathian's face went white as he heard the fierce, snarling rumble of the hradani's battle cries. Tomanāk! They were calling on *Tomanāk!* Was it possible they truly *were*—?

No! It was obscene even to think that, and he threw the thought aside as his men foamed up against the wall like the sea.

A Sothōii hurled himself at the wall, scrabbling up it on the run. The crude fort truly was little more than a heap of rocks, and its outer face was far from sheer. Men could scramble up it easily enough . . . but they were off-balance when they reached its top, and Bahzell Bahnakson's eyes were frozen brown flint as his huge blade hissed.

Despite the confusion, despite the noise, despite even his terror and excitement and need to concentrate on his footing, Sir Haladhan Deepcrag recognized the giant hradani from the parley. He saw the huge shape loom up, silhouetted against the sunset like a titan. Five feet of sword hissed in a sun-silvered flash, and then the first Sothōii to set foot on the wall flew backwards in an explosion of blood and viscera with his body cut cleanly in half.

It was impossible! It couldn't *happen!* Yet it *had* happened, and then Haladhan was stumbling up the wall himself while men shouted in rage and shrieked in pain and the ghastly, wet sounds of steel in flesh were all the world.

The first Sothōii rush slammed up the rock wall like storm-driven surf, but the Hurgrum Chapter of the Order of Tomanāk met it with another, deadlier wall, this one of steel. Attackers shrieked and died, or fell writhing in agony, their bodies slithering back down to trip and encumber their fellows, and even over their own war cries, the hradani heard the thunderous voice of Bahzell Bahnakson.

He leapt upward, driving his feet into the rear face of the wall to get more height, and his sword hissed with dreadful, rhythmic precision. The Sothōii were like wheat before one of Dwarvenhame's horse-drawn reapers, spilling away from him in a writhing wedge of severed limbs and lopped-off heads, and despite Mathian's earlier exhortations, they were unable to use their numbers effectively. There was only so much frontage, and Bahzell and his men had axes and swords enough to cover it all. The Sothōii were forced to meet them at little better than one-to-one odds, and it seemed impossible that any of them could possibly break through.

But they could. Individually overmatched or no, they swarmed forward, and here and there a hradani went down. Other members of the Order stepped forward to take their places, but a few Sothōii managed to wedge into the openings they'd made. Most died seconds later, but before they did, their advance had cracked the defensive front enough for the men behind them to strike at the flanks of other defenders. A gap opened in the hradani's line at the extreme left of the wall, and a roar of triumph went up as still more Sothōii stormed forward to exploit it.

"To me, lads! *To me!*" Hurthang bellowed to Bahzell's reserve, and went to meet the breakthrough. Kaeritha Seldansdaughter charged with him, and the two of them slammed through the confusion like a spearhead. They met the leading Sothōii warriors head-on, and Hurthang's axe struck like Bahzell's own sword. Dead men spilled away from him, and Kaeritha spun to her left, covering his flank as the Sothōii tried to flow around him. Their light armor and sabres were a better match for her shorter swords, but it didn't matter. She killed her first two opponents before they even realized she was there. Sheer weight of numbers pushed her and Hurthang back a stride then, but they wove a web of steel before them, no longer attacking but seeking only to hold, and then the reserve was there with Gharnal at its head, driving the breakthrough back.

Mathian of Glanharrow reeled, vision spangled by bursts of light, as the hradani broadsword smashed down on his helmet. His banner bearer was already down, hands clutching at the oozing hole where the spearhead of a daggered axe had punched clean through his cuirass, and Festian leapt desperately forward to cover his lord.

He lashed out at the hradani with his sabre and felt it bite on the other's thigh, but even as he struck, the hradani's sword smashed his light shield to splinters. He cried out as his arm broke under the blow, and the hradani struck again, as if he hadn't even felt the sword cut. Festian managed to get his sabre up to block the blow, but the hradani's heavier sword caught it right at the hilt and snapped it squarely in two.

The veteran hurled himself backward. It was all he could do, and he heard himself cry out again as his broken arm took the brunt of his fall. But at least he'd thrown himself out of the hradani's reach, and his desperate leap had knocked Mathian backward, as well. They slithered down the rough rock wall and the heaped bodies together, like a boy's sled on snow, and then Festian hit the bottom, stunned and barely half conscious from the pain in his arm, with Mathian beside him.

"Lord Glanharrow is down! *They've killed the Lord Warden!*"

The shouts went up from men who'd already seen Mathian's banner fall, and panic spread out from them like pestilence. Warriors who had surged forward into the slaughter atop the fort's walls felt the drive of those behind falter, and suddenly they were giving ground themselves, falling back and fighting only in self-defense as they retreated.

Festian saw it happening, as he'd seen it happen to one side or the other in too many battles, and knew it couldn't be stopped. Not, at any rate, by one middle-aged knight with a broken arm and no sword. He shoved himself back to his feet with a grunt of anguish and fastened the fingers of his good hand on Mathian's cuirass. Fresh agony lashed through his bad arm, but his heave brought the Lord Warden to his feet and got him staggering—still stunned by the blow his helmet had turned—away from the fort.

Bahzell saw the Sothōii break off, and a dozen of his own men started after them.

"*Stop!*" he bellowed. His deep voice cut through the bedlam, and they looked over their shoulders. "Back!" he shouted, pointing back down into Charhan's Despair with his gore-soaked blade. "Back into the fort, lads!"

For just a moment, he thought they were too carried away with battle fever to heed him, but then they obeyed. They scrambled back into the fort, and he heard Vaijon shouting for men to get their shields back up behind him.

But no fresh arrow storm came. The fight atop the wall had only seemed to last forever, but it *had* lasted long enough for the light to go. Even as the Sothōii fell back, the sun sank beyond the western cliffs at last, and darkness fell like an axe blow. The Sothōii archers no longer had light to shoot by, and Bahzell breathed a prayer of gratitude.

He looked out into the dimness, and a carpet of pain writhed before him. At least three hundred Sothōii lay out there, most dead but many wounded, and he bared his teeth. The Lord Warden of Glanharrow wouldn't be so quick to launch a *second* assault, he thought grimly.

But then he turned to survey the interior of the fort, and his jaw tightened. Twenty or thirty Sothōii had actually made it over the wall; all of them lay dead or wounded . . . but so did at least that many of his own. It looked as if half or more of the Order's casualties had been inflicted by the preliminary arrow fire, however. Now that darkness had taken the Sothōii's bows effectively out of play, their losses would be enormously higher than the Order's in any fresh attacks.

Which didn't mean they couldn't still take Charhan's Despair away from him in the end. But at least they'd wait until dawn to try if they had a shred of sense.

He drew a deep breath, then straightened his shoulders. Many of his men already knelt over the wounded, hradani and human alike, and he and Kaeritha and Vaijon would have plenty to keep them busy in the meantime.

CHAPTER THIRTY-FOUR

Sir Mathian thrust the surgeon roughly away and heaved himself up off the camp stool. The world swooped about him, but at least this time he managed to stay upright, and he lurched to the tied-back flap of the tent someone had managed to erect beside the field surgery. Chaos almost as wild as that inside his head swirled under the torches outside the tent, and he clung doggedly to a tent pole while he made his brain sort the confusion into some sort of order.

It wasn't actually as bad as it looked, he realized slowly. The surgery had been set up in one of the few wider stretches of the Gullet, but there was little room to spare. His men were packed tightly together in what space there was, and the crowd seemed to seethe and flow as messengers and stragglers trying to get back to their units pushed their way through the press. The unsteady light of the torches only made it look even more confused, and he clung to the pole as vertigo washed through him.

"Milord, you *must* sit back down!" the surgeon protested. "At the very least, you have a concussion, and there may—"

"Be silent!" Mathian rasped. He closed his eyes, and his head pounded as if a dozen dwarves with pickaxes were trapped inside and trying to get out. The force of his command to the surgeon didn't help the pain one bit, but at least the man shut his mouth. That was something, the Lord Warden thought, and opened his eyes once more.

"You—guard!" he called to one of the sentries outside the tent. He didn't recognize the man, but the guard turned at his summons.

"Yes, Milord?"

"Send Sir Haladhan to me at once!"

"I—" The guard hesitated, glancing at his fellow, then cleared his throat. "I can't, Milord. Sir Haladhan . . . didn't return from the attack."

Mathian clung even more tightly to the tent pole, staring at the guard, and his eyes burned. Haladhan? *Dead?* It couldn't be. The gods wouldn't permit it! But as he stared out into the torchlight and the chorus of scream-shot moans from the surgery washed over him, he knew the gods *would* permit it. Deep inside, part of him recognized that the attack on the hradani's fort had been no more than a skirmish compared to the slaughter of a major battle. But that recognition meant nothing at this moment. It had been Mathian's first taste of real combat, and the brutality and savagery of it had turned all his dreams of triumphant glory and vengeance for his father into cruel mockeries. He had never before known such terror, never imagined such horror, and now he'd lost Haladhan, as well.

But he may not be dead. He may still be alive out there . . . and is that any better?

He shuddered, picturing his cousin writhing on the rocky floor of the Gullet, sobbing while he clutched at the crossbow bolt buried in his belly or the sword slash which had spilled his intestines in the dirt. Or, worse, screaming as the hradani avenged their own losses by torturing the wounded.

Yet even as imagination tormented him, he realized he had to *do* something. A craven voice in the back of his brain urged him to listen to the surgeon, to sit back down and surrender to the man's ministrations, using his injury to hide from his responsibilities. It was tempting, that voice, yet he dared not heed it. He was Lord Warden of Glanharrow, and *he* was the one whose orders had brought all these men here. However right or wrong the decision had been, it had been his, and if he was to retain any ability to command them in the future, he could not show weakness now.

"Very well," he told the guard who was still staring at him. "What of Sir Festian?"

"He's with the surgeons, Milord." Mathian looked up sharply, but the guard shook his head reassuringly. "It's only a broken arm, Milord. He's having it set."

"Good." Mathian rubbed his forehead, jaw clenched against the pain. "Ask him to join me here as soon as he can. And pass the word to the other captains. I'll want to speak to them as soon as Sir Festian and I have conferred."

"Yes, Milord!" The guard saluted and hurried off into the confusion, and Mathian allowed the insistent surgeon to at least get him to sit back down.

"That's the best we can do for them, I'm afraid," Kaeritha said. She and Vaijon sat with Bahzell, and all of them clutched hot mugs of tea. Bahzell blinked, struggling with the aftermath of healing the wounded, and nodded. Vaijon said nothing. It was the first time he had ever touched the healing power Tomanāk granted his champions, and the aftereffects had hit him harder than his more experienced companions. He'd done well, though, Bahzell thought, reaching out to rest one hand on the youngster's shoulder. Vaijon looked up, half-dazed but blue eyes glowing with the joy of bringing life, not death, and Bahzell squeezed. Then he looked at Kaeritha.

"Aye, I'm afraid you've the right of it," he said. He didn't like the admission, but if they expended any more strength on healing, they would be useless if the Sothōii launched another assault. A part of him felt guilty for having seen to their own worst wounded before turning to the enemy. He knew some of the hradani they'd healed would have survived unaided while many of the Sothōii they had not healed would die, yet they'd had no choice. They needed every man they had—on his feet and ready to fight, not lying wounded in his blankets—and it hadn't been their decision to launch this attack.

"D'you think they'll come at us again?" a voice asked, and he turned his head to find Brandark at his side.

"I've no idea at all, at all," he said after a moment. "I'd not try it again before dawn in their boots, assuming I was wanting to try again at all."

"They might try under cover of darkness," Kaeritha pointed out. "They could creep in a lot closer, and they might think they could surprise us."

"Aye, so they might," another voice rumbled. Hurthang loomed out of the darkness and seated himself on a boulder beside her. "But we're talking of Sothōii here, Kerry, and for all that young fool as 'parleyed' with us isn't after having the sense the gods gave idiot geese, there's bound to be some older heads over yonder. And if there are, then they'll know as how hradani see nigh as well as cats in the dark. They'll not surprise us by creeping up unseen, come what may, lass."

"Which isn't to be saying they won't try," Bahzell said, "and from all I've had the hearing of, this Mathian of Glanharrow's fool enough to try almost anything. Still and all, I'm thinking you've the right of it, Hurthang. We'll be keeping a sharp eye on them, but if they've a brain in their heads, they'll wait on light for their archers to be seeing by."

"We should attack again *now*, while they're still licking their wounds!" Mathian insisted, and Festian turned from where he'd stood watching the surgeons through the tent doorway. His broken arm throbbed—he'd almost passed out twice while the bonesetter splinted it—and he felt as if the sobs of the wounded were a dark and restless sea on which he drifted.

"We hurt the bastards—I know we did—and there were fewer of them to begin with," Mathian went on. "And we've our own wounded to think about, lying out there where those butchers can get at them. We have to rescue them. And—"

"Milord, shut *up*."

The older knight spoke with cold, bitter precision, and the three words cut Mathian off like a sabre blow. The Lord Warden stared at the man who'd become his senior officer with Haladhan's disappearance, and his mouth worked like a beached carp's. The combination of his concussion and the open contempt in Festian's voice left him momentarily bereft of words, and the scout commander forged ahead into his silence.

"If there's a single thing you haven't done wrong, Milord, I can't think what it might be," the older man told him in a flat, biting voice that hurt far worse than any shouted imprecations. "Even leaving aside whether or not you've acted within the law, or whether or not you've set us all on a direct course for the Order of Tomanâk to invoke the Sword God's edict against us, you and that other young fool have managed to commit us to an attack under the worst circumstances you could possibly have arranged. I *warned* you not to come down the Gullet, but you wouldn't listen. I warned Sir Haladhan that there was a *reason* the hradani decided to fight here, but the two of you had to charge ahead—*on foot!*—and find out how defensible that position is the hard way."

"But—" Mathian tried to interrupt, but Festian cut him off with a savage chop of his good hand. No doubt the shock of his own injury had something to do with his tirade, but *gods* it felt good to finally speak his mind to this fool!

"I haven't finished, Milord," he went on with that same, cutting levelness. "As I was about to say, *if* you insist on pressing this attack at all, then for Tomanâk's sake—" his eyes glinted as Mathian flinched visibly at that name "—wait for daylight! The Horse Stealers are infantry; we're not. They're armed and armored to fight on foot; we aren't. If we try to take that pile of rocks away from them with head-on assaults, they'll massacre us, because we'll be fighting *their* kind of fight, not ours. Oh, we can *do* it, Milord, but you've already lost upwards of four hundred in dead, wounded, and—maybe—prisoners. We'll find that hard enough to explain to Baron Tellian without doubling or trebling the butcher's bill. And the only way to avoid doing *that* is to use our bows. If you insist on continuing this attack, then for the gods' sake at least stand off and lace them with arrows for an hour or two! Mount a few false attacks to pull them up onto the wall, then fall back and let the archers shoot them in the face. Do whatever you have to, but *don't* send in another Sharnā-damned charge without whittling them down first!"

Mathian bit his lip as fury mixed with the pain throbbing through the bones of his skull. How *dared* Festian speak to him with such cold contempt? Yet under the anger and the pain was the cold knowledge that Festian was the least of his worries. Even the minor lords who'd stayed loyal to him when Kelthys split his forces had to be shocked by their losses. Many were no older or experienced than he himself had been. They'd expected him to lead them to a quick, sharp victory—just as *he* had expected to do—and their failure to crush the hradani with their first rush must have stunned them almost as badly as their casualties had. No doubt they were thinking long and hard right now about their decison to follow him into what might, technically, be construed as treason. If he forced a break with Festian, his own senior officer, by insisting on mounting another attack immediately, he could lose all of them. But if he didn't do *something* to assert his authority and show he had command of the situation, he'd lose them anyway!

Give it up, a little voice whispered. *The whole thing's turned into a disaster. If you don't give it up, it's only going to get worse. Kelthys has already betrayed your trust in him—and taken those other gutless worms with him. And Haladhan—*

He shied away from thoughts of his cousin once more, and his jaw tightened. He had committed himself to this attack. He hadn't precisely *defied* Tellian to launch it, but he'd clearly done so on his own authority, and that could have dire consequences when the baron learned of it. The only thing that could possibly justify his actions was success. He had to break into Bahnak's rear and create sufficient havoc to smash the Horse Stealer's efforts to unite all the northern hradani under his banner. If he did that—or even if he only committed the *rest* of the West Riding's knights and armsmen to doing it—the Court faction which favored intervention would protect him. But if he let a handful of hradani bog him down while the rest of his force splintered—

But what if they are *the Order of Tomanāk?* a traitor trickle of thought demanded. *You're getting in deeper and deeper, you fool. It seemed so simple and exciting—so easy—when you and Haladhan played at plotting, didn't it? But it's not simple, and Haladhan's probably dead, and those* fucking *hradani are down there laughing at you!*

"Very well, Sir Festian," he heard himself say flatly. "We'll do as you suggest. Summon the other captains, and I'll inform them that we will attack again at dawn."

"Well, it looks like you and Hurthang were right." Bahzell turned his head as Vaijon stepped up onto the firing step beside him, and the young champion smiled crookedly at him. "They *are* going to wait for dawn."

"So it seems." Bahzell looked at the eastern sky. Only the very faintest hint of gray had crept into it, but the lip of the Escarpment was a bolder, blacker bar than it had been. *Another forty minutes,* he thought. *Maybe an hour, at the outside.*

He looked back down into Charhan's Despair. Hurthang and Gharnal had done their best to protect the wounded, hradani and human alike, from the arrow storm they all knew would soon be unleashed. Thirty-seven of the Order's hundred and twenty warriors lay dead, with another six too badly hurt to fight, and Hurthang had used the shields of the fallen to cobble up a sort of shield-roofed lean-to. Gharnal had supervised the movement of the wounded men into its protection, and the confused expressions of the nineteen Sothōii had put a grim smile on his face. Clearly none of the humans knew what to make of the care their captors had taken for their safety.

"I'm wondering if I should be sending you and Kerry out for another parley," Bahzell rumbled. Vaijon raised an eyebrow at him, and the Horse Stealer shrugged. "I'd no mind to try sending *anyone* out in the middle of the night, lad. It's easy enough to be missing a truce flag in daylight—especially when tempers are after running high. But the two of you are both after being human, and we've hurt the bastards hard." He gazed grimly out over the carpet of bodies, most stiff and cold now, but a few which had been too far out for the hradani to reach without drawing fire still twitching pathetically. "It might just be as the idiots would be listening to reason for a change, now that they're after knowing what the Despair will cost 'em."

"If you say so," Vaijon said dubiously. "I'm willing to try, but if they were going to listen to reason at all, then surely—"

He broke off, wheeling suddenly to stare up the Gullet as a confused welter of bugle calls spiraled into the darkness.

"—and the archers will open fire on Sir Festian's signal," Mathian told his vassals. Some of the faces looking back at him in the torchlight wore doubtful expressions, and he deepened his voice deliberately, trying to ignore the pain still throbbing through his skull.

"We'll let them work on the bastards for twenty minutes or so," he went on, "and then we'll launch a false attack. That should draw them out of any cover they may have found, and the archers will—"

The sudden, silver notes of a bugle cut him off in midsentence. It came from the east, from further up the Gullet, and his belly seemed to fall right out of him as he whirled towards the sound. It couldn't be!

But it was, and Sir Mathian Redhelm, Lord Warden of Glanharrow, felt his last chance to retrieve his fortunes crumble as the bugle sounded the personal call of Baron Tellian of Balthar, Warden of the West Riding, yet again.

Other bugles were sounding, and he heard the confused roar of voices as he stepped out of the tent and stared up the steep slope above his crowded encampment. There were more torches up there than there had been, and he clenched his jaw as a tightly clustered knot of them forged down the slope. Boots sounded behind him, and he looked over his shoulder as Festian came out of the tent to gaze up the Gullet himself. The older knight met his eyes for just a moment, then he looked away, and Mathian felt the last, shattered fragments of his glorious dream fall uselessly from his fingers.

CHAPTER THIRTY-FIVE

"What d'you suppose is keeping them?"

Brandark's elaborately casual tone fooled none of his listeners. He stood atop their rough rampart with Bahzell, Kaeritha, Vaijon, and Hurthang, gazing up the Gullet, and bright, cool sunlight flooded down over them. If anyone up there decided to fire a sudden flight of arrows, he could do enormous damage to the defenders' command structure. But somehow none of them expected that to happen, not after all the confused shouting and general bedlam which had followed those predawn bugle calls. Of course, they had no idea what *was* about to happen.

"I suppose they might have overslept after all the hubbub," Vaijon said judiciously, striving to match the Bloody Sword's tone, and Hurthang chuckled.

"So they might, but I'd not bet money on it. Still and all, *something* must have been after changing their plans, for I've not doubt at all that they were minded to be taking our ears."

"No more have I," Bahzell told him, "and—"

He broke off suddenly, and the others stiffened beside him as they saw movement up the Gullet. A group of figures emerged from the boulder field, and Vaijon smothered something that sounded remarkably like a curse.

"Tomanak! How in the name of all the gods did they get a *horse* that size through there?"

"They didn't, lad," Bahzell said softly. Vaijon glanced at him oddly, and he grinned as yet another rider picked his cautious way clear of the boulder field. "Those are coursers, Vaijon."

"But—" Vaijon began to protest, then stopped as the sheer size of the "horses" registered. There were dismounted men with them, and the head of the tallest man out there didn't reach the shoulder of the smallest of the half-dozen coursers. And then a seventh rider came around the boulder field, on a much smaller mount, and Bahzell laughed.

"Well, now! It seems I may've been being just a mite hasty. That fellow trailing along behind *is* on a horse, and one I'm thinking I know."

"You do, hey?" Hurthang looked at him skeptically, then shrugged. "So what are you thinking to do now?"

"Why, if they're minded to call on us all sociable like, we ought to be meeting them," Bahzell replied, and strode down the rough wall with long, swinging strides.

The others followed, all but Hurthang scrambling down with considerably greater difficulty, and he walked down to the foot of the slope atop which Charhan's Despair sat. Then he stopped and waited, arms folded, for the Sothōii to reach him.

It didn't take them long. Vaijon and Brandark, neither of whom had ever seen a courser before, stared at the huge creatures. It was impossible for anything that size to be simultaneously graceful and delicate, yet somehow the coursers managed it, and neither of them could figure out how. Bahzell, however, was focused on other concerns—like the tall, red-haired man in silver-washed plate armor mounted on the chestnut stallion at the head of the Sothōii party. The rider nodded to Vaijon and Brandark gravely, as if acknowledging a reaction he'd seen many times, but his eyes were on Bahzell.

"Good morning," he said. A neatly trimmed beard and mustache showed in his open-faced helm, and his voice was surprisingly light for such a big man, but it had the rap of someone accustomed to being obeyed. "You must be Bahnak's son," he went on, looking Bahzell straight in the face.

"Aye, I am that," Bahzell agreed, and glanced past him at the single man mounted on a regular war horse. "And a good morning to you, too, Wencit," he said.

"The same to you," the wizard replied calmly, wildfire eyes glowing. Then he smiled. "I told you I had an errand of my own to run on the Wind Plain, didn't I?"

"So you did," Bahzell said, then returned his gaze to the man on the chestnut courser. "And who might you be, if I might be asking?" he inquired politely.

"Tellian, Baron and Warden of the West Riding," the wind rider said simply. One of Bahzell's friends inhaled sharply, but he only nodded, as if he'd expected that answer.

"And would it happen it was you as was sending these lads—" he twitched his head at the bodies littering the slope "—down the Gullet?" he asked mildly.

"It was not," Tellian said shortly. Then he showed just a flash of white teeth under his mustache. "If it *had* been, I assure you the affair would have been better managed."

"Would it, then?" Bahzell cocked his head, then snorted. "Aye, like enough it would. Still and all, you're after being here now, aren't you just?"

"I am."

Tellian nodded, and it was his turn to let his eyes sweep the dead men. His expression was grim, but he said nothing for several seconds, and Bahzell waited silently. The Kingdom of the Sothōii was unique in that its highest noble rank after the king himself was that of baron. Legend said that was because the original Sothōii settlers had been led to the Wind Plain by a single baron who had escaped the Fall of Kontovar. According to the tales, he had refused to promote himself to count or duke as so many other refugee leaders had done, and that had set a tradition which the Sothōii still declined to break. Bahzell had no idea if the story was accurate, but whatever the reason, the man before him was one of the four greatest nobles of the Sothōii, with a "barony" anyone else would have called a kingdom in its own right.

"I was not aware of what Lord Glanharrow intended." Tellian's sudden statement snatched Bahzell back to the surface of his own thoughts. "Had I been, I would have commanded him to abandon his plans. In which case—"

He stopped again and shook his head.

"No, that's not quite true," he said in the voice of a man scrupulously intent on getting his facts straight. "I *did* learn what he intended, but not until Wencit arrived to tell me. And I regret to say I didn't believe him at first. Not entirely." His face darkened. "I made my own preparations, but I had my own agents keeping watch on Glanharrow, and I thought I was better served by their reports than by whatever Wencit might have heard from afar. What I didn't realize was that with one exception—" he turned his head and smiled briefly at another wind rider, this one on a courser of midnight black "—my agents had come to share Lord Glanharrow's intentions. And so, this—"

He waved one hand at the bodies, and Bahzell nodded once more. But the Horse Stealer's eyes were hard, and he twitched his own head back towards the fort behind him.

"Aye, and so this . . . and so the thirty-seven lads of mine dead back yonder, as well," he said grimly. Tellian's head snapped up, and his eyes flashed angrily, but then he clenched his jaw and chopped his head in a nod of his own.

"That, also," he acknowledged, and silence fell once more.

"So would you be telling me just what it is you're minded to do now you *are* here?" Bahzell asked after a moment.

"I don't know," Tellian admitted. "I never intended for this to happen, yet it has. Whoever began it, both you and we have dead to mourn, and here I am, halfway down the Gullet with an army at my back. Under the circumstances, many at Court—and in other districts of my own Riding—would say the rational thing to do is to press on. The war has been started, and we hold the advantage at the moment. And if we secure control of the Gullet so that we can pass men freely up and down it, we'll continue to hold it."

"Aye, I can be seeing that," Bahzell conceded levelly. "It's in your mind as how my father isn't one to be looking lightly at this, come what may and whoever was starting it. It might just be he'd be minded to be hitting back at the West Riding for it, but he's his hands full with Churnazh the now. So if you were to keep right on going, why, you might put paid to all his plans—even bring him down for Churnazh—and then you'd not have to worry at all, at all, about what he might or might not have been after doing. Would that be about the size of it?"

"It would," Tellian agreed with a grim smile.

"Well, I can't say as how I'm surprised," Bahzell said frankly, "for it might be I'd think much the same in your boots. But it's not so simple as all that. I told your Lord Glanharrow as how we wouldn't be moving for him, and no more will we stand aside for you. And whatever *he* may have been thinking, we *are* the Order of Tomanāk. So you be thinking long and hard before you're deciding to press on."

One or two of the men with Tellian stirred angrily, but the baron only shrugged.

"Whatever I may decide, Milord Champion, I, for one, have no doubt at all that you and your companions serve the War God," he said. One of the dismounted Sothōii made a sound of disbelief, but Tellian quelled any outburst with an icy frown. "When Wencit of Rūm vouches for someone's truthfulness, I have no intention of questioning it. But that still leaves us with a problem. You may belong to the Order of Tomanāk, but you are also all hradani." Vaijon stirred beside Bahzell, and Tellian paused. Then, for the first time, he smiled with a trace of true humor. "Well, *most* of you are," he corrected himself.

"And your point is, Baron?" Kaeritha's question was sharp, and Tellian turned to face her.

"My point, Milady, is that while you and I might be inclined to see this matter as a case in which the Order of Tomanāk intervened, precisely as it ought, to prevent an unprovoked massacre of those unable to defend themselves, others might not. I feel quite certain there will be some at Court who will see it only as a clash between hradani and Sothōii and be furious if I do anything but continue the attack. And there will be others who will fear, legitimately perhaps, that Prince Bahzell's people will see it that way, as well, and demand vengeance. That, after all, is the way of border warfare, is it not? Both sides can always justify present atrocities on the basis of past wrongs done to their fathers, or their grandfathers . . . or their great-great-*great*-grandfathers."

"So they can," Wencit put in dryly, "and especially if they're hradani or Sothōii." Bahzell and Tellian frowned at him almost in unison, and he laughed. "I rest my case!" he declared, and human and hradani darted looks at one another, then looked away quickly.

"No doubt the wizard is correct enough about that, Milord Baron," another wind rider put in, "but for myself, I'll trust a hradani—and especially a *Horse Stealer* hradani—no further than the end of my own lance." Bahzell's face tightened, but several others, especially among the dismounted Sothōii, muttered in agreement.

"Perhaps not, Hathan," Tellian said in a flat, discouraging voice, "but *I* am the one who must decide what happens here today, not you!"

"With all due respect, Wind Brother," Hathan said in an oddly formal tone, "the decision you make may affect all Sothōii. And we are both wind borne, you and I. If I may not speak my mind to you, then who may?"

Tellian flushed and opened his mouth as if to snap back an answer, then paused and closed it. He glowered at the other for a moment, then nodded grudgingly and waved a hand at Bahzell, as if resigning the conversation with him to Hathan. The other wind rider made a soft sound, and his courser flicked its ears and stepped daintily forward until it stood directly before Bahzell. Unlike any of the Sothōii, the hradani seemed almost properly sized for the huge creature, and he stood motionless, arms once again crossed, and met Hathan's gaze levelly.

"You claim to be a champion of Tomanāk," Hathan said finally, speaking to Bahzell as if no one else were present, "and Milord Baron and Wencit of Rūm both accept your word. Very well, so will I, hradani. Yet you might be ten times a champion, and still you would be hradani, and a Horse Stealer, and the son of the *ruler* of the Horse Stealers." Hurthang and Vaijon both stirred angrily, but Hathan ignored them, his unflinching gray eyes locked to Bahzell's. "My wind brother has said memories are long in border war. So they are, and I tell you this, Bahzell Bahnakson: the Sothōii will never forget that your people have raided ours from the first day ever we set foot upon the Wind Plain. Nor will we forget the very name in which you glory: Horse *Stealers*, the barbarians who raid our herds, who steal the horses we love almost as our own children and devour them like beasts of prey! What say you to *that*, Champion of Tomanāk?"

"Say?" Bahzell cocked his head, and his brown eyes were just as hard as Hathan's gray ones. "I'll say as how I 'claim' to be himself's champion because I am. But, aye, you've the right of it when you call me hradani and Horse Stealer. And Wencit has the right of it when he's calling hradani nigh as stubborn and long in the memory as you Sothōii. True enough all of that is, true as death, but you've set the cart before the horse for the rest of it, Wind Rider. Aye, we're after calling ourselves 'Horse Stealers,' and proud of the name, too, for never another name in all Norfressa was harder earned. But let's be telling the whole tale, shall we? Aye, we were after raiding your herds, and stealing your horses—yes, and eating them, too—for we'd no choice at all, at all . . . but it wasn't my folk as *began* the raiding." Hathan shifted in the saddle, and many of the other Sothōii muttered angrily, but Bahzell ignored them and glared straight into Hathan's eyes.

"My folk were here before ever yours came next or nigh the Wind Plain, Wind Rider, for none of the other Races of Man would have us. Warrior, woman, and child, we were driven off wherever we'd managed to fight our way ashore after the Fall, and if we were after dying in the wilderness, so much the better. And so we ended here, at the foot of the Wind Plain, on land no one else was wanting and too far from the 'civilized' folk for their warriors to be creeping up on us at night and burning our roofs over our heads while our children slept!"

The anger in his deep voice dwarfed the Sothōii's mutterings, and his brown eyes blazed like iron fresh from the forge.

"And what came of us here, Milord Wind Rider? What happened when first *your* folk brought their herds and horses to the Wind Plain? *My* folk remember, if yours are after forgetting. We remember the Starving Time, when your warriors came down off the Wind Plain like a pestilence. When the barns burned, and the harvests with them, and our babes starved at their mother's breasts. Aye, we *remember* it, Hathan of the Sothōii, and we're after taking our name from what your kind forced upon us, for we'd no *choice* but to raid your herds for food! It was that or be watching our children starve, and I'm thinking your own choice would've been no different from ours!"

"Nonsense!" Hathan shot back. "The earliest tales make it perfectly plain that it was your kind who raided *us!* And—"

"Excuse me, Hathan." Wencit didn't raise his voice, but something in it snapped all eyes to him. He paused a moment, as if waiting to be certain he had the attention of all of them, and then he shrugged. "I'm afraid Bahzell's version is the more accurate, Hathan," the wild wizard said almost gently. "Oh, his ancestors were no saints, but it was yours who began the war between you."

"But—" Hathan paused, mouth frozen in the open position. Then he shook his head. "But that's not possible," he protested. "All of our tales, all our histories—"

"Are wrong," Wencit said with that same note of gentle regret. All the Sothōii, even Tellian, stared at him in disbelief, and he sighed. "Unlike any of the rest of you, *I* was here at the time," he told them. "I warned Baron Markhos of the presence of Bahzell's ancestors when he set out for the Wind Plain, and I urged him to keep clear of them—to leave them in peace so long as they left *him* in peace. But he didn't. Like almost all the refugees, he hated the hradani for what they'd done in the Carnadosans' service. It didn't matter to him that they'd had no choice. It was simpler to hate than to understand them, and so when his scouts reported the locations of the Horse Stealers' ancestors, he waited until winter was near and the harvests were in, and then—exactly as Bahzell says—he ordered their barns burned to starve them out."

Total silence ruled the Gullet when he paused. The Sothōii sat or stood frozen in shock, and he sighed.

"It was an ugly time, my friends," he said sadly. "An ugly time for all of us. But I tell you this, Hathan Shieldarm: of all the Races of Man, the hradani's suffering at the hands of the Carnadosans was the cruelest. They were enslaved, driven and goaded by spells you cannot imagine, used and discarded and broken into slavering beasts which remembered being *more* than beasts yet could not fight the sorcery locked upon them. And then, when a handful of them escaped to Norfressa against all but impossible odds, the other Races of Man fell upon them and slaughtered them *like* animals, too filled with hate for what the Carnadosans had forced them to do to heed me, or Duke Kormak, or Ernos of Saramantha when we *told* them the hradani had had no choice.

"So, yes, they raided your herds, for your ancestors had left them nothing else to eat. And, yes, they slaughtered and ate your horses, as well as your cattle. Indeed, they *preferred* horsemeat to beef, for they knew how much you loved your horses, and they treasured anything they could do—*anything at all*—to strike back at the warriors who'd tried to exterminate them. It was your people who first called them 'Horse Stealer,' Hathan, but there was no name in all the world they would have preferred, for they, too, knew how to hate, and, oh but your ancestors gave them cause to."

He fell silent, and, one by one, the Sothōii turned away from him, looking at one another in shock and confusion. It never occurred to them to doubt Wencit's word, even though it turned everything they had ever been taught on its head, for he was Wencit of Rūm. And, as he said, unlike any of them he had *been* there.

Bahzell shared their shock, though in a different way. Hradani and Sothōii had each known for centuries how the other's version of history had differed from their own, yet none of them had ever expected the differences to be so suddenly resolved or to have the truth disclosed with such brutal directness, for it had never occurred to either of them to simply ask the one person who'd been there at the time. And now that the truth *had* been revealed, Bahzell had no idea what to do with it. It was almost worse than the bitter denials and denunciations his people and the Sothōii had hurled at one another for so many endless years, as if the proof that the Horse Stealers had been right all along was somehow almost immaterial. As if in some strange way the hatred and distrust between them and the Sothōii had been the only thing they truly *shared*, so that the destruction of its basis left them all bereft of rudder or compass.

But then, at last, Tellian stirred. He shook his head as if to clear it and looked at Bahzell once more.

"I don't—" He paused and cleared his throat. "It will take me some time to come to grips with what Wencit has just revealed to us, Milord Champion," he said finally. "And in many ways, I suppose which of us first offended the other matters far less than the history we have built between us since . . . and what we must build now." He smiled suddenly—a smile tart as alum, yet a smile nonetheless—and chuckled mirthlessly. "If I was prepared to believe that when I thought *your* ancestors had attacked *mine* without provocation, then I see no reason to change my mind now that I know it was *my* folk who were to blame. Yet I think those of my people who are not here today, who did not hear the truth from Wencit's own lips, will find it difficult to believe. Worse, some of them will *refuse* to believe, for to do so would require them to give up too much of the hatred in which they have invested their lives. And so, I fear, Wencit's history lesson, however accurate or well-taken, offers no simple solution to our dilemma."

"Aye, I'm thinking you've the right of it there," Bahzell rumbled. "But a solution we need, nonetheless."

"Agreed. Unfortunately, I see only one which my people could possibly accept."

"Ah?" Bahzell cocked his head. "And should I be taking it from your tone that you're thinking as how it's one *my* people *couldn't* be accepting?"

"That," Tellian admitted, "is indeed what I fear."

"Well, spit it out, man," Bahzell said impatiently when the baron paused once more.

"Very well, Milord Champion." Tellian drew a deep breath. "The only answer I can see is for us to end this right here, today, before it can escalate further. And the only way I can see to end it is with one side surrendering to the other. And since there are less than two hundred of you and over four *thousand* of us—"

He shrugged almost apologetically, and Bahzell heard Hurthang's teeth grind beside him. He himself said nothing for a full thirty seconds, and when he did speak again, it was in a very careful tone.

"Let me be certain as I've understood this, Milord. You're saying as how the only way we can be resolving this mess without a war is for us—the ones as were attacked without reason or declaration—to be surrendering to *you*, as were the ones *doing* the attacking?"

"Put that way, it certainly sounds . . . less than just," Tellian admitted. "Yet it's the only solution I can see. I have to *end* this somehow, either with a victory won by force of arms or with a formal settlement to which my own honor is pledged. If I don't, the Court factions which most hate and fear your people may well force King Markhos to order me to take still stronger action. But if you surrender to me, then I will be honor bound to protect you as the terms of your surrender provide, and not even Erthan of South Riding will want to push too hard in that case."

"So you'd ask the Order of Tomanāk to surrender so as to be letting you 'protect' us, is it?" Bahzell rumbled in a dangerous voice. "Well let me be telling you this, Tellian of West Riding! The Order's no need of your 'protection,' and the one thing I've never learned at all, at all, is how to be yielding my sword to another! So if that's after being the only 'solution' you can see, you'd best be calling up your dogs and finding out how many of them can die with us!"

Tension crackled, and then, to the amazement of every man present, Hathan Shieldarm laughed. Not scornfully or bitterly, but with a deep, rolling belly laugh of pure amusement. All eyes swung to him, and he bent over his saddle bow, laughing still harder. It took several seconds for him to drag himself back under control, and when he did, he leaned forward and murmured something to his courser, then dismounted gracefully, despite the courser's height. He stood for a moment, raised left hand resting lovingly on the courser's shoulder, and then walked around to face Bahzell. He was a foot and more shorter than the hradani, and he craned his neck to look up at him.

"Well, Bahzell Bahnakson," he said, with a bubble of laughter still lurking in his voice, "if it's only a matter of your never having learned to do it, perhaps I can demonstrate how it's done!" His own companions watched him as if he'd run stark mad, but he only grinned and drew his sabre, then flipped it up to catch it by the blade and extend its hilt to Bahzell over his left forearm. "Milord Champion, I yield to you a sword which has never known dishonor, and with it myself, as your prisoner."

It was Bahzell's turn to stare, and then he heard Tellian roar with laughter as delighted as Hathan's own.

"Of course!" the baron exclaimed. "All I need is a formal agreement—it doesn't matter who surrenders to whom!" He drew his own sword and leaned low from the saddle with a sweeping bow. "Milord Champion, I yield, and my men with me!"

"Here now!" Bahzell looked back and forth between Hathan and Tellian with a flustered confusion the prospect of a battle to the death had been unable to evoke. "Here now!" he protested again, and Wencit joined the laughter.

"I don't see the problem, Bahzell," the wizard told him between guffaws. "As Tellian says, what matters is that *someone* surrenders. And think what a glorious triumph it will be for the Order! Less than eighty of you taking four *thousand* trained Sothōii warriors prisoner!"

"Now just you be waiting one Phrobus-damned minute!" Bahzell snapped. "I'll not have the Order— I mean, it's not fitting that— Fiendark seize you, Brandark, will you *stop* that laughing before I'm after breaking your worthless neck!"

No one seemed to pay him the least attention, and, finally, the glare faded from his eyes and he began to chuckle as well. He shook his head helplessly, then waved both hands at Hathan and Tellian.

"Oh, put up your swords, the both of you! If you're so all-fired eager to be surrendering yourselves, then I suppose the least I can be doing is grant you parole!"

"Thank you, Milord," Tellian said with becoming seriousness. "Upon what terms will you grant it?"

"Well, I suppose we *should* be thrashing that out, now shouldn't we just?" Bahzell agreed. "It's honored I'd be to invite you into my tent to discuss it, Milord Baron—if I was after *having* a tent, that is."

"It just happens that I have quite a nice one which the former Lord Warden of Glanharrow brought with him," Tellian replied. "If you and your companions would consent to join me there, I'm sure we can work out the terms of my army's surrender—and parole—to our mutual satisfaction."

EPILOGUE

"Are you *sure* about this, Bahzell?" Vaijon asked quietly.

The two of them stood outside the tent in which Bahzell and Tellian had haggled out the details of the Sothōii's "parole" while what had been Sir Mathian's army struck camp about them. The men of that army were in a strange mood, one whose like Bahzell had never seen before. The most common emotion seemed to be sheer, unadulterated shock—the stunned disbelief of men whose world has just been turned upside down. Very few of them knew what Wencit had revealed about the early history of the hradani-Sothōii wars, but they *did* know their liege lord had just surrendered all of them to an enemy they outnumbered by fifty to one. And that they were about to struggle homeward up the Gullet, apparently in total defeat, from a foe who could face them with less than seventy swords.

But there was more to it than shock. There was hatred in all too many of the eyes which flicked constantly over Bahzell or darted to where Hurthang and Brandark stood talking quietly with Kaeritha and Wencit. Too many centuries of mutual slaughter lay between their people and Bahzell's for it to be any other way, and for many of them, the shame of their own "defeat" only made the hate burn hotter. Rancor and consternation held one another in uneasy balance at the moment, yet their hate also emphasized what Tellian had said earlier. Too many of the Sothōii feared what the united Horse Stealers and Bloody Swords might represent, and the fragile edifice the Baron of West Riding had patched together with Bahzell could still crumble into renewed and bitter warfare all too easily.

"Aye, I'm sure," he said after a moment, then grinned. "Or as nigh to it as any man could be!"

"Well, *I'm* not," Vaijon told him frankly. He looked away from Bahzell to glare at a Sothōii armsman who'd let too much hate show in his expression as he looked at the hradani. The armsman felt Vaijon's eyes and glanced in his direction, then turned quickly away, and Vaijon snorted. "You're going to wake up one night soon with a knife in your back if you go with these people," he warned Bahzell, "and I don't like the way they look at the *rest* of our lads, either!"

"'Our lads,' is it now?" Bahzell teased gently. He clapped Vaijon on the shoulder, and the human looked up at him with a sudden flash of laughter as he realized what he'd just said. But then the humor faded.

"Yes, *our* lads, and not just because they belong to the Order, Bahzell. They're good men, all of them. Some of the finest I've ever met, and I'm proud that *they* think of *me* as being one of theirs."

"Aye, well, I'll not argue there," Bahzell said softly, and squeezed his friend's—no, his *brother's*—shoulder gently.

"But we're wandering away from the point," Vaijon told him.

"Which is?"

"Which *is*," Vaijon said with a glare, "that you can't just go wandering off with this Tellian all by yourself! And before you say anything else, think about your father and mother. How d'you think *they're* going to react—or, worse, Marglyth!—when I come home and just casually announce that you've gone home to Balthar with your people's worst enemies?"

"Why, as to that, I'm thinking they'll be carrying on for a bit about idiots and fools and children as never look before they leap. And then Father will be having a bit to say about boulders and skulls, and I've no doubt at all that Marglyth will help him say it. But after that they'll both be stepping back and drawing a deep breath, and when they're after doing *that*, Vaijon, why, they'll realize as this may be the best thing that's ever happened yet betwixt us and Tellian's folk."

"Do you really expect me to believe that's going to happen?" Vaijon said skeptically, and Bahzell laughed.

"You just be watching my da, now, Vaijon of Almerhas! He's one as has more wit than hair, when all's said, and he'll see I'm after being right." Vaijon still looked unconvinced, and Bahzell sighed. "Look you, Vaijon. For twelve centuries, Sothōii and Horse Stealer have been slaughtering one another over this or that, and not a step closer to ending it have we ever come. Well, it's in my mind—

aye, and in Tellian's, too, I'm thinking—as how we've a chance to change that at last."

"You don't think anyone else is going to take the surrender of four thousand men to less than seventy seriously, do you?" Vaijon demanded.

"No," Bahzell said. "But if *Tellian* and I are treating it seriously, why there's no one at all, at all, can object without he's offered insult to Tellian's honor, on the one hand, or to the Order's, on the other. And *that*, Sword Brother, is why I've no choice but to be going with him, for if he and I *aren't* after acting like we mean it, then we've no pretext to be holding the others in check."

"But—"

"No," Bahzell said again, gently. "Think it out, Vaijon. Think it out, and you'll see as I'm right. And the fact that I'm champion of Tomanāk, and Horse Stealer, and son to the Horse Stealer as is probably collecting Churnazh's ears just about now, is the one thing as might just be making this work. Who better to speak for my folk among the Sothōii than a champion? And what Sothōii is like to be challenging the Sword Oath of a champion? But I'm after being my father's son, as well, and that's after making me a right fair choice as ambassador and envoy, as well. And don't you be forgetting that hradani and Sothōii both understand the giving of hostages in peace settlements, Vaijon! No, lad. With me in Balthar as Tellian's 'guest' to see to enforcing the terms of his 'parole,' we've a chance at last to be ending the constant fighting betwixt us, and himself wouldn't be so happy at all, at all, if one of his champions was turning his back on such as that, now would he?"

"I suppose not," Vaijon sighed. "But I *hate* thinking of you all alone among them."

"Hisht now! And who said I'd be after being alone amongst 'em?"

"What? But I thought—?"

"Well, that fool Bloody Sword yonder says as how he's always wanted to see a Sothōii city and spend some time comparing notes with their bards. And Kerry's been after reminding me as how her original business out here was with the Sothōii, anyway. So the two of them will be coming with me, and I've no doubt Father and Mother will be sending a few lads up the Escarpment to be giving me a bit of a guard to call my own."

"Really? Well, that's better than I thought. At least—" Vaijon broke off suddenly and frowned. "Wait. Wait just one minute! You said Kerry is going with you, too?" Bahzell nodded, a slight twinkle dancing in his eyes, and Vaijon's frown deepened. "I don't think that's a good idea, Bahzell. I mean, there's the chapter still to be organized, and if some of your Horse Stealers have had trouble accepting Bloody Swords now, think how much worse it will be when Bloody Swords who actually fought on the other side in the current war try to join us! *You* could probably talk them into it—or knock their heads together hard enough if talking doesn't work. And Kerry probably could, too. But without either of you—"

"Without either of us, they'll still be having *one* champion to be knocking heads together at need," Bahzell told him. "And," he added judiciously, "you'll probably be finding yourself doing that quite a bit, the first year or so."

"What?" It didn't seem to have registered for just a moment, and then Vaijon's eyes flew wide. "*What?* You expect *me*— You think *I*—!" He stared at Bahzell in disbelief edged with terror. "Bahzell, you can't be *serious!*"

"And why can't I just?"

"Because— Because I'm too young! And because . . . because—"

"Hisht, now!" Bahzell said again, and this time there was an edge of sternness under the amusement in his voice. Vaijon slithered to a stop, and Bahzell looked down at him with eyes which were deadly serious.

"Vaijon of Almerhas," he said sternly, "you were after being a right pain in the arse when first you set eyes on me, but you've come along nicely since. Mind, you've a few flaws yet, but then I suppose even *I'm* after having a few of those. And, aye, you're young. And human. But you're also a champion of Tomanāk, and one who's earned the respect of all our lads, as well. And a champion of Tomanāk, my lad, is one as does whatever it's needful to be doing. So it's back to Hurgrum you'll go, you and Hurthang and Gharnal, and it's the three of *you*, not me, as will be building the Order amongst my folk. For I've no doubt at all, at all, that it was for that very task himself was after sending you all this way with me."

"Indeed it was," a deep voice rumbled in the backs of both their brains, "and I'm pleased you finally figured it out. Surprised, mind you, for I'd almost given up hope you would, but pleased."

Vaijon had opened his mouth in fresh protest. Now it closed with a snap. He and Bahzell stood motionless for several seconds, waiting for that silent voice to speak again, but it seemed to have said all it had to say, and Bahzell smiled crookedly.

"Well, lad? Are you ready to be arguing with *him?* For if you are, I can tell you of my own experience that you'll be after losing in the end."

"Ah, no," Vaijon said finally, and drew a deep breath. "No," he said judiciously, "I don't believe I *will* argue with Him. But you owe me for this, Bahzell Bahnakson. You owe me quite a debt, and one of these days, I intend to collect it."

"Oh, and how would you be figuring as how *I'm* owing you a debt?"

"I'm astonished you can even ask that!" Vaijon said, and raised his hands, counting off points on his fingers as he made them. "First, you turn up in Belhadan and let me make a fool out of myself in front of an entire waterfront full of idlers. Then you let me drag you home to Sir Charrow and make an absolute ass out of myself in front of him and the entire chapter. *Then* you break both my arms, haul me off across half of Norfressa in ice and snow, fling me into the midst of a batch of barbarian hradani—the *shortest* of whom is taller than I am, I might add—hurl me into an attack on a temple of Sharnā where I wind up fighting demons *and* get my arm broken all over again, and now *this!* Oh, no, Bahzell! Trust me, you'll be *years* paying off all you owe me!"

"Oh no I won't," Bahzell told him, slapping him on his back with a laugh, and jerked the thumb of his other hand to where Brandark, Hurthang, and Kaeritha were walking towards them. "Oh, I've no doubt you might be feeling just a *mite* miffed over all those other complaints, Vaijon, but there's one favor I'm about to be doing for you as you'll be thanking me for for the the the rest of your days."

"Oh? And what would *that* be?"

"Why, I'm after taking Brandark with me," Bahzell said wickedly, "and just you be thinking what *that* means!"

"You mean—?" Vaijon glanced at the Bloody Sword and began to grin himself.

"Exactly. I've no doubt at all, at all, that you'll be finding your own set of problems, but just you remember when you do that you'll *not* be hearing some cursed song about "Vaijon the Fair" or "Vaijon the Noble" or some such foolishness. And that, my lad, puts paid to *any* debt I might be owing you!"

APPENDICES

THE GODS OF NORFRESSA

THE GODS OF LIGHT

Orr All-Father

Often called "The Creator" or "The Establisher," Orr is considered the creator of the universe and the king and judge of gods. He is the father or creator of all but one of the Gods of Light and the most powerful of all the gods, whether of Light or Dark. His symbol is a blue starburst.

Kontifrio

"The Mother of Women" is Orr's wife and the goddess of home, family, and the harvest. According to Norfressan theology, Kontifrio was Orr's second creation (after Orfressa, the rest of the universe), and she is the most nurturing of the gods and the mother of all Orr's children except Orfressa herself. Her hatred for Shigū is implacable. Her symbol is a sheaf of wheat tied with a grape vine.

Chemalka Orfressa

"The Lady of the Storm" is the sixth child of Orr and Kontifrio. She is the goddess of weather, good and bad, and has little to do with mortals. Her symbol is the sun seen through clouds.

Chesmirsa Orfressa

"The Singer of Light" is the fourth child of Orr and Kontifrio and the younger twin sister of Tomanāk, the war god. Chesmirsa is the goddess of bards, poetry, music, and art. She is very fond of mortals and has a mischievous sense of humor. Her symbol is the harp.

Hirahim Lightfoot

Known as "The Laughing God" and "The Great Seducer," Hirahim is something of a rogue element among the Gods of Light. He is the only one of them who is not related to Orr (no one seems certain where he came from, though he acknowledges Orr's authority . . . as much as he does anyone's) and he is the true prankster of the gods. He is the god of merchants, thieves, and dancers, but he is also known as the god of seductions, as he has a terrible weakness for attractive female mortals (or goddesses). His symbol is a silver flute.

Isvaria Orfressa

"The Lady of Remembrance" (also called "The Slayer") is the first child of Orr and Kontifrio. She is the goddess of needful death and the completion of life and rules the House of the Dead, where she keeps the Scroll of the Dead. Somewhat to her mother's dismay, she is also Hirahim's lover. The third most powerful of the Gods of Light, she is the special enemy of Krahana, and her symbol is a scroll with skull winding knobs.

Khalifrio Orfressa

"The Lady of the Lightning" is Orr and Kontifrio's second child and the goddess of elemental destruction. She is considered a Goddess of Light despite her penchant for destructiveness, but she has very little to do with mortals (and mortals are just as happy about it, thank you). Her symbol is a forked lightning bolt.

Korthrala Orfro

Called "Sea Spume" and "Foam Beard," Korthrala is the fifth child of Orr and Kontifrio. He is the god of the sea but also of love, hate, and passion. He is a very powerful god, if not over-blessed with wisdom, and is very fond of mortals. His symbol is the net and trident.

Lillinara Orfressa

Known as "Friend of Women" and "The Silver Lady," Lillinara

is Orr and Kontifrio's eleventh child, the goddess of the moon and women. She is one of the more complex deities, and extremely focused. She is appealed to by young women and maidens in her persona as the Maid and by mature women and mothers in her persona as the Mother. As avenger, she manifests as the Crone, who also comforts the dying. She dislikes Hirahim Lightfoot intensely, but she hates Shīgū (as the essential perversion of all womankind) with every fiber of her being. Her symbol is the moon.

Norfram Orfro

The "Lord of Chance" is Orr and Kontifrio's ninth child and the god of fortune, good and bad. His symbol is the infinity sign.

Orfressa

According to Norfressan theology, Orfressa is not a god but the universe herself, created by Orr even before Kontifrio, and she is not truly "awake." Or, rather, she is seldom aware of anything as ephemeral as mortals. On the very rare occasions when she does take notice of mortal affairs, terrible things tend to happen, and even Orr can restrain her wrath only with difficulty. It should be noted that among Norfressans, "Orfressa" is used as the name of their world, as well as to refer to the universe at large.

Semkirk Orfro

Known as "The Watcher," Semkirk is the tenth child of Orr and Kontifrio. He is the god of wisdom and mental and physical discipline and, before The Fall of Kontovar, was the god of white wizardry. Since The Fall, he has become the special patron of the psionic magi, who conduct a merciless war against evil wizards. He is a particularly deadly enemy of Carnadosa, the goddess of black wizardry. His symbol is a golden scepter.

Silendros Orfressa

The fourteenth and final child of Orr and Kontifrio, Silendros (called "Jewel of the Heavens") is the goddess of stars and the night. She is greatly reverenced by jewel smiths, who see their art as an attempt to capture the beauty of her heavens in the work of their hands, but generally has little to do with mortals. Her symbol is a silver star.

Sorbus Kontifra

Known as "Iron Bender," Sorbus is the smith of the gods. He is also the product of history's greatest seduction (that of Kontifrio by Hirahim—a "prank" Kontifrio has never quite forgiven), yet he is the most stolid and dependable of all the gods, and Orr accepts him as his own son. His symbol is an anvil.

Tolomos Orfro

"The Torch Bearer" is the twelfth child of Orr and Kontifrio. He is the god of light and the sun and the patron of all those who work with heat. His symbol is a golden flame.

Tomanāk Orfro

Tomanāk, the third child of Orr and Kontifrio, is Chesmirsa's older twin brother and second only to Orr himself in power. He is known by many names—"Sword of Light," "Scale Balancer," "Lord of Battle," and "Judge of Princes" to list but four—and has been entrusted by his father with the task of overseeing the balance of the Scales of Orr. He is also captain general of the Gods of Light and the foremost enemy of all the Dark Gods (indeed, it was he who cast Phrobus down when Phrobus first rebelled against his father). His symbols are a sword and/or a spiked mace.

Torframos Orfro

Known as "Stone Beard" and "Lord of Earthquakes," Torframos is the eighth child of Orr and Kontifrio. He is the lord of the Earth, the keeper of the deep places and special patron of engineers and those who delve, and is especially revered by dwarves. His symbol is the miner's pick.

Toragan Orfro

"The Huntsman," also called "Woodhelm," is the thirteenth child of Orr and Kontifrio and the god of nature. Forests are especially sacred to him, and he has a reputation for punishing those who hunt needlessly or cruelly. His symbol is an oak tree.

THE DARK GODS

Phrobus Orfro

Called "Father of Evil" and "Lord of Deceit," Phrobus is the seventh child of Orr and Kontifrio, which explains why seven is considered *the* unlucky number in Norfressa. No one recalls his original name; "Phrobus" ("Truth Bender") was given to him by Tomanāk when he cast Phrobus down for his treacherous attempt to wrest rulership from Orr. Following that defeat, Phrobus turned openly to the Dark and became, in fact, the opening wedge by which evil first entered Orfressa. He is the most powerful of the gods of Light or Dark after Tomanāk, and the hatred between him and Tomanāk is unthinkably bitter, but Phrobus fears his brother worse than death itself. His symbol is a flame-eyed skull.

Shigū

Called "The Twisted One," "Queen of Hell," and "Mother of Madness," Shigū is the wife of Phrobus. No one knows exactly where she came from, but most believe she was, in fact, a powerful demoness raised to godhood by Phrobus when he sought a mate to breed up his own pantheon to oppose that of his father. Her power is deep but subtle, her cruelty and malice are bottomless, and her favored weapon is madness. She is even more hated, loathed, and feared by mortals than Phrobus, and her worship is punishable by death in all Norfressan realms. Her symbol is a flaming spider.

Carnadosa Phrofressa

"The Lady of Wizardry" is the fifth child of Phrobus and Shigū. She has become the goddess of black wizardry, but she herself might he considered totally amoral rather than evil for evil's sake. She enshrines the concept of power sought by any means and at any cost to others. Her symbol is a wizard's wand.

Fiendark Phrofro

The first-born child of Phrobus and Shīgū, Fiendark is known as "Lord of the Furies." He is cast very much in his father's image (though, fortunately, he is considerably less powerful) and all evil creatures owe him allegiance as Phrobus's deputy. Unlike Phrobus, who seeks always to pervert or conquer, however, Fiendark also delights in destruction for destruction's sake. His symbols are a flaming sword or flame-shot cloud of smoke.

Krahana Phrofressa

"The Lady of the Damned" is the fourth child of Phrobus and Shīgū and, in most ways, the most loathsome of them all. She is noted for her hideous beauty and holds dominion over the undead (which makes her Isvaria's most hated foe) and rules the hells to which the souls of those who have sold themselves to evil spend eternity. Her symbol is a splintered coffin.

Krashnark Phrofro

The second son of Phrobus and Shīgū, Krashnark is something of a disappointment to his parents. The most powerful of Phrobus' children, Krashnark (known as "Devil Master") is the god of devils and ambitious war. He is ruthless, merciless, and cruel, but personally courageous and possessed of a strong, personal code of honor, which makes him the only Dark God Tomanāk actually respects. He is, unfortunately, loyal to his father, and his power and sense of honor have made him the "enforcer" of the Dark Gods. His symbol is a flaming steward's rod.

Sharnā Phrofro

Called "Demonspawn" and "Lord of the Scorpion," Sharnā is Krashnark's younger, identical twin (a fact which pleases neither of them). Sharnā is the god of demons and the patron of assassins, the personification of cunning and deception. He is substantially less powerful than Krashnark and a total coward, and the demons who owe him allegiance hate and fear Krashnark's more powerful devils almost as much as Sharnā hates and fears his brother. His symbols are the giant scorpion (which serves as his mount) and a bleeding heart in a mailed fist.

DAVID WEBER

<u>The Honor Harrington series:</u> *(cont.)*

Field of Dishonor

Honor goes home to Manticore—and fights for her life on a battlefield she never trained for, in a private war that offers just two choices: death—or a "victory" that can end only in dishonor and the loss of all she loves....

Flag in Exile

Hounded into retirement and disgrace by political enemies, Honor Harrington has retreated to planet Grayson, where powerful men plot to reverse the changes she has brought to their world. And for their plans to suceed, Honor Harrington must die!

Honor Among Enemies

Offered a chance to end her exile and again command a ship, Honor Harrington must use a crew drawn from the dregs of the service to stop pirates who are plundering commerce. Her enemies have chosen the mission carefully, thinking that either she will stop the raiders or they will kill her . . . and either way, her enemies will win....

In Enemy Hands

After being ambushed, Honor finds herself aboard an enemy cruiser, bound for her scheduled execution. But one lesson Honor has never learned is how to give up! One way or another, she and her crew are going home—even if they have to conquer Hell to get there!

continued ☞